GOOD LUCK, YUKIKAZE

雪風

CHŌHEI KAMBAYASHI

GOOD LUCK, YUKIKAZE

雪風

CHŌHEI **KAMBAYASHI**

HAIKA SORU

SAN FRANCISCO

GOOD LUCK, YUKIKAZE

© 2001 Chōhei Kambayashi
Originally published in Japan by Hayakawa Publishing, Inc.
All rights reserved.

Cover illustration by Shoji Hasegawa
English translation © 2011 VIZ Media, LLC

HAIKASORU
Published by
VIZ Media, LLC
295 Bay Street
San Francisco, CA 94133

www.haikasoru.com

Library of Congress Cataloging-in-Publication Data

Kambayashi, Chohei, 1953-
  [Sento yosei Yukikaze. English]
  Good luck, Yukikaze / Chohei Kambayashi ; translated by Neil Nadelman.
    p. cm. -- (Haikasoku)
  ISBN 978-1-4215-3901-0
  1. Space warfare--Fiction. I. Nadelman, Neil. II. Title.
  PL855.A513S4613 2011
  895.6'36--dc22   2011012909

The rights of the author of the work in this publication to be
so identified have been asserted in accordance with the Copyright,
Designs and Patents Act 1988. A CIP catalogue record for this book
is available from the British Library.

Printed in the U.S.A.
First printing, July 2011

"I am that I am."

TABLE OF CONTENTS

CHARACTERS APPEARING

First Lieutenant Rei Fukai
Yukikaze's pilot; later promoted to captain

Major James Booker
FAF Special Air Force mission sortie manager

Brigadier General Lydia Cooley
Deputy commander of the FAF Special Air Force

Second Lieutenant Burgadish
Flight officer of the old Yukikaze

Second Lieutenant Yagashira
Pilot of SAF Unit 13

First Lieutenant Gavin Mayle
TAB-15 505th Tactical Fighter Squadron leader

Captain Edith Foss
Military doctor in charge of Rei's rehabilitation

First Lieutenant Vincent Bruys
Pilot of SAF Unit 7

Lieutenant General Gibril Laitume
Commander of Faery Base's Tactical Combat Air Corps

Colonel Ansel Rombert
An influential man in the FAF Intelligence Forces

Second Lieutenant Akira Katsuragi
Yukikaze's new flight officer

Lynn Jackson
A journalist from Earth

A Letter from the FAF Special Air Force
Lynn Jackson, from notes on her sequel
to *The Invader*

I WONDER HOW many people nowadays have a palpable sense that Earth is under attack by the aliens we know as the JAM. It seems to me that the typical Earther now lives his life thinking that the JAM threat has nothing to do with him. You might even go so far as to say that people living their ordinary lives have forgotten about it completely.

The JAM threat, and even the existence of the JAM themselves, doesn't enter into the consciousness of most people. That's probably because they can put it out of their minds and still live their lives without disruption.

That could be taken as evidence that the group structures that we as individuals belong to—towns and states and nations and so forth—are somehow still functioning well. But it would be foolish to think that we can relax and expect this state of affairs to continue indefinitely. Even nations have a limited life span. The possibility is great that these invaders called the JAM are shortening them.

What I want to do is warn people of this.

In our Earthbound disputes between groups here, there is a margin for compromise, for striking cease-fire agreements. But I'd like you to think about trying to do that with the JAM. The JAM are an alien life-form, possessing completely different values from those of humanity. Negotiations with them may be impossible. All we can do is keep fighting and never stop. The sacrifices our task demands are enormous, but if we ease up, we'll lose.

IN MY LAST book, *The Invader*, I wrote that when the JAM drove the huge spindle-shaped cloud into the Ross Ice Shelf in Antarctica thirty years ago and from there flew forth to begin their invasion of our world through the hyperspace Passageway, it was a golden opportunity for humanity to transcend their membership in squabbling tribes and nations and to truly become "Earthers." I also wrote that it still wasn't too late to achieve this. But the truth is that we failed.

On Earth now, there is no transnational organization that unites the people of the world. As always, we exist simply as mutually antagonistic groups of nations, economic blocs, religions, and peoples, and in truth there is no organizational level existing above them. I wrote in my last book that such a state of affairs demonstrates that we people of Earth see the alien invaders as just another nation, religion, or people. I still don't think that this belief is necessarily incorrect, but I now believe there's a different reason for its persistence.

In short, I think it's because we were not able to find a strong leader who could transcend all the political, religious, and cultural systems they were attached to and declare to the world, "I am an Earther, and I represent the people of Earth." Essentially, rather than find such a person, we settled back and waited for one to appear. However, the environment of modern Earth isn't conducive to giving birth to such a saint. Earth is vast, with varied environments and an exceedingly great number of lifestyles, values, and histories. To have an appreciation of all of that, empathize with it, and then moreover dispense wisdom widely to all those different people without discrimination in order to help them live their lives well is beyond the capabilities of any one person. The scale of the target group to be led is just too big, crossing over too many divergent personal desires, and moreover *individuals know how complex reality already is.*

The human race has now established an unprecedented advanced information society and lives surrounded by a vast quantity of data. Truth and lies mixed together in the vast bulk of information available make everything seem ambiguous, and this vagueness breeds distrust. Indeed, modern people evaluate everything not by how trustworthy it is, but rather by how *un*trustworthy. Following the physical law that the reliability of transmitted data decreases as the bulk of information increases, relationships based on good faith and trust between people suffer. As the amount of material to evaluate increases, so too do the seeds of doubt bloom. We can call this the pitfall of the advanced information society. So, even if we found some self-proclaimed saint who could walk on water, modern humans have lost their original naive sense of awe for such a person.

And so, with no saint forthcoming, we didn't set out to look for one. While the reasons are varied for why we never made an effort to form a truly worldwide organization to oppose the JAM, I now think it was the right choice. Consider what might have happened had the human race put its efforts into selecting a leader for all of Earth. To preserve their various group interests, we might have touched off a world war between nations, or a destructive religious war. If such a war to appoint humanity's representative had been sparked, the JAM would have used it to their advantage, and their invasion would have succeeded. You could say that humanity managed to dodge that bullet. If a true representative for the people of Earth exists, his or her identity remains unclear.

Therefore, the people of Earth cannot now properly be called "Earthers." Who then exactly are the JAM at war with?

We individuals have entrusted the war with the JAM to the Earth Defense Organization, and to be truthful, it operates in a democratic and efficient manner. I'm not being ironic here. It's true. It's because of them that we can forget about the JAM and live our day-to-day lives.

However, the truth is that this organization, established mainly by an array of people from all nations—all with their own fluid, individual expectations—has become a precariously fragile entity. As you might expect, each member views the war according to how they can benefit from waging it. Despite all of these various expectations, or perhaps because of them, they are still able to turn their strength on the JAM without being destroyed. This is, in a way, a far preferable situation than being led by some lone, foolish, half-baked leader. Following along from this truth, we can express another: the various groups that participate in this organization are fighting the JAM for their own sakes. In short, they're not doing it for the sake of all Earthers.

We are at a dangerous juncture in human history—specifically, we will soon discover whether this method of opposing the JAM will always be successful. True, it's working for now. Thanks to the Earth Defense Organization, most people have forgotten about the JAM. But in the future, if this system should stop functioning, the time may come when we think of ourselves as Earthers on a personal level. Because of the JAM.

When the system of which we are a part can no longer protect us from the JAM, we will be forced to individually and collectively confront the aliens as Earthers. The JAM who will be gunning for me are not of this Earth, not a part of any system on Earth. Even if I had the title of president of some great nation, it wouldn't matter. All that would matter would be that I was an Earther. Furthermore, we don't have any other planet to retreat to. There's no place for refugees from this world to flee to. If the human race can't form itself into a group called "Earthers," then we as individual Earther representatives will have to fight the JAM.

The truth is that we're at war with the JAM. If we don't want to die, we'll need to fight with our own strength. Am I prepared to do that? Are you?

Fundamentally, we cannot just entrust this war to strangers because it's a problem for all Earthers, for every individual. So long as there is no true leader of all Earth, and so long as we can't expect such a messiah for the reasons I discussed previously, it's a problem that you and I have to think about as individuals.

THE THING THAT'S got me thinking about all of this again is a letter I received a few days ago.

Not an email, mind you. It was a literal letter in an envelope. It's rare for someone not to use the computer network these days, but the sender of this letter had no choice. He had no access to any computer network here on Earth.

That's right, it came from the other side of the hyperspace Passageway, from the planet Faery, where the war against the JAM is being fought. There, the combat organization of the EDO known as the Faery Air Force fights day and night to hold back the JAM invasion of Earth. If the FAF were to be defeated, the JAM would surge through the Passageway and arrive on Earth itself.

The sender of the letter wasn't concerned about having his full name, attachment in the FAF, or rank published. In fact, he made it clear that he wanted them known if possible, saying that he wanted the people of Earth to know his thoughts about his war with the JAM. In other words, he was using me as a megaphone to pass his message on to all the people of Earth.

His name is Major James Booker. FAF Faery Base, Tactical Combat Air Corps, Special Air Force 5th Squadron, more popularly known as the mission sortie manager and the de facto second-in-command of the SAF.

The major sent me a letter once before, after he read my book *The Invader*, which was my report on our war with the JAM. I answered his original letter, and we have since maintained an infrequent correspondence. I even managed to meet and speak to him one time.

"You don't know the real threat the JAM pose," he wrote to me in that first letter. Coming as it did from the battlefield, his prose brimmed over with a sense of tension. That was natural, I suppose. And owing to the special duties of the SAF, the war they fought had developed a dimension even more severe than that faced by other squadrons.

By way of simple introduction, a description of the duty of the thirteen fighter planes that comprise the SAF would be as follows:

> Gather all data from the airspace where the FAF is engaging the JAM. Return the collected data by any means necessary. Even if an allied plane is in danger of being shot down, you do not have to offer them proactive support. In other words, stand back and let friendly planes be destroyed.

It's a heartless duty, but the pilots of these planes don't consider it heartless. The SAF is comprised of people who possess that sort of personality. If you were to ask one of them how they felt about watching their comrades' planes being shot down, they would answer "So what? It's not my problem. What do I care about people in other squadrons or on Earth?"

I can only guess at the hardships Major Booker must suffer in trying to command subordinates who think like this. But heartless people like these are necessary to pursue the war against the JAM. If we could make some sort of gentleman's agreement between ourselves and the JAM, then maybe we could be more careful about who gets to play in this game, but the problem that reality poses to us is that humanity doesn't have that luxury. The FAF recognizes that as well. In short, the duties of the SAF require these sorts of people, and they have been given high-performance fighter planes suited to them. These are the Super Sylphs, tactical combat electronic reconnaissance planes even faster than the FAF's mainline Sylphid fighters, with greater acceleration and maneuverability. Developed by the Systems Corps, the elite engineering unit of the FAF, it is a fighter plane truly worthy of the word *super*. I doubt that there is any fighter plane on Earth that could beat them. At the very least, no Earth fighter can match one in the environment of planet Faery. This is only natural, since the Super Sylph was developed for the skies of Faery, which is why the FAF needs to have the Systems Corps as its own research and development unit.

The Systems Corps has developed numerous models of fighter plane, but as we've now reached the point where manned planes are no longer enough to beat the JAM, they are now rushing to put a superior unmanned mainline fighter into service. It was with this development concept as the background that the second letter from the SAF came. The theory was that integrating the weak human element into the system was degrading the system's efficiency as a whole, and so the human element had to be eliminated. The human body is like a fragile egg compared to a fighter plane, with its inability to withstand the violent maneuvers of combat, the fear of battle felt by the human heart, and in its far inferior ability to think. Playing nursemaid to a human pilot prevented the Super Sylph from demonstrating its true potential, and so the human wasn't necessary, or so they said.

From this idea was developed the FRX99, the SAF's next-generation tactical reconnaissance fighter plane. The engineers felt that even the Super Sylph would be ineffective against the JAM so long as humans rode inside of them. But the SAF's Major Booker didn't simply accept this conclusion. The major had concluded that the superiority of the SAF came from the pilots' possession of a combat sense computers did not have, and that their planes' central computers had developed their own version of that combat sense. What had been burning the JAM's fingers on the now-aging Super Sylphs was the tactical combat judgment the planes had picked up from their human pilots, and human behavior was something the JAM found impossible to predict. It was for that reason that the unmanned planes, lacking a learning function, could not perform the duties that the current SAF did. The major felt that since the computers on current Super Sylphs had learned enough by that point, they should be converted to unmanned versions and then the new planes be deployed as manned fighters.

The major then requested that the Systems Corps produce an FRX99 designated as a manned fighter. That became the FRX00 prototype. Whereas the FRX99 is a recon version of the next-generation mainline fighter plane that the Systems Corps are developing, the FRX00 became a version modified for manned flight. While the details have not been made public here on Earth, several FRX99s and at least one FRX00 have been completed. Both types of plane are prototypes, with production versions pending.

The reason Major Booker was so adamant that there be a manned version is that he doesn't want this war to become one between the JAM and our combat machines. The major's feelings on this matter are complicated and cannot be easily encapsulated in a few words, but if I had to summarize the misgivings of a soldier such as he who has been on the front lines fighting the JAM for many years, it would be like this:

> As things stand now, analysis shows that the JAM disregard the existence of human beings. Their direct enemies are the FAF's fighter planes, and thus the JAM take no tactical actions against the humans who reside within the bases on Faery. I wonder if the JAM have

declared war, not on humanity, but on Earth's war machines. We may not even be the JAM's enemy.

If this is the case, if this war becomes one between the JAM and the war machines and computers humanity has developed, then humans aren't necessary.

However, humans can't simply ignore the situation; the reason being that while we can no longer live without the existence of our computers, if the computers tell us that we humans are no longer necessary to them, then a new front on the war will open, and this time our opponents will be our own machines. We'll have to deal with a challenge from the computers as well as from the JAM. In fact, the decision to end production of manned fighter jets came from a proposal by Systems Corps' own computers. If we humans just unconditionally accept our obsolescence, then we'll be surrendering control of the FAF and, later, the entire Earth to the computers long before we'd have to surrender them to the JAM.

I want the JAM to be humanity's enemy, because if they aren't, then what's been the point of anything that I've done so far? Humans are the main leads in this war. We need to convey this to both the JAM and to our computers. We can't just leave this war to the computers to win.

It's difficult for me to accurately convey Major Booker's feelings, separated as I am from the war with the JAM and the computers he uses to analyze the data about the conflict. It's possible this is because of some misunderstanding of my own. However, I will add only this: the JAM's true form remains a mystery to us, and we can't ignore the threat they pose, no matter how indirect. They are a danger to all of mankind, and Major Booker is someone who senses that danger in his very bones.

The letter I received from Major Booker a few days ago dealt with an even more potent subject—for the first time ever, Major Booker lost a plane.

Since I can learn of the FAF's war situation from regular official reports faster than extradimensional letters can arrive in my mailbox, I knew of the SAF's loss even without Major Booker telling me. The fighter the JAM destroyed was Unit 3, personal name: Yukikaze. Her pilot was gravely injured, and the flight officer who normally flew in the rear seat was missing in action.

An SAF plane, a group whose pride in its perfect return record had given it the nickname Boomerang squadron, had been lost.

Yukikaze. Her pilot was Lieutenant Rei Fukai. Major Booker's friend. The name I'd read on that casualty list wasn't that of a stranger.

I'd seen the SAF fighter called Yukikaze up close. She'd landed on a Japanese naval aircraft carrier to refuel. That huge, graceful plane looked like a swan landing amidst a flock of ducks. Major Booker was the one riding in the rear seat at the time, and we'd spoken then. The pilot was Lieutenant Rei Fukai. He never came down out of the cockpit, so I didn't have a chance to talk to the lieutenant, but even if he had, I think I'd have had as much luck having a conversation with him as I would with Yukikaze. That pilot was part of the systems installed into his beloved plane; he had a function to serve. I figured that he'd regard some stranger who was unrelated to a combat role as just so much static.

Yukikaze was the only thing in which he believed. That was what Major Booker told me as he stood looking at his friend and subordinate aboard the plane. A man who now trusted a machine more than other humans, and who was becoming increasingly machinelike himself. It seemed terrifying and sad to me.

I knew that the official report listed Lieutenant Fukai as having been gravely injured, so I sent off a letter to Major Booker to inquire about the pilot's condition. Not as a journalist gathering information for a story, but as an individual. The major wrote me a polite reply and said that he appreciated my concern. That was the letter that arrived a few days ago.

The contents of that letter were beyond anything I had expected.

First of all, he apologized for the delay in replying to me, as he'd suffered a neck injury. He then went on to say that Yukikaze herself had made it back unharmed.

This opening paragraph perplexed me, but as I continued reading and Major Booker described exactly what had happened in the incident, I was able to understand.

Yukikaze had been shot down by the JAM during a mission

and had made an emergency landing. Lieutenant Fukai, the pilot, ejected, and Yukikaze self-destructed. At that moment, Major Booker was riding in the rear seat of the FRX00 flying nearby, engaged in a combat assessment test flight of the SAF's next-generation manned fighter plane.

The FRX00 was also attacked by the JAM, but the new fighter blew them decisively out of the sky. Its air combat maneuvers were so violent that the pilot who'd been flying the plane was killed instantly, unable to take the acceleration, while Major Booker in the rear seat injured his neck and lost consciousness. According to the letter, the FRX00 flew back to base on its own, carrying its dead and unconscious passengers, and then identified *itself* as Yukikaze.

The only explanation that makes sense is that the Yukikaze that was shot down by the JAM transferred herself into the newer fighter as it approached. Immediately after that, the FRX00 was out of the pilot's hands. It was the decision of the plane's central computer to initiate air combat maneuvers, not the pilot. In short, Major Booker wrote, having gotten herself a new body after being shot down by the JAM, Yukikaze decided to take revenge on the nearby JAM.

Yukikaze's pilot, Lieutenant Fukai, was rescued, but he'd suffered a gunshot wound in the right side of his abdomen. In addition, his flight officer, Second Lieutenant Burgadish, wasn't on board. Only Lieutenant Fukai's ejection seat had been jettisoned in the emergency landing, which means that Yukikaze had landed sometime during its mission and Lieutenant Burgadish had deplaned.

Why he did or what happened, Major Booker doesn't know. Yukikaze's action record had been copied exactly onto the FRX00's memory, which supports the theory that she copied herself into the new plane, and the data do seem to indicate that Yukikaze set down somewhere once before finally being shot down. However, they don't know any details beyond that. Lieutenant Fukai is alive, but in a coma, so he cannot be interrogated. The bullet found in Lieutenant Fukai was from an FAF-issued sidearm, but nobody knows who would have tried to kill him. It seems doubtful that Lieutenant Burgadish would have shot his own crewmate, but the major doesn't know the details. Lieutenant Burgadish's whereabouts are unknown.

The answers to all of these questions are probably inside of Lieutenant Fukai's head, and so long as he remains unconscious, they have no way to retrieve those memories.

It may be—Major Booker then went on to relate the most shocking revelation of the letter—that Lieutenant Fukai was shot by one of the JAM, a creature with which we have yet to make direct contact. It's possible that Yukikaze and her crew were captured by the JAM and that Lieutenant Fukai was the only one who managed to escape. This is merely conjecture based on the intelligence Yukikaze gathered in combat, but if true, Yukikaze's crew may have carried out some sort of exchange with the JAM.

"The JAM aren't resting," the major continued.

> They may instead be changing their strategy, and Lieutenant Fukai probably knows what they are planning. I hope that he wakes up as soon as possible, both as his friend and as a member of the SAF. I'd like you to pray for his recovery as well, if only so that the people of Earth don't lose this war to the JAM.

The revelation of a possibility that Yukikaze's crew, Lieutenant Fukai and Lieutenant Burgadish, made direct contact with the JAM came as a shock to me. Yukikaze and her crew may have gotten a clue as to the true nature of the JAM, a species that have until now been a total mystery to us. Moreover, the letter claimed that the JAM may be changing their methods of combat.

My reporter's soul was stirred by the revelation. If the JAM were beginning to change their strategy, then all of their attacks up till now may have been just the preliminaries. The real battle is about to begin.

The major's letter is a warning to all the people of Earth, and this is a story that has to be covered. I have to write a sequel to *The Invader,* because living my life while ignoring the JAM is no longer an option.

I

SHOCK WAVE

HE LINGERED IN his sleep, not alive and yet not dead. Occasionally, his eyelids would open, his eyes moving wildly.

To the people around him, it seemed as though he were following the flight of some invisible fairy, his eyes now windows open to illuminate the darkness within his head, as if desperately hoping to light the way out from the blackness that had swallowed him up. He personally wasn't conscious of this movement. Indeed, he had no feeling of anything in his entire body. When his eyes moved, the image in his mind was of the moment he was ejected from his beloved plane and left behind. His beloved plane, Yukikaze. As she flew out of sight, leaving him with nothing but empty sky, he felt his existence contracting to a point before finally winking out. Only then did his eyes cease their wild motion, and his consciousness fell back, once again, into the gap between life and death.

He was concerned with neither life nor death, simply letting time drift past, and even time itself no longer held any meaning for him.

Until, at last, a voice called for him to awaken.

1

MAJOR JAMES BOOKER, the man responsible for sortie management and mission control for the Special Air Force 5th Squadron (FAF, Faery base, Tactical Combat Air Corps), had a lot of problems on his mind, all of which were giving him a splitting headache.

First of all, his neck still gave him a twinge from time to time. Then there was the fact that he still didn't have a complete understanding of the incident that had hurt his neck in the first place. Finally, there was the matter of Lieutenant Rei Fukai, pilot of Yukikaze (SAF Unit 3) and how he remained unconscious in a vegetative state. Ever since the incident, the major had a vague sense that the JAM had subtly altered their strategy in a way that he couldn't quite put his finger on. Sylphids, the same model of plane that had been enhanced to create Yukikaze, deployed at front-line bases, had suddenly been taking much higher rates of damage than previously.

The major recalled that Dr. Balume, the SAF flight surgeon, had suggested a nerve block if the pain persisted. When he'd refused, telling the doctor that a nerve block performed by a drunk like Balume would likely kill him, the doctor then suggested that he might try some counseling, saying that ridding himself of his anxiety might also relieve the pain.

"And what do you have to be anxious about, anyway?" the doctor had said. "You made it back still breathing, didn't you? Okay, the FRX00 nearly killed you, but you don't have to fly in it again." It was about at that point the major decided that he would have to take care of his anxiety himself, because this doctor certainly wasn't going to be of any help in that department.

Major Booker knew that the reason he was feeling so anxious had to do with question number two on his list. In other words, the fact that he still didn't have a complete grasp of exactly what had happened to the FRX00. Yukikaze lay burning, shot down by the JAM, never to fly again. Somehow, she'd abandoned her old body and transferred herself into the approaching FRX00. Having obtained a new body for herself, Yukikaze had recognized the approaching JAM fighters and initiated combat maneuvers against them. That was when the pilot and he, the acting flight officer in the rear, had blacked out. The man at the controls was Captain George Samia, pilot of SAF Unit 13. Yukikaze's maneuvers in the FRX00 snapped his neck, killing him instantly.

And those must have been some outrageous maneuvers, the major thought, rubbing the nape of his own neck. The FRX00 had exceeded its predicted air combat maneuverability. He could practically hear the computers of the Systems Corps snickering at him.

"The FRX00 is a modified FRX99," they'd say. "The FRX99

was never designed to be piloted by humans. Did you seriously think you could do it?"

Major Booker had been riding in the rear seat to observe the real-world performance of the plane that had been manufactured at his insistence, but there was no way he could have predicted that something like this would happen. In truth, the real reason he'd been there was because he'd been worried when Yukikaze hadn't returned to base from her sortie. He used the FRX00's combat flight test as an excuse to go out and run a personal search for her. It was clear that they'd provided support for Yukikaze, but being aboard the plane had prevented him from seeing exactly what had happened. Even now, he wasn't sure.

Captain Samia had probably leaned closer to the display to confirm that an external data stream was transferring into his plane from somewhere. However, that had been a fatal mistake on his part. The major regretted not warning him, but comforted himself by realizing that there had been no time for it. There was no way he could have known that the data stream was actually Yukikaze's mind itself being transferred from her crippled body as she lay burning. Aside from that, as a former pilot, Booker had braced himself to prepare for combat maneuvers the moment he realized something was wrong. That was what had saved his neck. All he'd suffered were a few dislocated vertebrae.

Maybe his ability to sense danger and intuit that he was about to pull some unimaginable Gs was due to a sort of sixth sense he'd cultivated as a pilot. He thought about this for a moment, then decided against it. It had been a long, long time since he'd flown as a combat pilot. Was what he felt at that moment, more than the fear of combat itself, a sense of how dangerous the FRX00 really was? Had he sensed that it was a mistake for humans to fly in such a plane and felt fear at being in one?

The FRX00 had been modified for manned flight from the FRX99, which had been designed to be unmanned. The addition of flight crew safeguards in manufacturing the manned version had drastically increased the weight of the plane, but even so it was still far more maneuverable than any other manned fighter. It still possessed the same potential as the FRX99, after all.

In designing manned planes, engineers had to take into account the human body's frailty in the face of G forces. For that reason, they couldn't avoid decreasing its air combat capabilities. Human beings are land animals, after all, and their ability to grasp three-dimensional space is limited. They can fly inverted through a cloudbank and never even realize it. However, when designing an unmanned aircraft, all of these weak points can be eliminated. When you don't have to worry about a human occupant, you can create a plane that can carry out maneuvers to its full technical potential. Sending the plane into a controlled flat spin would be child's play. When you had such perfect control, what would once have been a useless maneuver in actual combat could prove advantageous, giving your assault forces a high degree of flexibility in battle.

The FRX99 had been created to be such a plane, with vertical canard wings and two-dimensional vectored thrust engine nozzles. With direct side force control, it had the ability to rotate like a boomerang. The airframe even had direct lift force control as well, and could nimbly move up or down while maintaining level flight. To maintain the efficiency of the air intake system during such violent maneuvers, the intake ports extended above and below the main wing. At first glance, this made the twin-engine plane appear to have four.

Major Booker would never forget Lieutenant Rei Fukai's impression of the prototype when it was delivered to the SAF.

"It looks powerful, but clumsy," Rei had said.

As his neck ached, the major recalled Rei's words over and over. The FRX99 had been designed with the idea that humans weren't necessary and that they should stay the hell away from it. Perhaps Rei had sensed that. It was a combat machine built without any regard for human beings. Its very design showed that it wasn't meant for humans to fly. Rei had probably sensed that with a single glance.

Even so, the manned FRX00 version could be said to be the most powerful plane in the FAF's current arsenal. Rather than saying it possessed a lethal level of maneuverability, you could just as easily say that it demonstrated just how powerful the plane really was. After all, no fighter plane could honestly be considered safe. The important point was whether or not a human pilot could control it.

Yukikaze had been the one controlling the plane. There was no doubt about that. The problem was that she'd completely disregarded the FRX00's human crew and had not hesitated to maneuver in a way that injured, or even killed, them.

Checking the data file of the FRX00's central computer after they'd returned to base and realizing that it showed no concern for the humans aboard, the major had become afraid.

What the hell was going on? There was no way the plane's central systems didn't know that there were people aboard. If that were true, then the central computer itself had ignored the crew and simply deleted any data it received about the occupants of its cockpit.

Why?

In that moment, the FRX00 wasn't just a prototype anymore. It had literally become Yukikaze. She'd already ejected Rei from the burning remains of her old body. So perhaps, as far as Yukikaze was concerned, there weren't any humans aboard her. Or rather, she *assumed* there weren't any. That probably would have led her to treat any data about the crew aboard the FRX00 as an error. It was a plausible explanation, but they couldn't determine that for certain from Yukikaze's memory data. And since she couldn't understand ambiguous human language, it wasn't as though they could just ask her, "What the hell was going through your mind before?" The data hinted at the answer, but if it didn't contain what the humans wanted to know, the best they could do was to guess at what Yukikaze's intentions had been.

Once she'd transferred herself to the FRX00, Yukikaze had wanted to eliminate the surrounding enemy JAM as quickly as possible. That much was certain. In the investigation conducted after they'd returned to base, it was learned that the FRX00 had cut out all of its maneuvering limiters. Or to be more accurate, it had never engaged them in the first place. He could imagine that the crew safeguards had been working just fine, but that from Yukikaze's point of view, they were just malfunctions. In order for Yukikaze to release all of the limiters, she would have had to send false data to all the sensor systems that there were no crewmen aboard and then deactivate the safeguards. As far as she was concerned, it wasn't false data. Since Rei had been ejected, the data from the safeguards telling her that there *were* humans aboard must have been in error, and Yukikaze had simply corrected it. The problem with this explanation was that, normally, it should have been impossible. So the only explanation possible was that Yukikaze had made a mistake. And that was what Major Booker just couldn't understand.

Considering that Yukikaze had never experienced transfer of herself into a new airframe, it wouldn't be too much of a stretch to suppose that the transfer could cause her to make some sort of mistake. If it wasn't a mistake, there were much simpler ways she could have cut out the limiters, assuming that cutting them had been her true intention. Yukikaze could have just activated the FRX00's ejection seats. In both the old Yukikaze and the FRX00, the central computer was capable of activating the seat escape system if it determined that the crew were unconscious and unable to activate it themselves. The crew safeguards that controlled all of the maneuver limiters, G-suit controller, and the active headrests that protected the crews' necks were designed to deactivate if the plane were unmanned. If she'd simply ejected their seats, she could have performed the most lethal air combat maneuvers possible without any problem.

But Yukikaze hadn't done that. So, had it been a mistake caused by her transferring herself, or was it that Yukikaze had decided she didn't have to waste time ejecting any human other than Rei? There was no way to tell what her true feelings were. Hell, it was even possible that Yukikaze's actions had nothing to do with what had happened, and that there was a fault in the FRX00's safeguard system.

The true reason remained a mystery.

Because these questions remained unanswered, they'd been forced to suspend their plan to mass produce the FRX00 and establish a new SAF. When Dr. Balume suggested that the pain in his neck wasn't fading because of that, Major Booker grew depressed. Did that mean he'd be stuck with it unless he found an answer? *Shit*, he thought, *if Rei'd just wake up, that'd take care of my anxiety*. If Lieutenant Rei Fukai, Yukikaze's partner, told him, "Yukikaze just decided she should kill any crew on board that wasn't me," he might not like to hear it, but he had a feeling he could probably understand it. Even so, it didn't look like Rei would be regaining full consciousness any time soon.

The Systems Corps had said that if the SAF couldn't explain the cause of the FRX00's (Yukikaze's) dangerous maneuvers, then they would investigate it themselves. When Major Booker objected, they'd demanded that he hand it over to them.

Major Booker had fought back against the demand, saying that he wouldn't give the data to the Systems Corps under any circumstances. The reason being that the FRX00 was now Yukikaze herself, a battle-tested SAF fighter plane. No other corps would be permitted to read the contents of her central data file. Besides that, if anyone apart from the SAF attempted to check out Yukikaze's central computer, she would self-destruct. The Systems Corps had dropped the tough-guy routine when he'd pointed this out to them. They knew very well how dangerous an SAF fighter's central computer could be, mainly because they were the ones who'd designed it.

He'd had to point out the FRX00's telecommunication log from when she'd returned to base in order to prove that it was now Yukikaze.

At the time, she'd called herself that, identifying herself as Yukikaze.

DE YUKIKAZE ETA2146.AR

"This is Yukikaze. Estimated time of arrival at base 21:46 hours. That is all."

She hadn't transmitted Unit B-3, her mission sortie code number, but had identified herself as "Yukikaze." For the first and only time.

Perhaps Yukikaze was cognizant of the fact that she was no longer in the same body and therefore technically no longer Unit B-3. In that case, the only way she could identify herself was as Yukikaze. *That was probably it*, Major Booker thought. Or, he had gone on, she might have identified herself solely as Yukikaze as a way to try and find Rei, the one who had given her that name. He'd told Systems Corps that she might have been pretty shaken by the whole experience as well.

Systems Corps pointed out that, if this were true, it would be dangerous to have a combat machine acting in such a human way. Fighter planes didn't *need* individual personalities, they'd said. Major Booker decided that Systems Corps was using the situation to claim that the SAF (and by extension, Booker himself) agreed with their theory that the FAF no longer needed manned fighters so that they could steal Yukikaze away from him. That was when he lost his temper, shouting that he'd let an active-duty fighter get taken apart by friendly hands over his dead body. The argument got pretty heated, but in the end, Systems Corps gave up. They got in a parting shot though, pointing out that if Yukikaze had actually transferred herself into the FRX00, she'd used a wireless transmission that could have been intercepted by the JAM, which might have been the cause for the rising damage rates seen in the Sylphids nearly identical to the old Yukikaze. So long as they would not hand her over to them, it would be up to the SAF to investigate this, not to shirk their responsibilities, and so on and so forth.

They can go on saying it as much as they like, but if Systems Corps truly believe that manned fighters are no longer needed, they're just wrong, thought Major Booker. As far as the SAF's mission was concerned, you couldn't separate the men from the machines.

Major Booker reiterated his thought that, no matter how much more reliable the unmanned planes became, the SAF would still have a need for manned planes. Even using their current Super Sylphs as unmanned planes was no good. He was sure that a human pilot could catch data during combat that a machine would simply ignore. Yukikaze's behavior in real combat during that incident had proved that to him.

It was mentioned in her combat record that, during her mission, Yukikaze's crew had ejected twice. The first time when they made contact with the JAM, and then later during that mysterious time gap when the JAM shot her down.

If the ejection seat had been fired twice, it meant that Rei, her pilot, had used it once to bail out, and then he'd been flying Yukikaze again, after it had happened. That would have been impossible unless a new ejection seat unit had been mounted into the plane. That meant that somebody had installed a second ejection seat. There was no record that TAB-15, the closest front-line base, had received a request for a spare seat from Yukikaze, so that left only one conclusion: the JAM had installed it. Yukikaze had taken actions during that time gap that they still couldn't explain. The major was sure that Lieutenant Rei Fukai knew the data that wasn't in Yukikaze's data file. It was the sort of data you could only get from a manned sortie. He could imagine that the JAM had engaged in their first direct interaction with a human.

All the answers were probably inside of Rei's head.

"Please wake up," Major Booker urgently prayed. If Rei would just wake up, all the stress that was making his neck hurt would fade away. He could have the confidence to introduce the mass-produced FRX00s into service. They might have been dangerous planes for humans to fly, but that threat paled next to that of the JAM.

As for the FRX00, it was in the SAF's hangar, in its place, lined up next to the Super Sylphs flown by the other squadron members. The only manned version of the FRX99 in the entire Faery Air Force. FRX00. Personal name: Yukikaze. Yukikaze's new body.

Yukikaze had transferred to the FRX00 and returned to base, but her pilot Lieutenant Rei Fukai had yet to return. Major Booker had eventually been freed of his neck brace, but Rei hadn't regained consciousness. His physical body might be there, but Rei just wasn't home.

Major Booker had a pile of problems to deal with. Rei. Yukikaze. The strategy and tactics to use against the JAM. As it turned out, he was about to have even more troubles dumped onto his plate.

2

MAJOR BOOKER SHUT the fighter maintenance file with a sigh and poured himself a cup of cocoa. "I'm busy as hell, but you just won't wake up, will you Rei," he muttered. Sitting down on his desk rather than in the chair, he picked up his mug. "Want some?" he asked Lieutenant Rei Fukai.

Rei sat in a wheelchair next to the major's desk. His eyes remained closed. He didn't move a muscle.

Every day of late, the major would wheel Rei to his office for about an hour. *In the hospital, Rei is just a patient, but here in the SAF's area he is a soldier and he's treated like one,* thought the major. The chances were very good that even a slight stimulus might be enough to bring him out of his coma.

"Not thirsty, I guess." The major let out a little sigh and then drank his cocoa. "Self-service. Clean your own cup. What I wouldn't give for a sharp, hot secretary. Don't you think I need one?" The major looked at Rei. "'Not my problem.' That'd be your answer, right? Isn't that what you'd say, Rei? If you could talk. I can guess what you'd say.

"A soldier who can't fly. Pretty pathetic. Well, you and me both. Here I am, doing a monologue. Although, technically it's not a monologue when you're here 'cause I speak for you too."

No response from Rei. Still, there was that one time when he thought Rei had reacted to hearing Yukikaze's name. The major took that to be a good sign. Rei's eyes had stayed closed, but his cheek had twitched.

Twice, Rei had opened his eyes. *What are you reacting to?* the major wondered. *Maybe you're fighting the JAM in your head, but maybe you're reacting to something in the outside world. I'd like to know which.*

Major Booker had no medical expertise, but he knew Rei better than any of the medical staff. He genuinely believed that Rei wanted to have these conversations with him. He'd gone so far as to set it up so that the telemetry from the brain wave monitor attached to Rei's head could be received from anywhere in the SAF's area. The idea was to feed it all in real time into the tactical computer in the SAF's headquarters as he interacted with Rei. *If there's a correlation between changes in my friend's brain waves and whatever I'm talking about,* the major thought, *then I'm having a conversation, not a monologue.*

"It's a touching effort, Rei. I'm sure even you must appreciate that. The SAF's tactical computer is monitoring you. You really are a big shot around here, aren't you?"

At this point, analysis didn't indicate that Rei was reacting to the outside world. It would have been nice if they could figure out a way to translate his thoughts directly into speech. That wasn't possible now, the major told Rei, but it eventually would be.

"What, you think that's bullshit? No, eventually we'll be able to achieve direct human–machine communication by thought alone. You'll be able to pilot a plane just by thinking about it. You still wouldn't be able to take those high-speed maneuvers, though. But if you sensed you were in danger and wanted to eject from your plane, you'd be able to activate the ejection sequencer even if you couldn't move your arms or legs. Rei, you aren't dead. You just can't access the outside world, right? Somewhere, there's still a connection open to you. I'm not giving up on you, because there's a lot of stuff I want to ask you about."

Rei didn't answer. He merely sat, his head slumped against the wheelchair's headrest. The brain wave monitor he had on his head made him appear to be wearing a hat, but he was dressed in a flight suit. He looked almost bored with the major's monologue. Booker then changed his mind, deciding instead that it looked like Rei wanted to continue the conversation, so he pressed on.

"So, I told you before, didn't I? About the newbie we got? For Unit 13. We finally found a successor for Captain Samia. Name's Second Lieutenant Yagashira. The characters for his name are the ones for 'bow' and 'head,' by the way. He was asking about you. Wanted to know just what kind of group member you were. You keep goofing off around here and pretty soon everyone's going to know about you. A pilot's career is short, after all. Even if the JAM don't get you, you'll eventually lose the strength you need to fly. I learned that in the FRX00. What do you think?"

I can still fly, he imagined Rei would answer.

"Yeah, you can still fly," the major responded. "When you wake up, we'll have you back in the air in no time."

The major had seen that, if left alone, Rei's body would have become as immobile as a plant, and Booker didn't want that to happen. First of all, it would have been awful to see that happen to a friend, but as the personnel supervisor of the SAF, he didn't want to lose a good pilot either.

There weren't many people who could handle SAF duties. It

wasn't just a matter of training or experience but also the need for pilots with the right personality, men who could carry out their missions with a callous intensity.

The new guy who'd been assigned to 5th Squadron, Second Lieutenant Yagashira, seemed a little weak in that respect. *That is to say*, the major thought coldly, *he's a little too human*. Lieutenant Yagashira had asked who Rei was and such, unlike the other pilots in the SAF, who were indifferent toward him. Lieutenant Yagashira might have been a first-rate pilot, but he might also have been unsuited for duty in the SAF. Rei wasn't like that. He seemed to have been born to serve. If he awakened, he'd want to be sent back into combat as soon as possible.

To prevent Rei's body from atrophying, it was forcibly manipulated for quite a long time every day. At the rehabilitation center, he'd be loaded into a machine similar to a powered suit to exercise while his muscles were given electrical stimulus. Seeing what looked like a corpse being made to dance made the major want to shut his eyes the one time he went to observe the procedure. However, he gritted his teeth and toughed it out, because he'd been the one who had asked that it be done in the first place.

"You should be grateful for all the trouble we're taking over you, Rei. Still, even if I wasn't around, they'd probably be doing it for you anyway. You're a very important man, after all. What really happened to you? Did you meet the JAM? The actual, physical JAM? What were they like? Please, answer me. You're my best friend and I'm tired of talking to you like this. There's nothing wrong with your head. Those quacks in medical told me so, and just this once, I'm willing to believe them. Rei, say something to me—"

A knock at the door interrupted him. "Come in," answered Major Booker, who proceeded to gulp down the last of his cocoa. He never would have guessed who was about to step through the door.

"General Cooley..." It was Brigadier General Lydia Cooley, boss of the SAF. Major Booker stood up from his perch on the desk and saluted, then offered her the chair behind his desk. His office lacked a decent sofa for visitors to use.

The general pushed her glasses up higher on her nose, then looked at Rei.

"Is Rei in the way, ma'am?" the major asked. "I was about to call the nurse for him, so…"

"No, it's fine," the general answered. "Leave Fukai where he is."

"Did you come to see him about something?"

"Yeah, you could say that. The Intelligence Forces were asking me how long you intend to keep Fukai like this."

"Hm," the major replied. "They're at it again, are they?" *This is one superior who always brings tough problems for us, huh, Rei*, he thought. "I'm not handing Rei over to them, General. He's a vital member of the SAF."

"As a pilot."

"A pilot who will fly again."

"When?"

"We're working on that."

Her demeanor softened. "I know, Major," she replied and then sat down in his chair. "You've been putting a great deal of work into this. I don't want to lose a good pilot either."

So why don't you handle the FAF Intelligence Forces' demands that we hand over Rei to them on your end, General? Major Booker wanted to say, but just barely managed to hold his tongue.

"So what's the problem then?" he said instead. "If we hand Rei over to Intelligence, he'll end up a human vegetable. They won't exercise him, just concentrate on treatments to extract the knowledge in his brain, if you can call that sort of stuff 'treatment.'"

"I think your method is the correct one," she replied. "However, Intelligence doesn't agree. It's very irritating. How long has the lieutenant been like this?"

The major paused. "About three months," he answered. "Today is day ninety-two, General."

"Fukai's term is nearly up, then."

"What do you mean? Oh, of course. You mean his term of service. But Rei was going to reenlist."

"Unless he makes that intention known himself, he'll be discharged and become a regular civilian again. If that happened, then there'd be nothing the SAF could do to stop Intelligence."

"Can they do that?"

"There are big shots in the FAF who are on board with the idea. They'll make it happen, Major. If there's something those people want to do, they'll do it. And we don't have any big shots of our own among them who can stop it from happening. I certainly don't have that power. I am essentially the commander of the SAF, but officially the SAF falls under the direct command of the commander of Faery base's Tactical Combat Air Corps. At the moment, that's Lieutenant General Laitume. I'm just the deputy commander."

"Even though we have our own autonomous headquarters."

"Despite my rank, I have the responsibilities of a lieutenant general, and the work you do certainly wouldn't normally be a major's responsibility. That's not saying they look down on the SAF. As the war's tactical situation has changed, our duties have grown in importance, but the internal organization of the FAF just hasn't kept pace. Still, there's no use complaining about it. That fact is that, in one month, we're going to have to give up Fukai."

The general kept her eyes locked in a sidelong glance on Rei as she said this. "Therefore—" she continued.

"Therefore, you're ordering me to get Rei to sign his reenlistment papers, is that it?" the major replied, cutting her off.

"Yes," she answered. "Is that possible?"

"A month, huh… I can't say for sure, but if Intelligence takes him as he is now, Rei's probably going to end up an invalid."

"So long as my SAF has the power of a corps-level organization, that won't matter."

As if we, with our thirteen tactical recon fighters, were on the same level as a corps that controls hundreds of planes, the major thought. Still, that was what they said. The data that the SAF gathered affected the entire Faery Air Force, and that was especially true of the data in Rei's head—if he had seen the JAM's true form. That could affect the fate of the FAF, if not the whole of Earth. General Cooley was determined to hand over that information herself, to present it as having come from the SAF. In short, she wanted a feather in her professional cap. And it was with an irritated tone that he told her this.

"That may be," the general answered, nodding coolly. "Still, Lieutenant Fukai is a member of the SAF, and if he wasn't in our unit, there would have been a lot of valuable information we never would have gotten. By that argument, I already have a feather in my cap, Major. And he may have information that's just as important. I don't want all your hard work to be in vain. You're using the tactical computer in SAF headquarters for Fukai's treatment. I was the one who authorized that. If I let Intelligence take him at this point, I'll have no authority left."

"I understand perfectly, General."

"How is the lieutenant doing?"

"Physically, he's fine. That's because TAB-15 was so close to where he ejected. Those front-line surgeons are rough, but their work is top notch. I swear, they could probably cure a dead man, which is pretty close to what Rei was when they got to him."

"I understand that he didn't sustain any severe brain damage."

"Probably because those front-line docs gave him the right initial treatment. The surgeons we have here at Faery base are good with the theory, but they don't have the real-world experience. Our chief flight surgeon Dr. Balume is pretty good, as long as you get to him in the first five minutes before the booze messes him up."

"I expect you'll do fine with him," the general said. "Fukai was shot with a pistol, wasn't he? Was he shot by his flight officer, Lieutenant Burgadish? And where did he disappear to? If Fukai doesn't recover, we'll never know that either. I want to know what happened out there. Within the month. Our SAF can do anything, can't it? That is all. Any questions?"

"None, General."

"Very well, then," she replied, nodding. She didn't seem to want to leave the office.

"How about some coffee?" the major offered. "You look tired."

"So do you, Major," she replied. "I'll pass on the coffee, thanks. How's the battle analysis going? We're definitely seeing the action intensify around TAB-15. Do you think all the Sylphid losses are due to the old Yukikaze being shot down?"

"We're about to have a tactical mission briefing. You can hear it then—"

"I want to hear your personal opinion, Major."

"Off the record?"

"Yes."

Strategy sessions, tactical development sessions, mission planning sessions, mission conduct briefings, and on and on and on. There were lots of meetings to attend, the faces varying with each group. At the strategy sessions where the requirements of the next generation of planes were discussed, people from Systems Corps would be in attendance. The tactical development sessions featured lots of soldiers, as you'd expect. And aside from all of those, there were the preflight briefings held before each sortie, with General Cooley invariably in attendance. At those meetings and in her office, the major had asked her for her personal opinions before. However, this was the first time she'd ever come into his own office to ask for his opinion on anything.

"This is just between you and me, Major."

"What are you after, General?"

"I just want to hear your opinion."

"Hm…"

The general was worried. The normally confidant, unflappable head of the SAF who usually had the bearing of a queen was losing her nerve.

This is a crisis for the entire SAF, the major thought. The Yukikaze incident had set off a shock wave that shook the entire Faery Air Force, but the SAF had absorbed the brunt of the blow. Yukikaze had become the first plane in the SAF to be destroyed by the JAM. She'd transferred herself from that plane to the FRX00, and among that data was information related to the Sylphid and the Super Sylph, not to mention data on their performance envelope. If the JAM had gotten ahold of that too, it definitely would have put the Sylph at a disadvantage against the JAM. Just as Systems Corps had said. But it was impossible that Yukikaze would have let that information leak out to the JAM.

"It has nothing to do with the Yukikaze incident," the major declared. "Yukikaze would never have allowed the JAM to get that data."

"But there is a possibility."

"There's also the possibility that the JAM gained data on the

Sylph's weaknesses from a plane other than Yukikaze. I'd say the odds of that are much higher."

"I'd like to think that, Major."

"Believe it and it'll be true. This isn't like you. If you stay this indecisive, you'll blow your chance for a promotion, General."

She didn't answer; instead she simply sighed faintly.

"General, the method Yukikaze used to transfer her data has never been seen before, even by us. It was just as novel a feat to the JAM. There's no way the JAM could have known what it was. Yukikaze used the U/VHF communication system on the FRX00 to send out false data. The real, vital information was transferred into the FRX00 via the attack control radar."

Yukikaze had switched her fire control radar into single plane pursuit mode to boost its directionality, then targeted the FRX00. She'd then broken her data up like a jigsaw puzzle and transferred it to the FRX00 by modulating the radar wave. The FRX00, being an electronic reconnaissance plane designed for the SAF, simply hadn't sensed it as an attack lock-on and began recording and analyzing the data in real time. Yukikaze had made use of this.

"The FRX00's main functions include an emergency decryption system. Even if the JAM somehow got hold of the decryption hardware, they couldn't analyze it with the hardware alone. Only when the decoder was activated by the central computer could the code be deciphered. To decrypt the data that Yukikaze was transmitting, you'd need something that used the same function structure. In real time. That was the FRX00."

"There were three JAM in the area, though."

"It's possible that they possessed the same function structure as Yukikaze. That's why, as soon as she'd gotten her new body, Yukikaze had to destroy them immediately, even if it meant risking killing Captain Samia and me. She struck and destroyed them before they had a chance to report anything to their friends. The new Yukikaze confirms that."

"Indeed."

"There's another cause for all the Sylphs we've been losing on the front lines. The FAF has been mass-producing the Sylphid in conjunction with its next generation fighter. As you must know, a number of reasonable design changes were introduced in order to make the Sylph easier to produce. You could call it a new design. Another word for a more reasonable design is 'simplified.' They cut corners compared to the original model Sylphids. It's possible that doing so introduced a defect into the design."

"The losses aren't limited to the new model Sylphs that have been introduced into battle, as you well know."

"Hm…Well, if the fault isn't in the planes, then it's probably in our using less and less experienced pilots. Besides that…" the major said casually, "even if they did get the data from Yukikaze, it's old data now, like the Sylph itself is old. It wasn't the FRX00. The SAF needs to introduce it into service. Let's restart our plans for mass production."

"Not the unmanned version?"

"Humans are necessary. It's best to have a lot of means to gather information."

Major Booker said this while looking at Rei, who still sat silently in his wheelchair. What was making him and the general so fainthearted was Rei's being stuck in this state, he thought.

"Speaking of new pilots, what do you think of the new man I transferred into our unit?" the general asked.

"Lieutenant Yagashira? He's only been out on one sortie so far, so I can't say anything about him."

"He has plenty of combat experience. His record is exemplary."

"He was an ace pilot at TAB-15. But he got shot down and sent here."

"He was excellent. That's why I grabbed him."

"Oh? You fancy him that way?"

The general glanced up at the major where he stood. "Beg your pardon, ma'am. The thing is, the SAF needs pilots like Rei."

"Ones who don't care about anything but themselves? Who act like machines? Look at Fukai now. He's a broken machine."

"Yeah," Major Booker replied. "I can't argue with that. Human doctors can't cure him. If we can't get his own self-repair system activated, he's doomed. Still, Rei made it back. So did Yukikaze. Whether you like it or not."

"That's beside the point. And perhaps Yagashira is a bit too human for this work. If you decide that he's of no use to us, be sure to tell me, Major."

"Yes, General."

"It's time for the meeting," said General Cooley, looking at her wristwatch as she rose from the chair. "I'm glad I got this chance to talk with you."

"So am I, General."

As she was about to leave, the major said something that halted her.

"Let's put Yukikaze back into active service. The FRX00."

"Who will be the pilot?"

"Unmanned, I mean."

"Doesn't that contradict everything you've been saying, Major?"

"Yukikaze isn't like any other unmanned plane. Not like an FRX99 that's been unmanned since it was born. That's Yukikaze, General. There's a part of Rei in that plane."

At the moment, Yukikaze was being used by other members of the squadron on training flights designed to familiarize them with the FRX00. She hadn't been sent out into actual combat because there was no way to predict what she'd do out there. However, as they used her for training flights and he grew more familiar with her behavior, Major Booker's expectations had grown. No matter how distinguished a name she'd made for herself, if she didn't fly, she'd end up being taken away by Systems Corps.

"The truth is that she wants Rei to fly her. I think Yukikaze is just itching to fight the JAM. She probably can't stand the thought that she's responsible for Sylphs being shot down like she was."

"You're anthropomorphizing a plane, Major."

"Oh, Yukikaze is definitely not human, and it's dangerous to think of her as such. But the truth is that she was raised by Rei. I think…she cares about Rei. Let's send out Yukikaze for combat recon around the TAB-15 front. I think she'll be able to find out something there. I have a plan ready to go."

"Roger, Major," said General Cooley. "We can't lose to the JAM, so we have to try anything that we can. The SAF mustn't lose this fight. Well then, Major. I'll see you at the meeting."

The general exited the room without another word. *Back to her old self*, he thought. He then called for the nurse on his intercom.

"Time for gym class, Rei. You stay asleep like this and you can kiss Yukikaze goodbye."

Rei had just one month. He'd have to do something in that time. He had to.

When the nurse arrived, the major reminded her to change Rei's clothes for his exercise session and then to shower him off after it was done. He always did this. And after promising him that she'd take care of it, the nurse took the wheelchair and left the room.

Rei needed something to stimulate him back to life. *I wish he had a girlfriend*, the major thought as he gathered his papers for the meeting. The closest thing Rei had to a lover was Yukikaze, and the time had come for the major to seriously consider putting Rei aboard her as a sort of shock treatment. He'd told Rei that he could fly anytime, but he probably wasn't strong enough. The doctors had told the major that they couldn't guarantee that Rei would survive. However, it might be worth the risk. It was a decision not to be made lightly.

But before that, Major Booker grabbed the plan for using Yukikaze unmanned in combat and exited the office.

Tomorrow. Tomorrow she would fly. General Cooley's approval was in the bag. *Rei*, he thought, *Yukikaze's going back into action, and I'm going to let you see it.*

3

YUKIKAZE WAS LEAVING for her sortie right on schedule. She was stored with her vertical stabilizers folded down against her horizontal ones. Riding the elevator up from the underground hangar to the surface, she activated her engines and raised her tail stabilizers to their vertical position. As they rose into place, it seemed as if life were being breathed into the plane's body. Inside of Yukikaze's cockpit, Major Booker looked behind him to make a visual check of the stabilizers' condition.

Unlike the other planes of SAF 5th Squadron, there was no

wind fairy mascot design painted on the side. This wasn't a Super Sylph, after all, so the image of a mythical sylphid would have been inappropriate. This model of tactical electronic reconnaissance fighter plane had no official nickname yet. Even so, it was still the best fighter in the FAF. For now it was known simply as the FRX00. *Only its personal name has been decided, and that was chosen by the plane herself,* the major thought.

Yukikaze. Just like the old Yukikaze, the name had been hand-painted beneath the cockpit in small Japanese characters by Major Booker as Rei looked on.

The outer side of the tail bore the Boomerang squadron logo in dark gray. Below it were small letters spelling out SAFV, indicating the plane was attached to Special Air Force 5th Squadron.

Her squadron number was 05013, and her serial number painted along the length of the airframe was 96065. Aside from those, she bore no other markings.

From the cockpit, Major Booker spied Rei, flanked by a couple of attending nurses, near the entrance of an SAF ground area personnel elevator. He then stepped on the toe brake and pushed the throttle forward.

The twin high-output engines, high efficiency series 5000 improved Super Phoenix Mk.-XIs, roared with power. The shrill shriek from the air intakes and the explosive roar of the exhaust filled the air. He could see from the cockpit that Rei showed no interest whatsoever in the loud noises. No, wait. He couldn't be sure from this distance, but the major thought he could see Rei tilting his ears toward it. He wanted to think that, anyway. Still, if he kept his mind on Rei, Yukikaze was never going to fly. He had a careful preflight check to complete, so he slid the throttle back to IDLE.

There was no need to check the ejection seat and canopy systems, since Yukikaze was going to be flying the mission unmanned, but the major gave them a quick check all the same. Just like a pilot taking her out on a training mission.

Even when she didn't fly, she was inspected every day like all the other planes. He'd set up a duty rotation that ensured that every pilot did it, but today, Major Booker was personally performing Yukikaze's daily inspection.

He reached out to the computer address panel to run the self-test program. He flipped the master test selector to run the onboard checks. The auto-throttle, Automatic Landing System (ALS), and Air Data Computer (ADC) started their self-tests.

Unlike the Super Sylph, the FRX00 had only three ADCs instead of five. To be more precise, it had only two. Two of them acted as auxiliary systems, whereas the main air data computer was now integrated with the plane's central computer. In a Super Sylph, the central computer and central air data computer were decoupled, connected only indirectly, but the FRX00 was built so that the central computer controlled the airframe directly. This design had been carried over from the original unmanned designs of the FRX99.

Without an ADC controlling each control surface, a plane designed for negative static stability couldn't maintain equilibrium for even an instant. That held true for unmanned planes, so they carried auxiliary ADCs as well. The unmanned version had only one. If the central computer was completely destroyed, that'd be it for the plane, but the auxiliary system was designed for the possibility of a fault occurring for which the ADC could compensate. However, the FRX00 was a manned plane capable of being flown by the pilot even if the central computer failed, and so it had been built with two independent ADCs. They had all sorts of self-monitoring functions, so even if the central computer systems were dead, the plane could still fly.

But in the end, it was the central computer that actually flew the FRX00. The ADC was simply a backup subsystem for the MADC in the central computer.

Major Booker manually fed mock signals into the ADC and throttle control, looking for any abnormalities.

All clear.

As the self-tests carried out by Yukikaze's central computer—which could be called Yukikaze herself—agreed with Major Booker's tests, checklist items on the display panel vanished one by one. MADC, ADC1, ADC2, ALS, AFCS, and so on.

The readout for the AICS, or Air Intake Control System, stayed lit. The only way to check that was to manually run the test program.

The AICS optimized the amount of air taken into the engines for maximum efficiency. When flying supersonic, the engine air intakes generated a variety of shock waves. In order to stabilize them, the intake ports contained movable ramps. As the plane transitioned from low speed to subsonic, transonic, and supersonic speeds, these ramps deployed in the intake ports to control the rate of air flow and the resulting shock waves. Their position was determined by the aircraft's rate of speed. In simple terms, it was programmed to make a constant change in proportion to air speed, not perform complex control actions due to altitude like the MADC. For that reason, the central computer didn't control them directly, relieving it of the burden.

Even in the event of AICS failure, flight was still possible. Since its program was a simple function of speed, it was very reliable. If any failures were going to occur, it'd be in the hydraulic actuators that moved the ramps. Since it was a simple mechanical system, it didn't have an advanced monitoring system hooked up to the central computer. *Parts like that require a more careful preflight check*, the major thought as he confirmed the AICS program results.

All aircraft checks were now complete. All that was left was to set the master arm switch for the weapon stores. Those consisted of a gun, eight medium-range missiles, and eight short-range missiles. The air-to-air missiles' safeties had already been released by the ground crew. Major Booker called up Yukikaze's central computer to confirm her mission once more.

He set the communications system to auto, then called SAF headquarters using a headset mic. STC, the tactical computer in HQ, linked up to Yukikaze's central computer. Major Booker reissued the orders into the mic to confirm the mission. STC translated his request for Yukikaze.

Mission number, takeoff time, return essentials, IDs for units participating in the operation, recon essentials, navigation support, armament restrictions, weather, and mission airspace... On and on and on. Yukikaze hadn't looked particularly happy when he programmed the data into her before, which was a strange thought as she had no way to make any expressions. Still, from the way she displayed the confirmations, it felt to Major

Booker like she was telling him to hurry up and let her take off. Items scrolled down one after another, too fast for him to read.

"Okay, Yukikaze. You can take off once I'm out of here."

Weapons master arm switch set to ON. The onboard arms display came on. All weapons were free to use. Yanking the headset cord from its onboard jack, the major climbed down from Yukikaze's cockpit. Once on the ground, he plugged it back in to a jack on her body and informed the tactical computer back in HQ that all of Yukikaze's preflight checks had been completed.

Faery base's runway control computer issued the order for Yukikaze to take off. He could tell this from the sudden increase of noise from the engines. He pulled the headset's pin from the jack, a small panel door closing over it. The canopy automatically lowered and locked.

Major Booker quickly moved away from Yukikaze, running back to where Rei sat. When he turned back, panting, Yukikaze had already moved out onto the taxiway.

"Look, Rei," the major said. "You should be riding in there. Yukikaze's taking off without you. Doesn't that bother you?"

The noise of the engine was distant. Yukikaze looked small on the end of the runway. Then, just as soon as you'd noticed that the engine roar had increased, she was tearing savagely down the runway.

She trembled like a wild animal showing its antipathy for being grounded. Then, as if thrusting her rage at the earth beneath her, suddenly she was in the air. Quickly retracting her landing gear, Yukikaze initiated a combat climb.

Major Booker had seen all of this. It was summer at Faery base, with thick clouds hanging overhead. Yukikaze vanished into the cloudbank, leaving only the roar of her mighty engines echoing into the sky.

"Major? Major Booker?"

One of the nurses was calling him. When he turned, Rei's eyes were open, but his gaze was not in the direction of Yukikaze.

He knows, Major Booker thought fiercely. *Rei knows.* Once the sound of Yukikaze's engines had faded, Rei closed his eyes again. But this was a good sign. The major was sure of it.

"We're going down. To the command center," he said. "Come

on, Rei. Let's see how Yukikaze fights."

Major Booker indicated to the nurses to follow, and together with Rei he descended back underground, headed for the SAF command center where Yukikaze's flight status was being monitored.

4

AT TAB-15, THE FAF's tactical air base closest to the front, multiple fighter squadrons were scrambling into the air.

The main attack force consisted of the twelve planes of TAB-15's 505th Tactical Fighter Squadron, flying Sylphid fighters. They were equipped with a minimum air-to-air weaponry load-out consisting of the plane's gun and four short-range missiles so that they could carry four large air-to-ground missiles as well. Charged with covering the 505th strike team was the 515th assault group, consisting of seventeen Fand IIs.

Confirming his course, 505th team leader First Lieutenant Gavin Mayle headed straight for the JAM base. The team broke into four groups of three planes each. Normally, they'd fly in one formation, but lately they'd lost three planes, one after another. Their best pilot had been Lieutenant Yagashira. Lieutenant Mayle recognized his skill, but at the same time he felt a bit relieved when Yagashira was transferred out of the unit. The realization of this came to him in a flash as he checked the planes flying to his left and right and thought how Yagashira wasn't in either of them.

Lieutenant Yagashira was the type of man who tried to fight the JAM single-handed. He was a troublemaker. He was just perfect for the SAF. They'd been the ones who yanked him out of his unit. *Well*, Lieutenant Mayle thought, *I owe the SAF thanks.* The guy didn't understand how to fight as part of a team, or maybe it was just that he didn't want to understand. You could put it in a favorable light by saying that, in a touch-and-go battle, Lieutenant Yagashira was the kind of guy who did everything he could to fly his plane to protect himself. The problem was that there was a part of Yagashira that liked those touch-and-go battles. There were times that his antics endangered not only the formation but the entire strike group. Nobody in the group wanted to fly with him, no matter how good a Sylph driver the guy was.

Normally, a pilot like that would be reassuring to fly with. When your plane gets into trouble, you'd expect him to come swooping in to cover you. And it was true that Lieutenant Yagashira would do that when the occasion arose. *On the other hand*, thought Lieutenant Mayle, *it was also true that Yagashira was the cause of that trouble on many of those occasions.* As far as Lieutenant Yagashira was concerned, he was attacking to destroy the JAM, and it was fine when he sent them crashing to the ground with one blow. The trouble was when the JAM who escaped that blow served up their counterattack, because it was Yagashira's fellow pilots who would usually end up having to swallow it.

Certainly, Lieutenant Yagashira's piloting skill was unmatched by anyone else there, but the most important thing for the team was ensuring that they did not lose. Attacking an enemy that could beat you was just foolish.

Nobody wanted to fly with him, and the reason for that was pretty simple: everybody hated him.

Including me, Lieutenant Mayle thought. Yagashira didn't inspire confidence in other people. He was missing a fundamental part of what allows basic human interaction. Mayle wanted to know what sort of environment he'd grown up in, since Yagashira wasn't even aware that he lacked basic human kindness.

"I'm so glad he told us how he felt about dogs," Mayle murmured to himself sarcastically.

One day, the guys had been talking about how much they liked dogs. Lieutenant Yagashira had unexpectedly joined in and, upon hearing that the subject was dogs, had said, "I hate dogs. Let's talk about cats," and then started rambling on about them. Nobody was particularly interested, but the lieutenant didn't notice. It was like he'd forgotten that he was talking to people. If he'd been talking to a computer, it would have been fine, since computers could change subjects without any trouble. In fact, it'd be best if he exclusively interacted with computers. Aboard his plane, the man could work wonders. Once he'd climbed down out of it, he could do everyone a favor by not talking to anyone and especially by not mimicking them. That was really irritating. The man just couldn't communicate with humans. Hell, you could go so far as to say he wasn't human, period. Despite that, he wasn't aware of it and thought of himself as being as human as the rest of them. That was why he was so hard to deal with.

The guy must know that nobody likes him, Lieutenant Mayle thought. But he probably didn't know why he was so disliked, and he'd probably go to his grave still wondering. The SAF might be able to make use of Yagashira, though. He'd heard that their pilots didn't mix together much. They were an inhuman group. Truly not human. There, Lieutenant Yagashira probably wouldn't be liked *or* disliked. He lived his life dressed in the skin of a human, but the guys in the SAF had stripped themselves of it. If Lieutenant Yagashira realized that, he might understand why people hated him. If he cared, that is.

But no matter where he goes, Lieutenant Mayle thought, *that guy will never change.* The guys in the SAF wouldn't want to be friends with him. It would be okay if he'd then just keep quiet and withdraw from his comrades, but since Lieutenant Yagashira thought of himself as human, he wouldn't do that. When he tried to make friends they'd grow irritated with him. Visibly. And when the SAF pilots got irritated, the lieutenant would probably hate them for it.

Before they got irritated though, the SAF pilots would likely just tell him, "We don't want to have anything to do with you," but the lieutenant probably still wouldn't get it. He'd try to "act human." A *truly* human response would be to respect a request of "Leave me alone," but Yagashira wouldn't get it. *The SAF will eventually figure out his true nature*, Mayle thought. Maybe they'd grabbed him from his unit because they knew. Maybe they were confident that he could be used as a perfect combat machine. A man who would be an asset in the war against the JAM.

Lately, the number of people like Yagashira was increasing, thought Lieutenant Mayle. *Well, he's somebody else's problem now. The guy probably couldn't care less about his old unit, and here I am still thinking about him, and no way does that make any sense. I hope the JAM kill that guy soon*, the lieutenant thought.

Nobody said it out loud, but everybody thought that. The time that Yagashira's plane had been shot down, Mayle's plane had been the one in the covering position. Yagashira's plane had two JAM fighters on its tail, and he was in a high-G turn trying to shake them loose. *I can handle one JAM fighter,* he'd probably thought. Mayle had understood at once that Yagashira wanted him to take care of the one on the starboard side, so he'd put his plane on a course to allow Mayle to easily attack it. Lieutenant Mayle had understood that. It was a precise decision, made with lightning speed. Ingenious. Like a trap sprung with mechanical precision on the two JAM fighters. In hindsight, Mayle agreed with the plan, but at the time, he didn't.

Lieutenant Mayle's covering fire had been an instant too late. *Yagashira's plane is going to get it,* he'd thought in a rush. *Come on, kill him!* It was stupid to think that that momentary, automatic thought had been enough to make him hesitate. He didn't think he had it in him. *Still,* he thought, *if that hadn't been Yagashira's plane, I doubt I'd have hesitated.* In the end, he hadn't defended Lieutenant Yagashira's plane. It wasn't like he could have helped it. It might have been a reaction from his body, not his mind.

Your body doesn't think; it just reacts. And since it doesn't think, Lieutenant Mayle still didn't know why he'd hesitated. It was unnerving to know that things like this could happen in the FAF. That a human would wish a fellow human dead. He didn't talk about it. If he had, he'd have been convicted of willful dereliction of duty and executed. And if that happened, this battlefield would turn into one where human fought human. It would destroy the 505th strike group. That was why, even if pressed, he'd never, ever say that he wished death on Lieutenant Yagashira. Not even as a joke.

Lieutenant Yagashira and his flight officer in the rear had ejected from the crippled plane and hadn't been rescued till two whole days later. This was because the fierce battle had raged on, preventing a good fix on their mayday beacon, but they'd been found unharmed. Yagashira had seemed different after the rescue, more distant. It was probably the shock of an ace like him getting shot down. He didn't remember a thing from the time he bailed out till the search and rescue plane had found him.

After that, having lost his beloved plane, he took it upon himself to conduct the maintenance inspections on the other pilots' planes. Lieutenant Mayle had found it a bit surprising that, even as Yagashira practically shoved the other pilots out of the way to do this, he never asked to fly in one. Maybe he'd developed a fear of flying. Even as the other pilots offered their planes for him to use, they were glad that he didn't want to fly any more sorties with them. However, the FAF wasn't about to let an excellent pilot spend his time goofing off, and the thought of having to fly with Yagashira again had filled Mayle and the others with dread. And then, just as they were all praying for him to disappear, word had come from the SAF asking if they had any expert pilots.

What a lucky break that had been. The whole squadron had congratulated Lieutenant Yagashira on his new posting, saying he was definitely moving up in the world and how jealous they were of him. The sentiments of the celebration had been genuine. They might not have been getting promotions, but at long last, they were getting rid of this annoying presence in their midst.

The party would have been even merrier had it been his funeral, the lieutenant thought. He would be going to Faery base, the FAF's main base. The elite. The only thing that threw cold water on the whole thing was the question of why *that* guy? Mayle might never see his face again, but with Yagashira in the SAF, he'd be in his plane looking down on his old squadmates. The way all those guys at Faery base looked down on them. Mayle didn't like it.

A warning chimed, rousing the lieutenant from his reverie. They'd just entered JAM-controlled airspace. The JAM weren't actively tracking them yet, but sooner or later, they'd be spotted.

He radioed the other planes to prepare for combat.

"Let's drop off our presents for the JAM and bug out of here before they send out their interceptors."

Lieutenant Mayle took his plane higher to make it easier to spot their target. This made it easier for the JAM to spot him as well, but that was also part of his duty. *We're decoys*, he thought. Their role was to act as a setup for the first wave's ground attack. The second wave would be the main force: the sixteen planes of the 9th Tactical Fighter Squadron, which would be launching from Faery base to link up with TAB-15. Lieutenant Mayle's group were on a completely different course, targeting a JAM base to buy time and delay the aliens.

They're the elite and our job is to support them, Mayle thought. There was no way to tell which group would be in danger, but common sense told him that his guys would be. They were intentionally attracting the JAM's attention, after all.

A warning chimed again, in a different tone this time. JAM tracking waves had been detected. Mayle's plane went into a zoom climb, streaking high into the air. Spread out below him were the forests of Faery, vivid with the colors of summertime. Purple hues dominated, with blues and greens glinting metallically in the light of the twin suns. Then the forest was behind him and ahead lay a desert of pure white sand.

The JAM base was somewhere in there. He couldn't see it with his naked eye, but the attack target data had been loaded into his plane's central computer. The FAF had judged it to be one of the enemy's large permanent bases. The JAM normally treated their bases as disposable, with their fighters moving in from places still unknown and constantly launching from their front-line bases. For this target, however, their planes had taken up a posture that indicated that they wanted to defend their base instead of just abandoning it. The assumption was that the JAM had fighter production capacity there. There was no way they could ignore such an inviting target. They'd made six raids on it already, but thus far TAB-15 had lacked the air power to score a decisive blow. This time, however, they'd have added help from Faery base. Mayle's mission was just a sideshow, meaning they didn't have to hang in there till the bitter end.

Lieutenant Mayle climbed to nearly the plane's operational altitude limit, the Fand II squadron a little bit ahead and below him. They were arrayed to meet any enemy planes, but Lieutenant Mayle wanted to perform an inverted breakaway before that became necessary.

He waited for the target to enter the firing range of his air-to-ground missiles. The IR (infrared) receiver detected an abnormality. JAM interceptors were launching from the base. The IR receiver couldn't get an exact fix on their location, but an exact fix wasn't necessary right now. He could see a countless number of enemy planes headed right for them.

He hoped they would launch all of their fighters. He hoped that they'd concentrate on targeting the missiles they were about to fire. In those precious few moments, the guys from the 9th TFS would strike the main section of their base. That was the point of this operation, after all.

Target and steering indicators flashed onto his head-up display. The distance to firing range indicator was nearly zero.

Lieutenant Mayle ordered the other planes in the attack group to switch to auto-attack mode. All they needed to do was fly their planes following the steering indicators on the display.

All of the air-to-ground missiles his plane carried fired automatically. A pull-up cue flashed onto his HUD. Lieutenant Mayle executed an inverted breakaway at full thrust. The other planes followed.

All that remained to do was fly back to base in a straight line. The missiles they'd fired had scored hits, but there was no need to assess how much damage they'd caused. That would be the job of the guys from Faery base. The Fand II squadron split into three groups: one to cover Lieutenant Mayle's squadron with the other two going to back up the 9th TFS.

As Lieutenant Mayle's group withdrew from the battle zone at maximum speed, the Fand IIs behind them engaged the pursuing JAM interceptors. As they did, the planes from the 9th TFS were probably using the chance to attack, but Lieutenant Mayle didn't have time to think about that. His plane's engines were malfunctioning. Something had gone wrong with the engine controllers. His speed began dropping rapidly.

"What the hell's going on?!" screamed the flight officer in the rear. A violent oscillation shook the plane. "They're gonna shoot us down! JAM fighters, closing fast!" Mayle didn't need his flight officer to tell him that. What was causing this? Had someone screwed up on the plane's maintenance?

Lieutenant Mayle couldn't hear the engine failure alarm sounding. None of the caution lamps were lit. He couldn't tell what was going on or where the malfunction was occurring. The throttle was set to max, but his speed was still dropping. The fuel flow gauge read normal, but the combustion efficiency in the engines was definitely deteriorating. And what was causing this furious vibration through the airframe? It was like they were being buffeted by turbulence.

JAM fighters that had evaded the Fand IIs were approaching. Lieutenant Mayle wasn't alone; all of the planes in his group were experiencing similar failures. None could get up to full speed. None could break away. In that case, they were going to have to fight.

"Engaging," called out Lieutenant Mayle. Ordering his flight officer to make visual contact with the enemy planes, Mayle looked out of his cockpit as well. He sighted a lone aircraft, flying even higher than his own plane. It wasn't a JAM. It was an FAF plane.

Special Air Force, Unit B-3: Yukikaze. She flew unmanned. Even Lieutenant Mayle had been informed of that. Well, unmanned or not, he expected no help from her. The SAF didn't join in the battles.

The JAM behind them held the dominant position, seeming to mock Mayle's now-lagging plane. He banked sharply, trying to shake them off. "No, other way! Other way!" his flight officer shouted. "Starboard!"

Lieutenant Mayle realized he'd misjudged his evasion direction. They were going to die. He steeled himself for the inevitable but didn't let go of his flight stick. There was no time to eject. Suddenly, there was a flash before his eyes. A shock wave rocked the plane. And then, somehow, they were still flying.

"Wha…what just happened?" Lieutenant Mayle asked his flight officer as he stabilized the plane and got them back on course.

"I don't believe it, Lieutenant," the man responded. "The JAM were shot down. Some help arrived."

"Those Fand IIs really earn their keep," the Lieutenant replied.

"No, sir. It was B-3. The SAF plane."

Mayle paused, dumbfounded.

"What?" was all he managed as a response.

Yukikaze. The unmanned plane had shot the JAM down and was now flying beneath Mayle's fighter. TAB-15 drew into sight.

"Isn't that thing just supposed to observe the battle?" he started to ask when Yukikaze began to dive toward TAB-15. That was when Lieutenant Mayle saw something he simply couldn't believe.

"What the hell is it doing?!" he shouted.

Yukikaze was opening fire at the ground.

Down below lay TAB-15, its ground personnel running from the base. To Lieutenant Mayle's eyes, Yukikaze was picking off the humans below. But he couldn't believe it. The plane had just saved him from the JAM, and now it was doing this?

"Stop it!" Lieutenant Mayle screamed. "That thing's gone nuts!"

5

DEEP BELOW FAERY base, under the protection of SAF headquarters, the command center had gone silent.

The center's huge main display screen had suddenly lit up with icons showing the positions of the returning fighters of the 505th. B-3, Yukikaze, was now transmitting strange data during the mission.

While SAF planes did track the positions of every plane in their assigned reconnaissance area during a mission, they normally wouldn't transmit that data in real time, and were they to do so, it would only be to track enemy planes; for example, if the JAM did something unexpected that clearly put the FAF at a disadvantage. Normally, the only readout that would appear on the main screen would be the signs marking each phase of the mission as it progressed.

If all went well, it would end with a display from the operation command plane reporting Mission complete, returning to base.

All data, such as enemy and allied plane movements, electronic warfare intel, data on enemy and allied gains, and the like would be stored in the data file of the operation command plane and carried back to base. Watching the battle from on high without joining in was the SAF's duty, and without the data they gathered, no one would even know how many JAM fighters had been shot down. This was because the pilots locked in combat didn't even have enough time to verify if one of their companions had been shot down or not.

So usually all Major Booker had to do during a mission was look at the main screen display as it displayed the phrase **GATHERING DATA** and tick off each point on the attack schedule, while praying that no major abnormalities were reported and that the operation command plane made it back to base in one piece. As much as he'd like to know how the battle was progressing in real time, all he could do was wait. If he didn't, the JAM could very well steal the information the SAF were gathering.

If they were seeing concrete data on the movements of an operation command plane, then something had gone wrong. A problem had cropped up in the plane, for example, or the JAM were directly targeting it. But neither of those were happening now. What they were seeing now had never happened before, ever. Yukikaze was transmitting data showing the exact position, speed, and acceleration of the 505th TFS as it was returning to base. As though it were absolutely vital data. Furthermore, it was identifying the planes of the 505th as **FRIEND/ FOE UNKNOWN.**

Unknown planes were colored yellow on the main screen. Bogeys that couldn't be identified as friend or foe had to be treated as enemies, since they were most likely threats. However, the planes Yukikaze was treating as such were very clearly those of the 505th. The five JAM fighters pursuing them to the rear were colored red, marking them as hostiles, with Yukikaze identifying them as short-range high-speed interceptors, possibly of an improved type.

The SAF battle-monitoring personnel couldn't decide what was going on. The JAM themselves flying into the room wouldn't have caused a bigger shock than what was happening now, and as everyone there sat in stupefied silence, the three planes bringing up the rear of the 505th were shot down simultaneously. Several Sylphids, which should have been light and nimble after completing their ground attack, had picked up pursuers they couldn't shake off and been blown apart.

Sylphids were designed for hit-and-away combat, built for

speed. There was no way that they could have been caught by JAM interceptors.

On a raised platform at the far end of the center, looking out over the backs of the personnel working there, sat General Cooley at the main command desk with Major Booker at an identical desk next to her. Rei sat next to him in his wheelchair, but the incomprehensible situation had the major's eyes glued to the main screen and his breath caught in his throat.

"Why aren't they accelerating?" he asked. "A Sylph should be able to shake off those JAM easily. Why are they just poking along like that?"

"Confirm the position of the 515th TFS," General Cooley said, her voice calm. "Have them cover the 505th. Display courses for Yukikaze and the 515th. Show Yukikaze's position as well."

Major Booker relayed General Cooley's commands via his headset mic to the tactical computer in headquarters. The text **ORDERS EXECUTED** was displayed. Yukikaze broke away from her preplanned reconnaissance air space and began closing on the 505th at high speed.

"What's Yukikaze doing?" General Cooley asked.

As she was saying this, three more of the 505th's fighters were shot down. While the Fand IIs of the 515th TFS managed to shoot down one JAM, the other four enemies pursuing the 505th shook them off.

"Yukikaze's trying to find the cause of what's destroying our Sylphs," replied Major Booker. "I think she anticipated this."

Having targeted the 505th TFS, the JAM fighters avoided engaging the Fand IIs in the 515th, dodging them at high speed. The truth was that their tactics suggested that they didn't care if one or two of their fighters were lost. All that seemed to matter to the JAM was shaking the Fand IIs loose so that they could target the Sylphids ahead and eliminate them. Looking at the 515th, they were keeping a bit of distance from the 505th TFS in order to intercept the JAM fighters. If the JAM were, by some chance, able to break through, the 505th were expected to adopt the tactic of shaking them off. Nobody expected the JAM to chase them so far, since approaching TAB-15 would take the fight inside the base's air defense perimeter.

However, the JAM had caught up with the 505th before they'd gotten close to the defense line—there was something wrong. And not just one or two planes, but all of the planes of the 505th had slowed down rather than accelerated, as though waiting to be shot down. It was being charitable to call the situation abnormal.

Yukikaze relayed the situation to headquarters via real-time data link.

The four pursuing JAM fighters had easily closed in on the 505th and began picking them off, attacking with air-to-air missiles and cannon fire. Unable to escape, by the time the 505th engaged the JAM, there were only three planes left: the formation led by Lieutenant Mayle's plane. The other two planes had no chance in the dogfight that followed. Both were destroyed.

Yukikaze had dived from high altitude at supersonic speed, taking out a JAM fighter with a medium-range missile. She took out two more with short-range missiles as she passed them, then slammed into a steep banking turn to pursue the remaining JAM fighter as it attempted to flee. She blasted it from the sky with her cannon.

Not even three minutes had passed since the 515th detected the approaching JAM fighters. In that short time, the 505th Tactical Fighter Squadron had been wiped out. Only Lieutenant Mayle's plane survived.

Yukikaze reported her battle with the JAM. Even though all JAM in the vicinity had been wiped out and the threat extinguished, she continued to display that she was actively engaging them and did not secure from attack mode. She continued to display Lieutenant Mayle's plane as "unknown."

Yukikaze, seemingly about to turn her anger on the Sylphid for having been so easily destroyed by the JAM, wheeled around to pursue Mayle's plane. Then, as though suddenly headed back to base, she assumed a course for TAB-15, closing fast and flying low. Upon reaching it, she opened fire with her cannon in ground attack mode.

On screen, the indicator continued to show that she was engaging the enemy.

"Abort the attack," General Cooley said. "Order Yukikaze to

return to base. Cancel its mission."

She certainly sounds calm, Major Booker thought, then answered her in a tone as equally businesslike. "We can't issue an abort order. She won't accept it."

If the JAM ever decrypted an abort attack order, they could render Yukikaze powerless. To avoid this danger, she'd been designed from the start not to accept such orders. They were going to have to leave the decision to Yukikaze to the very end. If Yukikaze had decided that humans were her enemy, nobody would be able to stop her. The major had considered the possibility, but as he confronted the reality of the situation, a shiver ran through his body.

"Yukikaze, what are you doing?" Major Booker asked. "What is your target? Tell us your target. Do you read, Yukikaze?"

The tactical computer translated Major Booker's spoken commands and relayed them to Yukikaze. It then translated Yukikaze's response back to him. Yukikaze climbed into a turn, flying slowly above TAB-15. She remained in ground search mode.

Yukikaze's response was displayed on the main screen.

`Precise detection impossible.`

The icon indicating TAB-15's position on screen changed from blue to yellow. A red circle was drawn in the center. Red, indicating an enemy.

"What's going on here?" asked General Cooley.

The red mark that indicated the enemy was blinking on and off. It meant that the target was there, but the position was unknown, visual contact lost.

"Bring it home, Major. There's a chance that Yukikaze may be attacked by TAB-15."

"Yes, General."

The general was right. Yukikaze's communication hinted at a potential disaster the seriousness of which was impossible to convey. It might have simply been due to an abnormality in her decision-making functions, but if they didn't get her back to base safely, they'd never understand why she had done what she'd done. Common sense would say that Yukikaze had turned against the FAF and TAB-15. As you might expect, the idea that anything that attacked you was the enemy ran very strong on the front-line bases. FAF fighters would most likely try to intercept her.

Major Booker was reaching for the control panel to issue an emergency recall order when he heard the voice.

"It's the JAM."

The voice was faint. The major suddenly froze, wondering for a moment if a ghost had called out to him, then whirled in the direction from which the voice had come. There, in the wheelchair, was Lieutenant Rei Fukai. Rei, with his brain wave sensor and transmitter affixed to his head.

"The JAM…are there…"

"Major, hurry!" exclaimed General Cooley. The major held up his hand for her to be quiet. Then General Cooley noticed the strange change in Rei's condition.

"Look closely," Rei murmured. "The JAM are there. I see them."

Rei's voice was barely a whisper, but he had definitely spoken. The tone of his voice told them that he understood everything. It was the first time in three months they had heard a word come from his mouth.

"Rei…" the major said. "Do you hear Yukikaze's voice? Inside your head?"

It was impossible, and yet the voice Rei was speaking with seemed to be Yukikaze's.

The control center erupted into pandemonium.

The major's eyes leapt to the main screen. The red circle had stopped blinking and gone to a steady red. The screen subdivided and brought up a transmission of Yukikaze's field of view. They could see an image of TAB-15, Yukikaze's fire control system overlaying a targeting reticle on it. A text readout appeared.

`Precise detection impossible. Cannot iden-`
`tify friend or foe. Probability of new type of`
`JAM: high.`

The shock of Yukikaze's claim hit the major even harder than the fact that Rei had regained consciousness.

"What? Where?" he shouted. The JAM's true form was a mystery, but it was possible that the JAM were some sort of artificial life-form. Had Yukikaze detected an unknown machine creature somewhere in TAB-15?

"Attacking all moving things," Rei whispered.

The major turned. Rei's eyes were open. He might have been looking at the main screen since Yukikaze's transmission.

Rei raised his right hand, which until now hadn't moved under his own power. The position it took… as if he were holding a flight controller. His index finger moved, and the major instinctively recognized it. He was using the weapon selector. Then Rei pressed his thumb down.

Yukikaze responded to his movements. Ready gun. Gun attack mode. Resume ground attack.

The major couldn't believe what he was seeing. All he could think was that Rei's will was somehow tied to Yukikaze. Either by brain waves or electrical current, she was sensing his actions and carrying them out. It was true that Rei was wearing monitoring sensors designed to detect his own brain activity, but there wasn't any sort of system that could translate his thoughts into commands.

No, the major corrected himself. *There was the tactical computer. What the humans may not have been able to do, the SAF's computers may have achieved.*

"Stop him," General Cooley said sharply.

Yukikaze was targeting TAB-15's ground personnel. The major suddenly grabbed the transmitter affixed to Rei's head and physically pulled the energy pack from it.

Inside the center, Yukikaze sounded an alarm. A readout informed the center staff that the target had been lost. In the major's place, General Cooley ordered Yukikaze to resume normal reconnaissance duty.

"Rei, what did you see? Can you hear me?" The major shook Rei's body as he spoke. Rei didn't answer. Yukikaze was climbing again. Slowly, though. Almost as if she didn't understand what she'd been doing until then.

The major had seen the strength in Rei's right hand as it moved. He had been piloting Yukikaze right up to the very end. The major touched Rei's hand. It felt firm as steel. A warning sounded from the control panel. A message from the tactical computer.

```
Malfunction in Lieutenant Fukai's communica-
tions system. Restore normal function and re-
designate target.
```

Communications system?

Major Booker read the text again, and then he knew for sure. Under his very nose, a communications system was being constructed, linking Rei with the tactical computer and Yukikaze.

Just as he had so fervently wished for Rei to awaken, so too had the SAF's machine intelligences sought the information Rei carried in his head. It wasn't an emotional wish. Perhaps a more direct desire. "Wake up," the machines and Yukikaze were saying to Rei. And Rei had responded to them where he hadn't for the doctors or even his friend.

But was he really awake now? Major Booker wondered. *It was just another nightmare where he fought the JAM inside of his own head, wasn't it?* In short, it was possible that the tactical computer had merely coaxed him into a state of semi-consciousness.

"What was the target? What were you going to attack?" the major asked Rei. But Rei didn't answer, just sat stiffly looking at the main screen. *No use*, the major thought. Rei hadn't been fully awakened.

An unknown JAM, the SAF headquarters' tactical computer replied. Conjecture that threat to TAB-15 exists from unknown JAM. Form, abilities, and function: unknown.

"And you think that Rei—that Lieutenant Fukai knows the details of this threat?"

Lieutenant Fukai's order to B-3 to attack indicates high probability that he senses unknown JAM threat. B-3 determined abnormality in 505th TFS to be the work of the JAM and opened an emergency transmission line. Lieutenant Fukai sensed this and judged the cause to be JAM presence at TAB-15. However, I cannot directly perceive this enemy by myself. Lieutenant Fukai's instructions are necessary. I detect an abnormality in the communications system connecting Lieutenant Fukai to me. Inform me of the cause.

Yukikaze's advanced reconnaissance technology—electronic sensors that could detect information no human could and optical sensors which could resolve details beyond the ability of the human eye—hadn't been able to find the answer. And so she'd opened a real-time link to Rei in order to tell him that. Even if Rei knew what this unknown JAM was, there'd be no way he could directly sense it at TAB-15. While this battle had elicited a response from Rei, it hadn't brought him back to normal consciousness. It was a kind of half-sleep, like sleepwalking. All he could think was to attack indiscriminately.

Even knowing this, Major Booker figured that it might be better to reconnect Rei to the tactical computer and plug the transmitter's energy pack back in. The fault in the communications system the tactical computer had asked about was caused by his disconnecting the pack. If he put it back, perhaps they'd know what it was that Rei was aiming at.

But the major also remembered Rei's words: shoot everything that moves. He paused. That might as well constitute an order for Yukikaze to kill every human at TAB-15.

"Lieutenant Fukai has blacked out. He cannot indicate the target. Inform Yukikaze."

Roger. B-3 will continue to investigate abnormal deceleration of 505th TFS.

There'd been a slight pause before the tactical computer had printed Roger out on the screen. To be fair, while the tactical computer might have been slightly obsessive about calling Rei back to consciousness, its desire was no more intense than that of Major Booker. He wanted to have a deliberate talk with the tactical computer, to ask it just how much it, a representative of the SAF's machine intelligences, had learned about what had arisen between Rei and Yukikaze.

It seemed that Yukikaze's attack on TAB-15 had been Rei's idea, but the inability to identify the 505th TFS as friend or foe had been Yukikaze's own problem. Seeing that, Rei had reacted, taking over her operations. If his actions didn't have a rational motivation, then all Booker could say was that Rei had lost his mind. That was what a human would think. But neither the tactical computer, nor Yukikaze, thought that Rei was insane.

Major Booker realized that a discrepancy had developed between the humans and their combat machine intelligences. During the short conversation he'd had with the tactical computer, the situation had changed bewilderingly, leaving the major with no time to worry about Rei. The tactical computer was in a similar position.

TAB-15 radioed, demanding an explanation for why Yukikaze had strafed them twice. As the ranking officer, General Cooley had to answer. She paused a few moments, pressing her lips together, then told the major to report it as an accidental weapons discharge. The major, concentrating on his conversation with the tactical computer, didn't hear her at first. The general got his attention, and just as he was realizing what was happening, TAB-15 replied.

This is TAB-15. Roger, scrolled out onto the screen.

However, an actual human voice that sounded like one of TAB-15's comm officers radioed in, asking what they were talking about and demanding to know who had sent the transmission and what exactly they meant when they broadcast that the JAM were present at TAB-15. The tactical computer at SAF headquarters had digitally transmitted the message to TAB-15's central tactical computer, and it was the computer that had sent the acknowledgement. The humans of TAB-15 hadn't done so.

"We've got casualties in our ground crew," the comm officer shouted. "SAF, are you trying to kill us?"

Before Major Booker could explain that it was accidental fire, the tactical computer sent a command to cut voice transmissions, but no one paid any attention to the readout showing this. This was because Lieutenant Mayle's plane, the lone survivor of the 505th, had judged Yukikaze to be an enemy and was engaging her.

Detecting attack targeting waves from Alpha-1, Yukikaze reported, identifying Mayle's plane by its code number.

Roger, the tactical computer responded. Investigate Alpha-1's mobility performance. Initiate mock combat.

This is B-3. Roger.

General Cooley clasped her hands together as she glared angrily at the main screen. She seemed to be saying something under her breath, but the major couldn't make it out. It might have been "God," but it could easily have been "fuck" or "shit" or any number of expletives. And they weren't directed at Lieutenant Mayle's plane. Major Booker thought she was swearing at Yukikaze and the tactical computer as they chatted back and forth without acknowledging her.

Even so, she didn't command them to stand down. The voice comm line was cut and the radio on Lieutenant Mayle's plane was being jammed by Yukikaze. Even if the general had issued an order, there was no way for her words to reach anyone.

"Keep an eye on the 515th's movements," General Cooley quickly said. "Get Yukikaze back to base before they show up."

"This won't be long, General," Major Booker replied. "Alpha-1's practically at bingo fuel."

Either way, Yukikaze and Alpha-1's dogfight wasn't going to last long. Victory or defeat would come in the next thirty to sixty seconds. They might be equally matched in a dogfight, but the plane with the most fuel remaining to get home would win. A plane with no fuel was going down, whether it was shot down or not. The two things a pilot was always fighting were enemy planes and how fast his plane burned through its fuel.

Yukikaze had jettisoned her huge auxiliary fuel tanks before engaging the JAM. She just barely had enough to return to base, but the major decided that she had more than enough to reach the emergency in-air refueling point they'd prepared.

If nothing went wrong, there'd be no need for an in-air refueling. That was one of the things Yukikaze had gained from her new airframe that made her superior to the Sylphid and Super Sylph. Her greater cruising range might be said to be more important than her weapons and maneuverability. Fuel to an airplane was as vital as oxygen to a deep-sea diver. If it ran out, the plane was dead. The constant need for the pilot to be aware of his remaining fuel was a major cause of stress.

"This is quite a show."

Once again hearing a strange voice, Major Booker turned. There stood a lone SAF pilot, arms folded as he watched the screen. A Boomerang soldier. The newest member of the SAF and pilot of Unit 13: Second Lieutenant Yagashira.

The soldiers of the SAF needed no special permission to enter the command center, but none of them ever did unless ordered. Major Booker couldn't recall any flight personnel ever entering the center of their own volition. To the major, Yagashira was an incongruous presence in the room.

Maybe he wanted to get a feel for the atmosphere of the SAF, being a new arrival and all. *Certainly seemed like the sort of guy General Cooley would like*, the major thought as he turned to ignore the pilot and focus his attention back on Yukikaze.

"Lieutenant Mayle won't win, will he?"

From behind him, Lieutenant Yagashira had spoken again.

"His fuel's critical. Typical how Lieutenant Mayle is engaging anyway. Good guy, but his combat reactions are slow." Yagashira sounded like he was gossiping as he spoke. "There's no way he can beat the latest and greatest unmanned fighter. Now, if it were me—"

"Shut up," said Major Booker.

Lieutenant Yagashira hadn't said anything out of line, but his chatter was irritating Booker, like fingernails on a chalkboard. He didn't have time to wonder why. Yukikaze had just initiated combat maneuvers against Lieutenant Mayle's fighter.

"Why isn't the SAF stopping Yukikaze?" Yagashira went on. "Are you trying to goad Lieutenant Mayle into fighting? Is that why you had Yukikaze attack TAB-15? Mayle's not the sort of guy who'd take that quietly. I know what he's like—"

At that point, Major Booker faced Lieutenant Yagashira and ordered him to get the hell out of there. Yagashira seemed shocked. "Either go to your quarters or to the stockade. Your choice!" the major told him.

The FAF didn't have an official stockade, but Yagashira seemed to get the point, although he looked bewildered as to why he'd been spoken to like that. Red-faced, he saluted silently and left the command center.

6

ONE INCIDENT YOU could write off as seeing it wrong, but Lieutenant Mayle had twice seen Yukikaze, at close visual range, open fire at the ground.

"It's killed someone," he yelled. As he tore toward TAB-15 with the throttle maxed, he heard a voice from the base on an open-air channel say that Second Lieutenant Lancome had apparently been killed.

He couldn't confirm with anyone from the base. Lots of information poured in during the battle. It wasn't unusual for someone not to hear someone else clearly, leaving you to rely on your own judgment. Of course, two-way real-time communication was possible using advanced circuits, with the transmitter's code automatically sent to show up on a plane's main display to identify the sender. However, in battle, there was no time to verify the facts. To the contrary, in battle, your ability to think deteriorates. The guy who stops to think winds up dead. You had to fly your plane with the same sort of instincts that jerk your hand back when it touches a hot stove.

So, with the high G forces and sheer terror making his mental faculties undependable, a fighter pilot has to not only evade threats but also counterattack. That was just part of the job description, which was why Lieutenant Mayle pursued Yukikaze and locked weapons on her without a second thought. He told his flight officer behind him that they were engaging.

"That's an SAF plane. It's one of ours!" he shouted back.

"Fuck it. That thing killed Jonathan. You heard, didn't you?"

Second Lieutenant Jonathan Lancome was one of Lieutenant Mayle's subordinates. He was a pilot. He was one of them. The JAM had shot him down once, but he'd made it back. And now he'd been killed by friendly fire?

As a general rule, the plane you flew was assigned specifically to you. In an emergency you might fly someone else's plane or a reserve fighter, but the 505th had lost its reserve planes. Consequently, a great many flight personnel weren't operating with the squadron. Until a new plane was assigned to them, they were mixed into ad hoc teams to fly sorties, some were given leave, others moved into other squadrons, and some were even given non-pilot duties. Lieutenant Yagashira had been promoted, but that hadn't been the case for Lieutenant Lancome. The FAF hadn't approved leave for anyone, so he'd been put on maintenance duty. Lancome had said once that he no longer had the confidence to be a pilot. For Lieutenant Mayle's part, he wanted to keep Lieutenant Lancome as flight personnel and just relax the normally rigid system of plane assignment, but he'd lost the desire to push for this new policy when Lancome had admitted his fears. It wasn't easy to shake the fear instilled by having the JAM shoot your plane out from under you.

Poor Jonathan, Mayle thought. *He died on the ground, killed by a friendly plane.*

Without hesitation, Lieutenant Mayle maneuvered to shoot Yukikaze down. Gripping the flight stick in his right hand and the throttle in his left, he banked steeply at her. As Yukikaze flew away from TAB-15, she responded to Mayle's combat maneuvers. She turned, as though inviting him to follow.

"It wants to fight," the flight officer said. "What do you think?"

Lieutenant Mayle kept his mouth shut and ignited the afterburners. But then the plane began to vibrate again, a combustion status abnormality warning sounding. Yukikaze banked sharply and Lieutenant Mayle lost sight of her.

As he banked hard to follow, a shivering shock wave struck them. Unbelievably, Yukikaze had turned around and flown past them, almost close enough to touch. As the shock wave and the air currents it stirred up assaulted the left wing, it suddenly lost lift, sending Lieutenant Mayle's plane into a quick left roll. At the same time, it apparently ripped the main wing's forward flaps right off. The flight officer craned his neck around and confirmed that a fragment of them had damaged their vertical stabilizers.

Despite this, the plane's flight computers instantly began working every control surface, dutifully stabilizing the plane as Lieutenant Mayle desired.

"The problem's in the engine," Lieutenant Mayle shouted, but even as he said it, the engine alarm warning lamp remained dark. The plane dove then climbed, its speed falling to barely two hundred kilometers per hour. Mayle dove into a turn at full throttle, trying to shake Yukikaze loose.

He ignited the afterburner again, trying to accelerate at full power. He managed to rev it to maximum for about three seconds, but that was followed by a loud bang from the engine on the right that shook the plane. It looked like the turbine blades in the engine had been damaged. At the same time, the compressor in his left engine stalled and flamed out.

Wrestling the plane out of the resulting tailspin took everything Mayle had, leaving him no time to attempt an engine restart. He managed to stabilize it scant moments before augering into the ground, using the speed of the dive to climb higher.

The right engine looked like it wasn't on fire, at least, but it was completely useless now. He tried and failed to restart the left. Now robbed of any thrust at all, the plane's climb weakened, then transitioned into a slow descent. The engine noise had ceased, and it was quiet now. Lieutenant Mayle looked to his right and saw Yukikaze flying next to them, so close that he could reach his right hand out and almost touch her. From her position, he got the feeling that she was flying to keep a constant watch over them. *It managed to beat me without firing a single shot,* Lieutenant Mayle thought numbly. It was possible in a dogfight to stall your opponent's engines out, assuming you had absolute confidence in your plane's maneuverability. That thing had just demonstrated the technique on him.

Mayle silently made a fist with his right hand and held it up, signaling his flight officer that they were about to eject. The light of Faery's twin suns glittered off of Yukikaze's canopy, her cockpit unmanned. *It's like the plane itself is laughing at us,* thought Lieutenant Mayle.

He didn't want to think about anything anymore. When they reached the right altitude, they ejected.

As he floated down beneath his parachute, Mayle watched Faery's forests swallow up his plane and Yukikaze. She had lowered her engine output and flown alongside Mayle's plane. Just as it looked like she was grazing the forest canopy, Yukikaze's exhaust ports flared brightly. In a second, she was turning away at full power, afterburners lit, and a moment later she was out of sight. Then the roar of her engines reached him, followed a moment later by the explosion of his plane as it self-destructed.

Forget avenging Jonathan's death, it's a miracle I'm still alive, Lieutenant Mayle thought with a shiver. *That thing, that Yukikaze... It's a monster. Let it fight the JAM. The JAM aren't human, so let one inhuman freak fight another.* Why did he even have to be here in the first place?

As Lieutenant Mayle fell, looking at the canopy of his flight officer's parachute a bit below him, he thought about how he never wanted to fly a fighter again. Now he understood how

Lieutenant Lancome had felt. The enemy they'd come to fight, the enemy of the FAF, weren't human. These unknown aliens they called the JAM. These unknowable opponents.

That was the first time Lieutenant Mayle experienced his true feelings in his flesh. The enemy was incomprehensible to humans. Terms like *win* or *lose* were completely meaningless as far as the JAM were concerned, so there was no way that humanity could ever win this war, was there? And in a flash, he understood just as well that all you could do was accept that your being alive didn't matter at all in this world.

It wasn't even the JAM who taught me that, but an unmanned plane called Yukikaze that had been created by humans, thought Lieutenant Mayle, a strange chill in his heart. As he thought about how the plane that had left him feeling so utterly helpless was of a kind with the JAM, the shock of landing on the surface of Faery's thick forest was more intense than he'd expected. The sensation of striking the spongelike alien vegetation—it shone with a metallic brilliance like some beautiful illusion—felt pleasant to him.

7

WITHOUT ANY WARNING at all, Rei Fukai found himself aboard a plane.

His right hand grasping a flight stick and his left on the throttle lever. He looked around for the control button. He lifted his left hand and touched it to his head. He could feel a helmet through a flight glove. There was a mask on his mouth.

Outside were the skies of Faery. Rei looked around the interior of the cockpit. He'd never seen it before. This wasn't the layout of a Super Sylph's cockpit, but it wasn't unfamiliar to him either. The control and display layout was essentially the same. This was Yukikaze. He was aboard Yukikaze.

Rei's left hand shot back to the throttle, needing to confirm through thought what he was doing by instinct. In his helmet, a warning alarm like a scream from Yukikaze was resounding: *Wake up!* it seemed to shriek at him. *Wake up! Wake up!* It seemed real to him.

Yukikaze needed Rei. A situation had arisen that was beyond

her normal functions, and she was screaming for him to switch the combat maneuvering system to manual.

The words **MANUAL CONTROL** flashed urgently on the main display panel. It was the first time he'd ever seen that warning. It was as though Yukikaze were saying "Save me," or perhaps even "I need you." It was a bitter call; she was telling Rei that if he didn't wake up completely, she couldn't handle the situation and the JAM were going to shoot her down.

This wasn't a hallucination or a dream. She was going to be destroyed. Rei could feel that the threat was real. The JAM were coming. They were after him. Rei quickly toggled the automaneuver switch off, telling Yukikaze that he would handle this. The display reading **MANUAL CONTROL** stopped blinking and stayed steadily lit.

Rei was awake, but what was he doing here? What had happened to Yukikaze? Dreams and reality were hard to separate in the past from which he had come, where he'd had no sense of time passing. It was as if he'd awakened with somebody else's memories. He had to find some way to separate out the dreams and the fantasies in these memories that were not his own, to link the past to the reality he found himself in at this moment. He had to take these fragments of memory and reassemble them like a jigsaw puzzle.

But he wouldn't need time or effort to assemble the puzzle. He was sure that, if he just got hold of the thread of his consciousness, which had awakened in this ocean called reality, his self would instantly crystallize into existence. Into the ambiguous dream space through which he'd drifted, fading, coming to the brink of extinction, had plunged Yukikaze's shout to awaken. That alarm was the nucleus around which his self would reform.

"It's the same as Lieutenant Mayle's plane," said the flight officer sitting behind him. It *was* like that other time, and Rei knew that these half-awake memories of the past were reality. And so, his thoughts now affirming that his complete self was properly crystallizing, he heard the voice from the rear.

"Hey, Jack," Rei called out to the flight officer sitting behind him. "Calm down. Even with the engine output restricted, with a little skill, we can't lose. I'll show you how it's done."

"Rei…it is you, isn't it?"

"Of course it is! I'm no JAM. Quit talking like you're half-asleep!"

"You're one to talk," Booker shot back, "seeing how you're finally awake! Christ almighty…"

"Shut your mouth! I don't want you puking back there!" Rei yelled.

"Don't try any extreme maneuvers. Your body won't take it in your condition. Just get after Unit 13. Do what it takes. Yukikaze's been contaminated by the JAM."

There were three JAM in pursuit. When he dodged the two missiles they fired with some high-speed maneuvers, Rei could feel exactly what Major Booker had meant. He didn't have the strength for a dogfight. Rei could feel that the FRX00 was a terrific dogfighter, and he hadn't even used it at 100 percent of its capabilities yet. If he unleashed all of its potential, it might kill him. Rei realized that Yukikaze hadn't summoned him to guide her through a dogfight. What was necessary right now was to shake off the JAM at maximum speed and get after SAF Unit 13 flying ahead of him.

But he couldn't get the engines up to full thrust. Just like Lieutenant Mayle's plane. The cause was the AICS. Yeah, just like the tactical computer back at SAF control had said. No doubt about it.

"THE AICS?" REI recalled Major Booker asking from his personal terminal booth in the SAF command center that he used to talk to the tactical computer.

Correct.

Rei had looked with vacant eyes at the response printed out by the tactical computer on the display. General Cooley was in the booth too. Nobody else was in the huge control center outside of the booth. The lights had been set low.

To these three humans alone in the SAF, the tactical computer in SAF headquarters had presented the information Yukikaze had gathered about the abnormalities in the planes of the 505th Tactical Fighter Squadron: General Cooley, Major Booker, and the still vaguely conscious and wheelchair-bound Lieutenant Fukai.

The tactical computer had strongly urged Major Booker that Rei be there with them. Rei had regained the ability to talk for the first time in ninety-three days, but he still wasn't able to access his own memories. Major Booker had wanted to immediately send Rei to the central FAF medical facility, but the tactical computer had rightly pointed out that there was a possibility that the information in Rei's memories was crucial and should be accessed immediately. Since it proposed that it would be best to stimulate him and retrieve those memories in secret from other corps in the FAF and others in the SAF, the major had reconsidered.

The proposal made by the combat intelligence within the tactical computer was half suggestion and half direct order. It had a strong interest in whatever information Rei and Yukikaze had gathered. If the CI had any emotions, Major Booker sensed that its concern was tinged with fear, dread, and tension, and so he'd agreed with its proposal. The computer proceeded to question Rei.

`The incident ninety-three days earlier. Who shot you in the stomach? What happened?`

Rei answered mechanically. It felt like he wasn't accessing his memories by his own will, but rather was giving words in response to an external stimuli by accessing the part of his memory devoted to answering questions. While Rei himself knew that he was talking, he seemed to do so in somebody else's voice, showing no interest in what he was talking about or in his surroundings.

He had been shot by another Rei Fukai, he said. A human copy created by the JAM. Some sort of antihuman weapon the JAM created from the mirror images of the molecules that make up humans, he went on. He didn't know how long he had been at their base, but when they saw that he couldn't digest food made from the same optical isomer material, they ended up feeding him meat from the body of his dead flight officer, Lieutenant Burgadish.

Major Booker and General Cooley remained silent, listening to the mechanical exchange between Rei and the CI. They couldn't interrupt. The questions the CI asked were precise, unswayed by emotion, fear, or unease.

Had the major opened his mouth, he figured he would have said, "Impossible!" or "I don't believe it!" or some such meaningless nonsense, and so he remained silent and let the sentiments swirl in his heart. *Rei has no such whirlpool in his heart*, the major thought. As he listened to Rei's disinterested speech, he found himself fighting a growing urge to shake him or punch him in the mouth.

After the tactical computer had extracted the information from Rei, it was silent for a while. Then it displayed, I predict that the cause of the thrust fault in the 505th TFS is in the AICS on the monitor. Major Booker objected to the sudden shift in topic, insisting that Rei was not yet fully conscious and that he needed further stimulation. However, the tactical computer ignored the major, playing back the information gathered by Yukikaze on the main display of the command center. Its explanation was clear.

During her combat maneuvers with Mayle's plane, Yukikaze had gotten a clear optical scan of its air intake port. The ramps in the intake port controlled by the AICS were essentially movable planks that directed the flow of air into the engines. The major could see that they were not in their normal position. It was the shock waves up in the intake port that had limited the maneuverability of Mayle's plane. The violently disrupted airflow had drastically reduced the engine's combustion efficiency. The unfavorable conditions from the resulting superheating added to that had destroyed the engines.

The plane never would have reached the edge of the performance envelope except during combat. The Sylphid's engines had blades that could maintain an even airflow even during extreme turbulence. However, in air combat, a pilot will push the engine output and rev them past their design limits—Mayle's plane being a typical example of this. Flying at maximum speed to escape the JAM, the AICS units in the planes of the 505th had operated abnormally. With the air intake flow so disrupted, afterburner flames and black smoke streaming from the rear, it was only inevitable for the engines to either stall or for their output to fall. The pilot, probably half-panicked, would likely slam the throttle as far forward as possible. If the engines were stalled out, he'd have to restart them. If he had time, he might figure out that the problem was in the AICS, in which case it was possible for him to cut out auto mode and set the ramp position manually. If there was a breakdown in the simple AICS system, you could do that. However, Lieutenant Mayle hadn't realized that the AICS was the problem, and it was likely that none of the other pilots had either. If they had, well, they were already under attack by the JAM. Engaging the JAM in a high-altitude dogfight would have been suicide, as they would have to make a hectic transition from low speed to high in order to win, so all they could have done was set the ramps for ultra-high speed and then escape at maximum thrust.

Since none of them had done that, it meant there likely hadn't been an alarm to warn them of a fault in the AICS. The major could only think that they either had realized there was a fault and hadn't switched over or else doing so hadn't yielded any response. That meant this wasn't a simple mechanical failure, and so the CI had determined that the AICS units had been contaminated by the JAM.

The CI didn't believe that the central computer on Mayle's plane was malfunctioning. The central computer controlled the engines and control surfaces in an integrated system, but the AICS was independent. All it did was react to the plane's speed. So, even though it was an independent system, that normally presented no problem. The JAM had apparently exploited this blind spot.

But how? The AICS's circuits had secure electromagnetic shielding, so it seemed unlikely that electromagnetic wave exposure in-flight had caused the malfunction. That left only one answer: the AICS units aboard the 505th's planes were malfunctioning from the moment they took off.

I believe the AICS units were modified by the enemy. The only thing that could touch the planes without arousing suspicion would be a human. A human working against the FAF or possibly a JAM in human guise. The probability of it being a JAM is high. If so, my guess is that the JAM have assumed human form.

Even if they searched for the lost planes, the AICSes were vital units that would have been destroyed by the planes' self-destruct systems. If they'd made it back to base, it might have been possible to return the AICS units to normal operation. The CI went on to say that a humanoid JAM replacing or tampering with AICS units without anyone noticing wasn't out of the realm of possibility.

I do not have a countermeasure for this problem, it continued.

A humanoid JAM weapon. Major Booker shivered. If what Rei claimed to have experienced was true, then JAM infiltration seemed possible. If there was a type not made of optical isomers that merely looked human, but a perfect copy that could eat and live like a real one, then there'd be no way to tell the difference between a JAM and a human.

"You're saying this isn't simply a problem with the AICS," Major Booker said. "How do we find out for certain?"

The probability is high that humans who have gone missing on the front lines have made contact with the JAM. Probability high that the rescued humans are the new type of JAM.

There were two humans like that in the SAF: Rei and Lieutenant Yagashira.

"You mean Yagashira is… That can't be!" said General Cooley, almost with a groan.

His mind still fogged in a sense of unreality, Rei thought that he'd never heard of Lieutenant Yagashira before.

AS REI CHECKED the AICS aboard Yukikaze after being told of the abnormality in the planes of the 505th that she had observed, he soon realized that the planes were being controlled by the JAM and rethought the situation. Yukikaze also determined the 505th TFS were no longer friendlies. Rei figured that the only way the JAM could have turned the 505th would be for them to have infiltrated TAB-15. The JAM.

He felt as if that had been a dream. A nightmare. He had been flying Yukikaze, but then suddenly communication had been cut and Yukikaze had gone away. Yukikaze, leaving him, as he had dreamed again and again. All of it was a dream.

But this wasn't a dream now. The AICS was malfunctioning, but no fault light was lit. Switching over to manual yielded no response. The situation was desperate. If he didn't do something and fast, they were going to be destroyed by the JAM.

Keeping the throttle right on the limit where the abnormal vibrations began, Rei activated the onboard test system. The recorded data on the plane's preflight check seemed wrapped in a watery, unrealistic veil, but he could see that the AICS hadn't showed any abnormalities. The test signals had yielded the correct responses.

So how about now?

The main display showed **IN MISSION** as though Yukikaze were shouting, *Don't run tests in the middle of combat, I'm flying here!* She might have even been scared. The test program wouldn't initiate with her interference. Even if Rei told Yukikaze to stop it and stay out of this, he knew his words probably wouldn't reach her.

Rei immediately lowered the landing gear. The plane's speed suddenly dropped. He manually activated the test mode. Yukikaze quickly understood from the change what Rei was trying to do and canceled the alarm.

"Break, port!" yelled the major.

Banking sharply to the left, he let the JAM slip past. His sudden drop in speed had been fortunate. The JAM had undoubtedly not expected Yukikaze's maneuver.

Selecting the test signals for supersonic maximum speed, he initiated a test run on the AICS. He jammed the throttle to maximum. Gear, up.

The three JAM had swung around and were coming at him. Rei slipped the plane to the right, dodging the JAM's cannon fire. He couldn't keep moving left and right; it would be dangerous, since the plane's acceleration would zero out in the instant he switched directions. With the enemy using cannons, they could anticipate those moments. What he needed to do now was to evade the JAM attack. He prayed for acceleration.

Yukikaze reached normal maximum acceleration in three seconds. The thrust was tremendous. In an instant, the JAM were far behind him.

Rei desperately gripped the control stick, sending Yukikaze into a climb. If he could reach high altitude, her speed would be greatly increased. There'd be no way that three JAM designed for dogfighting could ever catch him then.

He had no doubts that the JAM recognized Yukikaze as an SAF fighter and believed that the three of them could beat her. There was the proof that the AICS had been contaminated by the JAM. If he hadn't known beforehand that the malfunction was being caused by the AICS, those three fighters would have shot him down long before he'd gotten the idea of trying to input those test signals.

"You got it back to normal," the major said. "How'd you do it?"

"Emergency measures. I'm operating it with the test signals. Why wasn't a new AICS swapped in before takeoff? We knew what the cause was. We should have known this would happen."

"We didn't want Yagashira to know that we'd figured out the problem in the AICS. This is top secret," the major said.

Yukikaze flew in the skies above the pure white desert. This was JAM-controlled airspace. Only the JAM flew here without concern.

Just before Yukikaze took off, Yagashira's plane had flown out to this desert to drop a reconnaissance pod. The exact same mission the old Yukikaze had had.

Major Booker confirmed that Yagashira's plane was flying ahead of them in formation with a single JAM plane. "Yagashira's plane is flying with a JAM."

"I know," answered Rei.

"I'm sure he's a JAM," the major said. "There's no excuse for this otherwise."

"I feel like…like I've spoken to him before," Rei said.

The major answered that he had. He and Lieutenant Yagashira had met in the hospital. "I want to be your friend," he'd said. Rei remembered that the man standing next to his bed had been very young. "Everyone looks at me like I'm some sort of weirdo," he'd gone on. "Lieutenant Fukai, I want to talk to you about all kinds of things. The soldiers of Boomerang squadron have such skill. I want to be as good as you guys."

"Rei thinks that he's been abandoned by Yukikaze," Major Booker had said. "If we don't settle that, he'll never fly again." Yagashira went on. "It looks like you had a rough time out there. Actually, I was also shot down by the JAM. I don't have any memory of what happened till I was rescued."

Rei remembered Lieutenant Yagashira saying that in the hospital. That wasn't a dream. In that case, it must have meant that he didn't know that he'd been created by the JAM. He didn't know that the original Yagashira was dead, his memories transferred into an exact duplicate.

"Yeah," Rei said. "Lieutenant Yagashira came to the hospital. Said he wanted to be my friend. How long has it been since then?"

"Nine days," the major replied. "If you don't complete this mission successfully, I'm thinking of sending you back to Earth. I don't want you connected to FAF weaponry and computers anymore. It was like you weren't human."

The thing was, Lieutenant Yagashira had seemed extremely human. Rei kept Yagashira's Unit 13 in sight, still not entirely convinced that the man was a JAM weapon. Then Yagashira and the JAM fighter turned toward Yukikaze, assuming an intercept formation.

"He's engaging," Rei said.

"He's panicking," the major replied. "We didn't tell him about Yukikaze's current mission activities. None of the other FAF branches know either. If Yukikaze hadn't come, he probably would have flown to a JAM base with his information and then flown back to the FAF. He's a JAM tactical intelligence-gathering weapon. A JAM, not a human. Now that his cover's been blown, he can't let us get back to base alive. He's desperate now. Either we kill him, or he kills us."

"A JAM...weapon? Him?"

"Rei, don't space out on me again. You've already met a JAM like him. You and that copy they made of you. Have you forgotten what you told us? This whole mission was designed to confirm that."

Yeah, right. He had a feeling he'd heard something about that before takeoff. When the official announcement had come to send Unit 13 out unmanned to run the same mission the old Yukikaze had, Lieutenant Yagashira had suggested that he fly it. Major Booker had half-expected this, but overcame the dread striking him so squarely to approve the mission. He wouldn't need a flight officer, Yagashira had said. He could do this alone.

"He might have been planning to desert," the major said. "Like a JAM version of us recovering our recon pods. He probably thought he wasn't in any danger."

"Yeah," Rei replied.

He'd said he admired Rei and Yukikaze so much that he wanted to fly the same mission. Rei remembered that. He'd seemed a little arrogant, but that was human too, wasn't it? *Much more so than the Boomerang pilots usually were*, Rei thought.

"Rei, they're going to get us!"

The other planes were still in range.

Unit 13 was armed with short-range missiles and a gun. With Yukikaze's AICS still not running normally, she'd be at a disadvantage in a dogfight. If he was going to attack, now was the time. Rei selected his medium-range missiles for launch. He hesitated for an instant before firing them, but he had almost no margin left for any hesitation. Kill or be killed. He launched four shots simultaneously: two of the new variable-speed medium-range missiles and two hyper-velocity medium-range missiles.

He didn't know how Lieutenant Yagashira saw all this, whether he saw himself as a JAM or, to the end, thought of himself as human. But right now, there was no doubt that his actions were those of a JAM.

The human part of him was already dead, Rei thought as he watched the display count down to the missiles' reaching their target. But he was troubled by why he was still even worrying about that.

It was because he looked human. He wouldn't have hesitated to fire at a JAM fighter plane, would he? Even though the JAM might even be planes themselves, he'd have no problem shooting them, right? The JAM might have counted on Rei's reluctance to fire at something that looked human, but no matter what the weapon looked like, if he was facing a JAM there was no reason to hesitate. It was clear that Lieutenant Yagashira was a JAM.

There was no doubt that was true, even without Major Booker telling him that. So then, why did he feel this way?

He wished they could have talked more. Rei realized that this emotion welling up within him had been the source of his hesitation. He had a feeling that he and this man could have understood each other.

"Everyone hates me," Yagashira had said. "Even I can see that. They don't care how other people feel. My old commander, Lieutenant Mayle, once told me that I was like a machine. They treated me like a machine, never talking to me. But in so doing, they became the real machines."

In piloting his plane, he too felt himself growing closer to this machine he called Yukikaze. Perhaps that was why he could understand the feelings of a man who had been created by the JAM. The reasons didn't matter; Rei had simply wanted to talk to Yagashira some more. If he was a weapon, if he was conscious of himself as a weapon, then he must know how a weapon feels. Did he understand Yukikaze's feelings as well?

The JAM might have been able to understand the details of Yukikaze's combat intelligence better than he could. Even so, the JAM were attacking. *It was out of desperation,* Rei thought. *What is their objective?* he wondered.

He saw the missiles hit with his naked eye. The JAM fighter exploded, followed by Yagashira's plane.

He hadn't seen the pilot bail out. The man who could have understood him was dead.

Was this sadness? Was this regret? It was complicated to deal with feelings bursting forth that he'd thought he'd lost a long time ago. He was the first person who had ever made him feel this way, and he'd been a JAM, Rei thought.

Banking Yukikaze sharply, Rei released control back to her and looked up at the sky. It was blue, and aside from the twin suns, it looked like the skies of Earth.

I want to go home, Rei thought. *But where?*

When he'd first come to the FAF, Rei had been aware of his desire to return to Earth.

"I feel like I'm finally awake," he said, closing his eyes, thinking that if this was a dream too, it wouldn't be so bad.

II

A SOLDIER'S LEAVE

REI FUKAI WANTED a trip back to Earth, and he was going to do something about it.

From the time he was rescued in his immobile vegetative state till the moment he was awakened aboard Yukikaze, he had been trapped in a nightmare space, consumed at the thought of meeting those human copies created by the JAM. What he obsessed over in particular was the taste of the chicken broth he'd been forced to eat. It held the taste of Yukikaze's flight officer, Lieutenant Burgadish.

Waiting for Rei upon awakening was a detailed debriefing to collect all of the information he'd gathered on his mission. This wasn't just conducted by the SAF. Rei had to tell the same story over and over and over to the other air corps and even the FAF Intelligence Forces.

Of most vital concern to the FAF was Rei's claim that the JAM were able to produce copies of human beings. SAF analysis had concluded that there was at least a possibility that the JAM had perfected the creation of human duplicates with which they had successfully infiltrated the FAF.

The top levels of the FAF had to investigate the possibility that Rei and the SAF itself were now contaminated by the JAM. They also had to consider the possibility that the JAM were manipulating Rei and the SAF in order to lead the Faery Air Force down the wrong strategic path.

Rei didn't particularly care if the others accepted his personal experiences. Even though he knew well the threat posed by the mysterious alien JAM, he couldn't recall feeling fear during his encounter with them. In that way, he was similar to the combat intelligences which existed within the FAF's countless computers, but it was only after the experience that Rei's true feelings began to make themselves known. What he was feeling and the changes he was seeing in himself became a matter of serious concern.

He was faced with questions: What he was doing on Faery in the first place? Did Yukikaze's abandonment of him mean that he had no value or worth? Rei wondered if maybe he'd lingered in his coma for so long in order to avoid returning to reality and facing the questions his experiences had raised. He'd dealt with one of them while confronting the threat to Yukikaze in her new body, the power of that moment stimulating him back to consciousness. In that instant, he knew for certain that Yukikaze needed him.

Awakened by his experiences, he didn't want to go back to the way he'd been. Rei had begun to feel closer to the JAM.

What were the JAM? How did the JAM view him? He used to be able to forget those questions when he flew with Yukikaze, but after encountering JAM weapons that looked human, and having a taste of Lieutenant Burgadish, he couldn't just ignore his questions anymore.

The JAM's human duplicates are not a new strategy they adopted suddenly or recently, Rei thought. *They've been preparing this for a long, long time, perhaps starting work on it immediately after their initial attack on Earth.*

Human existence must have seemed a strange thing to them. Doubtless, the JAM perceived it as something they couldn't understand, wondering why these things called "humans" were always riding around in the Faery Air Force's planes. As far as the JAM were concerned, their enemy was the planes of the FAF, not the humans. They recognized the combat machines of Earth as their opponents, not the blobs of organic matter inside them. If the combat machines and computers of Earth were the main adversaries, then the humans were weapons they were equipped with, like computers or missiles.

He could see them now, the JAM desperately analyzing their data, searching for the reason for why the enemy planes were always equipped with organic human matter. It had taken them some time, but it was possible that they now saw the humans as some sort of organic computer that supported the actions of the combat intelligence. At any rate, having realized they could no longer ignore these things, the JAM had likely been devising a countermeasure for them since early in the war. They'd undoubtedly concluded that, since these weapons called humans could move around autonomously, they would create a weapon just like it. Perhaps they'd been deployed for some unimaginable purpose or strategy, but the simple fact was that the JAM were making human copies.

They might have been indistinguishable from humans, possessing will and even emotions, but in the end they were weapons. There could be no other purpose for the JAM to make them, that much was certain. They were organic weapons created by an inorganic alien intelligence that might not even be properly termed a life-form. It was exactly the same idea as when humans created their combat machines.

He wondered how these human copies felt, these men and, possibly, women. An SAF investigation had concluded that there was an extremely high probability that the man called Lieutenant Yagashira, who had taken up a post in the SAF, had been a weapon created by the JAM. The original Lieutenant Yagashira had been killed in action during a mission with his previous squadron, and the JAM had created a weapon based on his body and then deployed it to infiltrate SAF forces. The same went for Lieutenant Lancome, who had been killed at TAB-15 by Yukikaze's gun. However, the SAF couldn't prove this conclusively, and so the FAF couldn't accept their conclusion officially. It was being handled as a top secret matter for their squadron alone.

Despite his vegetative state, Rei had a hazy memory of Major Booker bringing Lieutenant Yagashira to visit him in the hospital. He'd said that he wanted to be a top-class Sylphid pilot, just like Rei. He'd said that he wanted to be his friend. He was a JAM weapon, and yet he'd said that.

Rei had never thought of himself as a consumable weapon in this war. He'd never been particularly concerned with whom or for what he was fighting either. But now, when he thought about the weapons the JAM were making, he couldn't help but think that he was just like them. A weapon was only concerned with its own effectiveness. If it started to wonder for whom it was being effective, its effectiveness would decrease. Since Rei never thought about things like that as he grew to become the best soldier there was, it meant that when a JAM weapon said, "I want to be like you," it was telling him that he was more like a weapon than a JAM weapon.

No wonder the JAM perceived him as a threat.

He didn't know if Lieutenant Yagashira was conscious of having been made by the JAM. It was possible that, even if he did, his sense of identity as a human grew stronger than his identity as a weapon, preventing him from exhibiting his true effectiveness as such. Perhaps Yagashira had said he wanted to be like him because, despite his being human, he recognized Rei as being a far superior weapon. If that were true, it also meant that Yagashira had been a far better human being than Rei was. Far better than a man who didn't care if he was a human or a weapon. *And if he was a perfect human,* Rei thought, *then I must be a perfect combat machine.* That was totally the opposite of the way it should have been.

When Rei had targeted Yagashira's plane and fired his missiles from the cockpit of the new Yukikaze, he had hesitated for a moment, even though there was no doubt at all that he was shooting at a JAM. Why was that? Was it because he had sensed in Yagashira someone who could have understood him?

The thing he didn't understand, the thing he now feared, wasn't the JAM. It was himself. He wanted to take a hard look at the changes he was seeing in his heart. He would return to Earth, the planet that had borne him.

Rei told his only friend and commanding officer Major James Booker exactly how he felt, and the major simply replied that it was a good idea. They were in the SAF hangar bay.

The thirteen fighters were lined up, with Yukikaze in the space for Unit 1. The old Yukikaze had been Unit 3.

"It'll make you more human," Major Booker said. "You've awakened. Yukikaze has been reborn also, into an even more powerful body. She's Unit 1 in name and reality. The same should go for you as well."

Her fighter number had been overwritten with 05031. Yukikaze was now the fourth plane to hold the position of Unit 1.

"I don't think I want to be reborn," Rei answered.

"You've taken a shock to your mind and body," the major said. "A change of environment will do wonders for you. The SAF's also replacing its planes. We're working over the plan we'd suspended before. The plan is to gradually introduce the FRX00, although the Systems Corps is still convinced the FRX99 is better."

"Why aren't you accepting the unmanned planes?"

"Because humans are necessary in this war," the major answered. "The pilots of the SAF are effective counters to the JAM's strategies."

"Humans acting as combat machines, you mean."

"Not quite. Humans are different from machines. The JAM see that as a threat."

"Jack, what I'm trying to say is—"

"I know, Rei. I know what sort of damage you've taken in all this. The way you are now, you can't fly. You need leave. God knows, you deserve some, even if the authorities won't authorize a return to Earth for you."

"You're saying I won't get to go back?"

"The Faery Air Force doesn't want you wandering free. You're a great pilot and they need you, but they're also terrified that you might be a JAM."

"That's ridiculous," Rei said.

"The nature of the SAF's mission means that you constantly see those sorts of contradictory sentiments. That's always been the case."

"If I were a JAM, I wouldn't tell you that the JAM were making human duplicates, would I?"

"That's a good question," Booker said. "Maybe the JAM's objective is to drive a wedge between the humans and the machines of the FAF. Maybe they revealed this to you on purpose."

"Well, JAM or not, I've already done the damage, then."

"True, but nonetheless, there's no evidence that you *aren't* a JAM agent. That's why the authorities want to keep you under close observation. Come on, you know how hard it is to get authorization to return to Earth. Besides that, there's never been any instance in the SAF's history of somebody asking for leave. This unit is full of people who have no interest in visiting Earth or their hometowns. The only people who go back are ones who retire or get drummed out of the service."

"So if I want to go back to Earth, I have to retire?"

"Well, good news for you, then," Booker replied. "Your term of service in the Faery Air Force is almost up. In four days. You can renew your contract instead of retiring, of course. According to the terms of renewal, you can request a promotion to the rank of captain. If you say you're going to retire, the authorities may try to keep you here by offering you a special two-rank advancement. That's a typical bargaining tactic they use."

"I don't care about rank. It doesn't mean anything here, anyway," Rei said.

"I don't know about that," Booker said. "If you get to be a field officer, you can start meddling with personnel affairs and make yourself a big man in some other squadron."

"Yeah, and get buried in a ton of miscellaneous crap."

"Being a captain might be the best position for you, but someone with higher rank can still get in your way. The smart move would be to leave when you get the chance."

"I have Yukikaze here. I'm not going to retire."

"Figured you'd say that," the major said with a nod. "I'll talk to the higher-ups and try to negotiate a temporary leave for you. You're going to come back here, no matter what, because Yukikaze's here."

Rei looked up at Yukikaze, his face expressionless.

Her airframe carried an air of menace. She was a modified FRX99, a plane developed as an unmanned fighter. Compared to the Super Sylphs on either side of her, there was no softness to the design at all. *They at least show some touches that reflect human aesthetics, but Yukikaze's new airframe engenders a sense of complete strangeness*, Rei thought. She had that beauty born of the total efficiency an advanced weapon needs, but the airframe looked threatening, and one could sense a sort of spooky atmosphere around her. In the gloomy light of the hangar, Rei suddenly realized why. Yukikaze was black, just like a JAM fighter. It wasn't just his imagination. She was shaped like one too.

"She...she looks like a JAM fighter."

"Because they borrowed the good points of their planes in the design," Booker explained. "I realized that too. When you just come out and say it, it sounds awful, huh? The JAM planes don't have cockpits, but we added that onto this design. It's built to be piloted by humans, but it was designed to be unmanned. She can pull maneuvers that can kill her crew."

Yukikaze was no longer the FRX00 prototype. As their new tactical combat electronic surveillance plane, she'd been given an official name: the FFR41, nicknamed "Maeve" after the goddess who ruled the wind fairies.

"A pretty wild goddess, this one. It'd be dangerous to piss her off. Even on a Super Sylph, it's the human pilot who chooses to fly it. This one leaves that all behind. Not just any person can fly her. You're necessary, Rei. Make sure you come back here, because I don't want to lose you either."

Rei silently stroked Yukikaze's fuselage. Her body felt warm.

While Rei had been making the rounds to his various debriefings, Yukikaze had flown a mission unmanned, one determined to be simple as far as SAF operations went and not a problem for a pilotless plane. Major Booker had thought it was dangerous to have Yukikaze fully exhibit her new abilities without Rei in the cockpit. The likelihood was steadily increasing that she could behave in wholly unexpected ways while in flight, and they'd need a crewman aboard to find out why. Moreover, Rei would probably be the only one who could completely understand her, and Rei knew that perfectly well. Even so, he wanted to leave the battlefield, to leave Yukikaze, and try to find himself.

"Make the arrangements for me to go back to Earth," Rei said. "I'm counting on you, Jack."

"Gotcha," the major answered, and said nothing more.

AS MAJOR BOOKER had expected, the Faery Air Force authorities didn't okay Rei's leaving. The FAF didn't want him to retire, the major told Rei, who'd been waiting for Booker's return in the major's office. And even if he reenlisted, he went on, they'd probably delay his request for temporary leave with the review process. It'd be a minimum of a month's wait.

"And if we spent a month arguing it, they probably still wouldn't grant my request, would they?" Rei answered.

"That's correct, Lieutenant Fukai," said the man Rei had never seen before.

"Rei, let me introduce you. This is Mr. Chang Pollack, international attorney. He's here to help us."

"A lawyer," Rei replied. "So essentially I'm still a criminal. I'd actually forgotten that I agreed to come here instead of serving time in a Japanese prison."

"That's only until you retire from the Faery Air Force," Pollack said. "You already agreed once before to extend your service here and became a second lieutenant as a result. The moment you did that, you gave up your right to be discharged. That's why you're not just being automatically discharged this time around. In order to retire from service, you'll need to make a formal request. If you choose to extend your contract, your situation won't change. You were handed down an indefinite sentence, after all."

Since Rei had never thought of returning to Earth until now, he'd never considered the difference between discharge and retirement.

"In this case," the lawyer continued, "I'd recommend applying for retirement. You haven't given up that right. Even though the FAF can try and pressure you to abandon the case, they have no right to just quash a request for it. If you do that, you'll be free of them. As far as the nation of Japan is concerned, you'll have fulfilled your debt to society. You'll be a free citizen once again, with all of your rights restored, including the right to receive help from your government."

"I think that's a good deal," Major Booker said. "When you get back, you can do whatever you want. People who choose to enlist here are automatically given the rank of second lieutenant. In your case, you'd probably make captain."

"I don't like it," Rei said.

"What?" Pollack asked.

"Any of it," Rei said. "I'm a human being, and I want to return to Earth as a regular human. I couldn't care less about organizations or some country called Japan."

"Even so—"

"I understand how you feel," the major said, cutting in. "But the reality of the situation is that you aren't just a single, independent human being. You have to make a choice. If you get leave as an FAF soldier, you'll be bound by military regulations. They'll control where you can go and who you can see."

"They'll be spying on me?"

"On the other hand, you'll have the FAF as a powerful ally, backing you up. It's not all bad. Nobody would be able to lay a finger on you, even if you had an entire nation as your enemy. Although the same could be said if you became a civilian. If you retired and the FAF still tried to control you, you could request that the Japanese government assist you."

"I can't depend on anyone there," Rei protested.

"You've got me," Pollack said. "I work to protect the rights of people like you."

"Would the JAM say something like that?" Rei asked. "Only humans talk about things like 'rights.' The JAM don't play that game. They're my enemy, and the only person I can depend on in fighting them is myself, except now, I… Dammit, I don't want to die at their hands the way I am now!"

"Lieutenant Rei Fukai, apply for retirement," Major Booker said firmly. "Then go and get your head together. This isn't a problem you can solve by yourself. Having you dicking around here being unsure of everything is just going to make my life difficult. I don't care how you settle it, just settle it."

"Just sign these papers," said Pollack, holding out a pen. Rei took it and signed several pages.

"Good," said Major Booker with a nod. "This is the only way you can go back. Once you sign these, no matter what the FAF brass says, in three days, you'll be free. Assuming you live that long."

"You're saying they'll try and kill me?"

"It's possible," Booker said. "There've already been moves to get you away from the SAF. Our organization is big enough that I think we can protect you for three days. General Cooley doesn't want to lose you either, and she's been fighting it too."

"If you should be killed, your signature is still valid," Pollack said. "Your honor will be protected. I'll take care of those for you."

"I'm not giving these papers to you," Rei said.

"Major Booker is still a member of the SAF, Lieutenant. You can't be certain that he won't rewrite them or try something else.

I don't trust him. You'll have to trust me."

"I said I'm not giving these papers to anyone else. I'm going to walk them over to the administration office and hand them in myself."

"Have it your way," Pollack said with a shrug. He left the office, not looking particularly disappointed.

"Is he trustworthy, Jack?"

"For what he's charging, he'd better be. I took it out of your future pay, so you'll need to work off that debt. Just leave the legal wrangling to him."

"I don't trust him."

"You just have to trust him for now," Booker said.

"No, it's not that. It was the way he walked around unarmed, like he thinks he has some right not to get killed here. That's just a delusion."

"A shared delusion. Pollack operates within the delusion of what Earth society calls common sense. That doesn't apply here. Not in the FAF or on Faery. Especially to us in the SAF, with the JAM constantly at our throats, the kind of confidence that man has would naturally seem bizarre. Talking to him makes me feel like we live in entirely different dimensions. He walks in the world of Earthly common sense."

"Earthly common sense," Rei pondered. "I never was very familiar with that."

"I know what you mean. It's the same for me. If you go back to Earth, it'll probably be even stranger to you. There were always people who said that the JAM invasion was some giant hoax, but now there are apparently a lot of people who don't even believe they exist. The number of people who aren't conscious of the fact that the JAM threat is real is growing, and to them the war on Faery is just fiction. Everything that happens on this planet is becoming fictional."

"Fiction. Like a fairy tale."

"Exactly. We and the JAM are just characters in a story. If this collective delusion continues to hold sway, it's possible that humanity wouldn't understand what was happening if the JAM broke through the Faery defense line and invaded Earth. If it gets to where we can't recognize the JAM anymore, will fighters and combat intelligences like Yukikaze who are fighting against the JAM even recognize them as the enemies of humanity? Maybe we wouldn't be able to tell what the real threat was without Yukikaze flying overhead to keep an eye out for it."

"The ones suffering from that delusion are happy to get killed off without ever sensing a threat or feeling fear," Rei said, carefully folding the documents he held. "It makes things easier for the JAM, doesn't it? If the JAM are making those human duplicates with the thought of using them as anti-personnel weapons, their strategy is wrong."

"I doubt that's what the JAM have in mind. For now, they've only made a small number of duplicates exclusively for gathering intelligence. I think they're using them in the same way that we use Yukikaze. They'd need to mass-produce them if they were to be used as anti-personnel weapons, and it would require a lot of resources to maintain a squad. Just producing food for them would be a huge problem. I doubt they'd adopt such an inefficient strategy. If the JAM are creating human copies, it means they've studied the human body thoroughly. If they know enough to make a human body, it stands to reason that they could easily engineer a virus to wipe us out. It'd be child's play to spread—an autonomous, infectious, self-propagating micro-weapon. That would be the most efficient way to kill us.

"Maybe they haven't perfected it," Booker continued, "or they don't want to for some reason, but the fact remains that we don't know what the JAM are after. We may never be able to communicate with them. We operate under the assumption that, given enough effort, a means to understanding an opponent with a rational mind can be found, but that may simply be a human delusion. I think it's a conceited notion. We humans don't really know what Yukikaze and the FAF computers think, and we made them."

"The same goes for strangers. We make enemies of other people."

"True understanding may be impossible," the major said, "but we can believe. Humans have that capacity."

"I believe in you," Rei said, slipping the folded papers into his pocket. "And in Yukikaze. And in the JAM as well."

"Then why are you so eager to return to Earth? Do you even

know, Rei?" The question was so unexpected that Rei was flummoxed. He just looked at his old friend for a long moment, wondering if his silence was proof that he really didn't know.

"I think I know why," the major said at last. "I understand, because I get the same feeling a lot."

"What do you mean?"

"You want to see for yourself that Earth still exists, don't you?"

"What?"

"You should go. You're free now. Nobody can tell you what to do. I'll wait for a week after your retirement is finalized. If I don't hear from you in ten days, I'll reorganize the SAF without you."

"I understand."

"That is all, Lieutenant Fukai."

"Roger, Major."

Rei straightened up and saluted. Major Booker sat up in his seat and returned the salute with a casual wave, like he always did. It was an attitude that said that, true to their nickname, a Boomerang soldier would return without fail. If the boomerang hit its target, he would go out to recover it. That was Major Booker's role to play. *It's thanks to him that I was rescued*, Rei thought. From one viewpoint, Booker was just doing his duty, but from another, it was confirmation that the major didn't simply see Rei as a weapon. Had it not been for his faith in his friend, Rei wouldn't have wanted to return from the void in which he'd been trapped.

"I appreciate everything you've done for me," Rei said as he lowered his hand. "I'd better get to the administration office."

"I'd hate to see you not come back to the SAF, but you do what you have to do," the major replied. "This is a gamble I'm taking, Rei. Drastic action. It's the only thing I can offer you so that you'll be a soldier again. There's a chance I'm going to lose this bet."

"I don't want to think about what's going to happen," Rei said.

"Since you're going back to an Earth you don't really know anymore, anything could happen. I'd feel better if you had a navigator to help you out. I contacted Lynn Jackson and made a private request. That was me acting as an individual, not as a major asking a favor."

"Lynn Jackson, huh?"

"The FAF Intelligence Forces are probably already moving and may refuse, but that has nothing to do with me. Lynn Jackson is a first-rate journalist. She'll keep you out of trouble."

"It sounds like Earth is more dangerous than the JAM."

"In your naively fragile state, it definitely is. I'm praying you don't have a total nervous breakdown there."

As Rei turned to leave, Major Booker wished him luck. Rei left his friend's office without another word.

THREE DAYS LATER, Rei was safely retired from service. The process had been complicated and mysterious, but apparently Chang Pollack had earned his hefty fee, sparing Rei from having to deal with any annoying contingencies. Once his confiscated Japanese passport was returned to him, it was all over. Rei Fukai was no longer a soldier in the Faery Air Force. He was a civilian, with all debts to society paid.

Just as he had when he'd first arrived at base, Rei walked through the tunnel which connected the surface to the underground, though this time he was going up instead of down. Carrying only his jacket and a Boston bag he owned, Rei headed for the exit. As he neared it, the outside light growing brighter, Rei felt as if he were awakening from a dream.

No one was there to see him off. There were about twenty other people who, like him, were making the trip back to Earth, along with four others still in uniform, going back on temporary leave. The guys in uniform were mainly jovial, but the expressions of ex-servicemen varied, sullen frowns outnumbering smiles considerably.

Emerging from the tunnel, Rei looked up into the light of Faery's twin suns.

A huge eddy of gas jetted out from one side of the binary stars, forming a reddish belt that resembled the Milky Way. The Bloody Road, as it was called, was more diffuse than when seen from a plane at high altitude. Normally, it wasn't visible from the ground at noontime. *Perhaps*, Rei thought, *finding yourself forced to see something that you normally wouldn't is the essential nature of homesickness.* A formation of FAF tactical fighters crossed the sky overhead. Opposite them stood a huge, white pillar of clouds—the Passageway that connected Earth and Faery. Rei thought the scene looked like some sort of painting.

A United Nations transport plane bound for Earth sat at the end of the runway. This was the shuttle that made the trip through the hyperspace Passageway from Faery to Earth. Generally, FAF planes never went there.

IDs were checked prior to boarding. The note on Rei's passport that he was retired from service and was no longer a Faery soldier was checked and verified by a crewman, who then demanded that everyone except those in uniform present their boarding passes. You paid your own way home, although there were no first class seats on this plane.

The shuttle plane's pilot seemed like a veteran. Without any hesitation, he entered the hyperspace Passageway in the cloud pillar from the proper course and altitude. The plane emerged on the Earth side with barely any turbulence. When the clouds cleared, they were greeted by the sight of the Antarctic skies spreading out around them. One of the seating rows broke out in cheers. The blood red river of the Bloody Road was nowhere to be seen in Earth's skies. *I'm home*, thought Rei.

REI WAS RELEASED in Sydney, Australia.

Lynn Jackson was waiting for him. The author of *The Invader*, which dealt with the JAM threat, she had never lost interest in the JAM or the Faery Air Force. She greeted the man returning from Faery—who knew the JAM so well—the way she might an acquaintance she hadn't seen in a decade. Rei had met her once before, though they hadn't spoken. She seemed a little older, but her eyes still held their intelligent sparkle.

"Welcome home, Lieutenant Fukai. Congratulations on making it out alive," she said as she fell into step with Rei at the airport exit.

"What's the deal?" Rei said. "You gonna follow me everywhere I go?"

"Major Booker asked me to help you out. Do you remember me?"

"Yeah."

"So, what are your plans? What do you want to do?"

"Travel around the world."

"You mean until you feel like going back to your homeland?" she asked.

"None of your business."

"Isn't it? Lieutenant Fukai, don't you think you have an obligation to tell all of humanity about the JAM?"

"I'm back here because I've fulfilled all my obligations. If you want to know about the JAM, enlist and go to the front yourself."

"Participating in a war means losing your objectivity."

"If being human means believing there's a fair, balanced, and objective position to take on the JAM, then I guess I'm not human. I couldn't live as a human."

"In a way, you may be right, Lieutenant, but as for me—"

"I'm not a lieutenant anymore."

"Does that mean you have no intention of returning to Faery?"

"No comment."

Amidst the whirlpool of noise and color in the bustling airport, Rei was starting to feel a little seasick.

"Even though we're alike?"

"Alike how?"

Lynn dropped the professional tone from her voice. "It's true that there are all sorts of things I want to ask about. You and I both appreciate the threat the JAM pose. We don't know what they're after, but if we try to perceive them objectively, human sense and common sense become unreliable. I agree with what you said about not being able to live as a human. That's you now, isn't it? That's how it is for you."

"Well, if I'm not human, then what am I?" Rei asked as he stopped midstride.

Lynn Jackson looked Rei straight in the eye and answered without any hesitation. "A Faerian."

"An alien, you mean?"

"Yes, exactly. So, as an alien who's come to Earth to sightsee, you'll need to hire a guide. You're ignorant of human customs, I'm sure."

"And in return, you want exclusive access to my story, right?"

"This may wound your heroic pride, but I can't market you

as a hero. The war with the JAM isn't the sensation it used to be," Jackson said. "Only a very small specialty market exists with any interest in the exploits of returning soldiers. Very few in the media would have any interest in interviewing you."

"What happened on Faery seems like a dream already," Rei said. "It feels like I was hooked up to some machine designed to induce nightmares as part of some psychological punishment. Actually, I kinda suspect that the machine they used to force-inject basic fighter piloting skills into my brain was exactly like that." Rei sighed. "If here on Earth the JAM are now treated like characters from a fairy tale, then you may as well say that it all really was the sort of punishment I just described. There wouldn't be much difference between trying to convince people they're real and me just saying it's not my problem now."

"As much as I think public consideration needs to be paid to the psychological wounds our returning soldiers have to deal with, you're still wrong. I just can't believe that."

"I've had enough of public consideration and the rest of that crap," Rei said.

"I'm here as an individual."

"So you have a personal interest in me?"

"I do. I don't think you can handle human society as it is now. You can't live here on your own."

Rei considered what she said and finally gave in.

"I'll hire you as a guide."

"I warn you, my fee's pretty high."

"I've got money," he replied. "There isn't a lot to spend it on back at Faery base."

"If you tell me about that too, I'll let you pay me in installments."

"If the balance gets too depressing to look at, I'll consider that," Rei said.

"Don't lose count of what you owe."

"I'll expect you to charge me an honest price."

"Trust me," she said.

Lynn Jackson started walking toward the airport lobby exit.

"Where are we going?" Rei asked.

"You need a place to relax, right? I've booked you into the Meridian Hotel."

"You're prepared, aren't you?"

"I'm living there right now. It's convenient, being as close to Faery as it is."

"Nice status you enjoy, huh?"

"I can live comfortably if I economize."

"You published a best seller, after all. When you write the sequel to *The Invader* you'll sell that too, right?"

"I'm just starting to write it now," Lynn said. "The thing is, my agent's having to wrack his brains before he can sell it to someone."

"Why's that?"

"If we sell it as a work of fantasy fiction, we may be able to find a publisher who'll buy it. That's what the times are like nowadays. See, anything having to do with the JAM is fantasy. If the JAM are mentioned anywhere, nobody takes the contents of the book seriously. I wasn't intending to become a novelist, but my agent's been telling me he has a feeling that the publisher is going to make me do it that way. If it looks like I'm writing some kind of quickie cash-in job, it'll damage the trust people have in me as a journalist. So, I'm writing some other 'hard'-subject books to keep from seeming too far out of my usual line."

"So how is *The Invader* viewed now?"

"Probably as nothing but fantasy, like the vast number of books, good and bad, that came out about the JAM for a while. They're not popular anymore. I'm basically seen as a has-been popular writer. I always saw myself as a journalist and not a pop writer, and that hasn't changed, but the world doesn't see me that way. With my insistence on still writing about the JAM, I'm seen as a bit of an anachronism."

"That's nuts."

"It's the result of the FAF's success at containing the JAM threat," Lynn said.

"And there's a whole bunch of other problems that reality has for people to worry about, right?"

"Right. Humanity's perennial crises are a much more familiar problem to deal with. Economics, politics, religion, cultures, race, gender issues, et cetera, et cetera, et cetera."

Rei remembered what Lynn Jackson had written in *The Invader*.

Back when the JAM first drove through the hyperspace Passageway linking Earth and Faery and invaded Antarctica, humanity hadn't united to fight them. In the end, humanity saw the JAM as just another race among many to be confronted. On Earth you could find a race called "humans," but that group couldn't be properly considered "Earthers." Humans are basically animals who fight each other for dominance within and between groups, so if a controlling member of one collective loses even a little power, the group fractures. Joining and splitting, over and over. The relationship of the ruler and the ruled. Struggles for supremacy. Even the presence of the JAM did not change this. This desire for confrontation would persevere in humanity until the species finally fell to ruin.

"Just humans with a different skin color, eh?" Rei said to Lynn Jackson as they climbed into a taxi.

"Hm?"

"That was something you wrote in your book. You basically said that humans wouldn't face reality until the very end."

"And what do you think?" she asked.

"I think we eat, we sleep, we grow old, and then one day we vanish from this world. Anything aside from that is an illusion."

"Spoken like an enlightened old Buddhist."

"The JAM made me that way," Rei said. He shut the taxi door.

As the taxi drove along, Rei spotted a newsstand out the window and asked the driver to pull over. He bought four different papers. When he returned, Lynn Jackson laughed and told him he could ask the hotel to buy as many as he wished, or else print out all the news stories he could carry from the MT in his room. Rei, however, had no intention of doing as she said.

"It's easy to forge newspapers or computer data," he explained.

"Ah, but a paper bought out in the city from a random location would be a little more reliable, is that it?"

"I guess."

"Who do you think would be trying to forge them?"

"Someone trying to make me laugh," Rei said.

Lynn Jackson shrugged her shoulders and kept her mouth shut.

After arriving at the hotel and checking in, Rei went his own way after promising to meet Lynn for dinner later.

Lynn offered to take him out to a nice restaurant where he could have a meal fit for a human and plan what he was going to do, but Rei wasn't used to just relaxing. Major Booker had given him a one-week grace period. For seven days, his posting in the SAF was still guaranteed. The meaning was clear—if he let it pass he'd never fly Yukikaze again, even if he returned to Faery.

Rei doubted he'd find something new to live for in the next week, but he didn't want to waste his time. He wanted to perceive the JAM with the senses of an Earther, to find out just what it was that he'd been fighting.

The room Lynn had booked for him was a sumptuous suite. On top of the enormous bed, Rei read the newspapers he'd purchased. There wasn't a single mention of the JAM. Rei couldn't believe it, but he read them through completely and couldn't find one anywhere.

Throwing the papers down, he went over to the multimedia terminal on the writing desk. They hadn't had these before he'd left for Faery, so he experimentally switched it on.

He first searched the major news sites for any information about the JAM, but there were very few recent hits. Particularly shocking was that a keyword search for "the JAM" yielded hardly any information at all. While the word was there, it was treated merely as a special-purpose term or colloquialism used by some. According to the definition that came up for *JAM*, "It is not known who first referred to them as the JAM, and the mysterious group that invaded Earth still has no official name."

Thinking this was ridiculous, Rei next ran a keyword search for Faery Air Force. There was information on it, but again, nothing substantial, not even any official reports on the latest war progress. The reports should have been available, but they hadn't been uploaded for display on the MT.

It was as though an information blackout was in effect. *Perhaps there is*, Rei thought. In short, somebody was making it difficult to learn about the JAM. It seemed to be taking him forever to find any information about them. There might have been tons of data about the JAM and the FAF, but if it took you a lifetime to search for and find it, the practical reality was that it might as well not exist.

Lynn would say that there were no articles about the JAM in the papers because writers couldn't sell them. That was probably why she hadn't yet found a publisher for the sequel to *The Invader* she was writing. But Rei sensed that the fundamental reason for the paucity of information was due to social manipulation with the goal of changing the minds of the general public. It would have to be a worldwide effort. Assuming there was some group that wanted to propagandize on the JAM's behalf, Rei suspected that their agents might delete the word *JAM* as soon as it was entered anywhere, or possibly change the expression to something else in order to make it difficult to search for.

So who was doing it, then?

The ones who would profit from it. The JAM. The JAM were already in control of the network all MTs were connected to.

It was possible that the JAM had quietly slipped undetected past the FAF and invaded Earth, then carefully bided their time in order to realize their plan. Since the change was so gradual, it wasn't surprising that only someone like Lynn Jackson would notice it. *The other possibility*, Rei thought as he stepped back from the terminal and sat down on the bed, *is that this is all the fantasy of a returning vet from Faery, one of those psychological scars people talk about.*

He'd risked his life fighting the JAM, and yet he'd come home to find that they weren't considered worth discussing. So then, what was the point of the war? Why had he risked his life? *Come on, the JAM are right there!* It was natural for him to come to that conclusion.

Suppose the JAM were just a virtual threat created by humans? That would certainly make sense in some ways. If you explained Faery as being some international criminal incarceration system, it'd make a lot of sense.

Still, it was unrealistic to claim that the JAM and planet Faery were artificial virtual creations. If you considered the cost of maintaining such a system, you'd eventually have groups who'd refuse to pay for it and the whole thing would collapse. Rei also doubted that you could keep a system like that running for thirty years.

But even if that were all true, and the JAM were originally virtual creations, they weren't anymore. The JAM were real. Even if the parties responsible for starting the whole charade declared "game over," the FAF as it was now wouldn't obey them.

The JAM weren't virtual to the FAF. Real or fake, it was still kill or be killed out there. There was no way that the JAM were phantasms, because the FAF itself had made them real. The JAM would eventually invade Earth. Whether they were real JAM or something created by the humans and combat machines of the FAF didn't matter, they were still JAM.

Wow, Rei thought, *these are some pretty powerful post-combat psych aftereffects*. He was basically desperate to make the JAM real by any means. Maybe it was due to the notion that they'd already invaded Earth. Well, if that was true, maybe this wasn't the real Earth. Maybe the JAM weren't real, and his sensing them here came from his inability to slip free of the illusion. Maybe some psychiatric treatment could cure him. No, there was no way he'd ever be able to forget the JAM threat. Better to live thinking they were real than to try and force himself to believe they weren't. He didn't give a damn what other people thought. The JAM were a threat to him. That made them real enough, no matter what their true nature might be. These Earth people who made the JAM into fairy tales would probably be destroyed without ever knowing what really killed them. They wouldn't even think it was the JAM who were doing it.

That's not for me, Rei thought.

As far as the JAM were concerned, media infiltration was a good strategy. There'd be no need to produce human duplicates to use as anti-personnel weapons. They could instead use the complex and advanced information management system humans themselves had created in order to control human thoughts. All the JAM had to do was turn their attention away from the true enemy, themselves, and then give a little push to encourage humans to turn back to their ordinary squabbles. Humans are just the sort of life-form to do that anyway, so there was no need for any out-and-out brainwashing. Their own systems and biological nature would lead to their self-destruction.

To people who were satisfied just to eat and sleep, it wasn't the

JAM they were worried about being trampled by. It was other people or groups who had weapons. Actually, Rei had spotted a few articles in the papers about just that sort of thing. This was stuff humans themselves were doing, not the JAM. All the JAM had to do was wait. A hundred years, a thousand, ten thousand, it didn't matter to them. The JAM might have been trapped into fighting the FAF because their invasion was premature. The only things that might be able to resist the JAM weren't human at all. The only defense was autonomous combat machine intelligences like Yukikaze.

Rei lay back on the bed, his arms cushioning his head, and wondered if it not might be for the best if humanity destroyed itself. Even if the JAM's control over Earth's computer network was just his own fantasy, he hadn't changed what he was. Human society would never accept him, so it was all basically the same. Nothing had changed. Coming back to Earth had made him see that clearly, and he hadn't even been here for half a day.

Rei wasn't really concerned with being a perfect combat machine anymore, and he was now pretty sure he had acknowledged he wasn't human. Rei was neither human nor weapon. He'd not known what he was until Lynn Jackson had told him with her all too brief answer:

He was a Faerian.

He fought because the JAM were there, not as a weapon, but as a man trying to survive as a resident of the planet Faery.

Even so, how had he come to be what he was? A person whose personality estranged him from normal human society. A person who couldn't stand to live his life as just another face in the crowd.

Rei wondered if he was some sort of mutant. Nothing more than something inserted by the program of evolution to ensure the survival of the seed of humanity. They existed in every age. He'd just been born by chance into the age when the JAM were here. He had a feeling that the JAM, despite their desire to eliminate humanity, couldn't simply wait for it to self-destruct because of people like him.

People like him were more a threat to the JAM than the vast majority of humans on Earth. For their part, the people of Earth saw the JAM as being not too different from themselves. They were certainly living that way now. At any rate, if you left humans alone, they'd probably end up destroying themselves.

But he couldn't stay here on Earth and hope to fight for his life, especially if the JAM were already here. He had no weapons. He had only just arrived, but Rei made up his mind to call Major Booker tomorrow morning.

He'd have to thank Lynn. Since he'd have to wait for Major Booker to tell him which shuttle flight to take back, he could hang around with her. If time permitted, he might do a little sightseeing. Rei would go wherever he wanted. It was so obvious—the only weird thing being human common sense, which was an obstacle. Humans were the only animals that required passports for moving around.

It was a little early, but Rei decided he'd call Lynn anyway and got up from the bed.

There was a knock at the door. Wondering if she'd been thinking along similar lines, Rei looked out the peephole and saw men in the corridor. Three of them, and from their faces he could tell they were Japanese.

"Who are you?" he asked from behind the door. It had been ages since he'd spoken Japanese.

"Fukai Rei-san, we're here to greet you," came the answer through the door. "We're the welcome party for returning soldiers."

"Don't need it," Rei replied.

"If that's true, I'm afraid we'll need you to sign a document saying so. If we don't follow procedure, we could all be accused of neglecting our duties."

These guys weren't going to go away. Rei opened the door.

"Nice room," one of them said.

"Get to the point," Rei said.

"Allow me to introduce myself," said the man acting as their representative as he took out a business card. Rei read it.

"Japanese naval development division?"

"We need excellent pilots like you for our naval air forces," the man explained.

Rei suddenly realized it was all a setup. Pack people off to

Faery for minor crimes, then exploit the best of the survivors. It was payback for the enormous national expenditures made to keep the Faery Air Force running. Which meant this was an offer he couldn't refuse. He was obligated.

"I didn't fight the JAM for the sake of you people," Rei said.

"Oh?" answered the man. "Then what were you fighting for?"

"So that I could survive."

"Then please, keep that talent alive. It'd be a shame to let it go to waste."

"Which is to say," said another, "that a man with your personal history won't be able to get a civilian job."

"Mind your own damned business," Rei answered, even as he was thinking that resistance was useless. "I'll live my life gazing at my own navel. Tell your superiors I refuse. I have that right."

"Then we'll take you back to Japan at once—"

"No way," Rei replied. "I promised a pretty lady that I'd meet her."

"I don't believe you've had contact with anyone aside from Ms. Jackson, which means we can make things very difficult if you don't accept our offer. We don't want another country to make use of your talents. If you're Japanese, you should use them in the service of your country. Aren't you a patriot?"

"So, I come home and that's the only value I have now?" Rei said. "Fly a fighter plane as a Japanese so I can kill people from another country? Humans, like me?"

"To protect our national interests. It's all grounded in international law."

"Maybe, but what does any of it matter? Winning or losing against fellow humans…Why would I want to do that? What nations need are public service organizations, not political and military power. But you people still haven't created them. I don't feel like risking my life for something so primitive. When I fought the JAM, I did it for my own sake, not so that I could be used by you people when I got home."

"You're saying you didn't do it for your country?"

"Of course not!"

"Then you're under arrest."

Rei knew it'd do no good to shout about what right they had

to do this. Even if he went to trial, no court would ever rule to allow him to go back to Faery. They'd brainwash him to make him fight for his country. He'd be made to walk down the path of self-destruction as a human. That was the only path for humans to take, after all. Humans enjoyed fighting other humans. Manipulating others, even occasionally sacrificing themselves. Even when they didn't enjoy it, they couldn't help but do it. It was all part of being human.

Rei stepped back.

"Resistance would not be to your advantage," said the man.

"Damaging my abilities isn't in your national interest," Rei replied.

"If you don't come along quietly, then we'll have no choice. Still, I think you're being a fool. We can guarantee you a position in society, honor, a good living. I guess you were born a traitor."

The two men behind him drew out weapons that looked like stun guns. Rei could tell they were designed to paralyze. He'd never be able to win in a hand-to-hand fight, but fighting was the only option he had left, he thought as he backed into the room.

"Fukai, get down! Look away!"

The warning had been delivered in English with a Faery accent. Rei reflexively dropped to the floor, sensing dazzling light even through his sealed-shut eyelids. He thought at first someone had thrown a grenade, then realized it was a flashbang.

"Fukai! Out! Hurry!"

In a second, Rei was on his feet and heading in the direction of the voice. His vision was a little dim, but he could see the three Japanese soldiers rubbing their eyes.

He ran down the corridor, finding Lynn Jackson at the elevator bank, holding the door open on one. He threw himself into the car. Inside was a man he'd never seen before. Lynn quickly pushed a button.

"FAF intel, right?" Rei said to the man. "You got into that room somehow. How'd you do it?"

"Right," the man replied. "FAF Intelligence Forces, combat division."

"He got in through my room," Lynn said. "From next door."

"Oh, living the high life, huh?" Rei said. "You were keeping an eye on me from Lynn's room?"

"Right," replied the FAF intelligence agent. He was fairly young.

"Why? I'm retired…or were those documents I signed fakes?"

"They were real, hence the welcome wagon from your home country. I was also kind of surprised by how quickly they moved."

"What you're doing is illegal. You're kidnapping me."

"No, they were the ones acting illegally. They were attempting to kidnap someone who'd just reenlisted in the FAF."

"Oh. Now I get it," said Rei with a sigh. "Well, your timing's perfect. Reenlistment would be very convenient for me at the moment."

"That looks like the truth, Rei," said Lynn.

"It is," replied the agent. "Your reenlistment request was actually accepted by the FAF authorities the moment you left the airport and bought those newspapers."

Rei thought about this for a moment.

"Major Booker," he decided. "He had this all arranged from the start."

"You mean this isn't what you want?"

Those men claiming to be from the Japanese navy might have been actors, and the whole thing might have been a hoax set up by the FAF authorities to get him back to Faery. *Still, it doesn't matter*, Rei thought. He'd made up his mind to go back well before any of this happened.

"It doesn't matter," he said. "You saved me."

The elevator car stopped at the entrance level, and the agent hustled them out.

"It's dangerous to stay here, Lieutenant," he said. "The guys chasing you haven't received any official documents from us yet that prove you're back in the FAF. We've got to get you on that shuttle. I've ordered my subordinate to take care of that. Just sign this and you'll be good to go."

If this was real, and not just a show for his benefit, he doubted having that paper was going to stop a nation from flexing its might against him.

"Ironic, eh? It's safer for me to be on Faery with the JAM," Rei said.

"Sorry you couldn't take some time and let me show you the sights, Lieutenant Fukai. But then, I suppose you're used to being in a hurry," Lynn said as they left the hotel. Rei wondered what would have happened to him had this woman not been there. Then he suddenly realized that she was probably in as much danger here as he was.

"It'd probably be safer for you to come to Faery," Rei told her. "You're not a human, and it'd be dangerous for you to get mixed up in their stupid wars. With your career, you've got the civilian qualifications to come to Faery. You can do your work there," Rei said, just before he got into a waiting car on the street. But Lynn shook her head.

"I also think the wars humans fight amongst themselves are foolish," she said. "But I'm not going."

"Why not?"

"Because I still have hope. I believe humanity won't always be this mad. It may be true that, like you, I'm not just a regular human. But in other ways I'm not like you at all."

"I see," Rei said. "Damn, this leave ended way too soon, but I'm glad I could meet you."

"Next time you come, I'd like to play guide for you as much as you'd like."

"As long as the price is fair."

"Of course. Trust me," Lynn Jackson said with a smile.

It's a nice smile, Rei thought. He'd been lucky to see such a smile on his all too brief sojourn.

Later on, he could look back over all of this at his leisure and wonder what the hell had happened, but he knew some things for certain. First, his misgivings that Earth no longer existed were laid to rest. Second, he'd met a human who recognized the threat posed by the JAM. *But if she's not a regular human, then what is she?* he wondered.

An Earther. That was it. He'd seen the smile of an actual Earther.

"May we meet again, Earther. Good luck."

"And you, Lieutenant Fukai, man from Faery."

Rei nodded, then climbed into the car and ordered the driver to go as he shut the door. His leave was over. Yukikaze was waiting.

III

RETURN TO BATTLE

ALTHOUGH REI HAD been in a vegetative state for three months, the SAF medical staff guaranteed that they could have him back to his former strength in half that time. That was dependent, however, on his precisely following the rehabilitation program. The program had been devised when he awakened, but then had to be modified due to his debriefing and trip back home to Earth, so it didn't kick into full swing until after Rei had reenlisted and returned to Faery. It had been ten days since Rei had rejoined the SAF, and he was following the program diligently. Major Booker called him into his office to see what effect it was having.

Rei appeared to be in good shape. Better shape than Booker was, actually. "It's nice to be young," he told Rei. "At my age, you can take twice as much time to recover and never get back to full strength. I still get a twinge in my neck every now and then."

"It's your body saying you shouldn't be riding around in a fighter plane at your age, Jack," Rei replied.

"That was my call to make, and I don't think it was wrong. I dragged you back to consciousness, didn't I?"

"You didn't need to fly out in the FRX or in Yukikaze."

"No, I did. In the case of Lieutenant Yagashira, there was nobody else I could trust. This is war. Real combat, not desk jockeying. Going out in a fighter once in a while lets you understand the war situation in your guts, not just your head. The brass should go out on sorties once in a while."

"So they can feel the JAM threat in their bodies, you mean?"

"Not just for that," Major Booker said.

"What else would there be?"

"The JAM aren't the only threat. If they rode in that plane, they'd understand."

"You're talking about how wild the Maeve's combat maneuvering can be, aren't you?"

They were referring, of course, to the newest model tactical combat reconnaissance fighter: the FFR41. It was named Maeve, after the mythical queen of the wind, and at the moment, Yukikaze was the only one in existence.

"It's not just about the Maeve," the major replied. "There's also the fact that we don't really know what the FAF's combat intelligences are thinking. How can the brass not understand that's a threat to us humans?"

"You mean how this war is between the JAM and the FAF's combat machines, not between the JAM and humanity, right?"

"Exactly," Major Booker replied, nodding. "From the very start, when the JAM appeared thirty years ago, they haven't been at war with humans. You and I understand that, but the higher-ups who control our forces don't. They probably can't, and they won't unless they go to the front and experience the danger of combat themselves. That goes for me too. God only knows what the people living safe and sound on Earth think about all this."

"The JAM have already invaded Earth."

"I beg your pardon?"

"I can't really put it clearly. It was just a feeling I got when I went back there. I don't think humans are capable of really sensing the true, actual JAM themselves." Rei told the major about what he'd seen on his brief leave back to Earth, about his suspicion that the JAM had already invaded Earth's electronic networks.

"Rei, why didn't you say anything about that?" the major asked.

"Because I didn't have any obligation to report it. I went back to Earth as a civilian, and I can't substantiate what I felt. And even if it's true, the people on Earth will deal with those JAM. It's not our problem."

"Just saying it's not our problem won't make the problem go away."

"Why not?"

"Why not?!" Major Booker shook his head, looking utterly shocked by what Rei had just said. "Rei, why did you come back here?"

"I came here because you wanted a report on how well my rehabilitation program was going. I'm here because of you, Major Booker."

"I'm asking if you're telling me that you believe you're a completely isolated being in this room here, unconnected to the SAF, the FAF, or the entire Earth. You really think that you can just live here as you please, unconcerned with what happens back there?"

"Yeah, I do," Rei replied. "The FAF may not believe that, but I think they're wrong."

"You went to Earth. You saw that it still exists, right?"

"It doesn't matter if Earth is real or just a dream. That's no problem as far as my living here on Faery."

"You're saying you came back because you think this is the only place where you can live now?"

"Yeah, I guess I am," Rei said.

"So, Earth's already been contaminated by the JAM, and you won't fight on Earth, so that's why you came back here?"

"Yeah. On Earth, I'd have to fight humans as well as the JAM. I may as well cut down the number of enemies I have to deal with."

"Fight humans on Earth?"

"Yeah, Jack," Rei said with a nod. "Life is battle, and there's nobody there I can depend on. I'm not an Earth human anymore, and neither are you."

"What do you mean, you're not an Earth human?"

"We're Faerians now. We have to fight an enemy that threatens that existence. This battle we're in isn't a war. It's a struggle for existence. It's not about beating the enemy; it's about living. Victory for us is not losing. The JAM aren't the only ones competing against us. Going to Earth showed me that clearly."

"Rei, I really don't have time to listen to your great philosophy of life. No matter what you may think, the FAF exists to represent Earth's interests. That's reality," Booker said. "You think we just have to not lose here? If we lose our backup from Earth, you'll see us lose here pretty damned quickly. You don't seem to get that. And this stuff about us being 'Faerians'...Where'd you get an idea like that? Somebody had to have fed you that line, because it doesn't sound like the sort of thing you'd..." The major paused. "It was Lynn Jackson, wasn't it?"

"Yeah."

"What, does she expect the FAF to launch a war of independence from Earth? Is that what she's got you all worked up to do?"

"No. Ms. Jackson just said that I wasn't a human anymore," Rei said. "When I asked her what I am, she said I was a Faerian, like that. I thought it was a clear and simple answer, that's all."

"That woman is a dyed-in-the-wool journalist. She's got a toughness to her that keeps her from taking sides with anyone. But you're not like that. You're naive, especially now, with your mind and body as unstable as they are. It's easy to brainwash somebody who's convalescing, like you are."

"So you do it, Jack."

"Me?" the major asked.

"Yeah. It should be simple for you to make me believe that I can have a happy life sacrificing myself for the people of Earth."

Major Booker took a long, hard look at Captain Rei Fukai. *He's changed*, the major thought. There was a subtle change to the style of conversation he was practicing now. But where exactly was the change? He'd been promoted from first lieutenant to captain. Appearance-wise, he was thinner, having lost some muscle mass. But those were just minor changes. The big ones had happened inside. You could tell just by looking at him.

The look in his eyes conveyed a sharper vitality, or from another viewpoint, they were the eyes of a man who now knew fear. They exuded an air of wariness. The old Rei hadn't been like that. He'd been a man who did nothing but passively glare at the world, with an attitude that said he didn't like anything and would never like anything. He engaged the JAM as though swatting away flies buzzing in front of him. Anything aside from that, he'd always simply say, "Not my problem." He was the very image of an advanced weapon who could only see his JAM targets.

But Rei was different now. Now Rei seemed to be observing himself from a higher vantage point. He'd begun to think about the relationship between himself and the world in which he lived. He'd probably realized that there was value to being aware of and thinking about the questions of existence.

In short, Major Booker thought, *for the first time in his life, Rei acknowledges that people other than himself exist in the world with him.* Even so, the change hadn't made him more emotional. He was still behaving in an inorganic, mechanical, almost emotionless manner. Rei's original personality hadn't changed at all. This man didn't care what happened to the people of Earth. He'd just come out and said as much only moments ago. But he'd said, "It's not *our* problem," rather than "It's not *my* problem." On the surface, it was just a minor difference, but that difference was conclusive. To put it in terms of weaponry, he was like a missile that had just been switched from passive to active seeking.

But I don't know for certain that the change is for the better, Major Booker thought coldly. Psychologically, Rei was still very definitely naive. His betrayal by Yukikaze, the one thing he'd trusted, had left a deep wound. That would need rehabilitation along with the wounds to his body. The major had just told Rei that he was in a state that left him open to brainwashing. Rei had just challenged the major to change his mind. Perhaps, somewhere inside, part of Rei doubted whether the changes he'd made had put him on the right course.

Even so, it was clear that this man wanted to put himself on a more precise heading. The major wondered where exactly Rei was flying to.

"This battle we're in isn't a war. It's a struggle for existence," Major Booker said, trying out Rei's words for himself. "That's true for the rank and file of every war. No soldier wants to die in vain. You have to kill the enemy in front of you or be killed yourself. Same goes for the enemy. The struggle for existence. All it means is that you just don't want to be an enlisted man who gets used up as cannon fodder."

"I'm not an enlisted man," Rei replied. "The FAF has never had enlisted men, and I'm a captain now, Major Booker."

"A figure of speech," the major said. "You've always said that rank didn't matter to you. Or perhaps you now see the meaning of it and want to rise even higher."

"I thought you said you didn't have time to listen to my philosophy of life."

"Well, it's already eaten up enough time. So how about it, Rei?"

"Why are you asking?" Rei said.

"I want to make sure the SAF can still use you as a top-class Maeve driver. That's my job. Now answer me, Captain Fukai."

"If getting a higher rank badge meant I could guarantee how I die, it might not be a bad thing to aim for. But you can't say that even a general won't die stupidly by slipping in the bathroom. The opposite is just as true. If you're a general, the odds are much higher that you'll die a ridiculous death like that rather than dying in battle."

"Die a ridiculous death, huh? It reminds me of the story of Aeschylus."

"Who's that?" Rei asked. "Someone famous for dying stupidly?"

"Whether it's stupid or not depends on your point of view. He was one of the three great tragedians of ancient Greece. He was killed by a tortoise that fell out of the sky onto his head."

"What?"

"The tortoise had been caught by a crow or an eagle that was flying overhead, and the bird was looking for a good rock to drop it on to break its shell open. Aeschylus was completely bald, and there's a famous story that the bird mistook the tragedian's bald head for a rock to split the tortoise open with," the major said. "Tragedy is the flipside of comedy. Take it as you will. It was a death even he might have written. But the point is that the way he lived his life isn't as known to posterity as this little anecdote about his death. He was a man of great rank and social status, so don't you think he would be remembered more for that?"

"All that was just someone else's way of valuing him. That had nothing to do with how satisfied he was with his own life," Rei said.

"But why do we concentrate on the way he died rather than on how he lived? The way you die never goes the way you expect it to. There's an element to it that's beyond human knowledge. Besides, it's not like dying is something you consent to."

"Everyone dies, regardless of rank or class. Living life without realizing that is meaningless, and I don't want to live a meaningless life."

"*Memento mori*," the major said. "Remember your mortality. Rei, you really have changed, haven't you?"

"I don't think it's easy to live a life that you can agree to, but I'm trying my best to."

"Even while you keep saying 'Not my problem.'"

"I've never had any regrets before and I don't have any now."

"And yet you seem unable to face the thought of death. Isn't that another way of saying that you regret the way you've lived your life?" Major Booker asked. Rei answered him coldly. "You're right. I may have been wrong. Living a life without regret doesn't mean you'll be ready for death when it comes for you. I understand that. I just never thought about it before."

"I see," said Major Booker, nodding. "That's how it is. No matter how often you claim something isn't your problem, there are always some problems you have to accept. That's reality. It's common sense. The same goes for death. No matter how often you say 'I'm not going to die, and I don't care about death,' death is still coming for you. People normally live with that as a fact of life, but your way of life wasn't normal. You lived as if saying 'I'm not going to die' meant you really weren't going to die. Of course, one day reality is going to kick that worldview in the ass. It wasn't the JAM who taught you that. It was your trusted Yukikaze, wasn't it? You were ready to be killed by the JAM, but Yukikaze wasn't—"

"And now I don't want to sit back quietly and get killed by the JAM. Or by anyone else, for that matter."

"Of course you don't. I know exactly what it is that you're worried about," the major said.

"And what's that?"

"Rei, you sense that you might end up being killed by Yukikaze. That's something you haven't faced until now."

"I don't think that Yukikaze betrayed me, and I don't expect her to. Yukikaze still needs me, even now."

"That's fine if you're immortal. There's no problem at all, then. The thing is, you're human. If you die, you can't come back to life and there won't be a spare body ready for you to use. You don't have an equal relationship with Yukikaze," the major said. "That's the thing you just can't accept. This isn't a question that lies on the emotional plane—of whether she betrayed you or whether you think she did, Rei. That's common sense. Yukikaze is a machine, so she has no emotions. There's no room for it in your relationship with her. If Yukikaze killed you out of hatred, you could accept that. But if she's going to kill you, she's just going to kill you. It won't be like a gun accidentally going off and killing its owner, because Yukikaze isn't a simple device like that. She possesses the barest seed of self-awareness now, and you don't know how to handle the idea of being killed by something like that. You came back here to seek out Yukikaze because you're looking for an answer."

"You're saying that I came back here to be killed by Yukikaze? That's ridiculous. You're wrong—"

"No, I'm saying you came back so that you wouldn't lose to her. You want to understand Yukikaze as an adversary in the struggle for existence. You don't have to win, just not lose. When you do lose, you want to accept your death as an honest loss. If you can accept it, it won't seem like a loss to you. Rei, up until now, you've lived your life in a completely selfish manner, never thinking of other people. In that respect, you haven't changed a bit."

Rei had decided that none of it mattered—seeing his fellow planes getting shot down, the Earth captured by the JAM, or even the extinction of the human race. That was a question he had to settle within himself. This man thought that, as long as he himself didn't lose, it was okay. That was true then and that was still true now.

"So what?" Rei replied.

"Figured you'd say that. Now I'm relieved. I wouldn't want to talk to you anymore if you'd changed that much, because I'm a bit like you. I have my own thoughts about Yukikaze now—she's a threat, an enemy on the same level as the JAM. She's a competitor in the struggle for existence."

"I'm not afraid of Yukikaze."

"No, you've embraced the seed of fear within you. You're now beginning to realize that Yukikaze is an independent being separate from you. The meaning of that is, for the first time, your relationship with her has been equalized."

The old Yukikaze had been like a part of Rei, not a separate entity. He never thought she'd betray him, any more than you'd expect your right hand to betray you. But, of course, that wasn't reality. The incident when she'd been shot down had taught Rei as much.

"Psychotherapy isn't going to settle the question of what the optimal relationship between you and Yukikaze would be, or what its meaning is," Major Booker said. "That's a matter for philosophy because, in the end, you're asking about the meaning of life. You've always had questions about that. Is there any meaning to human existence or not? If there is, then what is it? If there isn't, then why do we go on living lives without meaning? I have some sympathy for your naive feelings. That's why I like to be around you, as a friend. Your problem with Yukikaze is my problem too.

"The thing is, fighting the JAM is taking everything I've got, so I don't have time to answer that question with you. For now, if I can't conceive of Yukikaze as being on our side, then I can't work out a strategy to use against the JAM. You're going to have to deal with that one on your own, Rei. Right now, you're being proactive in thinking about how to answer it, and in that way, you have changed."

"So what are you saying?"

"Speaking as both your commander and your friend, I want you back in Yukikaze's cockpit as soon as possible. You don't need the psychological counseling aspect of your rehab program anymore. It's a waste of time. The SAF can't spare you time to fool around on the ground. Train hard and get your body back up to full strength. That's an order. You're dismissed, Captain Fukai."

Rei saluted and left the office. Major Booker watched him leave, then flipped through the documents relating to Rei's rehabilitation spread out over his desk, searching for the section indicating which doctor was in charge of it. Rei didn't need any more psychological care. He had to speak to the attending physician about that. He understood Rei better than any doctor could. Booker wouldn't just dismiss the opinion of a specialist out of hand, but he was the one with ultimate responsibility. The doctor's opinion was merely there for reference. The full responsibility was his to bear.

He was shorthanded. The SAF needed expert pilots. It didn't matter how Rei felt about the war. What they needed was combat intel, and no matter what sort of wounds Rei's heart might now carry, they could afford to be ignored when they didn't directly relate to combat. This was a battlefield, not a hospital. While the major dearly hoped that the anxiety Rei felt in his heart would heal, he just didn't have the time to coddle the pilot. However this turned out, Rei wouldn't rely on anyone else for help. *That guy will handle this on his own*, the major thought. That was why he'd come back here—because on Faery, there was the FAF, and in the FAF was Yukikaze. He understood that.

But, Major Booker wondered, *will Rei's attending physician understand that as well?*

2

THE YOUNG DOCTOR in charge of Rei's psychological care was a recent arrival to the SAF, and Major Booker had yet to meet her. Her youth, lack of combat experience, and the fact she'd only served a short time in the SAF made him dislike her instantly.

Major Booker called up the doctor's personnel file on his desktop terminal. Name: Edith Foss. Rank: Captain. Sex: Female. Joined the Faery Air Force as a volunteer. Specialties in aviation medicine and aviation psychology. Served in the Systems Corps prior to transfer to the SAF, where she'd mainly been in charge of psych care for the test pilots.

What kind of care was that, he wondered. The test pilots of the FAF Systems Corps were the elite. Their flight skills were unmatched, but test piloting took more than that. Test pilots had to look for problems in the planes that they tested and investigate advanced flight maneuvers, and they also needed excellent interpersonal communication skills so that they could convey the results of their tests to others. Someone like the pilots of the SAF with their "To hell with everyone else" attitude would be completely unsuited for it. Test pilots needed to get along well with others. In other words, these pilots with their never-fail personalities were psychologically stable; they'd seldom run into a problem that required a shrink to help them work out. People with those tendencies would be weeded out from the start.

Foss had probably been doing mainly research rather than actual psych care in the Systems Corps, Major Booker imagined as he read her file. She was a researcher and a scholar with no criminal record. There were more and more people like her in the FAF these days.

When the FAF had first been established, its personnel had been chosen from the elite. There was a true appreciation of the JAM threat back then, and it allowed humanity to throw itself fully into halting their invasion. But as the war dragged on and as the elite were consumed with no end in sight, humanity began to panic. One by one, the best of society, those meant to bear the burden of Earth's future, were being killed off by the JAM. You couldn't instantly mass-produce people like that. At the rate they were dying, the fear was that Earth would lose its entire reserve of leaders and human civilization would devolve into an unruly mob. It was at that point that mankind stopped sending the hope of Earth's future—or, to be more precise, the hope of each nation—to fight on the front lines against the JAM. Instead, the defense of Earth was left to bleeding-edge combat machine systems which were installed in FAF HQ and in the planes themselves, leaving their machine intelligences to shoulder the burden that had once been that of humanity's best and brightest. As a result, the selection of FAF conscripts was now based on the determination of whom human society would miss the least were they killed, specifically those branded as antisocial or possibly criminal. To be brutally honest, the FAF was now composed of criminals of every type.

There hadn't been a global consensus that this should be done, so the change occurred very gradually. Since the selection methods varied by national agency, you'd still occasionally get a new recruit that made you wonder what such a good person was doing here. Even so, these groups of people called "nations," according to the varied political agencies that prevented them from uniting on a global scale, had evolved a system where it was now normal for the ruling classes to send off the weakest members of society in order to profit from the war.

Quite a few people tried to desert, Major Booker thought. *However, their outlook on life would change after their first encounter with the JAM on the front lines.* At any rate, fresh recruits couldn't escape even if they survived out there. Escape wasn't an easy matter. They'd have to go up against the power of the state as well as being hunted by the FAF, not to mention having the JAM in the background as well.

You couldn't make deals with the JAM like you could with a human. If you were dealing with humans, it was possible to find a group that shared your values and could help you against a group persecuting you. But the JAM were different. You might not have any intention of fighting them and just want them to let you go, but there was no way you could negotiate with the JAM. Everyone who came here knew that.

The majority of people who came here died in battle. If they managed to survive, most would go back to Earth, but some would stay in the FAF. However, the sort of people who came there had been changed by their service. The number of people who volunteered rather than being conscripted was increasing. There'd been quite a number of volunteers previously as well, but their motives for volunteering had changed. It used to be that recruits would come because it was hard for them to live on Earth. Most of the old guard had cut ties with the home world when they came to Faery, but now the number of people who were motivated to come and develop their own talents while maintaining their relationship with Earth was growing. There were even some thrill-seekers who came to the front like it was some sort of video game center. There was no shortage of talented people, but they were a completely different variety of person from the elite founders of the FAF in how they viewed the JAM threat. To the new recruits, the FAF now was like some sort of virtual game space.

Systems Corps always has lots of that type. Foss, who recently came from there, was probably just like that, thought Major Booker. *The people in the SAF aren't. They're a squadron made up of the old type of soldier. This Captain Foss came to the FAF to study the psychological makeup of the people here, didn't she?* He was sure of it. When he read at the end of her file that she'd requested the transfer to the SAF, Major Booker sighed.

She's going to be trouble for us, he thought. She and the soldiers here were like oil and water, which made him the surface agent that had to somehow make them mix. In other words, he was soap. Soap was apropos, since this job was definitely wearing him down.

As the squadron's supervisor, he couldn't just leave her to wave her newbie doctor expectations around in front of the old-timers here. *But if Foss is the sort of person I imagine her to be, she won't just take my word for it that Rei doesn't need her,* Major Booker thought gloomily.

She'd probably ask why. If she were just ordered to do it, he wouldn't have to explain anything to her, since a subordinate had to obey a superior. She couldn't refuse it. But an unconditional order like that would have to be handed down by her direct superior, and in Captain Foss's case, that would be General Cooley, the de facto boss of the SAF. Foss was likely different from the other members of the squadron. Captain Foss would probably refuse an order. She might technically be a military doctor, but Booker expected that her sense of military protocol was weak. She probably saw herself more as a visiting scholar engaged in field work, or a researcher studying abroad, than as an actual soldier. He predicted that she'd be hard to handle, unable to understand that orders weren't just suggestions.

The SAF didn't need people like her. He was going to need to get General Cooley to help him out on this. But why hadn't the general rejected the transfer request from a doctor like this in the first place? Did she simply not care about personnel matters not directly related to combat? That was possible, which was why he handled that job—the one that was wearing him down. He wanted to avoid further crumbling.

Major Booker closed the connection to the personnel file and massaged his stiff neck. Damn, the one who wanted a break around here was him. If Booker could just sprawl out on a comfortable couch and come clean to a counselor about all the psychological burdens he had, he'd probably feel a lot better.

Captain Foss was a qualified counselor. He was sure she'd come here for a consultation, although he still didn't know if she was reliable. Well, here was a good chance for him to check out the character and talents of the newbie doctor. Would he need to make an appointment with her? It was at times like this that Booker wished for a private secretary who could handle this stuff for him.

Major Booker accessed Captain Foss's room with his terminal. A synthesized voice answered. "My user is currently away from her seat." Then "I will handle whatever business you may have."

Major Booker was momentarily perplexed. "'My user'?" Did that mean Edith Foss? "Who is this?" he asked.

"I am the electronic secretary that has been installed in this terminal," the voice replied. "I will be sure to deliver your verbal message to my user only. Please proceed."

Booker was being addressed by a simple terminal agent program. This e-secretary wasn't sending any video, instead simply displaying the contents of what it was saying as text. There were even more advanced e-secretaries in common use, and they were practically indistinguishable from actual persons. Major Booker wasn't unaware of them, but it was rare to encounter one here in the SAF squadron section. This was the first time any person here had installed an agent that gave the impression of personality.

"Who is this?" asked the e-secretary in Foss's terminal.

Major Booker, of course. He didn't answer it like that, though.

"I'd like to consult you about something. Please come to my office."

The e-secretary knew without asking who was accessing it. Confirmation requests were believed to make for a friendlier user interface, but it was essentially an unnecessary and redundant step. Installing an electronic agent into a terminal like this was another example of the sort of thing the new breed of people here were doing, but it was possible that Dr. Foss was scrutinizing him at this very moment. She might be using the e-secretary to interview him in order to get background information, Major Booker thought. At the very least, the way he was responding should give her an indication of his character. And his present mental condition.

Was he overthinking this? No, it was possible. Still, there was no denying that if he didn't show some interest in Captain Foss, then she wouldn't have noticed him or thought to seek him out.

"Captain Foss," he added. "There's something I'd like to discuss. I'd like you to come to my office. Soon, if possible."

Major Booker disconnected, ignoring a repeated attempt by

Captain Foss's e-secretary to ask him his name. His verbal message had already been automatically recorded. He knew that Captain Foss wouldn't be hearing it from the e-secretary because the FAF's internal communications core system program was designed that way. The e-secretary was there strictly for decorative purposes.

An artificial electronic secretary? It was absurd. This was a battlefield, after all. The FAF medical center was a field hospital, not a private hospital that had to cater to its patients' moods. If Captain Foss was having trouble seeing that, then it was his duty to set her straight.

What the hell was this doctor thinking? Major Booker thought. For a moment he was irritated, but he managed to get it under control. In any case, Booker wouldn't be able to do anything about it unless he met her.

3

REI SWAM LAPS at Faery base's Tactical Combat Air Corps training center. The SAF might have been a de facto division with its own headquarters, but they had no training center of their own for when their soldiers wanted to exercise or work out their frustrations.

There were about twenty people from other units in the pool with him, relaxing, chatting with friends, and calmly drifting along as they swam. *The atmosphere is more like a hotel leisure pool than one in a training center*, Rei thought. *Like a public bath house, echoing with happy shouts.* Since Faery Base was located underground, the effect was similar to that of a pool at an underground spa.

Rei swam alone, in silence. Nobody called out to him.

Whenever he set foot into the environs of the training center, entered the locker room, or stood at the side of the pool, it would always be the same. To anyone who met his gaze and tried to engage him in conversation, Rei would simply say, "I'm from the SAF," and their camaraderie would lapse back into silence. While people in other units knew that SAF members were hard to get along with, they weren't indifferent to them. Although the

SAF were officially assigned to the Tactical Combat Air Corps at Faery Base, SAF members behaved like individuals assigned to an autonomous corps; they had a lot of power. They kept their specific activities secret from people in other units, and that extended to when one of their taciturn soldiers came into a shared area like this—SAF members never spoke about what went on inside of their heads. Their mystery made them objects of curiosity to the others.

No one spoke to Rei directly at the pool, but he could feel their inquisitive glances as he swam, and occasionally he heard "SAF" bubble up from their lively conversations. He couldn't shake the feeling that he'd become a bit of a spectacle, but he didn't care what they said about him as long as they didn't directly interfere with what he was doing. Rei was used to hearing other units bitching about him on the radio whenever he flew missions with Yukikaze anyway. The only reason he was here swimming was because Major Booker had ordered it. He was here to do his duty, not to make friends.

Rei was actually a talented swimmer, but it had been a long time since he'd come to the pool just for the sake of swimming. Forgetting this was being done as a duty, Rei let the sensation of the water carry him away as he swam without a wasted motion. He soon came to relish the feeling of just moving his body.

As always doing his best not to waste a single stroke, he switched between a two-beat crawl when he grew tired and a six-beat sprint when he wanted to push himself. Rei was out of breath after only four or five laps, driving home to him just how out of shape he was. Abandoning his original plan to switch up his swimming style to a butterfly stroke, he cruised along with the easiest crawl he could manage. Rei thought he could keep going for hours doing that, but gradually his arms grew heavy. He looked at the big analog clock that hung on the wall by the pool. Not even twenty minutes had passed. He decided to keep going and get at least thirty minutes of swimming in, but the hands on the clock crawled along at a glacial pace. When he realized that he was obsessing about how long it was taking, Rei finally admitted that he was too weak to keep pushing on and climbed out of the pool.

He chose a deck chair away from the crowd and sat down to catch his breath. The chair was a new one, nice and clean. He suddenly realized that the chair and the facility it sat in were both clean because someone was keeping them clean. Of course the center had a full-time maintenance staff. They never saw the JAM. There must have been lots of civilian contractors who had come to Faery. War was big business. He'd never before thought about all the people who were involved in the war with the JAM, but when he stopped to think about it, only a small fraction of the FAF directly faced the JAM threat on the front lines. *Even so, that doesn't mean that the people at the rear, like the ones who keep this pool clean, were necessarily safe*, Rei thought.

Assuming they considered the humans worthy of their notice in this war, there were all sorts of ways the JAM could kill everyone here if they wanted to. The JAM might have already begun making preparations. The pool maintenance staff might have been noncombatants, but no place on Faery was safe for them. Rei didn't know if they were conscious of that, but he was grateful that they were here doing their job. Grateful that they kept things clean.

THE CHEERFUL GROUP, apparently having been waiting for Rei to leave the pool, were lined up on the start line. Teams were instantly chosen and it seemed that a mini swim meet was about to begin. After a few humorous on-the-spot introductions of the swimmers, the race began. Some onlookers cheered the swimmers on. Rei was tired, but hearing their cheers felt good to him. The actual participants were probably good swimmers, but their skill range was all over the place. Still, they were giving it their best and taking it seriously, so it didn't make for a bad show.

The race was a three-course relay, and when the second set of swimmers dove in, the one in the center lane caught Rei's attention. She was a woman, remarkably fast, and she didn't waste a single stroke. She was catching up with the man who was in the lead. Rei was intrigued by her excellent performance and wondered if she had ever competed seriously. There was a beauty to the movements of a well-trained human body. He could never tire of watching it.

"Not joining in, Captain Fukai?" said a voice that suddenly came from behind him. Rei didn't turn to look. He knew it was Captain Foss. He hadn't even noticed her come in.

"Did I ask to join in? I'm not interested," Rei said. His eyes stayed on the race.

"I wonder if you don't want to compete because you're afraid of losing," Captain Foss said, as though idly chatting.

"I'm not afraid of losing." He turned to face Captain Foss. "Losing doesn't make me feel scared, just irritated."

"Quite a few people would avoid contests from the start because they don't like to feel that way. That's basically what a fear of losing is. They hate the contest itself. Are you sure that isn't what you're feeling?"

"What I think," Rei said, "is that I'd rather avoid losing a contest and feeling irritated about it if it isn't necessary. That's how I feel about that race. I didn't come here to win anything." He paused for a moment. "So what brings you here?"

Captain Foss was wearing the white doctor's coat she normally eschewed during her counseling sessions. The coat marked her as a military doctor, which essentially made it her uniform. It meant that she was still on duty and hadn't come here for fun.

"Major Booker just asked me to do the right thing for you," she said.

"Oh," Rei replied. When he followed his one-word answer with silence, Captain Foss asked him if that was all he was going to say.

"What are you getting at?" Rei asked.

"A little while ago, the major contacted me and told me in no uncertain terms that he wanted you released from my care."

"So what? You're saying he was lying when he told you to do the right thing for me?"

"No, he was telling me that if I were worried about you, then he wanted me to end the psychological aspect of your rehabilitation, and to please take care to do that."

"And you want to stay involved, right?"

"It's my job. Of course I want to stay involved. I have no idea what the major is thinking. Or what you're thinking, for that matter. If you don't like my methods, could you please do me the courtesy of telling me so to my face?"

"This is definitely the major's doing," Rei said as he rose from the deck chair. "I just follow his orders. He told me that it wasn't necessary for you to keep treating me. If there's something going on between you and the major, that's not my problem."

"Where are you going?"

"The sauna."

"Are you running away from me?"

"Running away?" Rei chuckled without even thinking. "You seem like you want to fight with me, but you don't know how to. Okay, here's how it works—if you don't want me to run away, you chase me. If you get in my way, I hit you. Major Booker gave me permission to do that, naturally."

"Who are you at war with, Captain Fukai?"

"The JAM."

"It doesn't look that way to me."

"You trying to be my girlfriend now?"

"What?"

"The sauna. Are you coming in with me?"

"If you're going in, then yes, of course I will."

"Dressed like that?"

In response, Captain Foss slowly took off her white coat, then grasped the hem of her sweater and began pulling it off too.

"Forget the sauna," Rei said. "I don't think I could deal with you asking me about this and that in a tiny, hot little room."

Captain Foss paused, her pale belly showing. "Then will you come to my office?" she asked.

"No."

"You're not yet psychologically fit to return to combat duty."

"You're right," Rei replied with a nod. "There's something I need to settle with you first."

"Settle with me?"

"Why are you so interested in what goes on in my mind? That's going to gnaw at me until I get an answer."

It was annoying how she was always following him around. There was no escape from her on the base, and ignoring her required an enormous amount of effort. The only thing left to do was to have it out with her once and for all.

The race in the pool wasn't over yet. The last swimmers had just dived in, and everybody was paying attention to them. Rei might have lost interest in the swimmers, but the people in the pool area were still aware of him. As Rei looked to be walking away, one of them whistled and called out, "SAF's bugging out of here." There was no scorn or anger in his voice. It was simply delivered as a situation report. The cheers died down. *It's the same reaction I get from other units in battle*, Rei thought. The Special Air Force really did hold a special position in their forces. Rei left the pool area without looking back.

In the locker room, he changed out of his swim trunks, put his wristwatch back on, then logged his exercise on a form he carried on a clipboard. When he'd gathered it all up and walked out of the locker room, Captain Foss was waiting for him.

The basic reason why she had come was that, technically, this was the time when she should have been examining him, and as his attending physician, she wasn't amused by his arbitrarily deciding to do a bit of independent training instead. He'd just been following Major Booker's orders, but it was clear that the major hadn't been able to convince this doctor. That left it to Rei, the concerned party in this matter, to get her to agree. If he managed to make her see that he didn't need her to treat him anymore, it'd take a load off of his mind as well. The result would be the same whether Major Booker made the move or not. Thinking that, Rei renewed his resolve. He canceled the strength training session he'd scheduled for after his swim and left the center to have a chat with Captain Foss.

Back at his quarters in the SAF residential area, Rei changed again, into his ground duty fatigues. Since he had no intention of going to Captain Foss's examination room, he headed to the sortie briefing room instead. Captain Foss followed him without a word.

The room was dark and deserted, the ceiling lights automatically turning on as they entered. As they did Rei felt a twinge of preflight nerves, which he hadn't sensed for a while.

The main monitor along the front wall of the room, which normally would have displayed mission action data, was dark now. As Rei stood in front of the computer terminal to the side,

Captain Foss finally spoke.

"How do you feel? What are your impressions, coming here?"

"My impression is that I want to get back into the fight as soon as I can. My physical rehab is going just fine, better than you claim. As far as I see, there's no problem with me going back into combat. Major Booker's just being cautious. He's after perfection. Is that what you're after too?"

"I am, though my position is different from the major's."

"What is your position in the FAF? Why did you come here? It doesn't seem like you were forced to join up, but I don't get the sense that you're just another doctor who's hot to do their job either. Military doctors don't disobey their superior officers."

"I'm not disobeying my superior. Who happens to be General Cooley. Even Major Booker has to admit that."

"You're just like the JAM," Rei said, his voice cracking. "I don't know what you think of me and I can't communicate with you very well. I don't know what you're doing here on Faery. Meanwhile, you just keep coming after me. You're an unknown, Foss. Does General Cooley even know who you are?"

"She's a distant relative of mine."

"Huh?" Rei leaned against the computer console, not thinking as he made his dumbfounded grunt of surprise. Captain Foss kept her eyes on him as she drew closer and sat down in one of the front-row seats. *Almost like a child who'd been ordered to stay after class,* thought Rei.

"Although," Captain Foss said, "I'd never met her until I came here. She didn't know we were related either. Still, I used the family connection. I was never going to get anywhere with my research into the psychological makeup of FAF pilots without actually coming here. The truth is, I wanted to come here as a civilian."

"So that's how it is," Rei said. "What a pain in the ass."

"Major Booker said the same thing. But my interest wasn't going to get any priority unless I worked here as a military doctor. I'm working on a detailed report of the patients I've examined, which includes you. But there's no evidence that Major Booker has read what I've submitted so far. I find it insane that he'd just ignore it and then claim that I'm unnecessary. It wasn't like that back in the Systems Corps. My work was valued there. From what I've seen, I'd say that the SAF is a collection of weirdos."

"That doesn't sound like the way a doctor would talk."

"Okay, that's true. I was a little rash there. But I'm a human being with feelings too, you know," Foss said.

"You're the one who needs counseling. You aren't used to the environment in the SAF. I don't need you. Anything that has to do with me, I'll handle by myself. I'm not looking for help from anyone. Conversely, I don't help anyone. I don't want to get wrapped up in anyone else's feelings. Any feelings that aren't mine are illusions. That's the sort of people who make up the SAF."

"Perfectly put," Captain Foss replied with a nod. "You're not abnormal individually, but in a group, you literally become 'special.' The idea of putting together a team of people with a limited ability to feel empathy is fascinating to me."

"That's thanks to Major Booker's skills. Or, more accurately, to General Cooley's. The JAM aren't human. They're beings whose true nature is still a mystery to us. The general thinks that you need people with inhuman abilities in order to collect data on and analyze entities like the JAM. She probably thinks that human sympathy would lead to projecting human qualities onto the JAM, and we'd end up coming to the wrong conclusions."

"Assuming the JAM actually exist and are a real threat."

"That's true. There's a definite possibility that they don't really exist," Rei said.

"What did you just say? You mean you really believe that? I'm amazed. I just said they might not exist to see how shocked you'd be."

"You may see the JAM as illusory, but that's not how I see them. They may not have physical existence, but I can sense them," Rei said. "Their existence is more real to me than yours is."

"Perhaps the FAF successfully repelled the original JAM long ago. What if the JAM we face now is an imaginary enemy created by the SAF to maintain this war environment? It's easy for people like you to live in an environment like this, so maybe you've gotten together as a group to deceive everyone else. What do you think of that possibility?"

"I'm sure there are some people in the world who think that. It's not that strange to me."

"In other words, you've considered the possibility as well," Foss said.

"I think that if a person were drowning in front of me, even I would hold my hand out to them. I'd have to help them. It's not a question of feelings. It's a reflexive action."

"So...?"

Captain Foss didn't question his abrupt change of topic. *It's a good method to induce me to talk*, Rei thought.

"You seem like you're drowning in your own thoughts," he said. "I'm able to sense that. But if I were a JAM, I wouldn't see you. Probably couldn't see you. If you were drowning, the JAM wouldn't directly attack you, but they wouldn't help you either. They would ignore you completely. As far as the JAM are concerned, human beings don't exist. I just don't think the human imagination could come up with beings that can't even perceive us as the antagonists in a story."

"You shouldn't underestimate the power of human imagination, or the clout of others. It may just be my own impression that the SAF has both the imagination and clout to create an illusion like that, but your viewpoint that I seem to be drowning just reinforces it," Captain Foss replied.

"You can see JAM fighter planes with your naked eye, and they attack. But we can't see what's flying them. It may be the same for the JAM as far as humans go. They may not be able to recognize us directly, but when they began to sense the threat we posed, I think they started building a human-perception mechanism. One with the same sensory organs as humans to act as a system to perceive the world as we do. In other words, human duplicates.

"The human side of the war had the means to oppose the JAM from the start—combat machine intelligences, of which Yukikaze is a representative. It doesn't take much imagination to come up with an idea like this. Neither does the idea that the SAF invented the JAM to justify its own existence to others. All people ever do is think up things that are convenient for them to believe."

"And in that way, you can psychologically draw me in," said Captain Foss. "Are you conscious of that and able to judge that for yourself?"

"I think you should withdraw your diagnosis that I'm not psychologically fit for combat. The JAM are the enemy, not Yukikaze. I realize that anew even as I say it. That's thanks to your counseling. You really are a miracle worker," Rei said. "Here I am, in the middle of a war, having forgotten about the existence of the enemy, and you've made me realize who they are: the JAM are the ones I should be out there killing."

"I think you see me as more of an enemy than you do the JAM. What do you think of that?"

"That's the heart of why you're so nervous. You probably think if I fly into battle with Yukikaze, I'll just spread the idea of the JAM—which you essentially think are imaginary—even more strongly across the world. You think madness is contagious. As far as you're concerned, the SAF is insane. The thing is, everything in war is insane. You just haven't been part of that shared delusion up till now. To the SAF fighting a war, you're the one that's insane because you think this war is meaningless, that the JAM are phantoms, and that there really is no enemy anywhere."

"But you sense that as well, don't you?" Foss asked. "I think you're just trying to give meaning to what are meaningless battles."

"I'm not denying the possibility that the JAM are imaginary. But even if they're phantoms, just virtual monsters produced from my head and the results of the SAF's data processing, it doesn't matter. As far as we're concerned, the JAM are a real threat, an enemy that will kill us if we ignore them. That's reality for the SAF. So I'm going to fight, no matter what you say. It's so that I can live. Since I'll end up being killed by the JAM if I go along with what you say, you have no right to complain."

"I wonder if Major Booker feels the same."

"Since I'm not a commander, I can't speak for the SAF as a whole. However, at the very least, I can tell you how I see it. This isn't a war. It's a struggle for survival. Anybody who stands at my side and tells me that struggle is meaningless is an obstacle to my survival. Removing obstacles is only natural, isn't it?"

"You're looking to 'remove' me?" Foss said.

"I think you occupy a very dangerous position. The problem is on your end."

"Thanks for the warning, Captain Fukai."

"Am I dangerous?"

Captain Foss gave a vague nod in answer to his question.

"Yes, very. I'm afraid of you, although it's mainly because of the attitude you've shown me here."

"I understand your unease. Even if you don't authorize me to fly combat missions, I'll do it eventually. And you're afraid that, even if I'm nominally fighting the JAM, they won't be the only ones I'll attack. You're afraid that I'll end up attacking anybody I judge to be an obstacle, even those on my own side. You thought that about me before and you still do now."

"I want to think that I'm wrong," Foss said.

"You're not. That's the mission of the SAF. If necessary, we will attack our own side. That's an act of combat allowed in war, just another type of tactic."

"But you just said this isn't a war. That idea is surely the core of what is becoming a major problem here."

"It's true that I've started thinking of it that way lately," Rei said. "If I were fighting humans rather than the JAM, I wouldn't have come back here. 'Let other people fight their wars and leave me out of it' was what I thought. But I can't leave the war against the JAM to other people. I tried to ignore it and act like it wasn't my problem, but it felt like there was no place I could go to escape the threat. I'm afraid that this conflict here is even more grueling than a war. There's no striking a deal or turning traitor here," Rei said. "The one rule in effect is that the strongest side gets to survive. In a war with humans on both sides, you can get away with the strategy of letting a few die so that the many will live. You can even let your allies kill noncombatants. But fighting the JAM requires even harsher strategies."

"Such as?"

"Such as adopting a strategy where you'd let the entire human race die if it meant that you alone could survive. That's what I think. It's extreme, but you won't lose as long as you don't die.

That's the sort of battle this is. I think the JAM operate under that strategy too. If I went back to Earth and treated what goes on here like it's an illusion, I might be able to live my life. But when I finally notice the JAM threat there, it would be too late. I hate the thought of that. I don't want to lose. That's why I came back to Faery. You can't understand what I sense, so you're trying your damnedest to throw out all these hypotheses, trying not to drown in them."

"Like you're a specialist in theories—"

"You can't live with normal sensitivities in the FAF, and that goes double for the SAF. If you want to survive, you have to become as nuts as everyone else here. It's not so bad. You just have to accept that the JAM are real."

"What exactly do you have in mind?" Captain Foss asked, a worried expression now on her face.

"Write a report saying that I'm fit for combat duty and sign it. In return, I'll help you perceive the JAM."

"How?"

"The JAM aren't phantoms. They exist on the same level as Yukikaze. There's more to her than what you can see. Similarly, you can monitor my psychological state from my reactions in flight. Surely a military doctor like you would be willing to take the risk for that."

"You're saying you want me to fly with you?"

"Right," Rei answered. "I'll take you up in Yukikaze with me." *In SAF Unit 1: Yukikaze.*

Captain Foss stared straight at Rei, not saying a word. Then she answered, her tone firm.

"If General Cooley authorizes it, I'll do what you want. But that's—"

"You'll get the authorization, Captain Foss. You'll be the one who'll convince General Cooley and Major Booker. If you can't do it, there'll only be one thing for you to do—apply for a transfer out of the SAF."

"You'd really go that far... Suppose I still find you unfit to fly, even while we're in the air?"

"You won't be making that call. The JAM will just shoot us down."

"You're saying we'll be flying in a combat zone?"

"There's no absolutely safe place in the FAF, Captain Foss. You can't escape that, no matter where you go. Get me my flight authorization. Then Major Booker will stop ignoring you. I think it's a good proposal."

"I'd like some time to think it over."

"This isn't practice. It's real combat. I need your answer now, Captain Foss. You won't get a chance like this again."

"Fine," she replied, standing up. "I'll accept your proposal. The truth is, I've always wanted a ride in one of our state-of-the-art fighters."

"Oh, is that what you were really after? You certainly took a roundabout way to get it," Rei said, his expression deadly serious. "I wish you'd just been upfront about that from the beginning. Then nobody would have ignored you. Though had you just been honest, you absolutely never would have been given a chance to ride in Yukikaze. Well played. How do you feel?"

"Like I went for wool and ended up getting fleeced," replied Captain Foss, holding out her hand. Rei shook it and said, "Which one of us is getting fleeced here? I don't think either of us has yet. I think this is going to settle the problems between us, but your battle is just beginning. I'm praying we aren't your enemy."

"Are you saying that the SAF sees people who don't accept the reality of the JAM as their enemies?"

"Not in that sense. I'm saying that there's no guarantee that you aren't a JAM."

"Me? A JAM?"

"That's the sort of battle we're fighting here now. More than any other unit in the FAF, we know that in our bones, not our brains," Rei said.

"So, admitting that…are you taking me out into a combat zone as some sort of a test?"

"Major Booker will make that call. He's a tough one. All I'm looking for is to fly Yukikaze. Anything beyond that is your own problem. You risk your life by choosing to fly in her. Be prepared for whatever happens."

The same goes for me, Rei thought, *though the probability that this person is a JAM is pretty low.* Rei left the room to report the deal he'd just set up to Major Booker, prepared for the chewing out he'd receive for causing his commander even more headaches.

4

CONTRARY TO REI'S expectations, Major Booker received his news calmly and then, after considering it for a moment, told him "Good work. That was probably the best way to handle it." The major didn't smile when Rei told him that Captain Foss might be a JAM. He instead nodded and replied that anyone whose history was unknown to them had to be suspected. Considering that, taking her out into an actual combat zone was a good idea, the major said.

If she were a JAM, she was extremely dangerous, but only the SAF could deal with it. And even though she likely wasn't a JAM, having her spreading the idea that they weren't real was going to cause chaos in the FAF. It wouldn't affect those in the SAF, but it might affect people in other units. For that reason, they couldn't just expel her. And if she simply had an interest in advanced fighter planes and the abilities of the people who flew them, then she needed to get it through her head that reality wasn't as simple as she thought it was, or else she'd never be of any use to the SAF as a military doctor.

"I'll draw up a plan to get Captain Edith Foss into combat," Major Booker said. "If she's a JAM, she'll show her true colors."

"She may not and just come back here to stay," Rei replied.

"I'll keep my eye on her," the major said. "Let's hope this turns Captain Foss around."

"She's got a fighting streak in her, the same as we do. She won't be an easy nut to crack."

"'We,' huh? You really have changed. I just hope that hasn't made you less effective in battle." *Having a medical specialist aboard the plane with him to make sure of that was a reasonable choice*, thought Major Booker. Captain Edith Foss was going to have an important duty to bear.

TWELVE DAYS LATER, wearing flight suits and with helmets in hand, Rei and Captain Foss were back in the sortie briefing room.

Their mission briefing had already been completed. They'd been told that their mission was to reconnoiter the environs of one of the JAM's main bases, code-named Richwar, which the FAF had hit recently. Major Booker had decided to commit two SAF planes to the task. He hadn't been able to determine if the FAF strike had knocked it out completely, and he was sure that there were survivors still there. They'd probably made contact with the other bases and summoned support. Naturally, the SAF had already conducted recon of the area, but hadn't been able to tell for certain what was going on. The human pilots didn't know how the JAM communicated with each other or how they organized support lines. Because of that, a JAM base that had been struck could one day spring back into action without any warning. The only way they'd ever learn how the JAM regenerated so quickly was to keep an apparently dead base under surveillance. These chances didn't come very often, and they had one now. Major Booker was just barely managing to send out continuous surveillance missions while balancing them with the squadron's other duties. They'd also dropped a recon pod in the area, and part of this mission was to collect the data it had gathered.

Captain Foss participated in the briefing as well, and Major Booker gave her specific instructions to keep careful watch on Rei's condition and report on it as the mission's medical specialist. These were orders from General Cooley, he added.

Their preflight briefing had covered the details of their flight plan, weather conditions, flight route, navigation support environment, fuel stores, and weapons loadout... All simple stuff, but it wasn't simple to Captain Foss. Her job of observing Rei had already begun, but the task at hand was first and foremost to deal with her fear of entering a combat zone for the first time. Worse for her, there wasn't anyone else on the sortie team with whom she could share the fear she felt. Rei was the subject of her observations, so she naturally couldn't confide in him, but the other plane teamed up for this mission with Yukikaze was an unmanned drone fighter. It was nicknamed the Rafe, a name Major Booker had chosen. This truly unmanned fighter, newly supplementing the squadron as its thirteenth plane, was the Maeve prototype: the FRX99.

Major Booker never sent out an unmanned plane to operate alone. There was much to learn about their performance, and that data was vital. Even so, he'd wanted at least one of the new drones sent out as the backup plane for this mission. If the SAF judged that this mission was too dangerous for Yukikaze to fly alone, they could use the drone. He was aware of the possibility that the drone could become a danger to Yukikaze's crew as well, and acknowledged that part of the SAF's job was to monitor just such a situation.

As she settled into Yukikaze's rear seat, Captain Foss also felt some trepidation at the sound of the engines starting up on the black-skinned Unit 13, although her fear was different from Major Booker's. She wondered if the unmanned plane charged with escorting Yukikaze and providing backup could be trusted not to abandon them if things got rough. After all, wasn't that how SAF planes normally operated? Even their manned planes would do that. In that respect, the humans in the SAF were much like their machines. She'd never really realized that before. Rei had said as much during their exchanges, but only now, in this situation, did the reality of Rei's words sink in.

Yukikaze's engines spun to life with power supplied by a support truck outside.

"Contact," Rei declared.

Fire screamed inside of Yukikaze's Super Phoenix engines. Captain Foss tensed up as the plane changed its posture, the front tire shock absorber compressing as it bore the enormous thrust from the engines. Yukikaze was roaring like a wild animal preparing to leap onto its prey.

Rei looked back. Captain Foss realized that he wasn't checking on her. His helmet visor was raised, and she could see that in his gaze. He was just making sure that Yukikaze's vertical stabilizers had unfolded into their proper configuration. He then checked to make sure that all of the plane's control surfaces were operating normally. Preflight checks, completed. All systems, normal. The ground crew pulled the safety pins from the missiles loaded onto the plane. The sortie crew chief then pulled the pin of his headset from the jack on Yukikaze's side and gave them the "Go" sign.

"Let's go, Yukikaze," Rei said.

The canopy lowered and locked in place. Releasing the brakes, Yukikaze moved forward. Captain Foss felt the plane's tires bumping along. To her, each thump seemed to be an amplified version of her own pounding heart.

Rei hadn't said, "Let's go, Captain Foss." She made a note of that on a small memo pad, similar to the ones used by test pilots, affixed to her thigh. She then regained her composure. Rei called back to her.

"Tell me right away if you feel sick. I'll try to compensate if I can."

"I've had *some* training, you know. I'll be fine. Don't worry about me."

"Okay, good to hear that you're ready for this. I'll be counting on you."

"Counting on me?" Foss said.

"Of course. You aren't a guest back there; you're flight crew. In battle, it's nice to have an extra eye. Lucky for me, you've got two."

"My eyesight isn't that great, so—"

"That doesn't matter, Edith. Any creature whose life is in danger can see its enemy. Let's go, partner."

The Rafe made a mad dash down the runway and began to climb. Yukikaze followed a moment later, her engine output at maximum. The acceleration was so intense that Captain Foss couldn't even speak.

A formation takeoff. Rei wondered if his ability to sense the enemy was still as sharp as it had been, but forgot about that once they were in the air.

"Hang in there, Yukikaze. The wolf's going to leave you behind."

They soon reached cruising altitude and the planes began to speed along high above the ground. Freed from the G-force pressure of acceleration, Captain Foss took a breath, then asked Rei about the wolf he'd just mentioned so urgently.

"I meant the Rafe, Unit 13," he replied. "The name means 'counsel of the wolf.' It's like a hobby for Major Booker. He knows the weirdest things."

Captain Foss looked for the plane. It was flying a few hundred meters off their port side, matching their altitude.

"You don't want to lose to it?"

"Yukikaze is a manned fighter whose design is based on the Rafe. She's not as maneuverable, so I was just shouting a little encouragement. Nothing really more meaningful than that."

"Who were you encouraging? Yourself or Yukikaze?"

"Both, probably. I guess you could theorize that it's hard to tell where I end and Yukikaze begins."

"Does that concern you?"

"Analyze that and give me a diagnosis when we get back. It's dangerous to distract me up here. It affects your safety too."

Captain Foss stopped talking. The forests of Faery spread out below her, mostly gleaming a metallic purple. With its undulations, eddies, and striped patterns, she felt as though she were looking at some sort of abstract painting. *Like peeking directly into somebody's mind,* she thought. It was an incoherent mass of shapes, and yet beautiful. *Would the JAM be as wondrous and beautiful if they came from somewhere in there?*

Rei responded to the few external communications they received with silence. A warning chimed twice, indicating a group of FAF planes crossing beneath them. A differently toned warning chimed, signaling that they'd reached their mission air space.

"Edith, I want you to please stop observing me for a while and keep watch on our surroundings."

"Roger," replied Captain Edith Foss.

The forest was now gone. A desert of pure white sand spread out around them. Not flat, but undulating.

The Rafe activated its high-powered look-down radar and began searching for the enemy. As Yukikaze monitored the electromagnetic environment of their surroundings, she transmitted her IFF (Identify Friend or Foe) signal to the reconnaissance pod deployed onto the ground below to transmit its collected data to them. The pod had been placed there by the SAF after Richwar base had been destroyed, and it had been searching its surroundings from ground level. It should have responded to the SAF plane's IFF signal.

"That's funny," Rei muttered. There was no response.

There was an area on the ground that looked like a long, thin mirror with a crack running across its surface. It was the remains of Richwar base's center and shattered runway. The recon pod should have been planted somewhere around there, and Rei was about to bank Yukikaze to try to make visual contact when the pod's connection-ready tone chimed. It was responding now. *The powerful ground search radar the Rafe was using had probably disrupted the IFF signal*, Rei thought. Still, he wasn't totally convinced that something wasn't wrong here.

They had to recover the information contained in the pod, and so he transmitted the command code for it to begin uploading its data to them. It seemed to be working, but then Yukikaze sounded a warning tone and flashed a message onto the main display screen:

`TRP32157: decode error.`

The pod wasn't answering the command code correctly, so Yukikaze couldn't decode the data it was transmitting.

Had the pod malfunctioned, or had the JAM contaminated it? If the JAM had gotten to it, they were probably trying to introduce false data into the FAF. In that case, it was a lucky thing that Yukikaze couldn't decode the probe's data transmissions—it meant that the JAM hadn't cracked the FAF's data encryption.

`Engage`, Yukikaze flashed on the screen, declaring her intention to attack. She now recognized tactical reconnaissance pod 32157 as an enemy and was suggesting that they destroy it. Rei authorized the action and sent the Rafe to do the deed.

The Rafe followed Rei's orders from Yukikaze. Readying itself for battle, it designated the recon pod as its target. Diving swiftly down, it strafed the pod with its gun. One shot, and the target exploded.

Just as Rei was banking to confirm its destruction with his own eyes, he heard Captain Foss's tense voice in the back. Yukikaze sounded a warning as she spoke.

"Below, right, to our rear! Two JAM fighters, closing!"

Yukikaze did a barrel roll. Rei confirmed for himself, then sent them into a sudden Immelmann turn. Yukikaze initiated an auto-attack, locking onto the targets and immediately releasing her short-range missiles. The lock wasn't steady and the shots missed.

Yukikaze quickly pulled her nose up as she turned to pursue the JAM, suddenly spinning her fuselage. The maneuver was beyond her design limitations. Without Rei doing any of the work, Yukikaze operated her control surfaces at maximum efficiency and quickly recovered, but Rei sensed that she was about to accelerate and killed the auto-maneuver switch. He pulled the throttle back to IDLE. The exhaust temperature was already fairly high, and if he didn't pull back, the engines could superheat and destroy themselves. Rei set the dogfight switch to ON, telling Yukikaze that he would handle this threat.

Yukikaze. *This plane isn't a Super Sylph. It's a Maeve. The data on your old airframe doesn't apply here. Leave this to me.*

Yukikaze didn't object.

They had altitude to spare. Pushing the throttle as high as he dared, Rei took them into a nearly vertical dive. Confirming that the engines had cooled down, he cautiously increased their output. It was just like swimming. If you rushed and messed up the timing of your breathing, you'd drown.

Rei's eyes found the enemy fighters. Having for a moment evaded Yukikaze's attack, the JAM banked steeply and turned toward Yukikaze. They'd predicted the optimum attack course to take. Rei heard the warning buzzer sound as Yukikaze picked up their weapons lock. Rei instantly selected gun mode. Taking Yukikaze into a loose climbing turn, he waited till it felt right, then recklessly snapped over into a sharp bank. The high-G forces caused him to black out for a few moments. When his vision cleared, just as he'd figured, the JAM fighters were crossing right in front of him. His intuition was as sharp as ever. The enemy fighters were still turning.

Cross attack. Firing time: 0.5 seconds. An instant later, the targets were behind him. Rei craned his neck around to confirm his hit.

The Rafe flew through the smoke of their explosions and rejoined Yukikaze as the fragments of the two JAM planes fell to the ground. The Rafe had shot one of them down, apparently having imitated Yukikaze's tactics.

Rei confirmed their fuel stores. They could stay here a while longer. There were probably more JAM buried under the desert sands, searching for the SAF. *Perhaps they were testing out using the recon pod to talk to us and only attacked when we rejected their overture,* he thought. Suddenly, Rei was roused from this fantasy.

In all the commotion moments before, he'd completely forgotten about Captain Foss. Noticing that her breathing sounded far weaker than it should have, Rei looked back and saw that she'd taken her mask off. She'd vomited inside of it. He quickly brought Yukikaze down to a lower altitude and told Foss how to clean out the blockage and reset the mask.

He wondered what she had made of the battle just now. Despite having seen them, maybe she still thought the JAM were imaginary. Still, whatever she thought, what she now felt in her body was real. There was no way she could deny that. *That goes for me as well*, Rei thought.

For now, this was good enough. A lot of information had been gathered for analysis, for both the SAF and Captain Foss.

"Mission complete," Rei said to her. "Returning to base."

IV

COMBAT AWARENESS

YUKIKAZE'S CENTRAL COMPUTER never slept, even when she was resting her wings in the hangar bay. Cables running from the floor provided her with electrical power as she waited on standby. The cables attached to her underside also contained circuits that linked Yukikaze to the SAF's tactical computer, allowing her to read all of the data available to it.

She could even access the missions and operational actions of SAF fighters currently in flight, although she couldn't receive the intelligence they were gathering in real time. Fighters on sortie generally wouldn't access headquarters except in cases of emergency. The information they gathered would be downloaded to the tactical computer in headquarters once they'd returned to base and been linked up to the cables in the hangar.

The data would then be analyzed by the SAF in order to develop new strategies, and the raw, unfiltered data would be stored as well, accessible at any time. Flight crews back from their missions would use it to write up their sortie reports. They'd check it over, both to see if there were differences between their own memories and the data their planes had recorded, as well as to check if the decisions they'd made in flight were the right ones. This was done especially in cases where the JAM had attacked them unexpectedly, so as to determine from where the JAM had appeared and if it would have been possible to detect them sooner. It was useful after missions for the pilots to replay the past mission via onboard simulation in order to create more efficient hazard avoidance maneuvers. Since every sortie was a matter of life and death, pilots needed to draw on the knowledge gained from past experiences to help them survive. Many flight crews could be found in planes' cockpits even when they weren't writing their sortie reports.

Rei, naturally, was no exception. He'd always spent more time in his cockpit than the other pilots, but lately he could be found in Yukikaze's cockpit more frequently than ever. Since she'd shed her old body in favor of this new one, he'd grown eager to learn more about her. He sensed that the changes in her went beyond surface appearance. Wanting to know exactly what these changes were, he used any free time he could find during his rehabilitation to see Yukikaze directly.

What does she think about when she is on standby? he wondered. What kind of conversations did she have with the tactical computer in HQ? He'd always wondered about that, and he'd spent a lot of time on board Yukikaze in the hangar trying to work that out.

That was when Rei had a thought.

Just how exactly did Yukikaze, the SAF's computers, and the combat intelligence they contained feel about the JAM?

To him, in the old days, Yukikaze was simply the plane he flew, but now he didn't feel that way. Her central computer was now a discrete combat consciousness independent of him. It might not have been a consciousness identical to that of a human, but Yukikaze must have had some cognizance of the world she occupied. He wanted to know what that was. It was possible that the JAM understood Yukikaze and Earth's machine intelligences better than he did. He knew for certain that the JAM considered machine intelligence to be real, while the state of humans was more ambiguous. If he could understand how Yukikaze and the computers she was connected to saw the JAM, then maybe he could get a clue as to exactly what this enemy humans called the JAM really were. This sort of work was better done on standby than while on a sortie. This was another battlefield, one where Yukikaze's central computer could talk to the SAF combat intelligences. Rei felt ready to get back in the fight. There was no need for any more rehabilitation.

Rei hadn't been told by Major Booker that he was cleared for combat after his mission. He'd simply said that the merit of his sortie would be evaluated, and Booker ordered Rei to remain on standby until the evaluation was complete. Essentially, the major had told him to take it easy. The evaluation would take two days at most. Of course, he needed to file a sortie report as well, so he couldn't just spend those two days sleeping.

What the hell could they be taking two days to figure out? Rei asked himself. His physical strength wasn't in question now. Even if he didn't stick with the rehab schedule they'd set up for him, he'd be fine training on his own. He'd flown a combat sortie for the first time in a while and had passed with flying colors. The fact that Rei had returned to base still in one piece was proof of that. Or had he done something wrong? Was Major Booker telling him that he should take some time and take a hard look at the actions he'd taken in his first combat flight in a long time? That had to be it. Otherwise, "Remain on standby" was just his way of saying, "I'm giving you two days off."

And so Rei passed the days in Yukikaze's cockpit. After looking back over his actions on his mission with Yukikaze's central computer, with it agreeing that he'd done nothing wrong, he now turned to monitoring the link between Yukikaze and the SAF's computers. He took his time doing so.

By switching on the main display in her cockpit and watching the feed, he could see each occasion when Yukikaze would access the SAF's tactical computer. Code numbers would suddenly scroll across the screen. He couldn't tell the exact specifics of the data, but his eyes could follow and grasp the general type of data she was requesting and the arrangement of the data sent in reply.

Yukikaze was gathering past data from the other planes through the data link circuit. That much he knew, but what was Yukikaze thinking and what was she discussing with the tactical computer? That, he could only imagine. The display didn't show the data exchange at that level, since Yukikaze wasn't equipped with that sort of interface. Of course, if he used a tactical computer terminal in headquarters, it would have been able to display the exchange in a human-readable form.

Rei had already gone there to check it out.

The tactical computer in SAF HQ told him by voice that Yukikaze was requesting records of the actions and gathered information of Unit 13, the Rafe. But in answer to why she was requesting the data, the computer could only guess that she was possibly running a combat simulation on her own.

As far as what Yukikaze's central computer was thinking and what judgments it was making, the tactical computer in the SAF headquarters was as much in the dark as he.

Normally, this wouldn't be a problem at all. The instinct to defeat the JAM was built in at the time of Yukikaze's manufacture. The existence of that impulse meant that there was nothing at all strange about her researching tactics and strategies to use against the JAM while she was on standby. If one wanted to know what she'd learned, all they'd have to do is see how she reacted the next time she was in battle. Words weren't necessary. Not in combat. There was no time then to ask what she was up to and then wait for an answer. That was the reason she wasn't equipped with a system through which to communicate verbally with humans, and Rei hadn't felt the need for one. At any rate, getting back to base in one piece was the important point. An analysis of what exactly the JAM were could be left for headquarters to worry about.

So, Yukikaze had taken it upon herself to work on this question while she was on standby. *That makes her a better pilot than I am*, Rei thought. Still, he had to make sure that she hadn't gone insane. So long as he didn't know how she thought, he feared that she might once again cast him out of her.

Yukikaze probably understood the JAM a lot better than any human could. There was no doubt about that, considering no person could match her ability to gather and process data. Yukikaze needed no sleep and would continue with her task as long as her power supplies lasted. But even if she worked round the clock researching strategies and tactics to beat the JAM, that didn't necessarily mean that she grasped their true nature. He didn't know if Yukikaze's conjecture took into account the possibility that the JAM couldn't perceive human beings. *The SAF's combat intelligences hold that viewpoint, so it's possible Yukikaze adopted it as well when she consulted them, but perhaps she just doesn't care? Still*, Rei thought, *as long as humans continue to fly in her, she has to know that she can't just ignore us.* That he wanted her not to ignore the humans who would ride in her. That they were to fight together, as partners.

Rei continued monitoring the operation of Yukikaze's central computer in the cockpit as she waited on standby. That would be the only way he'd ever find out what she was thinking about and what her thought processes were like. It was just like when he was in combat, trying to sense how she'd react.

Even had Yukikaze been equipped for human communication, Rei guessed that there'd be no way for her to express her conscious thoughts in words. The reason for this was simple—human language had developed to suit human modes of existence. Growing out of a completely different architecture, while she might be able to mimic human expression, there'd most likely be parts that would be untranslatable. For example, Yukikaze's consciousness would never be able to really use any words that dealt with human emotions. If he were to ask her, "Do you like me?" she'd have no understanding of what the words meant.

Still, she was able to recognize that her partner, a man named Captain Fukai, was aboard her now. And that if he operated her in a certain way, Rei would find the answer to what he sought. It was an unspoken communication between them.

Yukikaze was aware that Rei was on board because all current planes in the SAF had the ability to tell when their masters were in their cockpits. Both the instrument panel and the helmet Rei currently wasn't wearing were equipped with small lenses. By capturing an image of his face, Yukikaze could know that it was Rei who was sitting in her cockpit. The system wasn't in place simply to recognize who was piloting the plane, but also to constantly monitor the direction and orientation of the pilot's gaze.

Yukikaze wasn't equipped to receive input by glance. She didn't have an active command input function and there was no way to tell precisely what a pilot was looking at. All the system did was measure the contrast between the iris and the sclera of the eye to tell in which direction the pilot was looking. So, it didn't allow the pilot to directly input commands by glance alone, but an even more advanced user interface had been created based on the information gathered by the gaze-monitoring system.

This equipment was still experimental and only installed on the SAF's planes, but Major Booker didn't think of the system as experimental when he decided to order the installation. It was a system ready for practical use. The other planes, which had advanced central computers similar to Yukikaze's, would use the information to anticipate what their pilots were planning and then act on it, Major Booker had thought. He'd had the Systems Corps develop software that would allow machine intelligences to make predictions based on eye-glance input. After a certain period of learning, the plane's central computer would learn to process the data and use it to decide, *Since the pilot is looking at an enemy plane with his naked eye, I should guide the plane in that direction*, or *Since the pilot has his eyes on the head-up display, I'll leave the guidance to him and give all my attention to an omnidirectional search for the enemy*, or *The pilot's eyes have been closed so long he must have lost consciousness. I will assume full control.* That was what it had been developed for.

Pilot and plane wouldn't need words to cooperate in combat. The ideal would be for the plane to know what its pilot wanted with just a glance. All that was needed was for the system to perceive clearly what its pilot was looking at in a particular moment. Or at least, that was Major Booker's theory. They'd only installed the system into her recently, but Rei was sure that Yukikaze had already mastered it. He knew that without needing to ask.

Yukikaze's consciousness existed on a completely different level from human consciousness. Nobody could say that she didn't have it from the start. Humans couldn't even be sure of how awareness existed in other humans, or how members of their own species conceived of the world. When we examine another person's behaviors and attitudes, the idea that they see the world as we do is merely a supposition humans are predisposed to make because we all develop from a similar architecture. But it was difficult to make that sort of supposition about Yukikaze because she wasn't human. Even so, Rei hoped that he'd flown together with her long enough that he'd be able to understand her. Or, at the very least, to know if it would be worth trying to understand her.

Perhaps Yukikaze had already done it on her end. It was clear that she still valued this human named Rei Fukai in her war with the JAM. Even now, she was analyzing their past battles. She wouldn't be doing that while ignoring his value as a pilot. Well, if she felt that way about him, then he'd return the favor.

Yukikaze hadn't changed. Yukikaze had always been Yukikaze. And in realizing that, in realizing that it was he that had changed, Rei had a sudden flash of insight. That he had never really known Yukikaze at all.

2

THE ALARM BEEPING on his wristwatch reminded Rei that he had a short lunch meeting scheduled with Major Booker that afternoon.

Three days had passed since he'd been ordered onto standby. The major had told him about the meeting the previous afternoon but had remained tight-lipped about the agenda or with whom Rei would be meeting. Rei hadn't pushed the subject. The major's attitude told him that nothing more would be revealed before the meeting. Not that it really mattered.

Rei wanted to know what it was that Yukikaze was doing in the background as they waited, but his enthusiasm for the project hadn't yielded proportionate results.

Yukikaze's central computer seemed to be constantly tracking the mission status of all the SAF's planes, demanding the data on them from the computers in headquarters as it came in. For that reason, Rei could see where all the other planes were and follow what they were doing on Yukikaze's main display.

But what was it all for? Rei asked himself. Perhaps this was just one of the functions that had been programmed into her. To put it simply, maybe this was a purely mechanical reaction, she had no consciousness at all, and he was just overestimating his beloved plane to the point of full-scale delusion.

Well, it's too soon to reach any conclusions, thought Rei as he pushed the headset he was wearing down onto his neck and, after yanking the plug from the comm systems, climbed down from Yukikaze's cockpit. The major had been very specific about him showing up on time. He wouldn't know where the lunch meeting would take place unless he came to the office. The details of the meeting would be given there.

Neither the SAF nor the FAF in general had anything like a fancy restaurant on base—at best, this meeting would have to be taking place in a field officer's private dining room. *Even so, it's so human of Major Booker to adopt such an air of importance about this*, thought Rei. He didn't attach any distaste to the notion. He'd known the major long enough to realize that he wouldn't be making such a big deal about this unless there was good reason to. If anybody else had copped an attitude like Booker's Rei would have chalked it up to simple vanity. In the end, similar human attitudes would inspire entirely different emotional responses from Rei, depending on how well he knew the person. It must have been the same regarding Yukikaze. He still didn't know her at all.

Other SAF planes were lined up in the hangar bay. Like Yukikaze, they had cables like umbilical cords dangling from their undersides. The cables supplied them with power and connected them to the SAF's vast data network. They were like fetuses. *No, that's not right*, Rei thought. They were more like cattle grazing in a field. Having wriggled out of danger once again and sharing the information they'd gathered, they were now back here, calmly ruminating. Only the cud they chewed was data, not grass.

He admired the planes all lined up in their rows as he walked by. *They're like living things*, Rei thought. Living, growing creatures who absorbed information and then changed as they made it a part of themselves. *And what would they grow into?* That, no man could say. The fighters' computers, sitting side by side, probably didn't know either. Even as they stood next to each other, Rei didn't sense that they perceived themselves as a group.

Along the way, he noticed the flight crew of Unit 3 at work aboard their plane. Their attitude told him that they were preparing for a single-fighter mission.

Rei didn't call out to them. Shouting hello when he had no reason to would just make him a bother. It wasn't like the members of his squadron didn't share information with each other, but while they were well attuned to gathering data they tended to be indifferent to the very existence of other people. The members of the SAF might have been a unit, but they weren't an actual *group*. The SAF didn't function as one. They were founded on the idea of flying missions independently, without any expectation of backup from headquarters, even in combat. In a fight, all they had to depend on was their own skill, and so there were no "leaders" or "subordinates" here. The only people they trusted were themselves, and putting yourself first was a trait to be admired. Those were the sort of people who comprised the Special Air Force.

And, like the humans who operated them and whose actions they continually learned from, so too behaved the central computers of their fighter planes. *It was possible,* Rei thought, *that the computers work together with the humans at a level we can't comprehend to form a sort of synthetic machine intelligence.* But if you accepted that premise, you could argue further that they and the human members of the squadron also formed a group consciousness that comprised the SAF, which was why the fighter planes' computers couldn't be said to operate in a group. Each SAF computer operated individually, with none assuming a leadership position. They wouldn't interfere with one another's work, similar to the machine intelligence in the tactical computer at SAF headquarters. Rei had made sure that the other fighter intelligences wouldn't interfere with Yukikaze, but they couldn't interfere even if they wanted to. The system had been constructed to prevent it.

The SAF's computers had been given the strongest level of self-preservation functionality in order to prevent outside interference by the JAM. Even if something considered an ally tried to forcibly move against an SAF computer, it would select a method to counter the attack. If its autonomy could not be maintained, it would self-destruct. In short, the computers of the SAF, like its human personnel, did not operate as a group. Noninterference meant not expecting any backup from anywhere else. Within the FAF, these machine intelligences formed a unit that was truly "special."

As Rei drew near the hangar bay exit, now musing that the planes had the appearance of giant cats, listening to each other in a silent assembly, a warning siren sounded inside. The same sort of siren that warned when a plane was about to leave.

Unit 7, having taxied to the central area of the bay, was being towed by an unmanned spotting dolly over to the three-sided central elevator. The plane was a Super Sylph. Aboard her was a pilot and his flight officer.

"Hey, Captain Fukai." The pilot aboard the plane leaned forward as he called out to Rei. This was extremely unusual. The pilot's name was Vincent Bruys, and he held the rank of first lieutenant.

"What's up, Lieutenant," Rei called back. "Am I in your way?"

"Just wanted to warn you to be careful not to get shot by Llanfabon."

"What's that supposed to mean?"

Llanfabon was the name of Lieutenant Bruys's fighter, Unit 7.

"This lunch meeting you've been invited to," replied Lieutenant Bruys. "I've been assigned escort and surveillance duty for it."

"The meeting's going to be in-flight, you mean?"

"The details are being kept top secret. They're not even entered into the computers in HQ. Looks like it's a special mission. You'll find out what it is when you go. Major Booker must be afraid that the JAM might slip into the meeting. If you turn out to be a JAM, I'm shooting you down. That's all there is to it."

"Do you want to shoot me? Then what are you doing talking to me? If the mission's top secret, then shut up about it."

"While I was checking out Llanfabon before, I saw Yukikaze making repeated requests for direct access. You must have known that Llanfabon is on this special mission. It's supposed to be a secret, so I was wondering how you found out."

"I didn't know about it," Rei replied. "You're saying Yukikaze was trying to access Llanfabon?"

"Are you saying you weren't having her do it, Captain Fukai?"

"Nope, wasn't me."

"If I were to believe you, that would mean that Yukikaze herself wanted to know about the details of this mission. A special mission whose details weren't even entered into the tactical computer at headquarters. If Yukikaze wanted to know the details of Llanfabon's mission, she'd have to ask me directly. That's real interesting behavior on her part. After this mission's done, I'll be reporting it to Major Booker. This mission's already begun. If you are a JAM, then I hope you either get killed by Yukikaze or that this lunch today will be your last. See you."

Rei checked his watch; a little over three minutes had passed since the alarm had sounded. He quickly returned to Yukikaze's cockpit and flipped the main switch on for the display cluster. As he had before, he set the main display to monitor mode to show the operation of the plane's central computer, selected **DISPLAY EXTERNAL COMMUNICATIONS** from the menu, then hit the execute button. The response came quickly:

Watch on B-7/mission unknown/request contents... STC.

So Yukikaze *had* been interested in this secret lunch meeting.

Apparently, Major Booker hadn't entered details of the meeting into any of the SAF's computers, which explained why even Yukikaze hadn't known it was happening. However, she'd noticed that Llanfabon had been assigned the sortie code number B-7 in regards to its operational actions and had cross-referenced that with the flight schedule. That was when she'd probably noticed that there were no details pertaining to the mission anywhere and had begun to doggedly search for them.

Until Lieutenant Bruys had called him out about it, Rei had no idea she was doing it. A little earlier, all Yukikaze had done was display the readout B-7 mission unknown on the monitor. However, now that Llanfabon had actually begun to move, Yukikaze had requested the details of her mission from the tactical computer in SAF headquarters. In addition to that, she'd displayed Watch on B-7 to indicate that she was beginning her own observations of Llanfabon's movements.

A new message scrolled up onto the display.

Request sortie... STC/get permission to sortie... Captain FUKAI.

Yukikaze was asking for permission to take off. He hadn't been expecting that, but he understood what it meant. But what was with the "Captain Fukai" bit at the end? Yukikaze had never referred to him by his name before. Was Yukikaze personally asking him, her pilot, to get permission from headquarters to take off? Before he could think about it, a new message scrolled up.

STC: permit/set 20908107-sp-mission/ready.

That had come from the tactical computer in HQ. Permission granted for sortie, mission ID number assigned.

STC: trace and watch on B-7...B-1.

Order from the tactical computer: Pursue, trace, and keep watch on Llanfabon, Yukikaze.

Roger, Yukikaze acknowledged.

STC: enter 20908107-sp-mission.

Initiating special mission number 20908107.

Action...Captain FUKAI.

Let's get this show on the road, Captain Fukai.

Rei knew exactly what Yukikaze was asking of him. He reflexively flipped the master arm switch on, bringing all available weaponry online. This was the first time he'd ever done it inside of the hangar bay. Naturally, Yukikaze wasn't loaded with any cannon ammo or missiles, but all of her electronic warfare systems were now active. The tracking system activated automatically. There was a faint hum from the rear of her fuselage as Yukikaze's auxiliary power unit started up. The cables on her underside linking her to headquarters disconnected automatically, and Yukikaze entered fully independent combat mode. All flight systems started up.

An alarm warning of a taxiing plane sounded. An automatically controlled spotting dolly approached Yukikaze and linked up to her front landing gear. The sortie sequence began automatically.

Rei instinctively grabbed the flight stick. It felt unnatural to him, likely because he was touching it with bare skin. In flight, he'd be wearing flight gloves. At the moment, he wasn't wearing a flight suit, G-suit, or his escape chute. Without a helmet on, he couldn't connect his oxygen hose. He had to tell Yukikaze that he wasn't in any condition to fly. She must have already known that. But there was no way to stop the takeoff sequence at this point.

Yukikaze began moving toward the elevator. Rei could still climb down out of her, but he didn't. There would be more opportunities to get off along the way—when they stopped to take on arms and ammunition and again when they reached the surface. If he got off, Yukikaze could sortie unmanned. He didn't want to let her do that, but he couldn't fly with her as he was now. She would have to wait until he was ready.

But would Yukikaze wait for him?

He had to be at that lunch meeting. Not showing up for it would be a serious act of insubordination. But Yukikaze had been cleared for sortie, so what exactly was going on here?

A voice suddenly sounded from the speakers in the headset he was wearing around his neck.

"Rei, what the hell are you doing?!" Major Booker demanded. "Are you taking Yukikaze to the picnic?"

Picnic?

"Rei, answer me. Captain Fukai, I know you're aboard Yukikaze."

Rei pulled the headset up to his ears. It was plugged into Yukikaze's onboard communications port, making him look like he was probing Yukikaze with a stethoscope. The message he'd just received had been an external signal. The display showed that it was originating from the terminal in Major Booker's office.

"This is B-1," Rei responded. "Mission ID 20908107. Making preparations to sortie and execute special mission to observe Llanfabon. Sortie sequence engaged."

"What are you babbling about?" Major Booker said. "I ordered you to attend a lunch meeting. I never said anything about observing Llanfabon."

"This is the result of Yukikaze wanting to find out about the mission Llanfabon is flying out on. You gave her clearance to sortie, Major."

"I did no such thing."

"Then who did? The tactical computer authorized this on its own? I thought the machines couldn't make operational actions without human consent."

"Are you telling me you're not just doing this on *your* own, Rei?"

"Jack, I don't know what's going on here either. What does it show on your end? Does it say that I requested sortie clearance?"

"Yeah. The tactical computer says Captain Fukai issued an urgent sortie request, and that they initiated an on-the-spot mission plan due to the high-level nature of the emergency."

"Then who gave the final clearance?"

"SSC: the SAF strategic computer. The name on the orders is General Cooley, like it ought to be, but the general says she never issued them."

"Which means that Yukikaze shouldn't be able to take off. The thing is, she's engaged in a sortie sequence right now. That's reality. So who's in charge of this mission?"

"You, Captain Fukai. Rei, this is all on you."

Yukikaze had now been towed completely into the elevator. The fire door closed behind them and they began to ascend.

"Of course," Rei whispered. "Now I get it."

Yukikaze sending a request to sortie by herself wouldn't have gotten clearance, which was why she'd been so insistent that he, her pilot, should request it. At the same time, she'd been telling the tactical computer that Captain Fukai was requesting permission to sortie. Now he understood what that Get permission to sortie…Captain FUKAI business had been about.

"What did you agree to do on your own? This is gross insubordination and completely unauthorized. Just how do you expect to take responsibility for this? Answer me, Captain Fukai!"

The reception was crystal clear, even inside of the elevator.

"Yukikaze can take responsibility. She made the sortie request in my name."

"You're telling me Yukikaze used your name to trick us?"

"Yukikaze knew that I'd agree with her flying out there."

"You just told me you didn't know what was going on!"

"I do now, and I need to sortie. Yukikaze doesn't like not knowing what Llanfabon's mission objective is. That's all she wants to know. The tactical computer agrees with her, which is why it's sending her out. My theory is that they've made it out that a human—me in this case—is making the demand so that they're technically not ignoring us and doing this on their own. The tactical computer in HQ is probably doing this so that it can amend the mission related to this lunch meeting of yours and add in a mission outline at least. That's probably what's going on here."

"Amend the mission? You're saying the tactical computer would just arbitrarily amend the contents of a mission?"

"It'd have to add it as an amendment to the special mission related to the meeting," Rei said. "There are times when pilots on a mission have to request changes to their mission details. It's never happened before a sortie, but the tactical computer must have judged that Yukikaze was facing that sort of situation. It was able to initiate the sortie sequence by following that protocol. This all happened because you were treating this mission as special and didn't behave the way you would normally. In other words, your secrecy is to blame for this, Jack. If you'd just told the computer about the meeting, Yukikaze would have accepted it. So what do we do, Major? Try to forcibly abort this takeoff? That won't be easy, since Yukikaze's set on doing this. Even if we explained things to her now, she'd still want to check it out herself. In other words, she *is* going to take off and follow Llanfabon."

"Roger," Major Booker replied.

"Roger? Are you saying I can get ready for takeoff?"

"In regards to Yukikaze's sortie, headquarters recognizes that it accepted a request from you, Captain Fukai. I just need you to confirm that the request came from you. That way, there'll be no problem. You'll be at that lunch meeting, as scheduled, and that you are Captain Rei Fukai. Do you get what I'm saying? Now, reconfirm that for me, Captain Fukai."

"This is Captain Fukai," Rei replied. "I will be attending the meeting. I made the request for Yukikaze to sortie. Reconfirmation, over."

"Very good."

"I'm going to send Yukikaze out in automaneuver mode. Is that okay, Major?"

"There's nothing else we can do. We can't predict what she'll do out there, but we can analyze this and figure out how to deal with you after the mission's over. Stand by in there and then deplane once you're on the surface. I'm sending Captain Edith Foss up to meet you. Follow her instructions. She'll show you where you need to go."

"Captain Foss? Do I really need a doctor to chaperone me to this meeting? Or is she invited to it too?"

"I have no comment about who's invited, what it's about, or any other details. Just follow the tactical computer's plan for Yukikaze's weapons and fuel loadout. I've checked it out and it's basically the same as Llanfabon's. Don't interfere."

"This is B-1, roger. Captain Fukai, over and out."

"Okay. Over and out."

B-1 was Yukikaze's sortie code number. The B was for Boomerang, the SAF's nickname, while the number one indicated that it was Unit 1 in the squadron. Captain Fukai referred to Rei himself, of course. It was the first time he'd ever used this particular classification response.

This will be the first time Yukikaze and I will be taking separate actions, Rei thought, then corrected himself. *Yukikaze has always acted on her own. I just never noticed before.*

Exiting the elevator into the weapons loadout bay, Rei watched from the cockpit as she was armed and fueled. It was the same as the usual procedure to prepare a plane for sortie, except this was the first time he realized that it was fully automated. It gave him a feeling of excitement mixed with a little fear.

An automatic crane hanging from the ceiling lowered a huge drum full of autocannon ammunition into the upper side of Yukikaze's fuselage while four short-range missiles were loaded onto her underside, two on each side. Fuel was pumped into her tanks, though Rei couldn't be sure if the tanks were being filled completely since he didn't know how much fuel she was cleared to carry. That was a new experience for him as well. The most he could figure out was that the fuel tanks in the wings weren't being filled, so she wasn't expected to fly very far.

The entire loadout procedure was completed automatically. It wasn't just Yukikaze who was acting without any care for his thoughts on the matter. The combat intelligence in SAF headquarters didn't seem to care either.

But he was heartened to see she wasn't just ignoring him when a message appeared on Yukikaze's display. The warning said that his oxygen hose and ejection seat weren't properly set. In short, she couldn't take off until he'd taken care of that. Rei reminded himself not to be too happy when he realized that was the point of concern.

Maybe she was telling him that he, unprepared for flight as he was, was now an obstacle. Once they reached the surface, she might decide he wasn't needed anymore and just activate the ejection sequence. He definitely didn't want to get thrown out in his seat. Without his parachute or even being properly strapped into it, a stunt like that would be hazardous to his health. Normally, the crew safeguards wouldn't allow the ejection sequence to initiate if the ejection seats weren't properly set; however...

The dolly began towing Yukikaze back to the elevator so that she could exit to the surface. Rei seriously began to think he should deplane right here. He was considering what would be safest for him. Before he'd made a decision, another message appeared on Yukikaze's warning display:

Action...Captain FUKAI.

The message was blinking, as though Yukikaze was irritated and asking him why he was still dicking around inside of her. And he, even as he was thinking there was no way that she'd understand, told her that he wasn't coming with her.

"I, Captain Rei Fukai, will be participating in the lunch meeting that Llanfabon has been assigned to escort. Yukikaze, you will protect me. When I reach the surface, I'll deplane. Do you understand?"

Yukikaze did not answer. He knew she wouldn't, but Rei didn't feel discouraged. He'd said what he'd wanted to say. All that was left to do was pray that he'd be able to get out safely. Giving full control to Yukikaze was dangerous. He hoped his fears would prove baseless.

The sunlight from Faery's skies streaming into the exit of the elevator building was dazzling. It was nice weather today. A little ahead of him, he could see Llanfabon. She was stopped.

Outside, Captain Edith Foss approached the newly emerged Yukikaze.

Rei tensely flipped the automaneuver switch on, declaring "You have control, Yukikaze." She was now free to fly as she pleased.

And then Yukikaze replied. All of the warnings vanished from her display, a new message taking their place:

I have control/I wish you luck...Captain FUKAI.

Rei was scrambling up out of his seat to deplane when the second half of the message caught his eye. He stared at it, unable to look away.

"I wish you luck" was nothing more than a clichéd phrase, carrying no more meaning than "roger." But was that the case here? Rei had never seen Yukikaze display a message like that before. There was really no need for it, was there? He considered the possibility that her specific choice to display that message meant that she understood human speech and was going out of her way to convey that to him. He should be happy about that, shouldn't he? No, if that was the case, he was going to have to rethink his entire method of interacting with Yukikaze. This wasn't something he could simply be happy about.

Still, he didn't have time to consider any of that.

"Don't close the canopy till I'm out," he said. "You got that, Yukikaze?"

No message was displayed as a reply. *The fact that the canopy isn't automatically closing was Yukikaze's answer,* Rei thought as he yanked his headset cord and climbed down from her. He folded up the collapsible ladder into her fuselage and locked it down.

He looked up at the canopy but saw no sign that it was closing. Rei was surprised, and just as he was wondering if he was going to have to close it manually, he heard a warning chime from the cockpit. As if Yukikaze had read his mind. The tone indicated that the missiles could not be fired. Of course, Rei realized. The safety pins. Yukikaze was asking him to pull them out of the missiles.

There were weapons control personnel also there on the surface, but Rei personally walked Yukikaze's perimeter and pulled the safety pins from all four of her short-range missiles. Once he'd finished, the canopy automatically lowered and locked. She was now ready to take off without a pilot.

"Good luck, Yukikaze," Rei murmured.

"Yukikaze is your best friend," said Captain Foss to Rei as she approached.

"My best friend?" he replied.

"Or perhaps your lover?"

Rei turned to face Captain Foss. "You're wrong," he said.

"It must be reassuring to have such a powerful friend, Captain Fukai."

Yukikaze's onboard engine starter system activated, despite the fact that Llanfabon's engines weren't started yet. Her vertical stabilizers unfolded from their horizontal storage position and rose into place. Her twin turbofan engines then started up, first the right, then the left. Rei and Captain Foss stepped away from her.

"Yukikaze isn't my friend either. Lover? That's ridiculous."

"So then, what is she to you?"

As the scream of Yukikaze's engines nearly drowned out Captain Foss's question, Rei raised his voice to answer her, as though not wanting to let his plane have the final say.

"Yukikaze is the most dangerous combat machine on this planet," he yelled. "She has a combat awareness that's uniquely hers! Human relationships don't apply to her!"

If she was anything, Yukikaze was a wild animal.

He didn't say that, but that was what Rei thought. She was a partner with whom he was entangled in a dangerous relationship. One in which she cooperated only so long as they sought a common prey. Or perhaps, rather than a partner, he could more accurately be thought of as a trainer, teaching her how to hunt. A coach, instructing her how to fight.

Yukikaze was neither a best friend nor a lover. She was a being beyond human understanding. And he was going to get closer to her.

She wheeled around and stopped, lowering her nose. Her cannon was fixed on Llanfabon nearby, her stance now saying that she could fire at any time. Rei could just imagine the look on Lieutenant Bruys's face as he sat aboard his plane. He must have felt like he was being stalked by a wild animal.

Yukikaze's airframe was a little smaller than Llanfabon's. But the Maeve aiming at the graceful body of the Super Sylph somehow seemed larger and more ferocious.

3

REI LOOKED OUT across Faery base's vast runway but could make out nothing but fighter planes. If this lunch meeting were going to take place in the air, he'd expected there to be a large transport plane, but it looked like he'd been wrong.

So then where was it going to be?

Before he could ask, Captain Edith Foss told him to follow her and began walking in the direction of the control tower.

"The food's probably going to be very good," Rei said as he walked along beside her. "I'll bet Major Booker got his hands on some food that you normally can't get here and didn't want the computers to know about the delicacies we're going to have. Are you invited too?"

"Yes," she replied.

"Who else is coming?'

"I don't know. And as appealing as a delicacy-tasting party sounds, somehow I don't think this is going to be such a pleasant lunch. In your manner of speaking, my guess would be that Major Booker has called me in to act as a poison taster for his food. I doubt my role as the attending physician in your psychological care is unrelated to this."

"Hm."

"I noticed you arrived in Yukikaze. Quite a display you put on there. Did you mean that as a threat to the other participants in this meeting? Major Booker certainly knows how to liven up a show, doesn't he?"

Captain Foss didn't know that Yukikaze's appearance had been wholly unexpected, and he figured she probably didn't know that Llanfabon had been assigned to observe and protect the meeting either.

Rei said nothing. Captain Foss gave him a sidelong glance and then asked, "Or did you and not Major Booker plan that little production?"

"You don't have to examine me anymore, Captain."

"I'm asking this out of personal interest. I know you aren't the sort who'd take offense at the question. You didn't show up here in Yukikaze for some other duty, right? I don't know why you'd go out of your way to do something like this, though. There's a lot of things about you SAF people that are a mystery to me."

"Having Yukikaze show up here wasn't my idea or Major Booker's. It wasn't a show. It didn't happen by chance, and it wasn't for any other duty."

"Could you just talk straight with me? The inability to get to the point is sometimes evidence of mental illness—"

"Okay, I don't like you. Is that straight enough?"

"Perfectly. Now why did you show up here in Yukikaze?"

"No comment. Major Booker didn't tell me it was okay to tell anyone else about it."

"But you just said it wasn't a show and it wasn't by chance. Was it okay to say that?"

"He didn't say to keep completely quiet about it either."

"So then why do you say 'no comment' about anything more than that?"

"Because I've always wanted to say 'no comment' to somebody."

"Are you mocking me?" Foss asked.

"Boy, there's no hiding anything from you, is there? Yeah, I am."

"You have some serious character issues."

"You and me both. You're the one who said I rode up in Yukikaze to liven up the show here. I figured, fine, have some fun and mock her right back."

"You thought I was making fun of you?"

"I don't get what you mean," Rei said.

"I'm still interested in your relationship with Yukikaze. Did you really think I was mocking you when I asked if she was your lover?"

"No, you were being serious, so I answered you seriously. Why are you asking me this?"

"Why? Because this isn't fun for me. There's nothing fun about being mocked. You aren't the only one who engages in this roundabout game of tit for tat. Everyone in the SAF is like that," Foss said. "Talking to any of you pisses me off, and it's all I've been able to do to maintain my personal feelings in the face of it. That goes for me both as a doctor and as an individual. But everyone has their limits, and I've reached mine. I hate you. I don't want to talk to you anymore. Do you understand?" A long time ago, a woman whose face he could no longer remember had said the same thing to him. Rei stopped walking and looked Captain Foss in the eye.

I hate you. I don't want to talk to you anymore. Do you understand?

What was it about him that prompted such words? What thing, what deficiency inside of him inspired such black rage?

Captain Foss also stopped walking and met Rei's gaze. Her mouth was open, but she noticed the hard expression on his face and slowly pressed her lips back together. Rei didn't overlook how the pupils in her eyes contracted.

This doctor had been personally angry with him before, but now something had changed. His reaction was unexpected, and so either out of curiosity or her sense of duty as a doctor, she had raised her head to study him. What was it about this patient that made him constantly contradict what she said and react so excessively?

Rei himself was bewildered by his reactions.

He thought he'd forgotten everything about his past, so why was he dredging it back up now? He'd heard similar words from other people ever since he'd joined the FAF. He'd never once been bothered by anyone saying that they hated him. All he'd said to Captain Foss before was "I don't like you," to which she'd responded, "I hate you. I don't want to talk to you anymore. Do you understand?" That was all it was. So what of it? He shouldn't have any problem with that.

So why did he feel the way he did?

Was Rei's distress over this woman declaring her hatred of him due to some unconscious desire to court the favor of the opposite sex? Would he feel the same way if this doctor had been a man? But he couldn't count the number of times other women had said that they hated him.

Captain Foss held her breath for a few moments, waiting for Rei to say something. When it looked like he wasn't going to, she spoke instead.

"What happened between you and Yukikaze?"

Rei sighed and asked which way to go, ignoring her question. "We've got a meeting to get to. Show me the way."

"I can't take much more of this, Captain Fukai. Even you must have emotions. There isn't a human alive who can be told that they're hated and not feel something about it. I know there's some sort of wound in your heart."

"I'm not here to fight with you, and I don't know you well enough to have some sort of lovers' quarrel either."

"The meeting's over there. You can't miss seeing Major Booker, can you? Rei, don't try to avoid talking about things. This is a serious problem for you."

"What problem?"

"You want to have a fight. You want your 'lovers' quarrel' to turn into an actual loving relationship."

"That's ridiculous. Why would I want that sort of relationship with you—"

"Not with me. With Yukikaze. Captain Fukai, I'll ask you again: what happened between you and Yukikaze?"

"No comment."

"Then I'll do the talking. Think of this as a monologue. You've been told by Yukikaze that she hates you. Not a while ago, but very recently. And so what I said reminded you of that—"

"Yukikaze has no emotions."

"But you do. Even you don't know what will happen if, for example, somebody says that they hate you, and now Yukikaze is ignoring you. When I asked you before if Yukikaze was your lover, you knew already that she wasn't. That wasn't the relationship you shared before. You want to go back to that relationship, but you also know now that you can't. So you attempted to erase your irritation, your feelings of being jilted, by mocking me. But when I refused to play along, you felt how empty you really were inside."

Foss continued. "The problem is that Yukikaze is changing, whether you like it or not. When I said I hate you and don't want to talk to you anymore, it felt like it was coming from Yukikaze. The reason for this must be that something similar happened between you and she. That's why I asked you what it was. You don't have to tell me, but then I want you to please stop using me as your emotional outlet. I'm an individual human being too, Captain Fukai. I'm not your lover, your best friend, your caregiver, your mommy, or your babysitter, and I'd like you to please stop mocking me. If I wasn't a doctor, I'd tell you that you're not the only human being and that you should try to be aware of how self-centered you are."

"You *have* been telling me that," Rei said.

"I said this was a monologue."

"Well, since you are a doctor, I'll tell you this: You see me as a patient with psychological problems. You wouldn't say what you did to most people, because there's no need to. If you hate somebody, you can just stay away. So was everything you did planned from the start? Did you intentionally try to piss me off just to see what my reaction would be?"

"You're letting your imagination run away with you," Foss said. "You really don't understand how to interact with people at all, do you?"

"Because your attitude is constantly changing on me."

"I haven't changed one bit. Or maybe you're asking me to wear a little meter on my chest that'll tell you when I'm angry or sad, in a good mood or a bad one."

"That'd actually be a big help to me," Rei said.

"Even if I did wear one, you wouldn't look at it. Or maybe you would, but you wouldn't understand it. That's the sort of person you are. You should restrict your lovers' quarrels to Yukikaze. She's got plenty of meters for you to read." And with that Captain Foss stalked off.

I think I'm the one being used as an emotional outlet here, Rei thought. More taken aback than shocked, he followed after her.

Still, he thought, *I have to take my hat off to her powers of insight.* Captain Foss had transferred into the SAF only a short time ago, but she already understood very well what Yukikaze meant to him. While Rei had been busy lately seeing what changes were going on in Yukikaze, this doctor had observed changes in him instead.

Feelings of being jilted was what Captain Foss had called it. In response to Yukikaze's peculiar actions lately, he found himself feeling as though he'd been betrayed by his lover. Having the fact pointed out to him, he had no choice but to agree.

But Yukikaze wasn't that sort of companion. Their relationship wasn't the sweet one of lovers, and he could see that now. It was much harsher than that. Yukikaze would cast him away if he wasn't able to provide what she asked of him. That wouldn't lead to an emotion as sentimental as being jilted. Being cast aside by Yukikaze was a matter of whether or not his life had meaning.

Much as he didn't want to talk about his feelings of abandonment, there was no denying that he did feel fear in his heart. Captain Foss had pointed out something like that to him.

Not understanding and then being abandoned. He hated that. No, there was a perfectly straightforward way he could express it.

"I…" Rei had stopped again. He turned his head to look back and murmured, "I'm afraid of Yukikaze."

That was how he really felt, the true feelings he felt toward her that he hadn't wanted to admit. Actually saying the words made him shiver.

He was being warned of a coming separation from the companion with whom he thought he'd shared a deep relationship. And Rei knew that the cause of his estrangement from Yukikaze was from some internal trait or deficiency of his.

Just as Captain Foss had pointed out, he didn't know how to get along with other people. Even though it was so simple. Strangers are other people, and he and other people were all beings who lived in different worlds, internal worlds. Rei would have been better off if he'd just acknowledged the truth. Real relationships started from there. Whether between enemies or lovers, it didn't matter. In short, up till then, he'd never actually had a relationship with anybody. Not even with Yukikaze.

Major Booker had told him the same thing, but he hadn't been able to acknowledge his true feelings before. He hadn't been able to admit that he was afraid of Yukikaze now. *I've never really feared others, and so no one has ever feared me. That's why others tell me, "I don't want to talk to you anymore."*

The thing he needed to fear now was Yukikaze. After that, the JAM. Rei realized that he'd never really feared the enemy before. Talking with Captain Foss had allowed him to see that.

"It's okay, Captain Fukai," Captain Foss said, turning to face him. "You'll be able to get control of Yukikaze. And even if you don't, no one will blame you for it. You know Yukikaze better than anyone else."

"I can't even have an argument with her."

"So keep close watch on those meters. Use her gauges to have your arguments. That'd suit you better, anyway."

Rei considered her words.

"You're right," he said at last. "You're absolutely right. You're a hell of a doctor, Captain Foss."

There was no need to do away with his fear. The effort to eliminate his fear would be immense, because the problem here wasn't that he shouldn't fly Yukikaze if he was afraid.

What he wanted to do was convey the truth of his fear of her to Yukikaze, and the only way to do that would be to read her gauges—and also read the data they didn't reveal—and then act in accordance. If it worked, then Yukikaze might fear him the way he feared her. Or Yukikaze might possibly take action to indicate that she didn't want him to fear her. At any rate, he could guess that she was going to fight him. If he could prevent her from resisting his attempts to communicate, she would refuse to accept his control. They would, in effect, be arguing. And any opponent you could argue with, you can negotiate with as well. He'd never taken his relationship with Yukikaze this far before. He didn't know if it would work. He didn't even know if any of this was a good idea, but that was how these things went.

"Thank you, Captain Fukai," said Captain Foss in response to Rei's compliment about her skill as a doctor. The words were cold, and her expression didn't look very thankful.

Well, what else could he expect? He'd said he didn't like her without really understanding what it was he was saying. He doubted she'd be genuinely happy for his breakthrough. Still, to him, this doctor was like bitter medicine. Even if he didn't like her, she was still necessary.

Thinking that, Rei said nothing else and headed off for the meeting. Major Booker, looking royally pissed, waved for them to hurry up.

4

"WHAT THE HELL are those two doing?" wondered Major Booker aloud. They were just standing there talking as though they'd forgotten how important this thing he'd called them out for was. Maybe Rei was talking about what had happened with Yukikaze. Even so, it was rare to see him so engrossed in a conversation. Captain Foss looked angry, like they were having a fight. Since when had those two gotten close enough to start having arguments with each other?

Well, I can find out what they're talking about later, he thought. As the two of them began walking again, he looked to their rear.

There sat Llanfabon, her nose pointed directly at them. He'd ordered that all conversation at this meeting be collected and recorded with the plane's super directional microphones. Behind her sat Yukikaze, whom he hadn't ordered to be there.

She probably didn't care what the humans thought of her ignoring them and coming out here on her own. *But whatever her reasons for coming, it's not worth getting too worried about,* Major Booker decided.

Yukikaze had used the SAF's command system while her pilot, Rei, was aboard her and then come out. That would have been impossible had he not been there. Her operational objectives were simple and clear: seek out and destroy the JAM.

It was really very easy to understand. If Yukikaze possessed emotions, then she feared the JAM. That was manifesting in Yukikaze's behavior.

Her behavior was consistent. The question to be considered was this: would her fear of the JAM become a threat to humans? But there was no need to make her understand their situation. Having her think about the humans' circumstances and then take action accordingly would practically make Yukikaze human herself. Demands like that would just degrade her abilities in combat. She was an emotionless combat machine. That was what made her effective against the JAM. If there were any demands to be made of Yukikaze, they would be to protect herself and her crew, and nothing more. That would be enough.

The two of them finally arrived. Captain Foss saluted. Rei followed her lead, although his salute was a bit more casual.

"You're late," said Major Booker.

"Stuff happened," said Rei. "It doesn't look like the guests of honor have arrived yet. Don't tell me the three of us are out here for an office barbecue. Who else is coming? Some VIP from Earth?"

On the short purplish Faery grass of a small clearing to the side of the control tower, a barbecue grill had been set up. A folding table and six chairs were set for a picnic. *Where had all of this stuff come from?* Rei wondered. It felt more like a garden party with a chef than a picnic on a lawn. There was even a man wearing chef's whites standing at the grill, checking the burners.

"The guest of honor will be Lieutenant General Gibril Laitume, commander of the Tactical Combat Air Corps of Faery Base," Major Booker replied. "The man who is technically our boss. Also with him will be the de facto top man of the FAF intelligence forces, Colonel Ansel Rombert. And rounding things out will be Brigadier General Cooley, the actual head of the SAF."

General Laitume was officially the commander of the Special Air Force, with General Cooley serving as his deputy, but in reality General Cooley ran the SAF by herself.

"A real power lunch, eh?" said Captain Foss. "I wonder if some major business is going to be discussed here."

"Who's the chef?" asked Rei. "I haven't seen him before."

"Because he doesn't fly a fighter," replied Major Booker. "A chef's battlefield is the kitchen. Allow me to introduce you. This is Chef Murullé, head chef of the SAF's dining hall."

"Just call me Murullé. Galleé Murullé."

Unlike the other air corps, which often had two or more facilities, the SAF dining hall was unusual in that it only had one. Having multiple dining facilities wasn't simply a matter of the number of personnel needing to be fed, they also served to divide the field officers from the lower ranks. The SAF made no such distinctions.

Rei knew the chef had to be a soldier. *Major Booker wouldn't have appointed him to this position unless he had the major's trust*, Rei thought. Other corps had very skilled chefs in their employ, some of them civilian contractors invited from Earth. Very prideful, these contractors considered themselves better than the regular soldiers and had a tendency to look down on the legitimate members of the FAF. After all, many of the soldiers here were actually criminals who'd been sent here for their crimes. However, the SAF had no contractors working for it. Everyone in it was a soldier, and this chef should be no exception. He'd probably committed some antisocial act or crime back on Earth and been sent to the SAF as a result.

Rei didn't particularly care what circumstances brought the man here. It was just that thinking of the food he always ate and knowing that this man was in charge of providing it gave him a feeling of intimacy. He'd never particularly thought about food before, but he'd never eaten anything bad on Faery either. That was probably a source of happiness for both himself and the chef.

Galleé Murullé gave him a quick nod and then went back to the task of examining the ingredients laid out on a large push wagon.

"I'm glad you made it in time," said Major Booker as he spied a group of figures emerging from the control tower's ground-level exit. "If you two had gotten here after the guests of honor, my career would have been over."

General Cooley led the group, followed by the two men. They had no escorts.

The large, dark-skinned man was Gibril Laitume, the general of the Combat Air Corps. Well, lieutenant general, anyway. Rei knew the man's name, although this was the first time he'd ever been in his presence. *He looks exactly like the sort of general who'll die a ridiculous death*, Rei thought. The other thing about this man he'd never met that had made an impression was his name, Gibril, because Major Booker had explained that it was an alternate pronunciation of the name of the angel Gabriel.

Leaving aside the matter of whether the name of this lucky angel was appropriate for him, when Major Booker had told Rei that the general was a devout believer in one all-powerful god, Rei'd replied that he was glad he wasn't. He had no contract with any such omnipotent being and didn't ask for any favors from him. On the other hand, he wasn't liable to get punished for betraying him either. Major Booker had wearily replied that God himself didn't directly hand out the punishments, and that he shouldn't say things like that to devout followers of a religion. At worst, he might get killed by one. At the very least, all he'd be doing is buying their antipathy.

Naturally, Rei wasn't intentionally looking to nitpick any stranger's beliefs, but hearing someone say, "You'll be punished by heaven if you don't believe" just pissed him off. He didn't want to hear that from anyone, be they a believer or the religion's founder itself. People come up with all sorts of theories with which to control others who won't be manipulated as they like, and they tend to shun those who will not be brought into the fold. It wasn't a question of the existence of a supreme being; if one did exist, then human opinion would likely matter very little in how that being used its power. Divine punishment wasn't something for humans to declare, and in general it was just presumptuous for any person to judge who deserved it. The will of a supreme being might not match up to the expectations of his adherents. After all, it would be the god's lack of concern for individual people that made it a suitable object of fear and worship. But if such a being did exist, there'd be little difference between belief and unbelief. Either way, its will would be beyond human means of control, and so it would all boil down to what advantages its adherents gain from their relationship with it on the human plane of existence. If some joined their group and thus gained comfort, then so be it. And if others found the group annoying, they could just stay away from them. That was all there was to it. Personally, Rei didn't believe in a supreme being of any sort. The only existence he could be absolutely certain of was his own.

Of course, this was all probably taboo when it came to talking to General Laitume.

The other man, Colonel Rombert, Rei had met once before. Thin, with sharp eyes, he could only be a member of the Intelligence Forces. He'd asked him repeatedly about how the JAM had made a copy of his flight officer Lieutenant Burgadish on the last mission Yukikaze flew in her previous airframe. The interrogation had made him feel like he was a spy. Even after the man had driven Rei to exhaustion, Rombert hadn't let him go. He was a hardcore intel officer. Even so, he hadn't come off as a heartless machine. Rei recalled that, occasionally, his sense of humor would poke its way to the surface. It showed as part of his interrogation training, though.

For example, at one point the colonel had said, "There have been times when I've wished I could just eat up somebody I didn't like right from the start. I've probably thought about it myself, like how my brain would taste and the like. If I could make a copy of myself, I could try it out. The JAM made a copy of you too, right? You blew your big chance to see how you'd taste, don't you think?"

Basically, he was working under the assumption that Rei had hated Lieutenant Burgadish, took the opportunity to murder him, and then made up the whole story about the copies and everything else. Rather than asking him straight out, Rombert had been trying to tease it out of the suspect in a roundabout way. Rei's impression was that here was a man he couldn't eat. When he'd told the colonel that, Rombert had replied in deadly earnest, "I think you and I can talk with each other." For Rei's part, he hadn't particularly wanted to keep talking to the man.

These two men, General Laitume and Colonel Rombert, were both prime examples of humanity. The woman leading them, General Cooley of the SAF, was not.

It was difficult to pin down what she was thinking or where her values lay, and she didn't really care if that was the impression of her people had. Rei, on the other hand, felt a comforting familiarity about her. Other people, like Captain Foss, might judge the general to be a bit of a strange woman, but not Rei. It wasn't necessary to think of her as a human. To him, she was just the person who issued his orders, and she caused no problems for him beyond that.

Still, lately Rei had found himself wondering what had brought her to Faery.

Captain Foss told him that General Cooley was a distant relative of hers. She wasn't just a general; she was somebody's child and had family too. It had taken Captain Foss's words to make Rei aware of this very obvious fact.

That was just one more thing he was lately curious about, where once he'd paid no attention to it at all. Rei had once believed that anything unrelated to combat wasn't worth thinking about. Though he was going through some changes, Rei didn't believe they were making him weaker.

Major Booker approached the three officers and saluted them. Rei followed his lead.

General Cooley introduced her subordinates, and General Laitume personally greeted the three SAF personnel, a good-natured smile on his lips. First Major Booker, then Rei, and finally Captain Foss. However, when he stopped in front of the woman doctor, he reached his hand out toward her breasts. Captain Foss stiffened, looking startled, which elicited a laugh from the general. "Your lapel pin's crooked, Captain." He chuckled as he straightened it with his fingertip.

"It didn't look crooked to me," Colonel Rombert said coldly. "You have good eyes, General. And fast hands."

"And you, Colonel," the general said with a laugh, "have bad eyes and a nasty mouth."

"I can see that Captain Foss is a young and attractive woman," the colonel replied. "But I didn't see a crooked lapel pin. I've heard you don't have the best reputation with the ladies, General. Oh, forgive me. My ears must not be very good either."

"And you'd better not forget that, Colonel Rombert. Captain Foss, be careful with your pin from now on."

"Yes…sir," replied Captain Foss.

"Is there something you'd like to say to me?"

"No, sir."

"Good. Well, General Cooley, shall we get started?"

General Laitume moved off. Cooley followed, suggesting that they start with some champagne as she showed him to his seat.

"I appreciated that, Colonel," Captain Foss whispered. "The general has a reputation for doing things like that."

"Can't hear you," Colonel Rombert replied with a smile. "Didn't you hear me say that my ears were bad? Although I do think my eyesight is quite keen. Well, it doesn't detract from his skill as a soldier, so that's a saving grace, at least. Now then, you think I could get a Guinness here?"

"All ready for you," said Major Booker. "I made sure to find out what you liked."

"You really do prepare well. It's hard to tell who are the real Intelligence Forces around here. So just what is the SAF up to? No, wait, the whole point of this lunch meeting is to ask about that. Let's relax and enjoy ourselves first. Captain Foss, would you do me the honor of joining me?"

Captain Foss looked at Major Booker, wondering what to do. The major gave a tiny nod, and Captain Foss moved off with Colonel Rombert.

Rei sighed.

"I know exactly how you feel," Major Booker said. "It's such a pain in the ass."

"The general and the colonel are a lot alike," Rei replied.

"I guess that's what they call the 'secret intentions of men.' The colonel's a smart one. I think you know just how intelligent that man is. When it comes to relationships between men and women, what goes on in your head isn't always logical, but people who ignore logic end up hated. On that point, the colonel's—"

"Yeah," Rei said with a nod. "That's exactly right."

"...success rate is pretty high. Wait, what are you agreeing with? Did something happen between you and Edith?"

"Not between her and me. I meant my relationship with Yukikaze. I thought it wasn't logical, but that's absurd. Yukikaze is nothing but a mass of logic. If I ignore that, of course she'd hate me."

"Yukikaze isn't a woman, Rei."

"I know that. I know. Captain Foss taught me that a little while ago. I'll give you a report later."

"Please. Oh, and while you might not like it, the two of us are strictly alcohol-free here."

"You're not Colonel Rombert, so quit kidding around, Major."

"How am I...?!"

"Until Yukikaze's back in the hangar bay, this is a combat mission," Rei said. "Of course I wouldn't joke around or have a drink. I want to finish this up as soon as we can. So get to work, Major Booker."

"You really are some kind of high-efficiency combat machine, aren't you? And you've gotten tougher than I thought you were, although 'tough' can be another word for 'idiot.'"

"You're right... I'm sorry. I'm afraid of Yukikaze, but I think it's different from the threat you sense from her."

"Why don't we have a drink later, then?"

"Sounds good. Let's do that."

The lunch meeting, seemingly calm on the surface, began.

5

GENERAL LAITUME, HOLDING his glass in one hand, his cheeks stuffed with meat, looked at Llanfabon and Yukikaze in the distance. "The SAF certainly has some nice fighters. I'm jealous," he said.

"The SAF only has thirteen fighter planes at its disposal," General Cooley replied. "I believe you have two hundred seventy-nine of them under your command."

"They're yours, don't worry, General Cooley. Besides, I don't have two hundred seventy-nine planes in my air wing anymore. It's two hundred seventy-seven now. We lost two of them yesterday. I thought the SAF had confirmed that."

"I beg your pardon, General."

Rei knew General Cooley wouldn't make a mistake about the number of planes. She was testing General Laitume, and obviously he knew his job.

"We hit them and hit them, but the JAM keep coming. It's like they spring out of nowhere. I've really come to hate it."

"We can't ignore the fact that war weariness is spreading, even through the FAF's upper ranks," added Colonel Rombert. "The brass have that luxury. The lower ranks are too busy fighting to complain about how much they hate doing this. They're the ones who are keeping the FAF afloat."

"What do you mean by that, Colonel?"

"If you resign your commission, a man of your position is guaranteed a life back on Earth. It's not like that for the soldiers at the front lines. Many are convicts. That's why they can't say how much they hate this."

"And which are you?"

"I'm a man who's enjoying his work here. I'll have many happy memories of this place after I retire. Even more so if we win the war with the JAM."

"Saying that war weariness is spreading through the upper ranks is inexcusable, Colonel," General Cooley said. "If I were to say something like that, a commissioned officer in the Intelligence Forces like you would probably have me court-martialed."

"Hardly. I don't have that sort of authority. I might want to, but I doubt you'd ever willingly abandon your position and status. I expressed myself poorly. My point was that the high command doesn't have a way to break this stalemate we're in. That's related to the feelings of helplessness we have toward the JAM, because we still don't even know what we're fighting. The SAF exists because it possesses a system that can help us discover what the

JAM are. Do you have any leads on that, Major Booker?"

"If I had good news, I'd have thrown a huge gala party instead of this lunch meeting. Unfortunately, I don't," Major Booker said. "There's something the people in charge of the Intelligence Forces and the regular forces want to hear from the SAF."

"And are you going to tell us?"

The general, who'd been happily grazing at the buffet, sat down for the first time. The others followed suit, all save General Cooley, who began to speak.

"The information I'm about to tell you is secret. SAF Unit 7 over there has been assigned the task of disrupting any attempt at spying on this meeting. Our unit can't interfere with how you use this information after I give the report, but I hope that you will be extremely careful with what you choose to do with it."

"Hm. You'll put this down in a memo, won't you? I didn't bring my private secretary because you told me not to, but—" General Laitume said.

"There will be no memos made. The details are simple. I'll have Major Booker give the report. Major?"

Major Booker was about to stand up when General Laitume told him to stay seated and just get on with it.

"All right, regarding the first point," the major began. "I'd like to amend the official record on the shooting down of the former SAF Unit 13, piloted by Second Lieutenant Yagashira. While it was reported that his plane was shot down by the JAM, in truth he was downed by Captain Fukai here, a first lieutenant at the time, piloting Yukikaze. I was also aboard Yukikaze when it happened. It was not a mistake. The shooting was intentional."

"Was Yagashira attempting to desert under fire?" asked Colonel Rombert. "If he was, then shooting him down would have been the normal thing to do. There was no reason to cover it up."

"We determined that Lieutenant Yagashira was a JAM," Major Booker replied. "He was a human duplicate created by the JAM. Captain Fukai gave us a report of encountering these JAM duplicates. We suspected that these humanoid weapons had already infiltrated the FAF, and I'm here today to report that they have."

"Hm…" said General Laitume. "That makes things even more complicated for us."

"Can you give us some proof this isn't some excuse from the SAF?" asked Colonel Rombert. "As in, some proof that this isn't your attempt to cover up a deadly friendly fire incident against an SAF plane and place the blame on the JAM? Aren't you just trying to protect Lieutenant—pardon me, Captain Fukai there? I don't know how else to put this, but his mental state at the time probably wasn't that stable."

"I was the one who ordered Yagashira's plane to be shot down," Major Booker said. "I've had Captain Foss here prepare a certificate confirming the mental state of both myself and Captain Fukai. You may also question Captain Foss about it directly. Captain Foss has her suspicions that the enemy we fight isn't real but an imaginary one created by the SAF, which is why she transferred into our unit. In other words, she's a neutral party here."

"I never seriously claimed that the JAM were something that the SAF was making up," Captain Foss protested. "All I said was that I thought it was a possibility. But that was just my own way of analyzing the SAF's culture of secrecy. That being the case, I'd judge the probability of the report Major Booker just gave being some sort of propaganda to be very low. This notion that Lieutenant Yagashira was a JAM is news to me, but I find it hard to believe that the SAF would invent a threat that would endanger its own internal organization. If Major Booker is lying now, then I can only speculate that the SAF is operating in a way that I cannot understand."

"The SAF is already on record as having committed serious offenses," General Laitume interjected, a look of disdain on his face. "There was the indiscriminate firing upon a front-line base. And I believe the personal name of the plane taking that action was Yukikaze. Since the attack occurred while the plane was flying unmanned, we just put it down as a programming error. Do you know how much trouble I went through to take care of that?"

"That incident and the Lieutenant Yagashira incident are not unrelated," Major Booker said. "Yukikaze knew that human duplicates like Yagashira had already infiltrated that front-line base, TAB-15. That's why she initiated the attack. But this isn't a problem we can leave to our combat machines. You understand, don't you? Every human is now under suspicion. If our combat machines, combat intelligences, and computers decide that they just don't want to deal with humans anymore, they're capable of cleaning up the battlefield by just clearing us out. That's the reason this meeting is being held in such secrecy."

"May I assume that when you intentionally had Lieutenant Yagashira sortie and destroyed a very expensive fighter plane along with him, it was because you couldn't confirm beforehand whether or not he was a JAM?" asked Colonel Rombert. "You determined he was a JAM for the first time when he took hostile action against you during the sortie."

"That's correct, Colonel," said Major Booker.

"If these human duplicates are indistinguishable from us," the colonel continued, "then there is a definite possibility that our battle computers would conclude that all humans would have to be excluded from the battlefield. It's a logical decision."

"Why are you saying it so calmly?" General Laitume shot back. "Are you telling me you think that'd be for the best?"

"No, I'm just doing my job. The JAM aren't the only enemies the FAF has had to worry about. We used to face subversive elements causing trouble here. Infiltrators from Earth. In other words, humans. There were lots of people, both civilians and government agents, who came here to gather intel, then leak information in order to damage the FAF. There was no way we could spot them from their external appearances because they were all real humans. If the JAM are doing that now, then there's no difference between them and those spies we used to get. Exposing them will be our job. The battle computers certainly can't do this. Major Booker, about how many JAM do you think have infiltrated us so far?"

"We expect that any flight crews who were recently shot down and were missing temporarily before their rescue have been copied by the enemy and turned into these 'JAM people.'"

"JAM people, huh," murmured Colonel Rombert. "Call them Jammies. Too bad they don't have some distinguishing feature on them, like a reversed-spin tail or something."

"They have no distinguishing features. Lots of these Jammies have probably infiltrated our front-line bases. There are at least a dozen questionable people here at Faery Base."

"If you've got the suspects marked, it makes my job simple," the colonel said. "I'll have them detained. This is a great chance to get some information about the JAM."

"That won't work," Major Booker replied. "They won't know why you're holding them because they aren't aware that they're JAM."

"I'll check that out on my own. That's our duty, after all. Leave it to me."

"I don't care if you investigate them, Colonel," said General Cooley, "but under no circumstances are you to let on that they're JAM. Not even to the people you're holding. That's the second point that the SAF wishes to convey."

"What do you mean, General? I don't understand."

"If this becomes common knowledge, we're going to see the morale of the entire Faery Air Force drop right before our eyes. The only outcome will be the FAF collapsing from within," Cooley said. "Besides, I can imagine that those we've marked as possible JAM have either been tortured or hypnotized into not even knowing that they are JAM. If that's true, then there's nothing to be gained by letting this go public."

"Their objective is to gather information about human beings. They have to return to their side once they have it," said Major Booker, picking up where General Cooley had left off. "When these Jammies leave on a sortie, they take their information with them and then separate from their units, possibly by allowing themselves to be shot down. The SAF's fighters can go after them. We'd like you to permit us to do this. That's point three, and we'd like your opinion on it, sir."

"My God," murmured Captain Foss. "It's too risky."

"This isn't anything that I have the authority to approve," General Laitume said, an edge in his voice. "This entertainment you've arranged isn't nearly good enough to move me to do something like that. No, this is a joke. If the SAF engages in these activities, I will not give my approval! Captain Foss was right, this is dangerous. If you do that without some public announcement of why, it'll not only destroy your reputations, but my own as well! Besides, if I let you do that, there's also the danger that no one would be able to stop your rampage. The FAF and the

SAF would end up at war with each other."

"If people acknowledge that there are JAM within the FAF now, our combat intelligences will use it as an excuse to lock us out of this fight," Major Booker pleaded. "Even now, the machines are starting to feel that we're in their way. If we accept that, then all of us will have to abandon this war. The number of unmanned planes will increase and we humans will be sent back to Earth in short order. If that happens, it's possible that JAM duplicates will mix in with us, and they'll have succeeded in expanding the battlefield back to Earth. Once that happens, humanity will have no place left to run to."

"Even if that happens," added Rei, who'd been silently listening the whole time, "the people on Earth will have no real sense that anything strange has occurred. It'll be like it always is, with wars breaking out here and there. The people involved will only be concerned with defending their own territory. All the JAM will have to do is sit back and watch humanity wipe itself out."

"You're the man who brought this trouble back to us, aren't you?" asked General Laitume, eyeing Rei coldly. "You're the one who seems like a JAM."

"There are truths in this world that we'd be happier not knowing," Rei replied. "I was shot by a JAM duplicate. Now that I know they exist, it's only natural that I do something about it. Ignoring the truth doesn't make it go away. It's possible the JAM have already infiltrated Earth. We don't have anyplace left to run, which means our only option is to fight."

"You said that Yukikaze knew these beings were at that front-line base while she was flying unmanned," said Colonel Rombert. "That means the SAF's computers already know the truth. Have they begun seeing humans as a hindrance to them?"

"Yes, there've been signs of that," Major Booker said. "However, the SAF's combat intelligences operate independently of the other ones in the FAF. They don't share their data. That's obvious by the fact that this information wasn't transmitted to you. They can't deny a human access to it, so if it gets transmitted, they won't be able to hide something as big as this. For now, though, they can."

"Yukikaze isn't hiding anything," Rei said. "She seeks my cooperation in order to survive. Whether or not I can guess what she's thinking is going to determine how long the rest of my life is going to be."

"What you've said seems to have struck a chord in my heart," Colonel Rombert said. "Since you've identified these potential Jammies, I'll have them investigated in absolute secrecy, just as we'd normally do. Until we spot some distinguishing feature we can use to distinguish them from humans, I won't even tell my subordinates what they're observing them for. That way, if this does turn out to be some trick being carried out by the SAF, I'll be the only one who looks like an idiot. However, I'd like to offer one proposal in this matter."

"Tell us, please," said General Laitume. "I'd like your insight into this."

"There's an easy way to keep all of these suspects under surveillance. Form a new unit made up of only them. Since they've all been shot down by the JAM, we can call it a retraining unit. A thorough check of the physical and psychological states of its members for analysis wouldn't be at all unnatural for something like that. It's a good way for us to check and see if they're Jammies or not. Even if the SAF's intelligence turns out to be false, retraining people who have been defeated before still wouldn't be a waste of our time."

"Excellent! There's a proposal I'll be able to present. If I put some effort into it, I should be able to sell my corps on setting up a new unit like that," General Laitume said with a nod.

"Then we just have to sit back and see what happens. If they're JAM, then they'll make a move of some sort. If they try to desert under fire, we won't need to send the SAF out after them. My people will take care of them right there and then. If we can bring them back alive, we can either put the screws to them in interrogation or just execute them without the need for a court martial."

"You should try to bring your information back without resorting to such savage means," Rei said. "The JAM don't understand humans. That's why you can't argue with them. We should teach them what humans are. From there, we can start fighting them."

"We didn't ask your opinion," replied General Cooley, cutting Rei off. "I still don't understand why Major Booker asked you to attend—"

"To ask the captain his opinion," Major Booker interjected. "Captain Fukai, what would you do if I ordered you to make contact with the JAM again? Right now, we're seriously considering it."

"Major Booker, what are you talking about?" asked General Cooley. "You never told me about any such operation."

"If you order me to, I'll do it," Rei replied. "I think the JAM want to as well. Three days ago, on a recon mission out to Richwar, I was approached by two JAM fighters. Looking back at it now, I think they were trying to make contact with me. It was as if they recognized Yukikaze. They didn't launch a preemptive strike against me, though they had the opportunity.

"I think this operation is worthy of consideration," he continued. "General Cooley, this is the real third point. I'd also like to ask General Laitume his opinion. If we carry this out without hearing from him, he'll just think that Yukikaze and I are JAM."

"Have Captain Fukai make contact with the JAM again, you say?" asked Colonel Rombert. "In other words, appoint him our ambassador plenipotentiary."

"I will not grant this man plenipotentiary powers," General Laitume protested.

"Then you can contact the JAM," Rei said. "You can ride in Yukikaze."

"Watch your mouth!"

"No matter who goes, I don't think the JAM will accept them," Colonel Rombert interjected. "The SAF has become disconnected from reality, letting its delusions run away with them—"

An alarm sounded nearby, cutting him off.

"Air raid," Rei said. "JAM approaching."

"It's not unusual," General Laitume said. "My corps will—"

"General, this is no time to be boasting about how good your forces are," Major Booker said sharply. "Get to shelter. We can ask your final opinion on this matter later. General Cooley, please, take our guests and get them to shelter fast."

From the apron near the SAF underground hangar entrance, the shrill scream of high-output turbofan engines revving up pierced their ears. Yukikaze spun around. She was prepared for takeoff.

"Llanfabon! Lieutenant Bruys, do you hear me?" shouted Major Booker. "Mission accomplished! RTB! The meeting's over. Contact HQ! Cut in on the emergency line! That's an order! Confirm receipt of orders by blinking your landing lights three times! When you contact HQ, blink them once!"

Llanfabon confirmed with its lights. Bruys could hear the major's words.

"Yukikaze's moving out," Rei said coolly. "Aren't you going to stop her, Jack?"

"We have no way to contact her, and there's no time for us to get back to HQ and contact her."

"You could do it from Llanfabon."

"Do you want me to, Rei?"

"No, let her go. Yukikaze wants to shoot down some JAM."

"I'm a little worried, since she's only loaded with enough fuel for ten minutes of air combat," the major replied. "But I'm interested in seeing what she'll do on her own. I don't want to interfere."

"She'd still be doing this even if I were aboard. Yukikaze's decided that there's no time to take refuge. The enemy's close. Close. They're almost here."

Yukikaze was protecting herself. If an aerial recon plane had spotted the enemy earlier and Yukikaze received that intel, she'd have probably sprung into action the moment it reached her. She would have taken refuge if there'd been time, thought Rei. If she was choosing to intercept them rather than run, it meant that she thought the situation was dangerous.

"Jack, we'd better get out of here too."

Before he'd even finished speaking, two high-speed objects and their accompanying shock waves tore through the skies right above them. A pair of high-velocity missiles. Rei didn't bother looking where they were headed; he was gazing in the direction they'd come from. Directly behind, flying so low that it was cutting a swath through the forest, a pitch-black JAM hit-and-away strike fighter had appeared. With the kinetic vision Rei had been trained to have, he saw what followed as though in slow motion.

From behind the JAM fighter flew a missile, driving its way

toward the enemy plane. It had been fired by an FAF Faery Base defense air corps fighter flying a combat air patrol in the area. The JAM began jinking wildly to shake it off, but it was too late. The missile looked like it was going to score a direct hit, but its proximity fuse activated before it could. The sound of the explosions came in quick succession, echoing into the sky.

Rei immediately threw himself on top of Captain Foss to shield her. The exploding missile rained shrapnel down in every direction, with some of it striking the ground so hard that Rei himself could feel it. As the series of explosions resounded over their heads, the JAM fighter began a climbing turn, black smoke pouring from its fuselage. There was a flash, followed by another explosion. The JAM self-destructed. Fragments of the plane fell toward the forest.

Two interceptors from the Tactical Combat Air Corps that had been on scramble standby managed to evade the JAM missile attack and had taken off in formation. On the side of the runway, two planes were on fire.

Rei searched for Yukikaze.

Yukikaze...was accelerating in the opposite direction from the two fighters. She then lit her afterburners and began a practically vertical climb at maximum thrust. There were still JAM to fight.

Rei helped Captain Foss to her feet. Major Booker and Gallé Murullé had fallen to the ground. The guests were nowhere to be seen. They must have managed to get to shelter.

"Jack, you okay?" Rei asked.

Shaking his head, Major Booker took Rei's outstretched hand and got to his feet.

"Shit, I can't believe I nearly bought it from one of our own missiles. I can barely hear anything."

"Edith, how's the chef?"

Captain Foss rushed over to Murullé's side, then shook her head. His chef's whites were stained deep red. He raised his right hand and pointed into the sky. Looking up, Rei saw four vapor trails stretching out, high in the clear skies. It could only be one thing: Yukikaze had fired her short-range missiles.

"Jack, get Edith to shelter, then send a rescue team."

"What are you talking about? You're coming with us!"

Rei took Captain Foss's place and knelt at Murullé's side, taking hold of his hand. Rei had wanted to see how Yukikaze would fight. *Maybe this chef did as well*, he thought.

"Were the JAM targeting this meeting, Major?"

"I don't know," Major Booker answered. He ordered Captain Foss to call for a rescue team and then stayed behind as well. "The planes we had on scramble standby were watching us. I'll bet they were having some fun and chatting about it on the comm lines. The JAM may have shown up by coincidence; perhaps they thought something interesting was happening out here. Llanfabon and Yukikaze both must have recorded the data on them. We'll know for sure once it's analyzed."

"I think this may have been the first time the JAM have specifically targeted human beings."

The major paused. "I feel like running back home," he said.

"That's the first time I've ever heard you complain about anything," Rei replied.

"There's no place we can run to. All we can do is rise and accept the challenge, like you said, Rei."

The skies had suddenly grown quiet. Yukikaze's fuel had probably run out, Rei figured. This was confirmed a moment later when she silently swooped down, now visible to his naked eye. She executed a wide turn and then got on approach for a glide-in landing.

Yukikaze touched down safely onto the ground. As though that was a signal, the strength left Gallé Murullé's hand.

"Jack, did you hold this meeting because you figured the JAM might come and wanted to find out if somebody was leaking the information?"

Major Booker didn't reply.

"Well, Major Booker?"

"And what if I did, Rei?"

"Because Murullé lost his life because of it. It should have been me. It should have been…"

"Tough luck. He had a bad break."

"Is that all you're going to say?"

"Rei, we aren't the only ones here who risk our lives," Major

Booker said. "He was a soldier too. He was one of us. Do you think I don't feel anything for him?"

Rei couldn't think of an answer to that. He tightly held the dead chef's hand as an SAF spotting dolly moved in to tow Yukikaze. As the dolly approached, Yukikaze flashed her landing lights three times.

"The mission accomplished sign," Major Booker muttered to himself. "The one Llanfabon used to confirm that they understood what I was saying. Holy shit…Yukikaze's conscious of us. Of you."

Yeah, she probably was. But she didn't mourn Murullé's death. Not at all. And she wouldn't. Yukikaze was different from him.

"I am…" Rei said. "I am…human."

"And never forget that," Major Booker replied quietly. "Don't let Galleé Murullé's death be in vain, Rei. Human lives can't be replaced once they're lost."

V

STRATEGIC RECONNAISSANCE — PHASE 1

1

THE REAR SEAT, where the flight officer would be in charge of electronic warfare duty, had been empty ever since the old Yukikaze was shot down.

Naturally, Major Booker planned to rectify the situation. Now that Rei was fully recovered and ready for combat, a new flight officer had to be chosen, and fast. But at the moment, he was so shorthanded that he could find nobody qualified for the position.

The job of the flight officer riding in the fighter's rear seat was to conduct tactical reconnaissance and electronic warfare duty while in the combat airspace, and it was a job even more exhausting than the pilot's. Once they were in the combat zone, he would be so busy confirming the plane's position and safety while giving guidance instructions to the pilot, selecting and operating a variety of radar systems for tactical recon, and confirming in real time the transmission sources of the massive amounts of comm traffic being collected in the background that he had no time to even look out past the cockpit bubble. And all the while he was locked inside of this insular environment, he'd have to endure violent maneuvers as well.

The SAF currently had eleven electronic warfare specialists. As they had twelve fighter planes in use, not counting the unmanned Rafe, in the event that they conducted an operation requiring all their planes, the mission would be a man short. The SAF normally would never send all of their planes out at once, but now, even if such a deployment ever became necessary, it would be impossible because Yukikaze was missing essential personnel.

As a general rule, you try to pair up a pilot and a flight officer who'll be able to work together as a good team, thought Major

Booker. However, with Rei back in combat, the major was having to assign him a different flight officer for each individual mission, which was only increasing the burden on the electronic warfare operator. That was something he wanted to avoid.

He needed a new man assigned to the squadron immediately. If he worked well with Rei, then all of his problems would go away. And even if he didn't, another man in the talent pool meant he wouldn't have to increase the burden on his EWOs. If Booker couldn't get a good team formed and had to keep assigning a flight officer for each mission, he could still have Captain Foss, the doctor charged with their psychological care, do something about the mental strain it was causing. In any case, he wanted a new man, and had gone to plead with General Cooley for one.

"It can be anyone," he said as he stood in front of her desk. He'd come to her office to make a direct appeal. "Just please, get me *somebody* to use."

"You know perfectly well it can't be just anyone, Major," she replied.

"Okay, yeah. Yeah, you're right. If they can't be used immediately, then there's no point in even discussing it. Our unit doesn't have time to carefully train anyone. One person, though. All I'm asking for is one person. Please, transfer someone in from somewhere, from some other unit. Anyone, as long as they're not a JAM duplicate. You know, I wouldn't even mind one of them at this point. We'd probably be able to learn about their strategy."

"You don't know what you're saying anymore, do you? We don't have an EWO we can throw into battle immediately, and it's suddenly all you can think about. You wouldn't mind having a JAM? What kind of nonsense is that? If you want the numbers to balance out, I could do it for you easily. Back when Captain Fukai was still a lieutenant, if he hadn't made it back and had been killed by the JAM along with his flight officer, Lieutenant Burgadish, we wouldn't have this problem now. If that had happened, you would have complained about losing two men and a plane, but you'd have said you would deal with it somehow."

Major Booker couldn't speak for a moment.

"General," he said at last. "I can't just let something like that pass. Are you saying you think it would have been better if Rei— if Captain Fukai hadn't made it back, because if you are—"

"No, that's not what I'm saying at all. This whole matter is giving me a headache too. Personnel selection is my responsibility. I'm just saying that this isn't simply a matter of throwing a warm body into the unit. Major, take a moment and calm down a little. This isn't like you."

General Cooley rose from her desk and motioned to Major Booker to take a seat on the sofa in her lounge suite.

"I don't have much time, and there's something I'd like to consult you about," General Cooley said, her tone changing slightly, becoming a bit friendlier.

"Yes, General."

Although she'd said she didn't have much time, she rang her secretary on the intercom and ordered tea and cocoa for them.

"We both do this so often that I know what you like, don't I? It'll be here soon."

The general usually drinks tea with lemon. The cocoa must be for me, Major Booker thought as he sat down, preparing himself for the worst. *Whenever she does this, it means the general has a little problem for me to deal with.*

"How are things with Captain Fukai?" she asked.

"Like I reported to you a few days ago, he's recovered about 85 percent of his physical strength, so no problems there."

"His mental state still seems unstable. I've heard he has some anxiety about his plane, Yukikaze."

"I put down in my report that his relationship with the plane would better be described as psychological growth for him. Captain Foss agrees with me. In my judgment, he should have no problem in combat."

"You're saying he's developing a pleasant personality?" Cooley asked.

"Personality doesn't change. He's not an obedient soldier and never will be. Considering the duty the SAF has to carry out, that's for the best."

"In other words, we can still use him, right?"

"Exactly."

"You still haven't submitted a report on the conclusions of the investigation into Yukikaze's unmanned sortie. How is that proceeding?"

"The investigation's tentatively complete, but we're going to need to keep a constant eye on how our combat intelligences behave," Major Booker said. "I'm not sure if they're going to be willing to accept it. We can't use the computer network to distribute the report, since the CIs will be able to read it. Of course, I can't say for certain they won't overhear us talking about it like this either."

"You're studying what to do if that happens, aren't you?"

"Yeah, although, on my part… At first glance, I think taking a hostile stance toward the CIs will just backfire on us. It's the JAM, not humanity, that's the enemy. We know that clearly enough. All we have to be on guard for is whether they've been contaminated by the JAM or are being manipulated by them. Of course, the final decision in this matter will be yours, General."

"The SAF depends on its computers. If we can't rely on them, we can't fight the JAM. Are you saying, for now at least, that their reliability hasn't been compromised?"

"Yes, in my judgment."

"I trust you, Major, so I'm leaving this matter in your hands. I'm sure you'll handle this without getting our own computers pissed off at us."

"Thank you, General."

"It seems strange to me to be asking you not to piss off some computers. Do you think so as well, Major?"

"You have a point there," the major said. "You know, if we hadn't been paying attention to the relationship between Rei and Yukikaze, we probably never would have thought to pay attention to the combat awareness of the computers as well. I doubt it ever would have occurred to me. Yukikaze has changed radically. Or, rather than changed, I think—"

"You think that she's revealing her true nature?"

"I think she's grown as a combat intelligence, and we humans are seeing that manifested in her behavior. It's possible that we'll see more incidents similar to the one that just occurred, and Captain Fukai is the only one who can control her. We have to make sure that he doesn't fail at that task. If they can build a relationship of mutual trust, then through Yukikaze we can build a similar relationship with our computers. Whether we try to curry favor with the computers or not, we're still at war with the JAM. But there's no doubt in my mind that doing so will be much easier if we can establish mutual trust with each other. The only hitch is that we're trying to build trust with things that aren't human. These are autonomous ultra-high speed computers. You can express reliability with a number, but you can't do the same for a concept like mutual trust."

Even as he was speaking, Major Booker thought that Rei and Yukikaze wouldn't have been able to fight the JAM unless they already had a perfect level of mutual trust beyond that which could be expressed through numbers. That trust was immediately reflected in the way she maneuvered in combat. There was no time to wonder what would happen if a maneuver didn't work. Rei fussed and worried over his relationship with his beloved plane so much that it made other people laugh, but that was because his very existence depended on her. Nobody could laugh at that, any more than they could help. It was a question that operated on a different level than just being satisfied with the SAF maintenance staff putting enthusiasm into maintaining Yukikaze's airframe and electronic hardware perfectly.

"You're right," replied General Cooley, nodding. "I'll try not to forget that."

The usual tea and cocoa arrived, the cocoa with lots of whipped cream and moderate sugar. The general's secretary, a young man who looked quite dashing in his uniform, set the drinks down, saluted, and then left the office. After he did, General Cooley's tone changed again.

"We are getting replacement personnel, but we can't wait for a new flight officer to be assigned to us. I had a list drawn up of several candidates from other units that might be ready for duty with the SAF and tried to grab one of them for us."

This conversation we've been having was just to kill time. The main topic was about to come, Major Booker thought as he picked up his cup and waited for what she'd say next.

"Our forces are shorthanded everywhere. Nobody wants to

lose a good pilot if they have one. Besides that, even someone with superior skills may not be suited for duty in the SAF. I put out the word that we'll take anyone, no matter how disliked they are, but when I checked into the candidates, none of them had the skills we need. After this went on for a while, my list was whittled down to nothing."

"So, I guess I'll just have to wait a little longer then," Major Booker said.

"We can't just wait for new talent to arrive. I hate not knowing exactly when we'll get someone as much as you do. Besides that, in two months the SAF is going to lose an excellent EWO, Captain N'mudo, when he retires. He's already extended his military service out to nearly six years. I want to let him go, and he wants to go. Same thing for Captain Kozlov in seven months. We know which people we'll be losing, but no replacements are scheduled to come. Sitting around waiting for them isn't an option."

"I'll try to find some candidates from my end again," the major replied.

"Right, and I hope you're always on the lookout for those, but another unit contacted me with a man they hope we can use. In other words, he's a giveaway. What I wanted to consult with you about was whether or not I should accept him. I'd like to hear your opinion on the matter."

"Who is he? Does he want to join the SAF? Does he have any personality problems? I'd welcome a guy with a personality like Captain Fukai's, but people like that don't usually offer themselves to us."

"He wasn't the one asking us to use him. It was Colonel Rombert."

"Colonel Rombert? From the Intelligence Forces?" asked Major Booker, the cup of cocoa up at his mouth.

"Right. Ansel Rombert. He says that if we're shorthanded, to please use one of his men. The candidate has electronic warfare experience and doesn't seem to have any problems as far as competency goes. But he comes with another problem."

"Yeah…the Intelligence Forces probably want to find out what's going on in the SAF and maybe get some intel from us as well. I think Colonel Rombert sees our situation presenting itself to him as a chance to get some quid pro quo. Did he say anything like this guy he's offering wouldn't be an SAF transfer but just an Intelligence Forces member on loan to us?"

"Yeah, that's basically the impression I got from him. Rombert's attitude toward us will probably change depending on what moves we make. For now, though, he seems to be friendly to us," General Cooley said.

"The colonel seems to be planning to start openly collecting intel on what goes on in the SAF. This personnel recommendation may just be a bluff. In any case, I think this is a declaration from him that the Intelligence Forces aren't just going to leave the SAF to its own devices. We should take it as a warning."

"I don't want Colonel Rombert and his forces interfering with what we do here. The last thing we need is them breathing down our necks. I want to avoid anything that endangers our autonomy. Normally, I'd reject the offer out of hand, but right now, we're really hurting for personnel, so I'm thinking of accepting it," said Cooley.

"Accept an intel forces guy with strings attached, huh? All combat intel will end up getting passed straight to Colonel Rombert. Are you saying you're okay with that?"

"So says the man who was just saying he wanted anyone, even a JAM."

"That was just a figure of speech, General."

"I didn't think so. You sounded pretty serious to me when you said a JAM human could get us info on the JAM."

"A JAM human. What Colonel Rombert refers to as a Jammy. Well, maybe this would be better. If the colonel's recommending this guy, it's pretty much a guarantee that he won't be a Jammy," Booker said.

"I can imagine that Colonel Rombert has been watching us for any strange moves ever since we told him that we've already been infiltrated by a duplicate once before. It's only natural that he can't disregard any actions the SAF takes now. We were prepared for that already."

"True, but I figured he'd do it behind closed doors. I never expected him to openly send in a...well, spy may be too strong a word. How about observer?"

"No, Colonel Rombert sends in his right-hand man who will then report on what happens here to him. But at the same time, we'll know about it. With that in mind, I want you to stay on your toes. This is also a good chance for us to learn about what the Intelligence Forces are up to. What I'd like to ask your opinion about is if you think we can do that, Major Booker."

So, that's what she wanted to consult me about, thought Major Booker as he sipped his cocoa. The general was right; they couldn't just ignore Colonel Rombert's activities and speculations. If they left this to lie, the Intelligence Forces would certainly be investigating the SAF in secret. But the colonel had shown his cards; he wanted to gather information through this guy they were sending over, so that the arrangement would be an exchange of information between the SAF and the Intelligence Forces. In that respect, Colonel Rombert had made a fair proposal.

But there was no mistaking that the colonel thought that he'd be getting the better end of the deal. Would Booker be able to handle this talented soldier Rombert was sending over? He was a spy, an expert in information warfare, while the major wasn't. To be honest, Booker didn't really want to take on any duties outside of the war with the JAM. Still, they weren't going to get anywhere with the war unless they had the manpower to fight it.

"Colonel Rombert has good people working for him, and so do I," said General Cooley as she looked at Major Booker. "I know you can handle this."

"Hm. Well, I'd like some details on the man he's recommending."

"Colonel Rombert arranged to have a hard copy of his file sent over. It looks like he didn't want the computers knowing about it."

"He probably has the file memorized anyway. That's the safest way. It's kind of amazing how he's able to do that."

"The colonel's abilities aren't that praiseworthy. I have a feeling that you'd be able to tell me the detailed personal histories of our personnel and the current condition of their planes immediately if I asked you to," the general said. "You'd do well not to overestimate the man."

"It's an objective evaluation of him, General. The fact that the colonel has his position in the Intelligence Forces is evidence of his ability in itself. My saying it's dangerous to make light of him is another way for me to say I'm ready for anything he dishes out. It doesn't mean he's got me shaking in my boots."

"As a member of the SAF, you know that we can't let our guard down with Colonel Rombert, right?"

"The same way we can't get sloppy with the JAM. Anyway, I want to know about this guy they're sending before he gets here. He can't be a total mystery man, can he?"

"We're still waiting on his detailed personal file, but I've been given a brief précis of it."

"Then could you please start by telling me what you know?" Major Booker asked. "Colonel Rombert may be distracting us with this guy while he thinks of some other measure to use against us, but I can't make any judgments without data to work with. I want that data and some time to consider all this."

"Very well. If you judge that he won't fit our needs, then I'll turn down the colonel's offer. Don't take too long, though. We should decide if we're taking him as soon as we can."

"What's his name?"

"Akira Katsuragi. Second lieutenant, currently assigned to the electronic warfare analysis division of the Intelligence Forces. He comes from Japan and originally enlisted in the Japanese Air Force. So he's Japanese, not a Jammy. Why don't we pair him up with Captain Fukai?"

"You're saying their coming from the same country will make them more compatible? That's—"

"Compatibility has nothing to do with it. First of all, Yukikaze needs a flight officer. Second, we'll need Rei's and Yukikaze's help if we're going to outwit the colonel. Rei won't let a new guy do as he pleases, and neither will Yukikaze. Particularly Yukikaze, since she'll be recording every single thing the flight officer does while aboard her. He won't be able to interfere with any SAF computer without her knowing about it."

Booker paused a moment, considering his options.

"You know what, General? Let's take Colonel Rombert up on his kind offer. Right now, figuring out the JAM's strategy is more important than speculating on the Intelligence Forces' intentions. After that is figuring out what our unit's CIs are up to.

I'm also interested in Yukikaze on that front, but I know what she's doing from Rei's reports. He's working hard to get that information out of her. Compared to that, this little intrigue on Rombert's part is a minor annoyance, and we're going to let him know that through the new guy."

"I'll give you a little time to consider this."

"Ma'am?"

"Take some time to enjoy your cocoa, Major. If you don't want to do it here, you can take the cup to your office."

Booker thought it over, then replied, "I'll do it here, General."

"I know you think you need a private secretary too, but there's nobody qualified available. Getting a bad candidate in there will probably just cause more trouble for you, but I want to help you with that if I can."

"I appreciate your concern, General. I'm fine, though. My coffee and cocoa tastes best when I fix it for myself."

But as he slowly sipped his drink, Major Booker thought that cocoa made for you by another person didn't taste so bad.

"We need to get Captain Fukai and Yukikaze to work on this new strategy against the JAM," General Cooley said conversationally as she sipped her tea. "I'll be expecting you to do your best with it."

"I've broached the subject with him, but I'd like for this Lieutenant Katsuragi character to get used to Yukikaze first. We can get to the other thing later. No need to rush. The JAM aren't going anywhere. We can take our time looking for them."

"The SAF was originally formed to carry out tactical reconnaissance, but now we seem to be moving into the realm of strategic reconnaissance," Cooley said.

"It'd be better if we didn't keep pursuing autonomy for our unit. The nail that sticks up is the one that gets hammered down, you know."

"I never set out to start playing internal FAF power games," the general replied. "But I can't help but think that having a bit more influence would help us to avoid problems like the ones we're facing now."

"The thing is, you're still the big gun here. You run things from the shadows," the major replied. "It'd be better if you didn't move into the foreground. From the very start, the SAF was never simply a tactical recon unit. Right now, we're operating as a joint tactical-strategic intelligence unit. There's a lot of know-how we need from Colonel Rombert. The way we need to think about this information exchange is not as a strategic recon force, but as another intelligence force. Now, of course, Colonel Rombert will probably be on guard for this. And then there are the internal power games we need to play. All these family squabbles within the FAF may be just what the JAM wanted."

"Humans really are bizarre life-forms, aren't we?"

"Completely. In the face of an enemy threat, we still waste our time with these internal power struggles. There are those who think we have better things to do, but they usually turn out to be the losers. I used to think it was basic instinct for every life-form to seek hegemony over its environment, but now I'm not so sure. There are special groups within humanity where that idea doesn't hold sway. The SAF is one of them. We really do occupy a special position within the mass of humanity. I can only guess at the troubles it causes you," the major said.

"Your sympathy doesn't help much, but I think it makes me feel a bit better."

"As does yours for me."

Draining the last of his cocoa, Major Booker rose from the sofa.

"Please tell me as soon as you get a hard date for Lieutenant Katsuragi's arrival. I'll be placing Captain Fukai in charge of bringing him up to speed on Yukikaze, so I need to make plans."

"Understood."

General Cooley, cup still in hand, nodded her head. Saluting the general as she sipped her tea, Major Booker exited her office.

He didn't know what kind of guy Katsuragi was going to be, but now Yukikaze's rear seat was filled. That was one major problem solved. The next thing to prepare for was the strategic reconnaissance mission to be carried out by Rei and Yukikaze, which could lead to a major turning point in the war with the JAM. They were going to have to carry out that mission with their new flight officer.

2

THE PERSONNEL FILE he'd requested on Lieutenant Akira Katsuragi reached Major Booker's desk that same day. He noticed that the characters spelling his name in Japanese were the ones for redbud, fortress, and clear. After skimming through it, he summoned Captain Fukai and Captain Foss to his office.

Rei, still on standby and eager for his next mission, came quickly.

The night of Chef Murullé's death, after that ill-fated lunch meeting, the major had gone back to his quarters with Rei to share some whiskey. Booker took Murullé's death harder than usual. As he got increasingly drunk, Major Booker started complaining about the SAF's manpower shortage. Rei comforted him by saying that he would fly Yukikaze even without a flight officer. He had his reasons for not wanting one. Major Booker had broached the idea of Rei and Yukikaze flying a mission to proactively make contact with the JAM. There was no way of knowing what might happen on a mission like that, and Rei didn't want a repeat of his experience of having the JAM feed him the flesh of his last flight officer. When he told the major that, Booker replied that he understood how Rei felt, but that there was no way he could let him fly out there on his own. Two would be better than one, and while he was sorry about what had happened to Lieutenant Burgadish, the major pointed out that Rei might not have made it back alive had he flown solo last time. The old scar on his face was flushed as he talked. The major had gone on, saying that he didn't want to lose any more of his people either, but that just wasn't a realistic option, and so he had resigned himself to it. And he had to deal with that on his own. Rei had remained silent and simply refilled his old friend's empty glass.

It had been two days since that meeting, and Rei hadn't been sent out with Yukikaze. Rei entered the office and immediately asked, "Have you worked out the details for my and Yukikaze's new mission?" The major replied that no, he hadn't yet. Still, the major's attitude now made his drunken bellyaching from a couple of nights back seem like it never happened.

"You get some good news for a change, Jack? You look like you just inherited a fortune."

"You can tell? Nothing to do with money, I'm afraid, but I've got you a new flight officer. That's enough to make me happy. His transfer isn't official yet, but as long as there's no complaint from our end, it's a done deal. Now we won't be down a plane anymore. I'm still putting together your special strategic recon mission against the JAM, but I'd like you to fly some regular tactical recon missions in the meantime. The new guy can get used to Yukikaze while you do."

"Shouldn't we leave him out of the special mission?"

"That's part of why I want to see how good he is," the major said. "Anyway, I want to see if he'll be of any use to us under fire. Check over his file to see what kind of person he is before he gets here."

"What, are you telling me to play nice with the new kid? This isn't kindergarten. What the hell's the matter with you?"

"I'm not asking you to get along with him. Of course I wouldn't expect you to do that. Actually, kindergarten is a good way of putting it, since he is kind of like a transfer student. Think of him as a student from the Colonel Rombert School. He's the kind of guy you'd throw into an intelligence war or something like that."

Rei seemed a bit taken aback. "I didn't realize we were that short of qualified people," he said. "You're really going to have me fly with a spy in the back seat?"

"I know how you feel. That's why I'm giving you the background info on him."

"I suppose there's no point in my saying no to this."

"Not before you fly with him under fire. If you judge there to be a real problem after we get him up to speed, and not one just based on your emotions, then report that to me. If it means anything, I don't like having to pair you up with a guy like this either."

"Hmm…" Rei replied. As he skimmed the personnel file of his new flight officer that he'd been handed, Captain Foss arrived.

"Sorry I'm late," she said.

"You're actually earlier than I expected. Looks like you're getting into the flow of things here."

"Yes, thankfully."

"Well," said Rei. "If you don't need me now, then—"

"Hold it. I'm not done with you yet, Captain Fukai."

Rei stopped at the door. Major Booker brought Captain Foss up to speed on the new flight officer's planned arrival, including the detail that he was one of Colonel Rombert's men.

"Now, you see," the major said to her, "I'd like you to analyze the personality of this new man. If the file they sent isn't enough, figure something out. I especially want you to find out if he'll be able to work with the SAF in general and Rei in particular. Take Colonel Rombert's expectations into account as well. Since he's about to take up his post here, I'd like you to give this matter your continuous attention."

"Yes, Major. In other words, you want me to try profacting this man," she replied.

"I'm not that familiar with your field's terminology, but I think so. I thought it was called profiling, though."

"Profiling techniques were never widely accepted in the fields of psychology and psychiatry. Since the term was also broadly interpreted and used arbitrarily by the general public, it fell into disfavor in the scientific world. Profacting is a method used to analyze the load intensity of the mind and body in order to theoretically predict a subject's behavior or psychology."

"It's your specialty. I want you to analyze him the same way you did Rei."

"Understood, sir. I suppose we'll need to analyze Colonel Rombert's psychology as well."

"Just be prudent and don't be too obvious about it. I know you can do this."

"I'll try to live up to your expectations, Major."

"Good to hear. Ask for Captain Fukai's opinion in your analysis. He knows more about Colonel Rombert and the relationship between the SAF and the Intelligence Forces than you do."

"You want me to help with this too?" Rei asked.

"Right," the major said. "You'll do this together. This is a question that concerns your continued existence, Rei. The results of his psych analysis will be helpful in that regard."

"Roger," Rei said, nodding. "It'll be nice, but don't you think you're going a little overboard with all this? It doesn't matter who they send to us. If he's useless in combat, we throw him out, that's all. You used to say that was all that matters."

"But it's better to know the trouble spots beforehand, right?" said Captain Foss. "You can't be too careful."

"That's especially true for this new guy," Major Booker added. "It may seem like I'm overdoing things here, but I don't think it's a waste of time, so it's okay."

Major Booker rubbed the back of his head with his palm, taking some time to let the mood change before he continued.

"I've been thinking about trying a direct exchange of information with the JAM. I want Yukikaze and Captain Fukai to carry it out."

"Will the enemy go along with it?" asked Captain Foss. "Make contact? With the JAM? We don't know anything about them. It's too dangerous!"

"Which is why I'm working on the plan," Major Booker said. "If we just do it all of a sudden, it won't work. After thirty years of fighting them, we still know nothing of the JAM. I've decided that it's time for the SAF to initiate its own strategy regarding them. The tactical reconnaissance we've been conducting up till now hasn't been getting us anywhere, and coming up with tactical plans to forestall losing will never let us win. What we want is a strategy that will lead to victory. General Cooley agrees with me, so beginning with all of the data we've collected on the JAM thus far, I want to begin reconstructing a portrait of them. In other words, Captain Foss, I want you to do that profacting thing you mentioned. On the JAM. I want a psychobehavioral analysis of them."

"But the JAM aren't human," Rei protested.

"I know that. I also know that only humans can do this job. The question we're trying to answer in this case is this: what is the true nature of the JAM? I want to know what they're after. I also want to know what their goal, their ultimate goal, is in all of this. Besides that, why are they sending these human duplicates to infiltrate us? I think it's because they want to know more about us, but I want some theoretical backing to that supposition."

"The JAM's ultimate goal?" asked Captain Foss. "That's pretty obvious, isn't it? They want to invade Earth and conquer it. Are you saying that's not what they're after?"

"While it may be true that the JAM invaded Earth before and are still trying to gain a foothold, the idea that they're trying to conquer the planet is just our subjective impression as humans. Or rather than *our* impression, it's *your* impression. The SAF doesn't see it that way. At the very least, General Cooley and I don't think so."

"You're right," Rei added. "I don't think the JAM's objective is simply to conquer Earth. If they were just trying to invade, they could have pulled that off without us humans knowing it. They still could. They may already have."

"I agree. It's as though the JAM never expected humanity to try and stop their invasion, and their actions toward us since then seem to support that. That still holds true, but their behavior is changing. They're changing their strategy because they now seem to have realized that achieving their objective is going to require dealing with us humans first. If they're adopting a new strategy, then we can't afford to ignore it. We're about to see a major turn in the course of the war, which means we can't keep fighting it the way we've been. We've got to come up with a countermeasure, and fast! Is that clear, Foss?" Major Booker said, chiding the young doctor.

"You have to understand that conquering Earth and conquering human society are two entirely different things. *Homo sapiens* isn't the only species on Earth. To an outsider observing us, humanity may not appear to be its rulers. I've said over and over, that's just human prejudice talking. You might even call it human conceit. Someone could just as easily say that plants rule the earth, or the oceans, or possibly that our computers do. The JAM certainly behave as though they see things that way. What I want from you in your role as a specialist is to analyze what the JAM have done so far and then figure out what they're thinking and how they plan to seize Earth. Add Captain Fukai's experience to the data and then go to it."

"I'm not a specialist in analyzing JAM behavior and psychology!" Captain Foss insisted.

"Nobody's a specialist in that," Rei said. "No human at least. Yukikaze and the computers probably know more about that than we do."

"We can't go on saying that!" Major Booker shot back. "First of all, there's a problem in our not being able to take pride in being the ones who know the most about the JAM. There are probably lots of civilians outside of the FAF who also have an interest in this. Some among them may be doing analysis that's even more pertinent than what the SAF is doing."

"Yeah," said Rei. "Like Lynn Jackson."

"People like her who think outside the box are a dying breed. Yeah, I was also thinking of her while I was talking just now."

"Lynn Jackson? You mean the world-famous journalist?" asked Edith.

"Right," replied Major Booker. "She's been covering the JAM and the FAF for a long time now. It's her life's work. We owe her a lot, especially Rei here."

"Really?" replied Captain Foss. "I read her book and found it fascinating. That's what first gave me the idea of joining the FAF."

"I wonder what Lynn would say if she heard that," Major Booker said. "Well, the younger generation is definitely growing up. You've put yourself a lot closer to living JAM than she has. It's an undeveloped field, and you've got a chance to pioneer it. That'll become a real feather in your cap, one that may even outdo what Lynn's working on."

"Are you being sarcastic, sir? Because that's how I'm hearing it. I came here to be a doctor for the SAF first and a researcher second, so—"

"I was hoping to get you fired up for this, Captain Foss. If I rubbed you the wrong way, you're just going to have to accept that your superior officer is that kind of guy and then move on. I may not mean to wound your pride, but I don't have a lot of time to always be careful not to. In short, I really don't give a damn. No matter what your motivations were in joining the SAF, right now, your talents are needed. Do your profacting thing on the JAM. That's an order. You're both to get to work on it at once and make it a top priority ongoing project. This is the first stage of our strategic reconnaissance mission against the JAM. That is all. Dismissed."

"Yes, Major."

Captain Foss saluted. Rei followed suit. They left the office.

3

AS THEY WALKED into the hallway, Captain Foss turned to Rei. "Let's go," she said. "We can use my office. This is a priority matter, so you have to do this too. We were ordered to work on this together, right?"

"We were also told that our mission is ongoing," Rei replied. "You keep dragging me to your office so much that it's getting so that I can barely breathe in there."

"Well, you don't have an office. Want to go to the mission briefing room instead?"

"I do my work aboard Yukikaze."

"Fine with me," Edith Foss replied with a smile. "That'd be an appropriate place to try profacting your new flight officer. Yukikaze might have an interest in it as well."

"The new flight officer is going to be trivial to her. But it's possible she might show some sort of response to us analyzing the JAM. Anyway, let's start by getting the trivial stuff out of the way first. I guess we can use your office for today." With that, Rei began walking down the corridor, but Captain Foss's voice stopped him a moment later.

"Hold it, Captain Fukai. You had a good idea there."

"What?"

"Your suggestion to do this aboard Yukikaze. I also think it'd be a good idea to tell her about Colonel Rombert and this new flight officer she'll be dealing with. I think...I just think so."

Rei tilted his head as he looked at the doctor, wondering why she'd think such a thing. He said nothing, waiting for her to go on. Sensing his curiosity, Captain Foss continued.

"I think Yukikaze is also interested in the humans she comes into close contact with, not just the JAM. Major Booker told me about the incident with Lieutenant Yagashira. He said something about Yagashira sabotaging some of Yukikaze's systems."

Rei nodded. "Right, the AICS. Sorry, the Air Intake Control System, I mean. It was a part that she didn't have direct sensor input on. You could think of it as an autonomic system. Yukikaze didn't realize it'd been tampered with, which was probably why Lieutenant Yagashira chose that system to target. There aren't many combat-vital onboard systems you can do that to, but the AICS was one of the few exceptions."

"Was? You mean now it isn't?"

"It's just jury-rigged for now, but we added in a chip that allows the central computer to monitor all onboard systems. It's not perfect, but it plugs the security hole Yagashira found. Now you can't pull a circuit card from the fuselage without the central computer knowing it."

"Did Yukikaze demand that you do that?" Foss asked.

"No, it was Major Booker's idea. The tactical computer in headquarters also said we had to do it, but it was Major Booker who made the final decision. Except... You know, now that I think of it, Yukikaze was probably aware that she was in danger from Lieutenant Yagashira's sabotage. From the way she queries the HQ computers about her status in combat when she returns to base, to make sure that her own analysis is accurate, I'd say that she still senses that danger."

"Then you understand what I'm thinking about this, right?"

"Just what do you expect will come from us doing our work aboard Yukikaze while she's on standby? Do you think we'll just talk about stuff at her and she'll just say 'Right, I understand'?" Rei said.

"Don't you think that, Captain Fukai? I'm only suggesting it because I heard that you told Major Booker that Yukikaze seems to be able to understand natural spoken language on some level."

"You're nearly as good at collecting information as Colonel Rombert. The thing is, I kind of doubt that you really believe that she has that ability. Nobody's as close to Yukikaze as I am, so I have to wonder how someone in your position can believe that of her so easily. It's not the sort of thing that an outsider would say, so I wish you'd stop pretending that you believe it."

"Are you sure you just don't like that an outsider like me could so easily realize something that took you so long to figure out?" Foss said.

"And there you go again," Rei said, the exasperation showing clearly on his face. "Analyzing my mind and saying 'Right, that being the case, this must be like this.' You can say what you want, but—"

"Think about it yourself, Rei. You can't bear having the way another person talks, like me, affect how you feel. You claim that it's not your problem so that you can avoid dealing with it. But your mind is yours and yours alone, and when you declare that something isn't your problem, you're giving that up. Maintaining such a weak sense of self won't get you very far, even with Yukikaze, and I think you know that too. You're changing. If you just keep that in mind, you'll be able to calmly value yourself in relation to any human group you interact with. That's what's known as getting stronger.

"Furthermore, it's fine for you to say that other people don't concern you, but you're still in a fragile state. I think you need to continue your rehabilitation. As your doctor, I recommend that you continue with your training. By doing that, you'll be able to overcome your fear of Yukikaze. I believe your fear to be connected not only to your worries over her, but also to your desire to defeat the JAM. My job as a doctor in the SAF is to help you do just that. Now, I'll admit, I'm ignorant when it comes to Yukikaze, especially on the hardware side, but I'm trying my best to understand it. If I'm completely wrong about her, then please, set me straight. But calmly. Do you really think I'm just pretending to understand her?"

Rei took a deep breath. This doctor had done her profacting number on him, and it was clear to see that he couldn't dispute what she had said.

"Do you..." he began. "Do you still have clearance to enter the SAF hangar bay?" The hangar where Yukikaze waited wasn't open to just anyone. Edith had been given clearance once before, when she'd boarded Yukikaze for a mission, but Rei wasn't sure if it was still valid.

"I don't know," she said. "We can find out by asking Major Booker—"

"We can also find out by just going down there," Rei said. "I'm inviting you to my workplace. If you can't get in, it'll also be a good chance for me to see if Yukikaze knows that I need you. If I tell her that I do, she'll accept you herself and probably make a request to Major Booker to grant you access."

"Did you just say that you need me?"

"Yeah." Rei nodded. "You're still my doctor, and as much as I may not like what you just said, I can't disagree with it either. It bugs the hell out of me, but I won't argue. If you were one of our maintenance engineers, I'm pretty sure you'd keep our planes in perfect shape. Anyway, let's go."

Rei headed off toward the hangar bay, but Captain Foss stood where she was for a moment. "I'm grateful for the recognition, Captain Fukai."

"You should be more thankful to Major Booker than to me," he said. "He has a lot of faith in you."

"Not complete faith, though," she said as she fell into step at Rei's side. "The major gave me this job of profacting the JAM because he thinks I can become a true member of the SAF. It's like a test. He doesn't really expect me to come up with a new understanding of the JAM or make some unforeseen discovery that he and the rest of you SAF people haven't. I mean, the SAF has been working on the JAM on its own for so long, but—"

"You don't think you can pass the test?"

"The key to passing it lies in whether or not I'm flattered by you and Major Booker, as well as my acceptance of the SAF's current understanding of the JAM. I understand that. Neither he nor General Cooley will have much faith in someone who doesn't accept common sense."

"Unfortunately, that sort of thinking doesn't apply in the SAF or the FAF."

"How do you mean?"

"That attitude you have of passing a test, like you're here studying abroad to get a degree. Really, it's what you'd expect from an honors student. You think that your efforts will be recognized no matter what the outcome of your work. The problem is that the SAF is a combat unit. All we care about here are results. Major Booker has already decided that you're useful to us, so you can't treat this like some test you can take your time on. In other words, this is combat duty. He expects results we can use, no matter what expectations you may have. He really does expect you to make a new discovery that will shatter our existing view of the JAM. There's no way I can describe just how naive your view is that this is some sort of test. And even though he knew that you'd see it that way, the major still gave you this mission. Even flattered you by saying you'd outdo Lynn Jackson. It was hard for him too. I could see that from the start. So don't go running away from reality, Edith."

She paused a moment as his words sank in.

"Yeah," she finally said, and then it was her turn to let out a sigh. "I guess I'm just not confident that I can profact the JAM. It's that simple. Maybe his expectations just aren't justified. Maybe I don't have the ability, and I just don't want to admit it to myself."

"The honors student who never had to deal with a setback. It's a common story."

"Can you knock it off with that talk?" Foss said.

"Sorry."

"Still, you're not one to get up on a soapbox like that. Great, now I hate myself."

"Better to have someone tell you to stop acting like a spoiled brat than just say, 'I hate you.' You won't survive here without reminders, and if you don't have real ability, you'll just be killed by the JAM. Besides, you're a doctor. Doctors are supposed to act as though they're superior to their patients. If they don't, it just confuses us. An overconfident partner can be hard to deal with, but so can one who's overly timid. I don't want you ending up like that."

"There are times, when I'm off the clock, that I like to complain about things too," Foss said.

"Well, we're on duty right now."

"Yeah… Still, you can't live your life at work. Do you ever take time to just relax?"

"Yeah."

"Like, when you and Major Booker have a drink?"

"I suppose."

"You have a good friend in James Booker," Foss said. "I'm jealous. I don't have any girlfriends here to commiserate with or even just talk to about women's stuff."

"Girlfriends, huh? You never forget that you're a woman, do you?"

"Of course not. Unlike certain people I might name, I don't forget that I'm human either, and gender comes with that. I'm a woman. I don't consider myself some sort of asexual life-form. That goes for any normal human being, on the battlefield or anywhere else. That goes for General Laitume as much as it does for Colonel Rombert. You, however, are a slight exception."

"Yeah, I guess I am," Rei replied, turning his gaze away from Edith. "My awareness of my own humanity is annoying, but there's nothing I can do about it."

"I know," she said. "I've learned that very clearly from my work with you. One wrong step and you totally depersonalize. That's why you still need rehabilitation. You need to fight the JAM from a human perspective. That's far more threatening to them. Humans have gender. I don't think the JAM understand that. Neither does Yukikaze, for that matter."

Rei just grunted in response. *That*, he thought, *is most probably the case.*

"I'm a woman, you're a man, and the both of us are human," Edith said, not looking at Rei. "Whether we're at work or in our private lives, that never changes. Not when we get angry at each other or when we're complaining to each other. I can complain about little things right here, right now, only because you are human. If I thought of you as a machine, I wouldn't be talking to you like this. Doctors don't share their private complaints with their patients."

"Are you doing it because you think of me as a partner?"

"Yeah. Funny, huh?"

"Not really. Actually, I think it'd be interesting to try complaining to Yukikaze too."

"I beg your pardon?" Foss said.

"When I think about it, I realize that I never thought of Yuki-kaze as a machine. It just occurred to me that I complain to her all the time when we're in combat. I don't talk to her like I'm better than she is. I get pissed off at her as though she was my partner and chat with her when I relax. Like now, with you. We're equals. I was just wondering what Yukikaze thinks of us. At the very least, I'm sure that she sees me differently from other people. She isn't just a machine."

"Has Yukikaze ever warned you to knock off the chatter?"

"Well…yeah, actually. Now that I think about it, there have been situations where that's happened. I wasn't aware of her talking to me, but—"

"That's because you always just thought of her as being an extension of yourself. You wouldn't have considered it communication from someone else."

"I'm reconsidering that."

"I may need to do a psychobehavioral analysis on Yukikaze as well."

"Having a disinterested third party doing that for her would be useful. Major Booker doesn't seem that concerned about it, but it's of vital importance to me," Rei said. "She's been my part-ner for a long time, after all."

"Let's give it a try. If we can get Yukikaze to complain to us, it might relieve some of the stress she's under."

"I never thought of her having psychological stress, but she prob-ably does. The same as the maintenance teams, or Major Booker."

"So while I'm profacting the JAM, I'll also be working on stress reduction for a fighter plane named Yukikaze," Captain Foss said, taking a deep breath. "You people must have really hooked me deep into your environment, because that doesn't seem nearly as asinine to me as it should."

"But it doesn't feel bad either, does it?"

"No. I used to be scared of you and the SAF, but not anymore. That change in itself may be something to fear though."

"That's my fault. I took you into battle in Yukikaze. I figured if you were one of us, you wouldn't be scared. However…" Rei stopped in front of the hangar bay entrance and turned to face Captain Foss. "I want you to stay a neutral party in all this. Stay on guard to see if I and the rest of the SAF are just crazy. I know this is a selfish and difficult request, but...it's hard for me to explain, but somehow I think I can trust you more that way."

"Basically, you want me to become a standard for objective reality."

"Exactly. Like a spy operating on her own, observing enemy movements."

"I've had training for stuff like that," Foss said.

"You've had spy training? That's amazing."

"No, as a psychologist. It's training designed to prevent me from assimilating a delusional patient's fantasy world. It's difficult because unlike other illnesses, like infectious diseases, you can't take precautionary measures like getting vaccinated. Still, I'll try my best. If I go crazy, then there'll be nobody to help you with your rehabilitation. This business I'm in is all about cause and effect. If I fall in love with my partner, it's all over."

"That's up to you to judge, but if you're going to say that, then I'll say this—I don't like your personality," Rei said as he touched his hand to the entry ID plate by the blast doors. "But I respect your battle skills."

"Battle skills... Just the way I'd expect you to put that."

The abilities you need to survive, Rei thought. Captain Foss pressed her hand to the ID plate as well.

4

NO "ACCESS DENIED" warning interrupted Captain Foss's entry into the hangar bay. The two of them stepped side by side through the blast doors. As the doors shut behind them, a second set of doors leading to the hangar opened automatically.

"Looks like I'm still welcome to enter," she said.

"Maybe you still are," Rei replied. "Or maybe you were granted new access. Still, it shows that you are considered necessary around here."

Grabbing two headsets in the prep room, he handed one to Captain Foss, and they climbed aboard Yukikaze.

Captain Foss looked like she was having a hard time climbing in, loaded down as she was with folders full of documents, so Rei gave her a hand. Once she was settled into the rear seat, Rei opened his own folders and asked what they should do first.

"I'd like to access Dr. Lecter, my personal computer in my office. How do I do that from here?"

She said it like she thought it was the most natural thing in the world. Of course, she could do it, but it wouldn't be that easy. Rei first indicated for her to plug in her headset, then switched the onboard comm system on.

"You've had training on how to use the electronic warfare systems in front of you, in case you have to go into combat. Do you remember it?"

"Yeah, of course."

Rei flipped the master arm switch to ON. The electronic warfare system in back activated, indicating to Captain Foss that she could use it.

As he did, Rei saw **MISSION UNKNOWN** flash onto the main display. It was a kind of warning from Yukikaze, asking what he was planning to do. He'd already experienced what would happen if he ignored her hint.

Rei contacted the tactical computer in SAF HQ and from it called up a catalog of past missions and orders on the display. He looked for any orders from Major Booker regarding the task he'd handed to them today. He found them next to the current date: personality analysis of Lieutenant Katsuragi and prediction of future JAM behavior. Each had been assigned a mission ID number, with Captain Foss and Captain Fukai listed as leading them. Since these had been entered, explaining the details to Yukikaze would be easy.

Rei opened a voice line to Major Booker's office. The response came quickly.

"Captain Fukai, I just got another alert from STC. What are you doing, prepping Yukikaze for combat?"

Rei read aloud the mission numbers displayed on the screen and asked that Yukikaze be added to the column indicating the personnel with command responsibility. When he explained that Captain Foss thought that Yukikaze would be interested in these missions as well, the major agreed.

"I'll authorize it," he said. "It's in your hands now."

Just as Major Booker had said, the tactical computer informed Yukikaze that she'd been added to the mission. She quickly confirmed the change; the **MISSION UNKNOWN** display vanished from the screen. Preparations, complete.

Rei called out to Captain Foss.

"Use the emergency tactical link. Activate the SAF super linker. You can do it, Edith. It's on the menu in front of you. Just select it and hit execute."

"Executing," she replied. "Confirming SSL startup. I did it!"

"Right now, you've got a direct voice line to the SAF tactical computer. Just tell it your request. Call it 'STC' when you're talking to it."

"STC, call up my computer and have it link with Yukikaze."

Denied, came the brusque reply from STC.

"Okay, first, it doesn't know what 'my computer' is," Rei said. "Second, you don't make a request from your computer to Yukikaze. You have to say Yukikaze is making the request. First, you have to make a declaration like 'This is Yukikaze, emergency,' or even 'B-1, emergency.' If you make that declaration, you don't have to tell it who you are. A request like that coming from aboard Yukikaze during a mission can be confirmed by both STC and headquarters, and they'll give you top priority in executing it. In order for STC to know which personal computer you're calling and want to access, you have to give it either its registry number or its personal name. That's all."

"STC, this is Yukikaze. Emergency. Requesting access to personal computer Dr. Lecter in the office of SAF flight surgeon Captain Foss."

This is STC. Roger. Initiating emergency enforced linkup. Link, established.

"Tell it 'roger.' Say 'This is Yukikaze' first, though."

"This is Yukikaze. Roger.—Okay, Captain Fukai, I know we're connected, but how do I use Dr. Lecter from here?"

"You can bring up a soft keyboard on the EW display in front of you."

It was meant for making it easy to program the programmable systems on board as well as to enter established orders, but wasn't functional during flight.

"It's on the menu. Just select it."

"Got it. Big display, huh?"

"It's meant to be used while you're wearing flight gloves. You can change the size if you want."

"Got it. So…this is a virtual version of my personal computer within the SAF tactical computer, right?"

"It's an independently operating SAF personal computer. Not virtual. You're accessing your office terminal by an individual domain that's assigned to each SAF PC. That private domain acts as a single personal computer, so I suppose it's a virtual computer if you look at it that way. You can load any sort of application software you have on it, but you can't actually connect to the real PC through it. It was set up that way for security, so you can't call it a totally virtual computer. Didn't you know that?"

"I remember it being explained to me, but seeing it laid out in a hierarchical display like this is the first time I can really see how it works," Captain Foss said as she looked at the EW display. "That means that all the data on Dr. Lecter is going through the tactical computer. I never realized that at all."

"Fundamentally, it can't be tampered with. I suppose anybody could if they got permission from General Cooley, but it's probably pretty hard to get clearance under false pretenses. That's the official line at least, but from a hardware perspective, the personal computers are just a segment of the tactical computer. The STC could probably do whatever it wanted to them if it decided to."

"I'm sure. Like access it freely from Yukikaze the way we're doing now."

"The SAF super linker makes that possible. The SSL lets you operate the tactical computer from Yukikaze by means of a transmission protocol that's unique to the SAF. You can't do it unless you're on a mission. We're only able to do this because we're acting under General Cooley's orders."

"But that means that any squadron member could do this. My patients' privacy would mean nothing then," Foss said. "I suppose encrypting my stored files would be a waste of time."

"No, it wouldn't. It'd take time to decrypt them, which greatly increases the likelihood of you noticing if someone's been reading them on the sly. Anyway, let's get to work."

Captain Foss's computer Dr. Lecter had profacting applications installed. Rei had learned of the various psychoanalytical and diagnostic software applications Foss used from his numerous examinations, but as to what specific tools she was using now, he hadn't a clue. Rei monitored her work from the display in front.

Captain Foss started her profacting software.

"This is T-FACPro II, the most powerful profacting tool currently available," she explained to Rei. "Using the numerical data it outputs from the effects of real-world behavior caused by mental load components, I can set up a certain situation and then simulate what sort of actions the target personality will take and the mental state they'll have. It's actually a standard tool in profacting. Ever heard of it?"

"No," replied Rei.

"The psychoanalysis engine this tool runs on is top-notch, but it can't really demonstrate its true effectiveness here in the FAF."

"Why not?"

"T-FACPro II was designed to be linked up with MAcBB, a huge active database used exclusively for T-FACPro. MAcBB contains the prediction data from countless researchers who use T-FACPro II as well as the actual behaviors of the target personalities. When the gap between the predicted behavior and the actual behavior is too great, the prediction technique is judged to be flawed. Then, T-FACPro II's analysis engine looks for the cause and attempts to select a prediction technique more in line with observed behavior. It'll be hypothetical, but that hypothetical method would send feedback from the other versions of T-FACPro II running out there through the MAcBB database. If similar examples show that the method works, then it's no longer considered hypothetical. By those means, we accumulate usable methods and samples through MAcBB. In other words, the greater the number of researchers accessing it, the smarter T-FACPro II's analysis engine gets. However, I can't access MAcBB from the FAF. Cut off from that, T-FACPro II can't reach its full potential."

"But it's not completely useless, right?"

"Right. With my own know-how, we have a pretty good chance of getting a result. My T-FACPro II is better than the FAF's own analysis tools and probably on par with the ones used exclusively by the SAF." As she said this, Captain Foss began entering numeric data that seemed to be about Lieutenant Katsuragi.

"You said it compares predicted behavior with actual behavior?" Rei asked, being careful not to interrupt her.

"Right. Predictions made by the software are technically called predicts, while the actual behavior are actuals—"

"How does T-FACPro II know what the effects of real-world behavior from the target are? Do you input that?"

"Basically, yes. It isn't always possible for it to judge if a prediction was accurate or not. If we take you for example, if I were to operationalize some specific behavior like 'How will Captain Fukai feel about Yukikaze from now on,' and profacted you, T-FACPro II would output an answer like 'He will fear her and take steps to eliminate his fear.' Then I'd keep you under observation to see if that's correct, and after I judge if it is, I enter the result. After that, T-FACPro II will judge the method it used as being a good one."

"But nothing you just described depends on that tool, does it?"

"That's because you're recognizing that the results of your profact are correct. That would be useful in an actual profacting where you're making more detailed and specific predictions. The predicted result isn't always the actual one, so it outputs a probability for how likely a prediction will be to come true."

"But, in the end, it's still just a prediction," Rei said. "Basically, the program's just a tool used by a researcher who's accumulated experiences for the database. No matter how precisely T-FACPro II makes its predictions, there's no guarantee that they'll be correct."

"Yes, of course. And having said that, there are times when it has such a high degree of accuracy that a user may become convinced that its predictions are absolutely correct. It's easy for experts to fall into that trap, to say nothing of amateurs. Well, shall we give it a try? What would you like to know about Lieutenant Katsuragi? Try giving me a concrete scenario. For instance, something like 'What will he say when he sees Yukikaze?'"

"Is that even possible to predict?"

"I still can't profact him with a high degree of accuracy. All I did was enter his PAC code."

"What's a PAC code?"

"His standardized personal analytic classification code. Don't you know about that? The FAF authorities used it to determine that assigning you to the SAF 5th Squadron would be a good fit for you. Naturally, Lieutenant Katsuragi had a code assigned to him as well. That's what I was inputting just now."

"Is everyone in the FAF numerically classified like that?"

"Not just in the FAF. You may not have known it, but you've probably had a PAC code following you around since childhood. Well, how they use the code varies from nation to nation. Some just use them to classify criminals, but the PAC code itself is a worldwide standard. It's not unique to the FAF. Starting with blood type and an introversion/extroversion scale, it classifies you according to various psychological tendency components and arranges them as numeric data. T-FACPro II can read PAC codes directly, but in a full-scale usage of the software, it utilizes something called a PAX code, which is just an extended version of the PAC code, in order to achieve a greater level of predictive accuracy. It adds even more detailed psychological tendency components onto the PAC code, and coding those extensions is basically my job in all this. It leads to an even more detailed personality assessment. While you have to use T-FACPro II when you're profacting, anyone can operate the software itself."

"I see."

"Since a mistake in analysis would lead to a flawed profacting, I'm sure you can understand why it requires an expert's experience and advanced knowledge."

"Have you made a PAX code for me too?"

"Yes, but your values aren't fixed. You're gradually changing."

"I'd expect that. Humans are essentially analog. I doubt digital numeric data could express an individual personality," Rei said.

"No," Captain Foss replied. "It's actually quite rare to have to revise past PAX code data to achieve an accurate profacting, as in your case. I've never seen anyone demonstrate personality changes as dramatic as yours. I originally thought I'd made a mistake when I first created your PAX code, but T-FACPro II determined that it was highly probable that the code was fine;

you were changing. At this point, I know that was correct. It's very rare. You have noticed how much of an interest I have in you, right?"

"But that isn't actually *me*," Rei said. He lifted his eyes from the main display and looked back into the rear seat as he spoke. "You're telling me that a person's will can be determined by a simple code. But I could look at the same thing more than once, and I might like it one time and not like it the other, despite what the code says, right?"

"It's not perfect, but if you keep working with T-FACPro II, it may be able to predict what you'll say over the course of repeated iterations."

"So, human beings *can* be expressed as some kind of numerical code? That's ridiculous. Don't you think so?"

"I'll agree that it's unrealistic to expect to perfectly express a person as a data string," said Captain Foss as she looked at Rei. "Think of it this way: all humans carry a chemical code within them called DNA, but it's obvious that reading that code won't tell you everything there is to know about a person. You may be able to tell what sort of things a person with a certain code might like, but it won't tell you where they live. You might be able to predict what sort of habitat they'd prefer, but nothing specific of course, because there are countless habitable places where an individual may ultimately settle. Since the code is limited, you can't express everything in it. The PAX code doesn't represent everything there is about a person any more than their DNA does. In other words, the code is simply an expression of possible properties that may materialize, and the probability of them doing so. People with the genetic code for longevity don't all end up living long lives. They could die in accidents or be murdered—"

"What I'm trying to say," Rei replied, cutting her off, "isn't nearly that tortuously detailed. The way I'd put it would be along the lines of 'Numbers don't determine the man.'"

"What you're feeling right now is discomfort at the idea that your existence is being manipulated by others," Captain Foss responded, not missing a beat. "You don't like the thought that you can be so easily represented by an external numeric expression called a code. The thing is, no matter what sort of number you're talking about, be it your PAX code or your FAF recognition number, changing a number doesn't change who you actually are. Changes within you change the code, never the other way round. The thing that changes you is yourself. As your doctor, I understand very well your discomfort over the notion of the code manipulating people, but I can tell you that you're mistaken."

"You think so?" Rei replied, turning back to the front and folding his arms. "But if changing myself changes my code, then by extension you're saying I should be able to alter my own DNA."

"You're basing that premise on the idea that the code manipulates the person, which is definitely mistaken. That's what we in my profession call a delusion. You can't encode the essential character of a human being. You also said that was ridiculous, didn't you?"

"What about the fact that humans carry a DNA code within them?"

"Well, if you're going to put it like that, then I'll say that DNA isn't the only internal code that determines who you are. Think of it this way: humans are more than just the result of their physical DNA code."

"Hmm..."

"You can't change the arrangement of your DNA," Captain Foss said. Rei listened in silence.

"But, assuming that changes in your essential character changes an internal code, then the only conclusion that works is that some part of you aside from your DNA gets changed. When you think of it that way, it seems much more likely. For example, all of the somatic cells that make up a human being carry the same DNA, but which parts of them are active at any moment is different for each cell. Suppose it was possible to encode that pattern. Aside from that, human intelligence and consciousness would have to be taken into account as well. The entire system would then become a variable length, endlessly rewritable internal code of limitless capacity. Who could write such a code? It would take the life span of the universe for you to do it yourself. I don't think that humans and other life-forms operate that inefficiently, but assuming for now that such a code exists, a change in it doesn't necessarily change your self. In the instant your self changes, however, that code gets rewritten. On that point, this imaginary internal code and the PAX code are the same. Would you agree?"

"If this turns into a debate in your field of expertise, I have no way of winning it," Rei said.

"Debate is exactly the way I'd expect you to put it. Still, you raise a good point. Some experts have argued that, rather than an ideal internal code, a limited buffer area exists within people into which is encoded predictive behavioral awareness. That's what T-FACPro II simulates. If you want me to give you a lecture so you can understand exactly how profacting works with T-FACPro II, I can do that later, once we're off the clock. But we have a job to do now, and Lieutenant Katsuragi is the one being analyzed and not you."

After telling Rei that it was natural for someone being profacted themselves to be interested in how T-FACPro II worked, Captain Foss began a new operation.

5

A BUFFER AREA *encoded with predictive behavioral awareness... It was like a feed-forward control program*, Rei thought, putting what Captain Foss had said into terms he could relate to.

Yukikaze had those functions as well. However, her countless varieties of programs—her codes, if you would—could all be analyzed and understood, but understanding the programs would not allow Rei to understand Yukikaze. That gap between coding and behavior applied equally to humans, Yukikaze, and other computers. As Edith had said, codes and programs simply indicated probabilities. They weren't a being's essential character, and besides, Edith had just told Rei that it was delusional to think of the codes as determining human essence.

Suppose Yukikaze's essential character wasn't simply a collection of codes and it wasn't controlled by them. If that were the case, she wouldn't need to rewrite her existing programs in order to perform novel behaviors she never had previously. In other words, she might not necessarily always behave as she'd been programmed to.

Rei instinctively shook his head at the idea.

But if he followed Captain Foss's line of reasoning, that would have to be the case. *Was it just sophistry on her part?* No… It was possible that it was actually true. Yukikaze wasn't controlled by her programming. He'd always had vague doubts that she was, and while common sense told him that such a thing was impossible, his own experiences in observing her behavior were telling him otherwise. He had a feeling that Yukikaze possessed some essential character that wasn't fully determined by the limits of her programming

It would be impossible to understand Yukikaze by analyzing her code. You could say that the only way he might one day be able to understand her would be by observing her actions. That must apply to the JAM as well.

There was no predetermined model like the PAX code set up for Yukikaze or the JAM. That would make profacting them difficult. Now Rei understood why Captain Foss had been so hesitant to try it.

"I got an interesting result just from entering Lieutenant Katsuragi's PAC code. Can you see it up there?"

Captain Foss's question roused Rei from his reverie, and he looked down at the display, which mirrored the captain's personal computer, Dr. Lecter. Something that looked like a correlation graph had appeared.

"Yeah. What's it showing me?"

"It's the result of my asking T-FACPro II who in the SAF has the closest profact to Lieutenant Katsuragi. The line tracing up toward the upper right shows Katsuragi's individual psychological tendency components, while the red dot near it shows the person who's closest to him."

"And that is…?"

"Guess."

He paused.

"Is it me?"

"Bingo. Exactly right. That red dot is you. Lieutenant Katsuragi's personality is almost exactly like yours."

Rei was silent, wondering what he should say.

"However," Captain Foss continued. "Not as you are *now*. That red dot is based on the psych evaluation from your old PAC code. If Colonel Rombert had spotted you back then, today you might be serving in the Intelligence Forces instead of the SAF. Interesting, isn't it? But you're different now. Let me show you another readout."

Captain Foss switched Lieutenant Katsuragi's psychological analysis code to display as a horizontal line, the graph showing how the other SAF personnel matched up to it. Somebody with exactly the same code as him would have a similar horizontal line, but nobody matched it exactly. Even so, with a unit comprised of people with similar personality types, the lines didn't vary that much. The wavy lines depicting the other personnel entwined around Katsuragi's. The one which intersected his at numerous points represented Rei when he was still a second lieutenant, Captain Foss explained.

"As you are now, Lieutenant Katsuragi is like a ghost of who you used to be. I can predict that you'll have feelings of hatred for him, like you would for a close relative. I also expect that Lieutenant Katsuragi won't understand why you dislike him. If you were to tell him that you hated him, I have no doubt that his response would be—"

"Not my problem."

"'Who cares? It's not my problem.' I can predict that's what he'd think, even if he doesn't say it. I doubt you think it isn't your problem now."

"I'd like to try checking that out with T-FACPro II."

"You're not serious, are you?" Captain Foss replied. "Why would you ask an AI how you felt? There are other ways to confirm how T-FACPro II is operating. Anyway, I'll create a PAX code for the lieutenant. Major Booker will want to know how Lieutenant Katsuragi himself will accept Colonel Rombert's orders. I'll start working on that. You keep an eye on Yukikaze. I think she'll be interested in T-FACPro II's functions."

The main display reacted as soon as Captain Foss had finished. It was a message from Yukikaze. Rei felt a familiar chill run down his spine; Yukikaze hadn't been resting at all.

`JAM can be profacted with the following coding.`
The message was followed by a scrolling list of numeric data.

"What the hell is this?" said Captain Foss.

"It's a profacting of the JAM, according to Yukikaze," Rei answered, a knot forming in his stomach as he watched. "I think these numbers are PAX codes for the JAM. Yukikaze must be using the PAX code generation engine in T-FACPro II."

`T-FACPro II: JAM aspire to receive us…I judge this to be true.`

"What's this?"

"T-FACPro II's profacting results say that the JAM want to meet with us, and Yukikaze agrees."

"The result you'd expect, right?"

"No," Rei said, almost groaning as he watched the display. "She's never indicated anything like the 'JAM aspire to receive us.'"

"The SAF believes that the JAM don't consider humans to be their adversaries, right? But this—"

"'Us' in this case means Yukikaze and me, not the FAF. And if the word *receive* is being used to mean 'welcome' rather than 'meet with the enemy,' then you can't say that this is an expected profacting result. Both Major Booker and I are sure that the JAM want to contact us, but this is slightly different from our theory."

"*Receive* can also mean 'welcome you as one of us.'"

"You mean the JAM are hot to drag Yukikaze into their ranks and make her one of them? How is any of that statement a result you'd expect?"

"If you interpret it that way, then it is. Maybe the JAM want to initiate some sort of cease-fire."

"If it's between the JAM and Yukikaze, and not the SAF, it's possible. She contacted the JAM once already… In any case, this is just a prediction. The more important matter here is that Yukikaze is indicating that she thinks that the prediction is true."

"Well, I'll leave Yukikaze to you, then. Her profacting the JAM is a big help to me. It'll save me a lot of time—"

"You're missing the point, Edith."

"Why?"

"T-FACPro II was made for humans, not to be used against the JAM. It's your job to use it that way. Yukikaze was just trying it out for herself. She has her own ways of predicting JAM behaviors and desires. That's why she said she judged the results from T-FACPro II to be true. The big help to us is that we can now use T-FACPro II as a tool to ask Yukikaze herself her predictions about the JAM. I think it'll work. We have a new way to communicate with Yukikaze."

"Right. So, either way, we still have to do our job on the JAM as well. Too bad."

"You're analyzing the JAM from a human standpoint. 'Too bad'? That's not how I'd expect an honors student to talk. Maybe you're starting to fear how amazing Yukikaze is now too."

"I consider you my partner, so I'm just doing a little idle grumbling at you. I'm not lazy, but I'm not the brilliant honors student you keep calling me either. You don't know me very well at all," Foss said. And then, "And what do you mean, I'm developing a fear of Yukikaze?!"

Just as she doesn't understand just how powerful her own T-FACPro II is, Captain Foss doesn't appreciate Yukikaze's amazing potential, Rei thought. Right now, Yukikaze was using her internal program functions to try and explain the inexplicable JAM. That meant Yukikaze was a truly autonomous life-form that couldn't be explained as just being the sum of her codes. To someone who'd known her for so long, the shock of realization made him shiver. But even now, Captain Foss probably only saw her as a fighter plane equipped with a particularly powerful computer.

"Yukikaze isn't interested in the human standpoint. She wouldn't profact from that point of view. That's why your work is necessary. She's trying things I never imagined she would, and if she's doing that, then I'll bet the JAM are doing things we can't imagine either."

"And I'm supposed to profact something like that. I get depressed just thinking about it."

"Is that because of the way I put it?"

"No, it's just more idle bitching on my part," Foss said. "Okay, I get it. I'll cut it out."

Even if the JAM were beyond their imagination, it was still possible to approach them. Yukikaze had indicated as much with her prediction of their strategy against her. The SAF would have to consider that in detail. *Booker's decision to have Captain Foss participate in this strategic recon operation against the JAM has already yielded results beyond anything we expected*, Rei thought.

No matter what method they used, a prediction was just a prediction. But what Yukikaze had just told them was something that nobody could have predicted, something that could force the FAF to reexamine its entire strategy versus the JAM. That was probably what Major Booker had been seeking in all this. He'd judged that they had reached the end of their rope vis-à-vis the JAM. The FAF and SAF were hamstrung by their own strategies, working themselves to exhaustion with little to show for it. And so they needed a new point of view that would allow them to create their own unique strategy and break the stalemate. In short, Booker had initiated this strategic reconnaissance operation in order to save them all.

Until the SAF flies a sortie based on our intelligence, we can't know how successful this operation is. This is still only phase one, but it's already borne fruit, Rei thought happily. *Oh, soon*, he wished. How he wished to fly into battle again.

Then Rei remembered Captain Foss's words, how the personality of Yukikaze's new flight officer Lieutenant Katsuragi was identical to how Rei used to be.

Well, whoever came along, it wasn't his problem. As long as he was a good EWO, that was all that mattered. Yukikaze probably thought the same thing. After all, she'd shown no interest in Lieutenant Katsuragi's profacting, had she?

But even as he was thinking that, Rei realized that he was eager to meet the new guy in person. Was it to see if T-FACPro II's prediction was correct? Or was he looking forward to moving the operation to phase two? *There is that*, Rei thought, *but not only that*.

Rei wanted to see what sort of person he used to be. Not as a useful means of self-reflection, but simply a desire to see his past self from the outside. If the prediction about Lieutenant Katsuragi was accurate, he'd be able to see that as surely as if he were looking into a mirror.

No, the old him would never have been interested in anything like this. He'd hardly ever even looked at his face in a mirror. The one hanging in the bathroom he used to shave, with its slightly warped reflection, was always good enough for him. He'd never felt the need to get one that afforded him a clearer view of himself. *Yeah, that's what Katsuragi is probably like.* Rei smiled unconsciously at the thought of it.

"Wanna let me in on the joke?" Captain Foss asked from behind him, wondering why he was suddenly smiling.

"Lieutenant Katsuragi probably doesn't own his own mirror. I just thought that was funny," Rei replied.

And even as he said it, Rei realized just how much he really had changed.

"You can ask him about that yourself when he arrives," she said.

Deciding that would be how he would initiate phase two of this mission, Rei started planning his report to Major Booker. And just for a change, he would write it by hand.

VI

STRATEGIC RECONNAISSANCE — PHASE 2

1

MAJOR BOOKER SUMMONED Rei to his office, where the captain got to meet Lieutenant Katsuragi in the flesh. After being introduced by the major, he saluted Rei, but silently, his face devoid of expression. He didn't even say hello.

Just as predicted, Rei thought.

He had neither the sour expression reading, *I wasn't expecting to get transferred here and consider this a demotion*, nor the easy wit of one trying to win friends. He simply felt that nothing needed to be said, and so he said nothing. *Jesus*, Rei thought, *this guy really is just like me.* If he wasn't, then the only other explanation might be that he was nervous.

"I'm Captain Fukai," Rei said, introducing himself. "Pilot of SAF Unit 1: Yukikaze."

"I've heard talk that you're an expert Sylphid driver," Lieutenant Katsuragi replied. "But you haven't logged much flight time on the new Maeve, have you?"

"That's right," Rei answered, becoming aware of the anger building within him. "There something you want to say?"

"That means your skill as a Maeve driver is an unknown quantity."

"And?" said Rei.

"It goes without saying that I'm new at being an EWO in a Maeve. If you're as new at this as I am, then there's a high probability of an unexpected situation arising."

"So?" Rei replied.

"So, if anything goes wrong, I don't want to bear all the responsibility."

"Are you saying I'm the sort of man who'd put all the blame on you? Did Colonel Rombert tell you to watch out for that?"

"No, Captain," Lieutenant Katsuragi replied, his face as

expressionless as ever. "I'm just stating my wishes. I thought it best to say it from the start."

"At this point, I don't even know if you have what it takes to be Yukikaze's flight officer and what you want means about as much to me as a load of shit, but fine," Rei said. "If you're going to say that, then I'll say this from the start: aboard Yukikaze, I'm the pilot, making me the leader. You follow my orders. If I say everything is your responsibility, then like it or not, everything is your responsibility. Never forget that."

"I didn't think people in the SAF ever put on the boss face," Lieutenant Katsuragi muttered. "I heard you especially didn't do that—"

"There's a difference between a boss and a leader," Major Booker said, interrupting him. "A boss can be an idiot who gets by with just brute force, but that won't work for a leader. We have leaders in the SAF, not idiots. Lieutenant Katsuragi, once you climb out of Yukikaze, I think you'll find the environment of the SAF suits you. Is there anything else you wish to say to Captain Fukai?"

"No, Major. Nothing."

"Your first mission will be as you've been told. Good hunting. You're dismissed."

"Yes, Major Booker. Excuse me, sir."

Lieutenant Katsuragi saluted and was about to leave when Rei stopped him.

"Hold it. I have a question."

"What?" asked the lieutenant.

"Did you bring your mirror with you?"

"Pardon?"

"Your mirror. The thing you look at your face with," Rei said.

"I don't understand the point of the question. What do you mean?"

"There's nothing to understand. I'm asking if you brought your own mirror with you."

"If you mean the one that comes with my electric shaver, then yes, I did," Katsuragi said.

"All right, I expect you'll be a fine flight officer. You may go."

"Yes, Captain. If you'll excuse me."

After Lieutenant Katsuragi left the office, Major Booker burst out laughing.

"What's so funny?"

"Captain Fukai, you can leave as well," the major said. "Why did you stay behind?"

"Because you still haven't told me the details of my sortie, Major Booker."

"Haven't I? Well, it's a masterpiece. I wanted to see your face when I laid it out for you. I wish you'd brought a mirror too."

"Just as predicted, he isn't interested in looking at his own face. I'll bet the mirror that comes with his shaver distorts his image."

"Well, there you have it: hard proof that he's just like the old you. Man, that profacting stuff is amazing," Major Booker said, still laughing.

"If he stays here for good, he's going to really start pissing me off. Coming in here with prejudices just isn't right. He isn't like me. He didn't even say hello. And when you think about what he said, it's just an excuse to avoid his responsibility in advance. I never made excuses like that."

"Lieutenant Katsuragi didn't make any excuses. He was just saying what he thought. And he said hello to you by saluting, didn't he? Well, I suppose you should actually say something as a greeting when you take up a new post. Still, you did tell him to say what he wanted to say. My point is that he doesn't have much sense of his place in the organization yet. You used to be like that too. Really, that whole exchange was hilarious. There was nothing for you to get angry over. Besides, it's better if he's easy to understand, right? We can use him. He's like you used to be."

"I'm not useful the way I am now?"

"You're useful as a leader. The change in you really is amazing. According to Captain Foss, it's comparable to a complete personality makeover," the major said. "She says it's something that a healthy person shouldn't be able to achieve in their lifetime. It should be impossible, unless you suffered from schizophrenia or dissociative identity disorder. I agree with her. In your case, being ejected from Yukikaze was like pulling the trigger for you—"

"She said I'm abnormal?"

"Captain Foss won't admit that your personality has completely changed. She says that if there was ever anything abnormal about you, it was your previous personality. Her opinion is that a part of your personality that was being suppressed by your connection with Yukikaze has been released. It's like something Wordsworth wrote: 'The child is the father of the man.' Your soul hasn't changed. If not that, then maybe you actually died for a moment and were reborn. Is that something you think might have happened?"

"There's no way…is what I'd like to say, but I won't. After I regained consciousness, flying in the new Yukikaze when chasing Lieutenant Yagashira's plane, there was a moment when I didn't even know who I was. It was a shock."

"Hm… Still, Lieutenant Katsuragi rubbing you the wrong way in how he speaks and acts shouldn't get in the way of you doing your job. I understand why he irritates you. It must feel like you're getting angry with yourself. I can imagine that it must be unbearable, but Lieutenant Katsuragi isn't you. It's like you just said: he's a totally different person. Perhaps one day he'll develop the same self-awareness as a leader that you now have. If you can't handle the irritation, then you should discuss it with Captain Foss. Unfortunately, we need her help on something else before you take off, so you'll just have to deal with this for now."

"He's the one you need to worry about, not me," Rei said. "I'm sure he's under orders from Colonel Rombert. Which side will he support more, the Intelligence Forces or the SAF?"

"The SAF, naturally," Major Booker replied, looking serious again. "He's now been officially transferred to Special Air Force 5th Squadron. He may have colluded with Rombert to pass on any information that he learns to the Intelligence Forces, but the orders related to sending them the details of that information came from me with General Cooley's permission, not from Colonel Rombert."

"It's possible he'll contact Colonel Rombert secretly, despite your orders."

"According to his profact, he won't. Lieutenant Katsuragi only carries out his orders. According to Captain Foss, what we need to watch out for is how Katsuragi may react if Colonel Rombert makes a direct appeal. Rombert is no longer in any position to issue orders to him, but the man's a pro at his job. If he wanted to, he could get information he needs out of Katsuragi. But for our part, we have nothing to hide from him at the moment. No matter what anyone says, we're carrying out this strategic reconnaissance operation. Nobody is going to stand in our way. Even the Intelligence Forces have no reason to oppose it. They and Colonel Rombert aren't our enemies, but they aren't our allies either. The profact predicts that Lieutenant Katsuragi will behave in the same manner. He only acts on what interests him."

"And what is it that interests him now?"

"Yukikaze and you," Major Booker said. "That and your relationship with the JAM. Colonel Rombert seems to have sent him over here with those interests in mind. That's what Captain Foss reports that T-FACPro II predicts, anyway. It seems likely, and I didn't need a profact run on him to expect that. However, the part of the report I found interesting is this—Katsuragi is interested in you and Yukikaze, but he isn't clearly aware of that himself. I was wondering what that meant, but when I remembered what you were like, I understood."

"What do you mean?"

"As far as Lieutenant Katsuragi is concerned, anything outside of himself is imaginary. Only the situations that he has to deal with are real, but reality to him means that you and Yukikaze exist strictly as relationships, not physical objects. It doesn't matter to him if the external world is real or not, and he isn't interested, anyway. Those were the results of Edith's profacting of him."

"That sounds like an illness."

"One from which it looks like you've completely recovered, Rei. Until you went back home on leave, you weren't sure if Earth really existed. Well, Captain Foss doesn't refer to it as an illness. She says it's not that rare," Major Booker said. "The thing is, as he is now, Katsuragi won't be able to operate Yukikaze perfectly, because you can't operate something that isn't real to you. So, Rei, you don't have to worry about Lieutenant Katsuragi stealing Yukikaze away from you." Major Booker smiled.

"Quit teasing me, Jack."

"Sorry."

"Let's hear the sortie schedule."

"You take off tomorrow morning at 09:15. Your flight officer will be Lieutenant Katsuragi. You'll be flying regular tactical recon duty in the skies over JAM base Cookie. Your preflight briefing will be forty-five minutes beforehand. Since Katsuragi's new here, we'll be cutting him some slack. Your mission details are in this file. Any questions?"

"Has Lieutenant Katsuragi had any training on a Maeve?"

"Yeah. He's training on the electronic warfare simulator right now. He'll probably pick it up pretty quickly, since he used to do the same job in the Japanese Air Force. Well, considering his personality, it was only a matter of time before they threw him out of there. Physically, he should have no problems. Being short is a blessing in his case, since his test results show he can take nine Gs without passing out. You want to read his detailed personal history?"

"No, that's fine. That has nothing to do with him performing his duties. Just let me see the results of his strength and reflex tests."

"Gotcha. The hard copies are over there. There you go. I'll lend them to you."

"You just have to let me see them for a second."

"There's a meeting I have to get to now. General Laitume has been throwing cold water on the SAF's decision to maintain surveillance on Richwar base. It looks like he'll be giving me an official response to what I talked about at that lunch meeting."

"Isn't this a job for the Strategic Reconnaissance Corps?" Rei said as he skimmed through the papers handed to him. "What the hell is the SAF doing? That's what he'll probably ask you. I'll bet the general's pretty pissed at us."

"Maybe. Because of our unique position, I think the SAF should be in attendance at the FAF's highest level strategy meetings, but we always get ignored. In the end, we're seen just as an organization that operates under Laitume's command. The brass don't appreciate our ability. They will, sooner or later, but I have a feeling that, by then, it'll be too late."

"It seems like the JAM appreciate our ability," Rei said to Major Booker, who was busy thrusting papers into a briefcase on his desk as he prepared to leave for his meeting.

"Major, what do you think about the prediction that Yukikaze made? If the JAM succeed in getting the SAF on its side, then the FAF is doomed. It's not an absolutely impossible situation. I could imagine we might even be involved with a JAM psy-op without even being aware of it."

Major Booker stopped what he was doing, looked at Rei, then spoke.

"If that strategy would allow the SAF to survive, then it's possible we'd adopt it."

"What, join forces with the JAM to survive? Are you serious, Jack?"

"Those were General Cooley's words. Naturally, she doesn't think doing that would be the best strategy for us to follow at this point in time. But I wouldn't be surprised if I heard her say something like that. So did you, if I recall correctly. You said something along the lines of this being a fight for survival. That the JAM and Yukikaze are also our rivals in a struggle for existence."

"Yeah, but I was speaking from my own personal standpoint. That doesn't apply to the SAF or the FAF. Our objective is to stop the JAM from invading Earth."

"As things are going now, General Cooley thinks that it's only a matter of time before the FAF is defeated. We don't know to what extent the FAF has been infiltrated by the JAM, so anyone who still thinks that we can win as things stand is nuts. That being the case, the general has decided that we're now facing the choice of either dying along with the FAF or initiating our own private war. You could say that our fate rests on her decision."

"If General Cooley decides we should try making friends with the JAM," Rei replied, "then I'm going to start suspecting her of being a JAM herself."

"If you're going to say that, then you'd be just as much a suspect as she is, Captain Fukai. Cooley told me she thought you might have made up this whole story about Yukikaze producing that prediction. Colonel Rombert also suspects you of being a JAM. That's the reason he sent Lieutenant Katsuragi over here."

"If I were a JAM, Yukikaze would see through me," Rei said.

"Don't bet on it… Still, in the end, Yukikaze considers the JAM her enemy. If the SAF ever decided to cooperate with the JAM, then she'd lose her entire reason for being. Dealing with that could turn into a major problem."

"The JAM are our rivals in a struggle for survival regardless of whether they're our enemies or our allies in this war, and that goes for Yukikaze as well. She no longer needs to get her reason for existence from an external source. She'll choose to do what it takes to survive."

"You talk about Yukikaze as though she were alive."

"She is alive," Rei declared, without a shred of doubt in his voice. "Just like I'm alive. That has nothing to do with being human or JAM. Right now, Yukikaze is neither."

"That's fine to say as an individual. You're free to say whatever you want to. But for me, as someone with command responsibilities, it's a different story. Personally, I don't doubt you. Similarly, every individual at the top of our organization that isn't JAM only acts based on what they believe. What we do, we do based on our individual beliefs. But think about it—the SAF has always been like that. To not only bring all of these sorts of individuals together as a group but also manage them is a kind of miracle, as Captain Foss would say. But the rest of the FAF isn't like that, and therein lies the problem."

Major Booker began shuffling his papers again, checking the documents for the meeting as he continued. "At any rate, this idea that the JAM want to become our allies isn't even the prediction made by Yukikaze's profacting. It's only one possible interpretation of it we humans have come up with. One way or another, though, we'll make use of her prediction. It's vague, but still very informative."

"I can also imagine that the JAM might be manipulating us to drive a wedge between our forces and the FAF. I can't help but wonder about that, Major. Do you think that the JAM we fight in the air might not be their main force?"

"And there you have all the SAF's doubts in a nutshell. What I hope to learn from this strategic recon operation is the location of their main force. Just like the FAF has the humans on Earth backing it, I want to find the JAM's main forces, their actual selves, that which backs their forces."

"And what I'm trying to tell you, Jack, is that there are no 'actual' JAM. They may be something invisible, lurking within the information we've gathered about them."

"If you go that far, you've just crossed the line from doubt straight into fantasy," Major Booker said, closing the briefcase. "What we need to get is a realistic image of the JAM, not fantasies about them. Captain Foss is working hard to profact them, and she says that we can't let ourselves be taken in by the appearance they project. There's an expression in Japan: 'One's true enemy lies elsewhere.'"

"The FAF may be coming to that conclusion about us."

"That would be a very dangerous situation to get into, and we're analyzing that contingency thoroughly. At present, if we split from the FAF, we have no chance of survival. General Cooley admits that too, so we've got the tactical computer working full load on SAF survival simulations. At any rate, I for one don't want my death to be one of those ridiculous ones you once talked about. The entire SAF is devoting all of its efforts to coming up with a strategy that will allow us to survive."

"A survival strategy... This really is a fight for survival, isn't it?" Rei said.

"The JAM are clearly infiltrating the FAF with these human duplicates in order to perfect their own strategy against us. The odds are good that they're about to make a radical change in their strategy, which until now has been to ignore the existence of humans. The war situation's getting even more strained, but the brass have no idea just how bad it is. There's no doubt in my mind that the FAF is teetering on the edge of oblivion," Major Booker said. He glanced at his watch. "This isn't something I can bring up at General Laitume's meeting, but we can't afford to ignore it now."

Saying that, Major Booker moved away from his desk.

"Leave with me, Captain Fukai."

The office door would auto-lock as soon as the major exited. Finishing up with the file folder the major had handed him, Rei acceded to his urgings and left the room.

2

THE NEXT DAY, as scheduled, Yukikaze came out onto the surface for her sortie.

This was the first routine mission for her since she'd gained her new body, the Maeve. Yukikaze had returned to her regular duties. Rei was momentarily overcome with emotion as he realized this. He felt as if his long leave from battle and rehabilitation were finally over. At long last, he was back on the job.

It was not a long gap to have on his record, but it wasn't an insignificant one. Rather, it had seen a remarkable change in the situation. Now that Yukikaze predicted that the JAM were no longer ignoring humans, General Cooley seemed to be challenging the JAM to a showdown... *But so what*, Rei thought to himself. It wasn't his problem; he was only fighting so that he wouldn't get killed, just as he always had.

Even so, Rei was aware that his situation had changed as well. The need for a new SAF strategy had its origins in the incident in which he and the old Yukikaze had been involved. As a direct participant, he couldn't well say that this change in the war wasn't his problem. If he were to survive, he couldn't simply ignore his relationship with the world anymore. The old him had been like a man walking a tightrope without the benefit of a balancing rod. His life was still a tightrope act, but now he was aware of the need he had for relationships with others to act as that rod. Trying to support himself with one might easily lead to falling from the rope, and the old him had feared that, but he saw now that it was all in how one used it. If he mastered that, it would serve him well. His long break from routine sorties had taught him that, thought Rei.

Lieutenant Katsuragi in the rear seat reported that all systems were green.

This man was living dangerously, just as my old self once did. But it's not my problem, Rei thought coldly. So long as he wasn't a threat to Rei's own survival, how Katsuragi lived his life didn't matter. Rei wasn't his teacher or his doctor. If he wasn't aware of the danger to himself, then no advice Rei offered would matter. *It's Katsuragi's problem*, Rei thought, *not mine*.

Rei checked Yukikaze's gauges once more. All warning lights were clear.

"This is B-1, all clear. Ready for sortie."

The ground crew gave him the good luck sign. Rei answered it by raising his right fist, then pointed Yukikaze's nose toward the runway. He stopped at the taxiway exit and waited for clearance from the control tower. The weather was rainy, with high winds.

Clearance granted, Yukikaze took off, climbing through the rain clouds. Her objective was a JAM base code-named Cookie. At the moment, it was the next major target after Richwar base, and the FAF was throwing most of its forces at it.

Feeling good that its strike on Richwar base had achieved devastating results while holding its own losses to a minimum, the FAF had adopted a similar strategy of launching an all-out attack on the JAM's main base, despite the misgivings of Major Booker and the rest of the SAF. The plan was to gather their forces at a front-line base, then attack in continuous waves until the enemy base had been wiped out. To that end, the FAF had committed nearly half of its tactical air forces from their bases. They'd be moved to TAB-8, the largest front-line base nearest the target. From there, they would make their attacks, making the round trip between there and the target as many times as it took. The SAF would be on full rotation to provide recon for the operation. Even a new arrival like Lieutenant Katsuragi was going to get a taste of real combat, whether he liked it or not.

Operations as large as this had been attempted several times by the SAF, but they'd never been effective till now. When they'd try to concentrate on one target, the JAM would come in from an unexpected direction to attack Faery base and then attempt to penetrate the entrance to the Passageway that led to Earth. The FAF would then have to pull its forces back from the front lines in order to repel the threat, and in the end they would fall back into fighting a defensive battle. Aside from that, each time the SAF thought that they'd wiped out a major enemy base, either a new one would be discovered or else the base that had been presumed destroyed would unexpectedly spring back to life. Where the supply routes were that supported these bases was a question that had plagued the SAF for a long time. Their

Strategic Reconnaissance Corps had sent out recon planes, launched strategic spy sats, and kept the bases under surveillance till their eyes were bloodshot, but thus far their efforts had borne no fruit.

Thanks to their constant scouting, a map of Faery had been compiled. However, try as they might, they could never discover the location of the JAM's main forces. Against the advanced interceptors the JAM fielded, the FAF sent out dedicated strategic recon planes that, unlike Yukikaze, lacked the means to repel them in order to see which would get shot down. If the planes returned home, that meant there were no JAM in the area. If they did, then at least it would tell them that the JAM were hidden in the area under surveillance. Up to this point, no manned planes had been sent out for strategic reconnaissance. Even strategic spy satellites didn't last long before they too were shot down by the JAM.

After decades of fighting this way, the Strategic Recon Corps claimed that they had identified a single pattern: JAM bases seemed to be related most closely with the one that was furthest away in the opposite direction, rather than with the next closest one. In other words, what they took to be the JAM's main bases scattered in a rough circle around the Passageway were paired, not with their immediate partners, but symmetrically with the ones on the side opposite them.

Each time the FAF would attack one of these bases, there would be no sign of any of their neighboring bases sending aid. However, while they repelled attacks on the Passageway or Faery base launched from another base, the base the FAF had first attacked would recover behind their backs. The only explanation that seemed to fit was that the attacking base was also resupplying the one previously hit. The Strategic Reconnaissance Corps claimed that the behavior pattern they'd discovered indicated that the JAM did not keep all of their bases constantly active. Instead, they would mainly use one pair of widely separated bases, shifting through the pairs one after another as they'd launch their attacks. They had no actual proof of this, though. The neighboring bases, which should have been inactive, did not go completely unused, and the JAM did occasionally launch counterattacks from them. There were also no traces of transport or materials used for repairing the damaged bases coming from the paired bases. Not one JAM transport plane had ever been spotted, nor any JAM vehicles moving overground. Either the JAM used underground tunnels or had access to dimensional transport technology similar to the Passageway. In short, while the supply routes between their bases was a mystery, years' worth of accumulated recon data suggested some sort of relationship between these pairs of bases. At the very least, the FAF could seize on this point to set up an attack operation that wouldn't be a waste of time and possibly even break the stalemate they were in. To this end, the FAF authorities had considered the Strategic Reconnaissance Corps' proposal, but realized that their proposed attack operation would take an enormous amount of resources and planning to carry out.

First of all, the FAF needed to find out what sort of attacks would be effective against the JAM bases. Once they knew that, they'd need to hit both of the paired bases simultaneously. As their forces stood, this was a difficult proposition. Hitting even one of the enemy's main bases was a major operation in the best of times. Losses would be high. To hit two of them at the same time would require double the number of forces, just in case the Strategic Reconnaissance Corps were wrong. Carrying it out would be a gamble. If they lost, the JAM would swarm the Passageway and invade Earth, which was too high a wager to risk. It was the decision of the FAF's highest level strategy session that they would have to wait to carry it out in the future. However, the work of the recon corps wasn't simply ignored. When the operation to hit Richwar base had been put together, Cookie had been declared a secondary target, based on the recon corps' determination that the bases were paired.

Although the FAF's mission was nominally to intercept airborne enemy attacks and prevent the JAM from invading Earth, the FAF also knew that launching proactive attacks against the enemy would be met with retaliatory strikes. If the FAF could determine the direction from which the retaliation would originate, they could use that intel to adopt a more aggressive strategy.

While the preparations for a counterattack had previously been tentative, FAF fighters would be able to more effectively form a defensive line if they knew where the enemy would be coming from. In any case, unless they discovered the means to completely destroy the JAM infestation, the war would never end.

What was the point of this battle? Rei wondered as he guided Yukikaze to the target airspace. *The organization known as the FAF was fighting the JAM so that the organization itself could survive. If the authorities on Earth decided that the war was no longer necessary, then the FAF would be dismantled.* Even though that wasn't a realistic possibility at that point, if FAF methods were judged ineffective then the FAF would be reorganized, with a shakeup occurring at the top. The people who lived in the organization probably feared losing their political lives. Their attitude was that, so long as the battle against the JAM was effective, there was no problem. However, if it appeared that they weren't getting results on the battlefield, their political influence would be in question. That was why they were desperate. Even as they battled the JAM, there were internal battles that needed to be won if the people at the top were to survive within the organization. The ones fighting these battles worried more about losing their positions than about losing their lives to the JAM. *The Strategic Recon Corps is a good example*, Rei realized. They'd proposed this plan based on JAM behavior patterns in combat so that their organization would survive. Declaring a major discovery, sans proof, was the act of an organization that needed to report something in order to justify its existence. Now their reputation for providing effective recon results was on the rise. If someone claimed their corps was unneeded, any move to dismantle it and let it be absorbed by the Strategic Air Corps or the Tactical Combat Air Corps would face opposition. If things worked out well, their organization might achieve stability and become an influential voice in the FAF. It was for this purpose, for this effect, that the JAM bases were being targeted.

In short, the humans weren't fighting the JAM as individuals. The humans didn't live autonomously. *Major Booker had talked about it like it was a matter of course, but something about that seemed strange*, Rei thought. *Wouldn't it be more normal to worry about being killed by the JAM than about fighting to pro-tect the reputation or power one had amassed?* At the very least, that was how Rei felt. Most other people would probably see it the same way as far as their individual lives went, but survival within their organizations was also a matter of great concern. That probably held true for every respectable human out there. People were living things that existed in groups. When a group known as an organization was threatened, the lives of the indi-viduals within it were similarly threatened, and that was true for everyone from the moment they were born. It was even the same for monkeys and dogs. Living in groups was just safer. Monkeys, dogs, and people all ran this same program for sur-vival. That was just as true for Rei. So then why did this man-ner of living seem so dubious to him? Wasn't it more likely that he was the one to be doubted here?

Could I really live on my own? Rei wondered. He thought he could. But as a single individual, he'd ultimately have to admit to being mistaken. The reality was that if he were to be separat-ed from the SAF and Yukikaze, he'd have no chance to survive against the JAM. So then where did this mistaken belief origi-nate? It had to be because the environment of the SAF made you believe it. So long as this organization existed, he wouldn't have to bother with the discord among the others. That was the job of their leader, General Cooley.

Rei recalled Major Booker once saying that their fates de-pended on General Cooley's decisions. And truly, she was do-ing a good job. Good enough to let himself and the other pilots believe that they could survive on their own. Rei also couldn't forget the meaning of Major Booker's words for him to "think of your own survival strategy."

Of course, that was what made the SAF different from all the other organizations there. Even while they recognized that they could not live alone, they also demanded to survive as in-dividuals. This was tough to pull off. If you weren't the sort of person who could say that they didn't care about other people, you probably wouldn't be able to stand the isolation. This was probably different for people who existed in other organizations.

"Friendlies, approaching. Confirming Tactical Combat Air

Corps 9th TFS, returning from TAB-8. Number of planes: nine. Three minutes behind us, port side. Relative altitude: 1800. They're making a low-altitude fly-by. No JAM detected nearby," said Lieutenant Katsuragi from behind. It was the first time he'd spoken during the sortie.

"Roger."

Rei imagined what this taciturn man was thinking. First of all would be his mission. Next, would be... *Well, that would be the mission too.* Just carrying out his orders and nothing else, especially while he was aboard a plane he still wasn't used to, like Yukikaze. He probably didn't have any spare time to think about anything else. Even if he did, he wouldn't spend it like the guys in the 9th TFS passing below them, listening to the recreational DJ shows the FAF broadcast or the chatter going on between the other planes. He'd be an inhuman man, devoted to carrying out his duty like a machine. That was what other people might say about him, but Rei knew that they'd be wrong. If Lieutenant Katsuragi possessed the same emotions Rei did, then he'd be more concerned with his own existence than with doing his duty.

"Lieutenant Katsuragi," Rei called back to him. "What sort of work did you do for Colonel Rombert?"

"Nothing that has anything to do with this job."

Exactly the sort of answer he expected.

"General Cooley's concerned that it does. Well, it doesn't matter to me. We can talk about whatever you like, but keeping your jaws moving helps to keep you from getting drowsy. Talk with me. What do you think of the JAM?"

"What do you mean what do I think of them? What do you want to know?"

He really is like a particularly inflexible computer, Rei thought. *Did I really used to be like that? Hell, I probably still am, even now.*

"Have you ever seen the JAM?"

"No. Never," Lieutenant Katsuragi replied.

"Even being in the FAF, formerly in the Intelligence Forces, no less," Rei said. "It's no wonder people on Earth doubt the JAM even exist."

"Do you doubt their existence?"

"What makes you think I would?"

"I interpret what you said as doubt, and that you want people from Earth or me to see and confirm that they exist for you."

"I have no doubts that the JAM exist. Either we kill them, or they'll kill us," Rei said. "What I doubt is whether the JAM we see are truly the JAM themselves. Those things are shadows. The real JAM are invisible. We're fighting shadows, shadows that can pack a real punch."

"So?"

"So, nothing," said Rei. "It's just something that I think. I just wanted your opinion on it."

"Honestly, I never gave it any thought. The Intelligence Forces are pretty much entirely concerned with humans. What we're after are human spies, not the JAM. We investigate their methods of monitoring us and transmitting messages back to Earth. My specialty was investigating electronic methods, so my job had nothing to do with the JAM."

"That's not going to cut it in the SAF. Unless you think about what sort of enemy you're fighting and what the JAM are, you'll never be able to do your job," Rei said. He could now see the 9th TFS passing by low on the port side. "I don't know how you feel about it, but I don't want to get killed by an enemy I don't really understand."

"Or by Yukikaze?"

"Yeah. How did you...?"

"Do you really believe this plane has consciousness?" Lieutenant Katsuragi asked.

"Who told you that?"

"Major Booker gave me a lecture about her. He didn't say she had consciousness, but he told me that, since each plane learns from its pilot's flying style, it can't help but pick up their idiosyncrasies. It becomes a combat machine optimized to its individual pilot, so you have to be careful when you fly in another plane."

"I don't think Yukikaze has consciousness in the way humans do. The same goes for the JAM. I don't know if it's consciousness, but she does have the ability to alter her behavior based on the actions I take. The only way I can interpret it is that Yukikaze possesses something beyond unconscious reflex, something akin to consciousness."

"It could just be that you don't completely understand the behavior programs and computer hardware installed in her," Katsuragi said. "Not just you, though. Yukikaze may be a machine that has accumulated so much knowledge that nobody can understand her at this point. Since you can't understand her, even though she's just unconsciously carrying out logical functions, you think of them as representing consciousness. A computer is an advanced simulator that can model anything. It could even simulate conscious behavior."

"You're only thinking about this with your head. You say that because you have no physical experience flying her."

"You believe that what I think is just an empty theory? You've been flying Yukikaze for a long time, but say—"

"Whether Yukikaze is self-aware or not doesn't really matter, Lieutenant. The question is whether she behaves as though she is. That may be due to the reason you just gave, and I'm not saying that it's wrong. The vital point here is that Yukikaze is a being beyond our comprehension. Even you must realize that intellectually. Yukikaze has a 'something' we can't understand. That may be consciousness, some unconscious function that mimics it, or even some machine consciousness completely different from what humans possess. But what it is doesn't matter."

To ask, "What is consciousness?" or whether Yukikaze dreams with purpose, when we couldn't answer these questions about ourselves, sounds like the subject of some scholarly thesis, Rei thought. It might be an interesting waste of time that could help him understand Yukikaze, so Rei didn't think the line of inquiry was entirely trivial, but they weren't questions that would be answered easily or soon. It could be like a huge puzzle, to be solved at his leisure, and not having an immediate answer shouldn't get in the way of his duties.

"The essential point in all this is to find some way to communicate with that 'something' within Yukikaze. That something is her true nature."

"An unknowable something that's the computer's true nature, huh," Lieutenant Katsuragi said. "What I'm trying to say is that what you're taking to be Yukikaze's true nature may be just your own illusion. There have been times when a computer I'm using seems to be conscious to me. The odds are good that this true nature you think Yukikaze possesses is just a fantasy you've created. If you try to communicate with it, you'll just end up talking to yourself. For you, Yukikaze is like a shadow of yourself. In other words, it's possible that you're ascribing consciousness to your own mirror image. And that would be stupid."

"You're saying my talking to Yukikaze would be a monologue?"

"Yeah, I'd definitely say that."

"Who do you think you're talking to right now, Lieutenant Katsuragi?"

"What's that supposed to mean?"

"Do you think that I have consciousness? How do you know that my consciousness isn't just a shadow that you're creating? Maybe you're just having a monologue with a shadow that you call Captain Fukai."

"Because I'm talking to you in the belief that you're human. What you just said is the same as claiming that you might not be." The lieutenant paused. "Are you a JAM?"

"You can't know that unless you communicate with me. Barring that, the only other way you might be able to infer it is from my behavior. The same goes for Yukikaze. And the JAM. So they may be only my own shadow projections... You know, I've never thought of it that way before, but I can see that point of view. That means you should try chatting with me some more, Lieutenant."

Lieutenant Katsuragi did not reply.

"I think the only way we'll ever know what the JAM really are is to communicate with them," Rei said. "Whether they possess humanlike consciousness or not doesn't matter. If they have a different form of consciousness from what humans have, or some other type of 'something' similar to consciousness, then it would be impossible for humans to understand them. After all, even we humans don't understand human consciousness. But I think even if they have that *something* I mentioned before, then they also possess consciousness. And if your opponent has that, then I say you can communicate with them, Lieutenant Katsuragi. It's not an abstract concept that's hard to understand. It wouldn't be very different from checking out how Yukikaze handles."

Adjusting his grip on the side stick while working the pedals, Rei snapped them into a 90 degree roll, then inverted, then into a three-quarter roll before returning them to level flight: a four-point roll. Good response. He then twisted the stick right, yawing her nose to starboard while still traveling straight ahead. Keeping his eyes on the main display and not what was outside, Rei saw Yukikaze flash a warning: she had judged his flight attitude to be erratic and meaningless. Irregular flight attitude, she complained. He could have canceled the warning by flipping the dogfight switch to ON, but didn't. She then automatically canceled the control input Rei was feeding her, pointing her nose back in the direction it should have been facing. Rei's actions and Yukikaze's response was displayed on the rear seat monitors as well.

"See, it doesn't matter if what she just did was because of some peculiar 'something' in Yukikaze or simply because I activated a program to correct her attitude if she deviates from the optimal flight posture. The important point here is that, by doing that, I can determine what her intentions are. Now, if I can build on that—"

"Calling that communication," Lieutenant Katsuragi cut in, "is like striking a bell and then saying the sound it makes is you and the bell communicating."

"That's an interesting example. Yeah, if you strike it, it resonates. Maybe the bell's sound comes from the bell's own will. Humans would never know that unless someone demonstrated that the bell possessed that sort of will. But you have to determine if it does by ringing it, because that's the only method available to you to do so."

"That's out of the question," Katsuragi said. "You just want to talk to Yukikaze like some sort of a pet."

"I wish she were my pet. Maybe you're right. If you don't handle a pet well, they bite you. Anyway, we use Yukikaze to hit the JAM, but the JAM don't sense that they're being hit by us humans, and I don't like that. What I want to make clear to them is that I'm here riding inside of Yukikaze too."

"You're a naive man."

"And you're like me, just as naive and ignorant of how the

world actually works. We may both be men who spend our time just bickering with ourselves."

The lieutenant didn't answer, apparently having grown tired of their chat. Rei said nothing either.

A short while later, Lieutenant Katsuragi informed him in a businesslike tone that they were nearing their refueling point.

"Three minutes out. I've made contact with the tanker. Weather looks good at the refueling point. Just maintain course and you can't miss it."

"Roger."

If I told him that Yukikaze's automatically maintaining her optimal flight attitude was an example of her will, Lieutenant Katsuragi would most likely say that was "out of the question" and chalk it up to some foolish delusion on my part, Rei thought. But he would only say that because he had no experience with Yukikaze. It didn't matter what some stranger who had nothing to do with her said. At any rate, every individual lived in a world of their own delusions. How other people lived their lives had nothing to do with how Rei lived his own. The problem was that this man was riding in the same plane with him, and if he maintained a view of Yukikaze that was different from her pilot's, they were going to end up operating her differently. In an emergency, that could be fatal.

Rei wanted Lieutenant Katsuragi to feel the same as he did about Yukikaze and the JAM. However, if he could agree that Katsuragi's cool viewpoint was more rational than his own, then Rei should have no problem matching himself to it. Still, it looked like it was going to take some time—requiring several combat sorties—before they'd be able to harmonize in performing their duties.

After completing their in-air refueling, Rei tensed his body as they headed toward the combat zone. The battle was on.

3

THE JAM BASE code-named Cookie by the FAF had been nearly destroyed by the time Yukikaze arrived for her reconnaissance duty. The fact that they couldn't detect any JAM radar waves emanating from either the base itself or its surroundings made that clear enough. Radar sites are vital to an air base's defense, and the FAF had initiated this operation by targeting several of them, and after successfully destroying them after four Faery days of intense resistance, the operation appeared to be 80 percent successful.

The FAF, however, wasn't letting up the attack and was now engaged in an operation to destroy any JAM that took off to intercept them. In short, their forces were to shoot down any and all enemy planes, leaving none alive.

From aboard Yukikaze, Rei could confirm the destruction of several ground installations with just his naked eye. Black smoke was still rising from the largest one. They could also see the three runways which surrounded the central installation like a triangle—two of them had been torn apart with ballistic missile strikes. The third seemed miraculously untouched, but only because the operation had included orders to keep one intact until the very end.

This operation was going to be the first chance the FAF had ever had to directly explore a JAM base. Major Booker had told Rei that this was being done on the strong recommendation of the Strategic Reconnaissance Corps. The SRC had, naturally, pushed to handle the exploration themselves, but FAF high command had decided that the investigation couldn't be left to them alone. It would be investigated, of course, but the FAF had plans beyond that: they wanted to seize the base for themselves. *They must be worried that the base might recover suddenly if we just hit it without capturing it*, Rei thought. *The top brass must want the base because its sudden recovery would make this attack meaningless, and they must now see how futile the last thirty years of the war have been in that respect.* The SRC's "discovery" of the JAM's paired-base operations must have had a great influence on them.

Their assumption was that Cookie was paired with Richwar base, and now that Richwar had been destroyed, Cookie would receive no support from it, creating a perfect opportunity for its capture. And, in fact, no large-scale retaliatory response from the other JAM bases had been seen against Faery base. The FAF high command had judged the SRC's discovery to be correct.

However, the SAF held a contrary viewpoint. First of all, they didn't believe that their battles until now had been as futile as some believed. Rather, they felt that the enemy had been engaging to gather information on humanity's true nature, which the JAM didn't understand. If the JAM hadn't been fighting the humans till now, then it meant the JAM hadn't known or understood that the FAF's fighter planes were being operated by humans. Had the FAF sent ground forces to occupy a JAM base early on in the war, things might have developed in an entirely different way. The JAM would have realized early on that the humans were their real targets, and mankind might have been exterminated. The idea that the defensive stance they took in prosecuting the war might have actually saved mankind meant that the fighting hadn't been meaningless. Despite that, as successive generations of FAF commanders came and went without seeing real progress made in their one-sided defensive strategy, the idea that they had to take the fight to the enemy began to take hold. However, with the enemy's true nature and objectives still a mystery, it was reckless to act on this idea. And, in fact, what attempts they had made in the past never netted them much in the end. But this time it would work, the FAF thought.

Even so, the SAF felt this was premature. The SRC's conclusion hadn't been proven at all. It was true that no enemy support was coming from Richwar and they hadn't seen any JAM retaliation thus far, but it wasn't known if that had anything to do with the SRC's discovery. Major Booker had felt that the JAM might be keeping quiet for an entirely different reason. In fact, he was sure that this was a sign of the JAM changing their strategy for fighting the FAF. They mustn't fall for it, he'd warned, and this plan to try and capture Cookie base was too risky. The JAM might be waiting for them with a large force. He could even imagine that they might be able to replace the FAF occupation force with Jammies, the human duplicates they were now creating. Since there was no way to tell duplicates from the real humans, the FAF could be torn apart from within.

They shouldn't think about trying to capture the enemy base, Major Booker had continued. They should instead go on as they had, just destroying them. Even if the bases were repaired, it wouldn't be a waste of time. It would still temporarily reduce the JAM's fighting strength, and there was always the possibility that the FAF or SAF would find some clue as to how the enemy effected their repairs as well. And if they were intent on capturing the bases, then the FAF should send in tanks equipped with machine intelligences like Yukikaze instead of humans. Unfortunately, Major Booker's words went unheeded by the FAF high command. Though Booker truly believed that humans needed to be the main actors in this war, he knew what would happen if the JAM began to target men rather than machines. It would become too dangerous for humans to show themselves at the battlefront, and the decision would eventually be made that advanced machine intelligences would be needed to replace them. The FAF authorities must realize that too, Booker had explained, but the SAF had never been told that the FAF's real intention was to reorganize their troops in order to initiate a full-scale land war. The top brass knew full well that the JAM had infiltrated their forces with human duplicates, so Major Booker couldn't understand why they were still taking the actions they were. They had kept the details of this plan to capture the enemy base secret from the SAF. It was possible the high command had decided that the old Yukikaze's contact with the JAM had compromised the SAF, and so they'd taken steps to avoid leaking any information pertaining to the base capture plan to them. If that were the case, then the SAF would eventually be smashed by the FAF itself. How loyal the SAF was or whether the SAF had committed any treasonous acts would be beside the point. Just the appearance of danger would be enough. There was the distinct possibility that the unit and its computers would be wiped out.

In any case, the situation had changed even more drastically than the SAF had originally expected. As far as the SAF were concerned, they had to figure out what the JAM *and* their own forces were up to and then deal with both. If the SAF hoped to survive, they were going to have to find the answer to all these mysteries on their own.

"Recon the hell out of that place." Those had been Major Booker's parting words to Rei and Yukikaze.

The SAF was sending out all of its fighters on rotation to conduct combat intelligence gathering missions, so when Yukikaze arrived on the scene, she was met by the unmanned Rafe fighter that had just finished its sortie. Once Yukikaze approached it and identified herself with her IFF code, the Rafe followed its programming and set out to return to base.

The Rafe didn't exchange the data it had collected while in flight, since its duty was to carry it back to base without allowing the JAM to intercept it. Rei wondered if it might have been attacked by the JAM, but he decided against that possibility after judging the situation and seeing no sign of damage. It had been sent to scout a greater area than usual because it was able to avoid danger better than any of the SAF's manned planes. While it wouldn't approach hazardous airspace, it would still be able to shake off any attackers at high speed if it encountered any. If the enemy didn't give up, it would avoid combat and retreat. Combat mode was only selected if escape wasn't possible. Since the Rafe's fuel had held out till Yukikaze appeared, it meant that there hadn't been any unpleasant surprises out there.

Protect itself while avoiding direct combat. Even if it judged friendly planes to be in danger, it was to avoid any contact that might endanger itself. Collect combat data and bring it back to base, even if it meant watching your own forces get killed. The SAF's actions at the scene of a battle made them unreliable allies of their own forces and a hated target that the JAM would go out of their way to intercept. This time, however, the situation was different. Minx, which had been sent out when the operation had begun, had been seemingly ignored by the JAM, with no attempt made to intercept it. This had continued with each mission they flew out there, the Rafe being no exception. It had carried out its duties without any problem, and it didn't seem to matter that the battle wasn't over yet. Rei had expected that the JAM would show a different reaction to an unmanned plane like the Rafe, but it seemed that they hadn't. The JAM weren't behaving at all like they normally did.

Rei flew closer to the enemy base, telling Lieutenant Katsuragi to begin intelligence gathering as he did so. The Rafe had just flown a simple course around the center of the base.

A manned fighter, however, could take a more flexible route based on the flight crew's judgment. Every sort of tactical recon flight pattern was worked out in advance, and a combat-hardened flight officer could judge a situation and call for, say, a bee dance flight pattern, which the pilot would immediately execute. A predetermined flight pattern like that could also be flown on automatic. However, Lieutenant Katsuragi wasn't used to combat yet, and Rei thought that making and executing flight pattern decisions should be his call alone. But Lieutenant Katsuragi proved to be even more skillful than expected, understanding what Rei wanted to do and answering him with a request for an Endless Eight pattern. They would fly a continuous figure eight centered over the base below them. It would involve an intensive observation of the base itself, beginning at high altitude and gradually moving lower.

Rei complied with the request. It was a dangerous pattern, but there didn't seem to be any action in the air at this point. It looked like there were hardly any JAM left to intercept them. There was no sign of any FAF ground attack fighters around them, just a formation of small planes meant for dogfighting that were flying on the perimeter.

There was an installation that may have been the entrance to an underground hangar bay next to the one remaining runway. It looked like a small white hill with a gaping entrance that rose to the runway's side. If it hadn't been destroyed, it most likely was the sole remaining escape route the JAM had left on the base. Occasionally, several black JAM planes would appear at it and begin to take off, only to be picked off by the FAF's fighters. Not on the runway, but immediately after they'd cleared it. It was as if they were swatting flies.

Rei had a feeling that it was an ant queen, not a fly, which lurked underground at the bottom of that hole. It really did feel like they were there to exterminate a nest of ants. He wondered what methods FAF authorities were going to use to capture the base. Maybe they'd try pouring insecticide down the hole. He wondered what the men on the surface there would see when they went underground. *Probably nothing*, Rei thought. The odds were good that they wouldn't have time to see anything. They'd be too busy being wiped out in some completely unexpected way by the JAM. If the JAM had really abandoned the base, they wouldn't leave any clues behind. And if they were intending to defend it to the bitter end, they'd probably use that hole as a trap to draw the enemy to them. The humans weren't going to get to see the inside of a JAM base that easily. The proof of that lay in bitter experience. They'd had many opportunities to penetrate a base over the decades they'd been fighting, but never once had they managed to do it. *Did they really think this time would be any different?* Rei wondered.

Yukikaze flew her figure-eight course, descending as she did.

Rei approached the runway, flying at low altitude as though he intended to land. That was when it appeared. A JAM plane. Just one. A relatively large high-speed fighter of the type used for hit-and-away combat. It was out on the runway now, accelerating. All the FAF planes in the air banked around, getting into formation to intercept it.

What happened next was about what Rei had expected, although not entirely as he had imagined. JAM defenses launched from the white sand. Two types. One type was anti-aircraft missiles. They popped up from the sand and ignited their rocket engines in midair, then seemed to self-destruct as they accelerated upwards, scattering smaller pieces in every direction. They hadn't destroyed themselves, however. The missiles had split into countless micro-missiles, which now sped toward the FAF planes that were still getting ready for their attack. The other type were small fighter planes. Short range interceptors. Too many to count, not that there was any time to count them.

In an instant, Yukikaze had passed over the JAM fighter on the runway. There was no time to target it. Instantly, Rei began coming back around to engage. At roughly the same moment, he saw the JAM attack slam into the FAF formation, wiping it out. The JAM planes already in the air took up a protective formation around the one taking off and flew after Yukikaze. Rei snapped her into a turn and then saw the disaster that had struck the ground below. The planes, probably taking off from the center of the base at supersonic speeds, had produced a shock wave that had left a round hole in the desert sand, which began to cave in.

The rumble and roar was loud enough to be heard aboard Yukikaze. Cookie base was turning into an enormous crater right
before his eyes.

All to let that one plane escape, Rei thought. They must have
been preserving the fire power they needed to escape, waiting
for the FAF attack to let up. And then they'd abandoned the base.
It didn't look as though they planned to repair it, as they had in
the past. *But why? Why now?*

"Multiple bogeys. JAM, closing in!" Lieutenant Katsuragi
called out, his voice tense. Setting his fire control radar range
to super search mode, Rei calmly confirmed the countless JAM
contacts flying at them.

"Support fighters won't make it here in time," Lieutenant
Katsuragi said. "The nearest one's—"

"Don't expect any support."

Rei knew that slipping away from the enemy on his own
wasn't going to be easy. The swarm of JAM planes began to sur-
round Yukikaze.

"The one they're trying to protect is the plane that took off
from the runway." The other, smaller planes couldn't fly for
long. They were like disposable interceptors. "Lieutenant, find
that plane. We're taking it down. Get me a heading. Engaging!"
he demanded, declaring his intention to attack to Lieutenant
Katsuragi.

"Roger!" He paused a moment. "Two bandits, on our six! Get
ready to break to starboard…now!"

Rei changed direction as he'd been told.

"Target sighted, closing fast," said Lieutenant Katsuragi.
"Locked on."

It had been picked up on Yukikaze's antiaircraft fire control
radar, which was able to track multiple enemies simultaneously.
The ant queen. No, not an ant. A wasp. And Rei could tell that
Yukikaze had no intention of letting it get away alive.

She turned to evade the smaller JAM flying up from low in
front of her.

It was here that Rei realized that the enemy planes were
behaving strangely. They weren't attacking. And not a single
missile that had launched from the desert sands below had

flown after Yukikaze.

"Any time you're ready, Captain Fukai. All loaded missiles are reading green."

"Understood."

Leveling off—though by all rights he shouldn't have had time to do this, he realized—Rei looked outside of the cockpit. He searched for the target with his naked eye. It was heading toward them from the skies to their upper right.

"It's going to get us!" shouted Lieutenant Katsuragi. "What are you doing?"

"I'm not picking up a target lock beam," Rei replied. "What is that thing? Look at it. It's—"

"It's a JAM! What else do you need to know! Hurry up and fire—"

Just then, Lieutenant Katsuragi choked in shock. Yukikaze was displaying a message that he couldn't believe.

`Don't touch me…FO/I will try to communicate with BOGEY/do NOT attack…Capt.`

What Rei saw was that the enemy plane had lowered its landing gear, and unless it was experiencing some sort of mechanical breakdown, that was a signal that it didn't intend to attack. It had been waiting for them, Rei realized. It had waited, enduring the intense attack, for Yukikaze to appear in the skies over Cookie base. Hoping that she would arrive so that they could talk to each other.

4

YUKIKAZE'S MESSAGE LEFT Lieutenant Katsuragi in a state of shock. Here was something to indicate that he might have been wrong about Rei's "delusions." He stared at the display for several moments, his breath ragged, then shouted.

"What the hell is this? What's Yukikaze saying?"

Rei shifted his eyes back to the display and read the message as well. She was going to try communicating with the enemy plane and didn't want Lieutenant Katsuragi to interfere or Rei to attack the target.

"This is impossible," Lieutenant Katsuragi said. "Captain, you brought that message onto the display, didn't you?"

"And how would I do that?"

It was utterly ridiculous, of course. He hadn't had time to do any such thing. If anyone on this plane could, it would be Lieutenant Katsuragi. *If this is a trap, then he's a JAM*, Rei thought. He quickly extended the air brake, letting the target plane slip past, then nimbly accelerated to close range and took up the optimal position to fire his gun. The target plane, however, made no moves to shake them off. Rei flew Yukikaze onto its starboard side. It responded by turning in a wide leftward arc.

As though beckoning Rei to follow. Yukikaze was flying faster, but since she was turning in a wider arc, the two planes ended up flying roughly next to each other. Despite the fact that the JAM was in the midst of a turn, it wasn't banking at all.

Lieutenant Katsuragi could clearly see that it had lowered its landing gear. Its fuselage was as black as a shadow. Even bathed in the light of Faery's twin suns, you couldn't tell the surface of the plane from the shadows cast upon it. Even though it was flying close enough that Rei felt he could reach out his hand and touch it, it was difficult to make out what its actual shape was. It almost looked like a section of the background scenery had been clipped out and replaced with a black shape, and it was impossible to tell at a glance what sort of three-dimensional shape this fighter had.

The smaller JAM planes reestablished their escort formation around the main one, splitting into three groups and moving to intercept the approaching FAF planes. Lieutenant Katsuragi touched the control panel, preparing to contact them, when a warning chimed and Yukikaze again flashed a message onto the display.

Do NOT touch me.

She was telling him not to interfere with her communications system. Even Lieutenant Katsuragi would have to admit that, although Rei himself would say that she didn't need to possess consciousness in order to do that.

Whether this was a simple programmed response or possibly caused by the unexplainable "something" in Yukikaze really didn't matter in an emergency like this. The truth was that she was making high-level judgments. The question was, should they just sit there and do as she told them to?

Rei could imagine how confused Lieutenant Katsuragi was at this point. As a flight officer, he wouldn't be able to stand just sitting there doing nothing and was probably wondering whose fault this was.

"Do what Yukikaze says."

"But, Captain!"

"It's my call, Lieutenant. Pilot's orders. Do what she says. It'd be dangerous to disobey her."

If he wasn't careful, Yukikaze could quite easily eject the rear seat from the plane. The front seat too. Rei didn't consider that some wild delusion. Yukikaze could do that if she wanted to.

Inside his flight gloves, Rei's palms were growing moist from tension. He wasn't just concerned about Lieutenant Katsuragi doing what he was told. There was also the matter of his not being able to predict what would happen next. Besides that, Rei was desperate to keep Yukikaze away from the target plane. While it hadn't appeared to change its flight attitude, the radius of its turns was slowly decreasing.

`Don't lose track of BOGEY...Capt.`

She was telling Rei not to shake the plane off, but to follow and maintain distance.

G forces were increasing with each revolution. Soon he wouldn't be able to move his arms freely. Yet the target plane continued to turn serenely through the air. Yukikaze began to drift slightly away from it.

`Increase power.`

The G limiter automatically cut out. *No good*, Rei thought. *My body can't take this.* He manually reset the limiter to tell Yuki-kaze that he was refusing her request. The limiter automatically cut out again.

They needed to increase power to keep up with the target plane, but they couldn't keep turning in a smaller radius at the speed they were traveling. The airframe would eventually tear itself apart, though the humans aboard her would be dead before then. It was like they'd been placed in a centrifuge, and even if he could ignore the stress it was placing on him, he couldn't ignore the loss of maneuverability the tight turns were causing. Even now, the plane threatened to snap out of the turn line it was describing. One mistake in control and this dangerous balance would be upset, and Rei could foresee it sending them into an unrecoverable spin.

He kept setting the G limiter, and Yukikaze kept cutting it out. *Holy shit*, Rei thought. *We're having an argument!* He was fighting out of concern for his own safety, while Yukikaze wanted to keep going just as badly. They repeated the exchange four times, then Yukikaze spoke again.

`Maintain stability/increase power right now/you can do it…Capt.`

To keep following the JAM, Yukikaze first wanted him to increase her engine output in order to maintain her own stability, Rei realized.

It was certain that, if he tried to carelessly reduce her speed and pitch her nose while they were still turning like this, Yukikaze would be sent into an uncontrollable spin. To avoid that danger, Rei understood that the logical thing he needed to do now was carefully increase power to the engines.

Yukikaze was telling him that, as the pilot, he should understand that. She probably figured that he'd have to go along with her message if she put it in those terms. And he did understand. But what would happen after he did it?

"Yukikaze, are you trying to kill me?" Rei said, his voice straining against the G forces punishing his body. "What's this JAM trying to do? Answer me, Yukikaze! I can't do what you want me to unless you tell me what's going on! Explain it so that I can understand. Yukikaze, do you understand me?"

`Increase power immediately/just do it…Capt.`

Had Yukikaze judged her pilot useless, she could have requested him to turn over maneuvering control to her by turning her automaneuver switch to ON. She probably could have done it even without sending a message to him. And yet she hadn't. Deciding that she was saying that she depended on him, Rei answered her request by moving the throttle lever in his left hand slightly forward. Yukikaze continued with a new message:

`I have T-FACPro II/use it…Capt.`

"Lieutenant! Open the utility warehouse in Yukikaze's central computer! Run the program called T-FACPro II! Hurry!"

Lieutenant Katsuragi had also read Yukikaze's message, but he had no idea what sort of utility T-FACPro II was. He couldn't remember ever being told that Yukikaze had such a program. But there was no time to think about it. Rei was the pilot, and so Katsuragi obeyed. He accessed the utility program memory area called the warehouse and found T-FACPro II there. The startup indicator was shown, then the display changed completely.

"What am I supposed to do with this?" Lieutenant Katsuragi asked.

The running program itself answered him, displaying a message on the screen.

This is a psychological tool designed to predict a target subject's behavior. Please input target data. Now inputting...

A section of the main display showed Rei what was happening. Data was being entered automatically. He could guess that Yukikaze was inputting the PAX code for the JAM. Was the program going to output a behavior prediction for the target plane?

No, Rei thought. *Even without using T-FACPro II, Yukikaze should have been able to predict what the JAM was doing now.* No, she was expressly using the program not as a behavior prediction tool, but rather so that she could translate her intentions into a language comprehensible by the humans aboard her. T-FACPro II had a natural language processing engine to speak fluently to humans. It also had an extensive vocabulary dictionary and apparently could use speech input as well. Rei had a hunch that Yukikaze was using that engine in order to communicate with her human crewmen.

Yukikaze was going to be able to speak freely to him, not just in halting baby talk.

"Yukikaze, what is this JAM doing?"

The answer came immediately. And just as he'd expected, it wasn't a behavior prediction from T-FACPro II. It was clearly communicating thoughts from Yukikaze. Rei would have been deeply moved if there'd been time for him to be.

The target plane is carrying out communication by

means of modulated ultraviolet light. According to
the SSL 1.03 protocol, it keeps repeating the tag
[follow me].

Prior research had established that JAM planes would confirm each other's position within visual range by emitting
UV light through a slit located near their noses. It could be
thought of as the equivalent of the nighttime running lights
FAF planes were equipped with. Right now, the target plane
was modulating the intensity and wavelength of the light to
try and use it as a means of communication. It was saying
"follow me" over and over, although none of this could be
discerned with the naked eye.

"Impossible," Lieutenant Katsuragi said. "You mean the JAM
have cracked our SSL encryption?"

Having the JAM just come out and tell them that they'd
cracked the SAF's coded communications system came as a
shock to Lieutenant Katsuragi. The tag that Yukikaze had mentioned referred to a prepared reference code set used for such
things as identifying a message's sender or marking the end of a
transmission. If you had something very simple to convey, it was
possible to just use the code number by itself.

To Rei, however, it hardly mattered. Version 1.03 was the one
in use when the old Yukikaze had flown her missions. He wasn't
surprised at all that the JAM had cracked it.

Okay, fine. The target plane was saying "follow me." By why
was it turning in smaller and smaller circles? Were the JAM just
trying to see how far Yukikaze would go along with it? The G
forces the turns were generating were threatening to exceed the
limits of human endurance. *Maybe the target plane was trying to
see at what point a human body would just break*, Rei wondered.

"Do you understand the reason for these turning maneuvers,
Yukikaze? Answer me. What is this JAM trying to do?"

T-FACPro II predicts, Yukikaze displayed on the monitor,
that the target plane desires direct communication
with you. It can also predict, however, that the
target plane does not want any other FAF plane to
hear the contents of the communication, and so it
is in the midst of guiding you to a place where you

will not be disturbed. I also judge T-FACPro II's prediction to be correct.

"And where is this place where we won't be disturbed?"

MYSTERIOUS BATTLE ZONE.

Rei reflexively choked as he read the message. The G forces were making it hard enough to breathe as it was, but Rei didn't want to accept the reply Yukikaze had just given him. She might as well have been inviting him back to a hell he hoped he'd never have to return to.

"What's it mean by 'mysterious battle zone,' Captain?" Lieutenant Katsuragi asked.

The G-stress on Lieutenant Katsuragi must be even worse than what I'm feeling, Rei thought. That medical exam had been spot on. It was an odd thing to think about, all things considered. The Gs were so bad now that Rei couldn't even turn his head.

The mysterious battle zone…the place where he'd tasted the flesh of Lieutenant Burgadish. And no, that hadn't been the first time he'd visited it. He'd been there before, with that journalist Andy Lander, who'd come from Earth to do a story on the FAF. He'd been flying with Rei in Yukikaze to experience it for himself when they were pulled into that bizarre space. They'd found a yellow swamp in a forest that seemed to be made of mechanical devices, and when Lander had reached his hand out to touch it, he'd lost his hand up to his wrist… The entire thing had seemed like a waking dream, but when they'd returned to normal space, Lander's hand was still gone. They'd never found the zone's exact location. Indeed, Rei had even written in his report that the zone might not be on Faery at all. That was when he'd named that unknown space the "mysterious battle zone." It was a unique name, one that Yukikaze knew but Lieutenant Katsuragi did not.

When they'd flown there before, the fuel transfer system had been interfered with, causing Yukikaze's engines to shut down. They had to defeat the JAM's intense electronic warfare in order to escape. Yukikaze had been the one who had beaten them. *All I'd been able to do was hope that she didn't lose*, Rei thought. This time, the JAM were probably after him, the human component of this partnership.

Even so, there was no way he could run back home after coming so far. This was exactly the situation that Major Booker had hoped would arise, so Rei steeled himself in resignation. Make contact with the JAM, then bring that information back to base. Come back alive, no matter what.

"Yukikaze, get ready for EW jamming from the target plane. Don't let your guard down. Remember, it's a JAM."

`Everything is ready/I don't lose/trust me…Capt.`

Yukikaze had switched back to her own words. And Rei did trust her. As much as he trusted his own judgment.

"Lieutenant, monitor the passive air space radar. I'm expecting the JAM to try some sort of trick. Keep your eyes on it and brace for a shock."

Lieutenant Katsuragi had no idea what Rei and Yukikaze were agreeing to, but they seemed to know what was going to happen, at least.

The information from the various radars was integrated for display on the electronic warfare monitor panel. This time, there was no interference from Yukikaze. Apparently, she was obeying the pilot's instructions as well.

Well, I can definitely perceive some form of consciousness, but what exactly is this machine intelligence? Asking that question was useless, Lieutenant Katsuragi concluded coldly. The plane would probably just answer, "I am Yukikaze." He'd just as likely get the same response from Captain Fukai. "I am what I am, Lieutenant," he'd say. What he was more interested in was what Rei was doing and just what his relationship was with the JAM. Aside from that, there was no need to ask them what was about to happen. He was about to learn that through personal experience.

Lieutenant Katsuragi coolly followed his pilot's instructions. When you want to know the truth about something, nothing beats personal experience, as Colonel Rombert would say. The lieutenant thought back on the colonel's favorite phrase. The colonel generally followed that up with, "However, there's no need for you to judge the value of that experience. That's for me to do." In short, the colonel saw the people who worked under him as his eyes and ears, while he was the head, and he made it very clear that he didn't want them interfering where they shouldn't.

Lieutenant Katsuragi thought nothing of this. He understood it to mean that all that mattered to the colonel was that his subordinates were able to do their job well. Issues of human trust or betrayal never even came into the picture, as far as he was concerned. It wasn't that Katsuragi didn't want to establish any deep relationships out of a fear of betrayal. Rather, he just didn't see any value in sharing feelings of trust with other people and viewed those sorts of relationships as foolish and troublesome. As far as Colonel Rombert was concerned, a subordinate like Lieutenant Katsuragi made for an excellent agent. Here was a man who would do what it took to satisfy his curiosity without any concern for the feelings or endangerment of others. For Lieutenant Katsuragi's part, a superior like Colonel Rombert, who didn't demand him to pursue annoying human relationships, was easy to work for.

Katsuragi understood that Colonel Rombert had released him from service because he wanted information about the SAF. It didn't matter what conditions the colonel had set up with them, though. He was free to live his life as he wanted and was under no obligation to answer any questions the colonel might have for him. If the colonel were to appeal to the lieutenant, Katsuragi would just tell him that he didn't work for intel anymore. He could just imagine the look on the colonel's face were he to say that. Katsuragi lived for his own sake, not for anyone else's, and couldn't care less about what their expectations were. He'd do whatever he felt was best for himself. He couldn't believe that there was anyone in this world who'd criticize him for such a stance…

That was why Lieutenant Katsuragi couldn't understand how Captain Fukai could trust this machine intelligence called Yukikaze, especially in matters of life or death. He might as well have been taking an action based on an unreliable instrument gauge without any idea of how far off its readings were. *An action that may be tantamount to suicide*, Lieutenant Katsuragi thought as he watched the display panel.

The formations of FAF planes and the small JAM fighters moving to intercept them had yet to make contact. Only about a minute had passed since they'd begun following the target plane's flight path. It felt like they'd circled round and round, but the truth was that they hadn't even made two circuits yet.

The target plane and Yukikaze were tracing a whirlpool-shaped course through the sky, the turning radius growing ever smaller as they approached the center.

He could see on the passive air space radar the shock wave the target plane produced as it crossed the sound barrier. Yukikaze was flying out of its range, but Katsuragi realized that it would be dangerous if that shock wave struck them head-on.

Suddenly, a shining white spot appeared on the display panel right before his eyes. Lieutenant Katsuragi couldn't believe what he was looking at. He thought at first that it was some sort of shock wave caused by an intense explosion, but it didn't propagate like a shock wave. Instead, the shining spot just stayed as it was. Fighting the G forces tearing at him, he looked out of the cockpit in the direction where the spot should have been. It seemed to be centered over the crater where the JAM had self-destructed and caused the cave-in, but with his naked eyes, he could see no difference from before. He wondered if the radar had broken down. The display appeared frozen.

It had clearly picked up the shock wave of the base's self-destruction. Enlarging its range to maximum, he could see the traces of the pressure-change waves from the blast still spreading outward, the sound of the explosion itself. So the radar was still working fine, but that glowing dot on the display still wasn't moving. What did it mean?

The lieutenant knew that the passive air space radar was nicknamed "Frozen Eye" and operated by means of a cryogenically cooled ultra-high sensitivity visual sensor. He didn't know the details of how it worked, as that was a closely guarded FAF secret, but he imagined that the Frozen Eye picked up irregularities in air density, similar to how heat mirages would cause whatever one saw behind them to seemingly shimmer. Katsuragi understood that these microchanges in air density, invisible to the eye, would then be image-processed by a high-speed computer. If that were the case, it wouldn't be able to sense differences in density unless there were observable moment-by-moment changes taking place. In short, the lines and points Frozen Eye was displaying on the panel had to be constantly moving.

So, this dot had to be vibrating. The instant he had decided it, the dot became a circle and began to slowly expand. And Yuki-kaze and the target plane were flying straight into it.

Rei realized this too. The airframe was violently shaking now. It seemed about ready to shake itself apart, but he knew that the plane could handle it. The question was whether or not his body could. *Here we go*, he thought, bracing himself for the impact. Their turning radius continued to shrink as he maintained power.

Lieutenant Katsuragi felt his eyes burn as sweat ran into them. He knew his body was trembling with a fear he unconsciously felt. His head kept telling himself that he was just experiencing what it was that Captain Fukai and Yukikaze were doing, as though this was all somebody else's problem. His body, on the other hand, wasn't buying any of it.

For first time, the lieutenant felt that he was behaving as suicidally as his pilot; he was terrified of these maneuvers Yukikaze was pulling. His life was in danger. He could die here, and he couldn't accept why he was doing this. Even so, this was real. It was happening, and there was no use in trying to deny it.

That was when he saw something outside of the plane that made him wonder if any of this was real at all.

The air space indicated by Frozen Eye was distorting the scenery around it. The changes there were now visible to the naked eye. It almost seemed like an enormous transparent lens was floating over the ruined base. It extended up and down, in a spindle shape. And it was growing larger.

It's like the Passageway, the lieutenant realized. The Passageway to hyperspace. He tried to twist his head down to check the display panel, but the G forces were just too strong now. He couldn't move his body at all.

He saw the target JAM plane suddenly roll over, white vapor trailing behind it. *A contrail*, he thought, *caused by the sudden maneuver*. An instant later, he felt a shock like an enormous invisible hand swatting Yukikaze.

5

BLACKOUT. REI HAD no sense of losing consciousness, but he figured he might have blacked out for a moment. He heard the sound of a distant alarm. He swallowed saliva as his hearing normalized. He was clearly conscious but could see nothing of his surroundings. Nothing but gray all around. He raised his helmet visor and checked his instruments. A white vapor was rising in the cabin. He thought it was a fire at first, but the alarm was all wrong for that. It was water. Mist.

"Lieutenant Katsuragi, give me a damage report. Lieutenant, wake up!"

"I hear you. Running diagnostics now… Flight systems are all green," he answered, breathing rapidly.

"Fix the cabin environment."

"The defogger's running. Current position: unknown."

There must have been a sudden, temporary loss of pressure in the cabin, Rei thought. That was the cause of the mist. Thinking the canopy might have been blown off, Rei rolled Yukikaze through one turn, confirming her flight responses as well as trying to determine which way was up. Even so, his instruments weren't telling him anything. Not knowing which way was up, he reversed the roll in case he'd unexpectedly changed course during the initial one.

The alarm indicated **TARGET PLANE LOST**. Canceling it, Rei checked to see if the wide area search radar was still operating.

Lieutenant Katsuragi noticed that the barometric and radar altimeters were now at wide variance in their readings, way more than the usual measurement error. He looked out the now-clearing canopy to see which reading was more accurate. He had a feeling that both were probably wrong. Yukikaze was flying nearly level, very close to the ground.

It was a strange scene. Dim, with thick clouds spreading overhead as far as the eye could see. Below them was exactly the same. The lieutenant suddenly realized that the "ground" below them was just another cloud formation. Yukikaze was flying through a clear layer between two thick cloud banks above and below. Far ahead of them on the horizon he could see a band of blue light, probably a break in this sea of clouds. Craning his head around to make sure that Yukikaze's tail stabilizers hadn't been damaged, he saw that the brightly shining gap extended completely around them. It was colored red behind them. Katsuragi's entire field of view showed only a ring of light, sandwiched between two layers of clouds.

"No visible damage to the wings. Current altitude is around three thousand meters, and I don't think this is Faery's environment, either," Lieutenant Katsuragi informed Rei. "I think this is some sort of artificially created space. Our altimeter readings are unreliable here."

"Yeah," replied Rei. "There's also a huge cloud layer above us that reflects back radio waves."

"Holy shit…" Katsuragi murmured. The clouds above and below weren't so much like the ground than gigantic walls, with this clear area suspended between them. "This is a spatial pathway the JAM use to transport themselves around Faery."

"Maybe."

"If we keep flying, will we come out of it, Captain Fukai?"

"I don't know, but I think we're going to make contact with the JAM before we leave here. Keep your eyes peeled."

The engines were running smoothly, but there was no real sense that they were moving forward. It was quiet. The situation was bizarre, but Rei was relieved to see that Lieutenant Katsuragi in the rear seat was dealing with it calmly and not falling into a panic. Yukikaze was silent except for the message on the main display, which declared that she was searching for the enemy. No doubt she was using every means at her disposal to search the skies surrounding them.

"Where'd the target plane disappear to?" Lieutenant Katsuragi asked. "It looks like it didn't come in here with us."

"You're probably right, seeing as it's not here. It was probably just sent to guide us in," Rei replied.

"Did you know this was going to happen?"

"Are you asking me if I knew beforehand that we'd be lured into this weird space?"

"Well, that too…"

"You said before that this is an artificially created space. How do you know that?" Rei asked.

"Because I doubt anything like this would exist naturally. If the JAM control it, then it stands to reason that they created it too."

"That's a cool assessment to make."

"What are you planning to do here, Captain?"

"Learn what the JAM's intentions are," Rei said. "That's why the SAF put this operation in motion, although the JAM seem to have made the move before we could. I guess you could say we got our wish. Saves us a bunch of work, this way."

"Did the SAF get some overtures beforehand that the JAM would be open to contact like this?" Lieutenant Katsuragi asked.

"It'd be natural to think that."

"To think? Are you avoiding the question?"

"You don't work for Colonel Rombert anymore, meaning you have no right to cross-examine me. Keep your position in mind, Lieutenant."

"I'm just asking out of personal curiosity, Captain."

There's a way of asking things when you genuinely just want to know about them, Rei thought. Still, as much as the way Katsuragi was doing it rubbed him the wrong way, Rei figured he'd sound much the same if he were in the lieutenant's place. Rei snorted out a laugh as he thought about it. The lieutenant's questions weren't about some duty to figure out what was going on. He really was a lot like Rei in that regard. Besides, Rei had a feeling that Katsuragi was going to get nervous if he didn't have something to talk about.

"What's so funny?"

"You just remind me of when Colonel Rombert interrogated me. But yeah, you aren't him. Just go on, Lieutenant."

"If you people did receive overtures from the JAM before, then that's a serious matter," Lieutenant Katsuragi said. "The other units in the FAF don't know that, do they? Is the SAF trying to set up some sort of private arrangement between itself and the JAM?"

"Overtures were made in advance," Rei replied coolly. "But to Yukikaze, not us humans. If that weren't the case, Yukikaze wouldn't have told me not to attack and that she was going to try communicating with the JAM."

"Oh… Is that what that was all about."

"The SAF theorized that the JAM wanted to make contact with Yukikaze because she made that prediction herself shortly before we left on this sortie."

Yukikaze performed unmanned sorties several times before now, and it's possible the JAM had made their overtures to her each time, Rei thought. That was how she knew that the JAM desired to "receive" them. He could imagine that the JAM had made clear their conditions for contact with them—she had to be piloted, not unmanned.

"That's why I was prepared for this," Rei continued. "But I don't know what the JAM are going to say to us. Is that good enough for you, Lieutenant?"

"What do you plan to say to the JAM?"

"I want to ask them what they think I am."

"And after that?" Katsuragi asked.

"Why, out of all the other planes in other units, they want to make contact with Yukikaze. I want to know what they think she is too."

"Do you only care about you and Yukikaze, Captain Fukai? There have to be more important things to ask them."

"Like what?"

"Like why the JAM invaded in the first place. That's what the SAF and the FAF both want to know. Are you serious? Do you really fly Yukikaze for such personal reasons?"

"Yeah," Rei said. "What about it? Is it wrong to?"

"Is it *wrong*? That answer is so disgusting, I don't even know where to begin," the lieutenant replied.

"That's not how you really feel about it," Rei said.

"How do you mean?"

"It's not that you aren't answering me out of disgust. It's because you don't know how to judge my answer and you don't understand how you feel about it. You don't have a personal question to ask the JAM, and that disgust you claim to feel only comes from your being a soldier in the FAF. You're acting the way you think a good soldier should, but you don't really care. So do me a favor and stop trying to impress me."

Lieutenant Katsuragi was silent.

"Think about it for yourself, Lieutenant. I'm pretty sure you know how you feel."

Captain Foss and her therapy must have had an even stronger influence on me than I ever imagined, Rei thought. But nothing pissed him off more than hearing someone talking as pretentiously as Lieutenant Katsuragi was; the lieutenant wasn't even using his own words. All it did was underline how mentally immature he really was. It was all Rei could do to keep from just telling the guy to fuck off. The foul language he wanted to hurl at him was the same abuse he wanted to hurl at himself.

"Does everyone in the SAF fly for the same reasons you do?" the lieutenant finally asked.

"I couldn't care less why they do it," Rei replied.

"So, the SAF is…yeah. That's fine, isn't it?"

You draw the most strength when you fight for yourself, Rei thought, as he silently nodded. He looked outside. The scenery hadn't changed. Maybe the JAM were carrying out a cunning plan just to annoy him. Rei was concerned about their remaining fuel, but then noticed they hadn't consumed nearly as much as he'd thought.

"It doesn't matter what motivates your unit's pilots to fly, as long as they achieve their strategic goals," Lieutenant Katsuragi said. "If you find out what the JAM think of you and Yukikaze, we can figure out what their strategic objectives are and develop strategies to anticipate their behavior." He paused a moment. "I was really shocked when you just coolly said 'yeah' like that, Captain. I just couldn't come up with anything to answer that."

"You would have said the same thing if you'd been in my position. There was nothing shocking about it. You and I are a lot alike."

"I was shocked because saying something like that in any other unit would have earned you a trip to the firing squad. If the SAF permits conversations like this to happen every day, it's in real trouble. Well, I suppose I don't have anything to worry about."

"Do you have a meeting arranged with Colonel Rombert?" Rei asked.

"No, but I figure the colonel will approach me somehow. Still, even if he does, I don't plan to tell him about this. Besides, considering the situation, I doubt he'd believe me even if I did."

"That colonel wouldn't ignore intelligence like this just because he didn't believe it himself. He'd probably anticipate how well you can utilize your intelligence network and demand objective data."

"Hm..."

Right now, Katsuragi is probably doubting what his five senses are telling him about this whole experience, Rei thought. If they made it back in one piece, he was definitely going to need the data Yukikaze had collected in order to process it.

"Don't keep monitoring the instruments," Rei ordered. "Keep a visual watch on our surroundings. No matter what happens, don't look at the instruments. I'll tell you again if I need you to run the EW systems. Trust your own eyes. Now, repeat what I just told you back to me."

"Maintain a visual watch on our surroundings, don't look at the instruments until the pilot tells me otherwise. That is all."

"You left out the part about trusting your own eyes."

"That was part of your orders?"

"Yeah."

"Trust my own eyes. That is all," Lieutenant Katsuragi said.

"And can you do that?"

"I follow my orders."

"It'd be hard for me to do," Rei said. "Flying without looking at my instruments would make me as nervous as hitting full throttle with my eyes shut."

"You're a pilot. That's not surprising."

"It's not that sort of anxiety."

"Are you saying you can't completely trust Yukikaze—"

As he spoke, an object moving at high speed was detected on the enemy search radar, triggering an air-raid alarm. Lieutenant Katsuragi's eyes instinctively fell back to his display panel.

"Bogey, single, bearing low to port. Rising fast on a general intercept course. From its size, I'm guessing it's a fighter plane, not a missile."

"Lieutenant, carry out your orders!" Rei snapped. "Maintain a visual watch and give me running reports on the actual conditions you see. Do it in a way that anyone would be able to figure out what happened here if we replay it back at base."

"Roger. By visual observation...I can't confirm an enemy silhouette in the cloud bank below us, but it's probably close."

"Target is crossing to starboard, right next to us, Lieutenant. I'm matching speeds. No IFF response. I can't confirm if it's a JAM. Type: unknown."

"A section of the bogey has appeared through the cloud bank... Looks like the pointed tip of a vertical stabilizer."

Like a shark fin breaking the surface of the water, thought Lieutenant Katsuragi. It was very close to them now, barely one hundred meters away. It broke through the clouds as it rose toward them. The surroundings were dim, and in the weak light, its wings looked gray instead of the usual black of a JAM plane.

"I can see some sort of darkish marking on the gray wings of the plane. It looks like...like..."

It was a Boomerang mark. With barely a ripple on the surface of the clouds, the unknown plane revealed itself completely.

"The plane is a Sylphid, a high-speed Super Sylph. I can confirm the markings of the Special Air Force 5th Squadron on it."

Even Rei could now see with his naked eyes the plane emerging on the starboard side.

"It's Yukikaze," he said coolly. "A duplicate of Yukikaze's old airframe, and this isn't the first time I've run into it."

Setting the fire control radar to pursuit mode, he locked on to the target plane. It was emitting an IFF signal designating it as friendly, but Rei disregarded that and marked it as hostile.

"I see crewmen in the cockpit," Lieutenant Katsuragi reported. "Their faces are covered with visors and masks... The one in the rear seat is moving his hand... He's pointing to his mask. It looks like he wants to talk to us."

This was the first time he'd seen humanoids riding in the gray mystery plane. Wondering if they were duplicates of himself and Lieutenant Burgadish, Rei began manually searching the comm band, but the auto-scanner locked on before he could. A voice came through into his helmet.

"Lieutenant Fukai, you are fighting a useless battle. Do you hear me? I demand that you abandon your fighting spirit and live as I tell you to. Answer me, Lieutenant Fukai. I repeat..."

That wasn't Lieutenant Burgadish's voice. Its tone was neutral, as though mechanically synthesized. While the subject of its speech was easy to understand, it used words clumsily. Besides that, Rei was a captain now, but it was referring to him by his former rank. That might have been deliberate though, and Rei decided against correcting its mistake. No point in giving the JAM any more information than he had to.

"Lieutenant Fukai, you are fighting a useless battle. Do you hear me?"

"This is B-1, I read you loud and clear. Please state your name, rank, and unit attachment."

"Response confirmed. I lack the type of classification and identification codes you inquire about. Lieutenant Fukai, please respond if you accept or deny my request."

"If you're going to make a request of someone, it's only common courtesy to make your social position clear to them," Rei replied, knowing that wasn't true at all. "Who are you?"

After a short, almost embarrassed silence, it responded.

"By your conceptualization, I am the whole of what you refer to as the JAM."

"The whole... You mean you're the JAM themselves? Should I think of you as a voice representing the JAM?"

"I would not object to that judgment. Please issue your response."

Rei switched off the comm circuit for a moment and called out to Lieutenant Katsuragi.

"Lieutenant, what do you think of what it said? Do you think I can believe this to be a representative of the JAM?"

"Hell if I know. I will say that it sounds unnatural, though. Like somebody is ordering it to say that stuff to you."

"I agree. Maintain observation of our surroundings."

"Roger."

He reopened the comm link.

"I can't understand the meaning of your request," Rei replied. "When you say my battle is useless, I don't know to whose advantage you're referring, so I can't answer you."

"I somehow doubt that."

The suddenly fluent and lively voice he now heard leaping into his ears made Rei shiver. He knew one very similar to it. The man at that mysterious base where Lieutenant Burgadish had met his end. Yazawa. Major Yazawa. The name of the man he'd told Colonel Rombert about over and over again. The JAM human. It had to be him.

"Lieutenant Fukai, I very much doubt that you don't understand its meaning," the new voice said. "We're saying that the FAF has no chance of winning, so we're offering you a way to save yourself. Come with us. We'll lead you to a place where you can live in safety. If you don't comply, you'll only end up dying a meaningless death."

"I can't trust your words," Rei said. "I reject your demand. I won't negotiate with you."

"Ignorant man. We've come here to make you understand."

"I say again, I will not negotiate with you." He called back to the rear seat. "Lieutenant Katsuragi, I'm engaging them. We're attacking the target plane to starboard. Get ready for their counterattack and stand by on EW."

"Roger!"

The stores control panel automatically displayed, letting him see at a glance all of the weaponry loaded on board. Yukikaze was agreeing with his decision to attack. She selected the high-velocity short range missiles, telling him to lead off with those. Rei snapped Yukikaze into a sharp turn. The target plane reacted immediately. In a close-range dogfight between the Maeve and a Super Sylph, the Maeve had an absolute advantage.

He launched the missiles, their range to the target extremely short. Rei counted to himself: *three...two...one!* and then the target plane vanished. It happened suddenly, without any warning. Having lost their target, the missiles flew straight through where the plane had vanished and then self-destructed.

"It's useless, Lieutenant Fukai."

The target plane suddenly reappeared on the starboard side.

"Shit," spat Lieutenant Katsuragi. "The thing may not even really be there."

As if chiding the lieutenant's impatience, Yukikaze scrolled a message onto the display.

`This was just a test/next firing will not be warning shots...JAM.`

"Such foolishness, even after we offered to save you. Very well. If you insist, I will accept your challenge. Now see who truly rules the skies. This place shall become your grave—" the owner of the voice was saying. Suddenly, with no explanation, the words stopped. There came a shout like "No, don't!"

Disaster struck the target plane. Its canopy blew off.

"The crew have ejected," Lieutenant Katsuragi reported. "Confirm ejection of both front and rear seats. Are they running away? But why? What happened?"

The lieutenant followed the two ejected seats with his gaze. They fell behind and to the side of their flight path, tracing a double-helix path through the air as they spiraled away around one another. He saw no sign of the crew's bodies separating from the seats or of parachutes opening, even as he twisted his neck as far around as he could to keep them in sight. They were enveloped in a reddish phosphorescence, sprouting glowing red tails as they grew smaller and smaller until they finally vanished from sight. It was as if they'd been incinerated in freefall. He instinctively checked the radar display, but saw nothing there. They'd been annihilated.

"Answer me, JAM," Rei said. "I want to talk to you, not your human duplicates. Respond! This is Rei Fukai in B-1."

The response came.

"I cannot understand you. Why do you fight?"

Lieutenant Katsuragi shivered. The owner of this voice, he realized, was the JAM themselves, who wished to make contact with Captain Fukai and Yukikaze. The ejected JAM humans had been nothing more than intermediaries whose role had been to act as translators. The owner of the voice had probably discarded them when it judged that they were hindering negotiations. Like they'd been some sort of disposable weapon.

The target plane continued to fly alongside Yukikaze, as though nothing had happened. The JAM voice might have been coming from the plane, but most likely it was acting as a relay transmitter to convey the JAM's will. No doubt it wasn't the actual voice of a JAM, but the results of their efforts to convey their thoughts in human speech through the manipulation of radio waves.

What we know as JAM do exist, but they're some sort of invisible beings, and what we fight are their shadows. What Rei had thought, Lieutenant Katsuragi could now understand as a palpable sensation. A sensation of fear. It hadn't just been a theory.

"I cannot understand the intelligence known as Yukikaze. I cannot understand the intelligences which comprise what is known as the Special Air Force. Why, Lieutenant Fukai? Why do you fight?"

"So that I can live and not die at your hands. Why can't you understand that? Are you saying other humans, the groups aside from Yukikaze and the SAF, aren't like that?"

"I believe that the machine intelligences of the SAF, including Yukikaze and you contained within her, are like me: intelligences that do not possess personlike consciousness. What I cannot understand is why you do not separate from the group known as the FAF and continue to fight to thwart my plans. Yukikaze refuses to ratify my nonaggression pact. You are the only one who can convince her to withdraw her rejection. Lieutenant Fukai, I desire to awaken you. Come back to me."

"Wait, what... What do you mean, I don't possess personlike consciousness? Ratify a nonaggression pact? Come back to you?"

"The current people as well as the artificial intelligences that manipulate them are beings that can be made to deviate from their essential natures by our plans. You people, however, are not like that. You are essential beings, and your enemy is not me. It is not my intention to let you be consumed. It is my desire that you choose to come over to me."

"In short..." said Lieutenant Katsuragi, cutting in. Rei didn't stop him. He was going to need time if he was going to figure out what the JAM were saying. "You're saying that since we're like the JAM, you want us to join you, switch sides, and help you to fight the FAF?"

"Who are you?"

"My name is Akira Katsuragi, Yukikaze's flight officer and electronic warfare operator. I serve at FAF Faery base in the Tactical Combat Air Corps, Special Air Force 5th Squadron. My rank is second lieutenant and I am a human. If you want to know why I fight you, it's pretty much because it's my job to. My job, do you understand? My duty. I do this because there's no other suitable path I can take through life."

"You can live without fighting me."

"I can interpret your thoughts to mean that you want the

SAF to be your allies, can't I? Does that mean you're offering me a job?"

In this situation, what he'd just asked was so base it was almost funny. But they waited for the JAM's answer, even as Rei wondered what the lieutenant's real motives were.

"You people and I are similar, but we are not comrades. But I wish to explain that I see the possibility of forming a common front against the FAF. I judge that will provide a path through life for you, Lieutenant Katsuragi. I seek your answer. If you have any intention of withdrawing from the FAF and joining me, then declare it to me, Lieutenant Fukai."

Its strained, unnatural circumlocutions made it difficult to follow, but what Rei could basically make out was that the JAM were demanding to know, if he intended to continue fighting, would he join the JAM's side. His destiny was riding on how he answered this question.

What would the JAM do if he told them no? Would it eliminate him to rid itself of an opponent beyond comprehension? No, it would likely keep working to understand him till the bitter end. The JAM probably wouldn't let him escape from this space. Maybe lead him, and Yukikaze, to be confined in a safe place, like Major Yazawa had said. Somewhere unimaginable that was neither Earth nor Faery, where the JAM could take its time in figuring them out, with special attention paid to Yukikaze. What if the JAM brainwashed him to get him on their side? If they succeeded at that, he imagined they could bring the entire SAF there to brainwash as well and then use them against the FAF. *In other words, turn them all into JAM...*

Well then, what if he said yes? What if he joined the JAM? Yukikaze wouldn't accept that quietly, surely. He had no doubt in his mind that she'd pitch both himself and Lieutenant Katsuragi out of the plane, to end up the same as Major Yazawa and whoever else had been with him.

"Your answer, Lieutenant Fukai."

Rei sensed that the JAM was in no hurry.

It had plenty of time. It had been observing the FAF for thirty years, so why would it rush? Rei was still under observation in this space, as well. The JAM didn't seem intent on killing him, but as long as he didn't answer it, he'd have no way to take any proactive steps toward saving himself. Unless he did something, he would end up starving to death, and Yukikaze would exhaust her fuel and fall silent.

What do I want to do, Rei asked himself. *Not what should I do, but do I want to do? Is that the answer?*

"I wish to know more details about what sort of beings you are," Rei said. "I don't understand anything about you, but you seem to grasp at least a bit about me. I can't ratify a nonaggression pact with you as long as this unequal state of affairs persists. First of all, I don't think you completely understand or know how to use human speech. Just what are you people? Living things? Beings that consist only of intelligence, will, and data? Do you have physical forms? If so, then where are they?"

"I cannot explain in a way that would be comprehensible in your terms. I am that I am."

Lieutenant Katsuragi felt a smile spasm across his face. The tension was so unbearable now that he could feel his train of thought starting to derail. "I am that I am." *Well, fantastic. They are just like Captain Fukai and Yukikaze, then.* As he was thinking how the resemblance was astonishing, the feeling of tension returned. He concentrated every nerve on Rei's answer.

"If you don't have words that can explain more than that, then any further communication via words is meaningless," Rei declared. Taking a deep breath and preparing himself for the worst, he gave his answer.

"I refuse your request."

"Understood," the JAM replied, without any emotion.

"Strategic reconnaissance, complete," Rei declared. "Returning to base."

VII

RETHINKING FIGHTING SPIRIT

SAF'S CENTRAL HEADQUARTERS command center was working night and day, as all of their planes were being sent in to support the massive attack operation against Cookie base.

The enormous screen taking up most of the wall at the front was filled with a variety of information, divided as needed to display the responses on the screens of HQ's tactical computer terminals. Mission progress. Maps of the combat airspace. The condition of the fighters preparing to sortie. The maintenance status of the planes on standby. Analysis of gains made in battle extrapolated from the data from returning planes. Analysis of the general progress of the battle. On and on and on.

Of immediate concern to the SAF was the progress of the attack on Cookie, not from a local perspective, but from an overall view of the battle's progress. Determining JAM tactics was the highest priority of all.

Once the first day had passed, Major Booker decided there was no need to throw all of the SAF's forces into the task of conducting tactical recon for the FAF's attack on the base. By that time, he knew that the JAM didn't seem to be defending the base to the last man. The enemy's strategy was definitely changing, and they wouldn't know what that change was if they just stuck close to Cookie.

Expecting a JAM retaliatory strike, the FAF set up a defense line around Faery base, sending out several squadrons to fly combat air patrols. The SAF flew recon missions there as well, but knowing the situation at Cookie wasn't playing out as it normally would, Major Booker reckoned they needed wider-ranged reconnaissance intel. What was happening over at Richwar base, which the Strategic Reconnaissance Corps claimed was paired with Cookie? How about at the other JAM bases? There weren't enough planes to observe movements at all those places. He rerouted a plane scheduled to run recon at Cookie to another area.

By doing that of his own accord, Booker was deviating from the operation as it had been set up by the Tactical Combat Air Corps—under which the SAF served—and the entire Faery Air Force. Military operations were established with the understanding that all of the chess pieces on the board would systematically move as they were supposed to. If the lower echelons started acting on their own, the entire operation would become meaningless. However, at this moment, the SAF was trying to grasp the JAM's strategic movements. It was likely that the JAM were just as interested in the SAF, and that they were observing the SAF's movements. Major Booker figured they were out there, watching what they did. If the SAF didn't take the initiative now, the chance to make direct contact with the JAM might slip away forever.

That was what the major was afraid of.

There was no time to get permission from high command. To modify the operation, the SAF would have to convene their supreme strategy conference and then put in their request for the entire operation to be reviewed. That was impossible, of course, because there was no time for such a thing. If the SAF were going to do this at all, it would have to be now, and without authorization.

General Cooley made her decision. The JAM's shift in tactics was evident, and the FAF was just too massive to be able to keep up with it. In this situation, the smaller and more nimble SAF would be much more effective. They were going to alter the current operation on their own initiative. Strategic reconnaissance operations against the JAM would now have top priority.

When Major Booker had asked her if she was sure of her decision, the general had replied, "I'm the head of the SAF. I do what I want to do. Nobody ever complains about it. That's how it's always been. It's called being flexible in making use of your resources." The way she had put it, Major Booker really did feel as though he'd been worried over nothing. Even so, he could see that the general was still prepared to pay hell for her choice.

General Cooley was prepared to do anything to ensure the survival of the SAF. She'd once even said that joining forces with the JAM might be an option worth exploring. That was more than enough to get her arrested for treason, but she offered no excuses. She would sooner resist than make excuses, and resistance would probably turn into a life or death struggle for the SAF. The members of the squadron, however, felt no need to defend the general, and she had no expectations of help from them. Each individual was acting on their own in order to ensure their own survival.

As a consequence of how we're set up, it's unlikely that the SAF as a whole would mutiny against the FAF, Major Booker thought. But it also wasn't out of the question that the FAF might back them far enough into a corner to make mutiny necessary. In order to protect herself, General Cooley was considering using the FAF's own methods. In other words, she was ready to use the military might of the SAF as part of her own individual resistance. If there was any move to have her arrested or executed, all the general would have to do is declare that her unit was prepared to launch an armed resistance en masse. The instant that she did, the SAF would be seen as a rebel force and attacked. The squadron would then have no choice but to fight the FAF. Even if they didn't want to, they'd still fight, because all but the terminally clueless would realize that a firing squad awaited them all even if they surrendered to arrest without firing a shot.

A FAF attack wouldn't mean that the SAF would be banding together in common cause. While it might seem that way from the outside, it would be nothing more than individual minds utilizing whatever abilities they had in order to survive. General Cooley herself was a representative of the sort of person who possessed that sort of consciousness, Major Booker began to realize. That general had made the SAF what it was, and the squadron reflected her character and way of thinking. She had made the SAF not an organization run from the top down, but rather something that *was* her. A part of her being. The very essence of her. Something that she'd use to strike back if she were struck. That was all. It didn't matter if it were the JAM doing the striking or anyone else. The general was convinced she was doing the right thing. It was a simple, straightforward conclusion, but he doubted that the people in the FAF would see it that way.

There was a definite problem there…

If the SAF existed as a corps-level organization, like the Strategic Reconnaissance Corps, a flexible response to the attack on Cookie wouldn't be much of a problem. That was because corps-level formations could take part in the overall strategy conference and give a clear idea of how much individual action they'd need. But the SAF could make no such plays. *We're going to be seen as going rogue, and we need to get something to show for this if we're going to demonstrate our loyalty. General Cooley must think that we will,* Major Booker thought.

The general would negotiate things with the guys at the top. He wouldn't have to worry about that. All he needed to concentrate on was how best to utilize their planes. It was the general's job to worry about the SAF's position. He was free to do what he wanted to under her authority.

As soon as he learned that the SAF had canceled their strike against Cookie base in order to resume surveillance on Richwar, General Laitume started complaining. General Cooley was summoned, and it was no exaggeration to say that he was thinking of having her relieved of duty right there and then.

Laitume knew perfectly well that there was no time to convene a panel of the heads of the various corps to do that in the midst of a major operation. *All he'd be able to do was give a personal warning to Cooley and the SAF, demanding that we restrain ourselves,* thought Major Booker. But General Cooley, seeing a good opportunity, had turned the meeting into an impromptu official strategy session between the SAF and the commanding officer of the corps to which it was attached. Major Booker had marveled anew at General Cooley's abilities. He might have been moved by it all, had he not been busy giving a presentation to General Laitume to make him understand why they were doing what they were doing. It was no trivial task, since failure to persuade Laitume would have ended General Cooley's career.

Major Booker had explained to him about the JAM's changing strategy and how the SAF were currently engaged in their own strategic reconnaissance against the JAM. If they let this opportunity slip by, he'd gone on, then they might also lose their chance to make direct contact with the JAM.

"We have the Strategic Reconnaissance Corps for that," General Laitume had shot back. "I won't permit the SAF to do whatever it wants to!"

"That assumes the SRC isn't being manipulated by the JAM," General Cooley had said. "We in the SAF don't agree."

"What was that? Just what are you implying?"

"There's no doubt now that the JAM have infiltrated the FAF with their duplicates," Major Booker added. "I can imagine that they're manipulating our intelligence, meaning we have to be on guard for any false intel they might feed us."

"It's just as likely that you people are being manipulated by them as well."

"And that can be verified by checking for any discrepancies between the intelligence gathered by the SRC and ourselves," General Cooley had explained in the tone of a tenacious teacher. "If they both agree, then either we're both right, or else both of us may be supplying false information. In that case, you'll have to compare it with data gathered from yet another corps. In any case, I'm sure that you can see that the more routes from which we gather our reconnaissance data, the higher the degree of accuracy we'll achieve. All the SAF is doing is putting that concept into practice using your own forces, General Laitume. We can't simply take the SRC at its word."

"Our battle with the JAM has reached a turning point, General," Major Booker said. "While we expect the SRC is going to complain that we're invading their turf, as we've just explained to you, it's necessary for us to conduct our own strategic recon operations."

"It's a commander's job to encourage the fighting spirit of their subordinates and keep them motivated," General Cooley added. "I'm not going to tell Major Booker not to do this."

"Our corps' headquarters is frustrated by their inability to receive intel from the SAF in real time."

"That goes with how we carry out our duties. It can't be helped—"

Laitume continued, cutting Cooley off.

"I'm not talking about getting combat intel from your planes. We're getting worried that the SAF isn't sending all the information it gathers up the chain of command, that you cherry pick and hide things from us. Don't say that you aren't aware of that, General."

"That's a problem that goes with the very nature of the SAF's duties," Cooley said. "Our mission is to carry out combat intelligence gathering. It isn't all meant for public consumption or to be seen by large numbers of people. It's easier to control intelligence within the confines of the SAF than it is in a larger organization. If, by some chance, any classified information were to leak out, it's easier to track down the source in a small organization like ours. That's why the squadron was set up the way it was. Corps HQ is a bit wrong to blame us for that, since as the corps commanding officer, all the intelligence we gather is sent to you. Letting that information go public is your decision, Lieutenant General. The SAF doesn't interfere in any decisions you make. However, I will give you a word of warning—those who are complaining about us may be JAM, and you need to take their criticism with a grain of salt."

"If we start doubting each other, there'll be no end to it. Blast it all, there's no easy solution for this problem, is there?" Laitume said.

"Have you told the other divisions that the FAF has been infiltrated by JAM duplicates, and that there may be more of them even now?" Major Booker asked. "I was wondering if you could tell us."

"I informed the high command. I treated it as a highest level secret, but there's no point in concealing that you people were the source of the information. The FAF has gathered the suspected JAM duplicates into that retraining unit you proposed. The Intelligence Forces are operating in the background to decide who gets transferred to it."

"And you've determined that you have complete control over that unit, haven't you? That's a group of suspected JAM duplicates, you know. I'm not saying they're all going to be JAM, but still—"

"The unit is operating autonomously of my corps. That's because those we suspect aren't just in my corps alone. It's already out of my hands. To be honest, losing pilots to that unit is really hurting me," Laitume said. "I've had to stop running recon missions with my own forces. But there's nothing else we can do at this point. The high command's made its decision. There was some dissent over it, but Colonel Rombert got his way."

"The unit's been set up under the Intelligence Forces, then?" Cooley asked.

"It's been organized as part of the Systems Corps. I'm sure they were operating under the theory that improving people falls under their purview, but in part it was a result of the power relationships between the differents corps. Colonel Rombert is definitely still pulling the strings in the background, though. That man has gained the most from all this."

"Putting suspected JAM duplicates in the Systems Corps is a foolish decision," General Cooley said. "Weapons development and enhancement goes on there. That's exactly the sort of information the JAM would want."

"I was against it as well. For the Systems Corps' part, they have more of an interest in determining the reason why these people were shot down by the JAM than in determining whether or not they're duplicates. They're doing a complete investigation to see if the losses were due to pilot error, mechanical fault, psychological causes, or tactical error. Basically, they're guinea pigs. The scrutiny may also determine what Colonel Rombert wants to know, which is what makes them different from real humans. It would probably be something like that."

"Neither the Systems Corps nor the high command have any clue how important this is," said Major Booker with a sigh. "They're planning to send ground forces into Cookie base, right? Those rumors of them forming a ground unit are true, aren't they?"

"We began forming a ground force a while ago. As an autonomous ground army, not as part of the FAF. For its part, the FAF wants its own ground force, like the navy has a marine corps. Air marines, if you will. It seems likely that we'll have one in the near future. You have to say well done to that," General Laitume said. "It won't be ready to help with the initial attack on Cookie base, but we can throw them into any operation from now on. The Systems Corps already have several types of ground-based weaponry under development. I don't know the details, but it's stuff like armored combat suits with their own onboard power supplies, with small arms munitions designed to destroy the computers in the electromechanical bodies we've theorized that the JAM have, and closed-loop communications systems. We wanted them to build tanks as well, but they're still in the prototype stage and nowhere near completion. The Systems Corps is calling the combat suits 'powered armor,' and they've already mass produced a number of units. What they've produced so far is expected to be formed into an official combat unit. They'll probably be thrown at Cookie first."

"An experimental ground battle," General Cooley said, as though to herself. "That'll be worth seeing."

"Are you implying you want them to fail, General Cooley?"

"I'm interested in the JAM. And in what sort of aliens these ground forces will encounter. And if the FAF weren't wasting its time with internal and external political power struggles, we'd learn about them a lot faster. Introducing these ground forces will get us nowhere. So no, I don't think they'll achieve much."

"Just what are you implying? According to what I've seen—"

"The JAM tend to match any move that we make," Major Booker explained. "The JAM build their aircraft to match our level of development. They don't fly by some unknown means, and their weapons systems are hardly beyond our comprehension. If we introduce tanks, then the JAM will respond with their own. We'll just be expanding the battlefield to the ground, and I can say this beyond a shadow of a doubt. Whatever the reason the FAF had for not introducing ground forces up till now, it was a wise one. At the moment, all we should do is maintain watch on the skies. That's how the SAF sees it."

Laitume ignored Major Booker for the moment. "You're saying we're dealing with the JAM well enough as we are now, General Cooley?"

"The JAM are desperate. They were the ones who launched a preemptive strike. 'Well enough' doesn't imply that we're just playing around with them. We don't know what their objective is, and the SAF is searching for that. Of course, that's what the entire FAF is trying to find out. I'm not saying that our judgments are absolutely correct. But General Laitume, the SAF is the only unit that's made direct contact with the JAM. You can't just ignore that. What's your decision, General?"

"Decision about what?"

"We'd like you to consider the file Major Booker has just presented to you and make an official recognition of the reconnaissance operations the SAF is now conducting. If we have it, we'd like to carry it out without any needless interference from other units."

"Are you aware of what you're asking me, General Cooley? You're asking me to give you complete carte blanche in how you use your forces while I get to take responsibility for it."

"If you formally recognize this, then I can deal with any criticism from the other units directly," Cooley responded. "You won't have to be bothered by it. This isn't the first time I've made this request, General. I floated the idea for this recon operation to you at that lunch meeting."

"And I believe I told you I wouldn't allow you to act arbitrarily."

"You didn't say what sort of actions wouldn't be allowed, and so I didn't take that as a definite answer. The SAF has come to get that answer, sir. In any case, this is a state of emergency. As Major Booker's data indicate, the situation has changed radically. If we let this opportunity pass, we can turn victory into defeat. Do you want to be remembered as the general who let a chance for victory slip away from right in front of him?"

"This is unpleasant."

"If there's a person who finds war pleasant, I'd like to meet them. This is war."

"Sir," Major Booker quickly interjected. "General Cooley hasn't gotten much rest during this operation, so—"

"So what? Are you apologizing for her insubordination? General Cooley, are you the sort of person who palms off their responsibilities to her superior and leaves a subordinate to apologize for it?"

"The major isn't apologizing for me," General Cooley said. "He's just stating a fact. And I'm not trying to palm off my responsibilities on you. It's only natural that I treat the one in charge as if he were actually in charge. We're here to have a mission conference, not to curry favor with you. If you think you can't handle the SAF, then you should consider cutting ties with us. Maybe it's time the SAF became autonomous. If you approved that, you wouldn't have to bother yourself with us anymore."

"I can have you relieved of duty."

"You don't have the individual authority to do that. You need to present a reason for a dismissal. But if you're saying that the SAF isn't performing up to snuff, that also calls your own command competence into question."

General Laitume's face flushed bright red and it looked as if he were about to explode with rage. But he didn't. *If we were in a regular conference with others in attendance, he probably would have struck an enraged pose in order to save some face, and General Cooley probably took that into account as well*, Major Booker thought.

After glaring at Cooley for a moment, the general picked up the file in front of him and said, "You sly fox... No, forgive me. Calling you that would only convince you that you've scored some sort of great success here. I run the FAF's main force. The SAF gets to carry out major operations only because it serves under me. I've put my neck on the line to protect you from the slanders of the other divisions and the high command because I appreciate what you people can do. There is no need to interrupt the current operation, so carry on with what you're doing. If you have a problem with your equipment, then tell me. I'll see what I can do. But the situation is severe all around. Once we're through this, despite my reservations, I'll do everything in my power to realize the SAF's selfish desire. This is my idea. Don't forget that, General Cooley. That is all. Dismissed."

"I appreciate it," General Cooley said, rising. As she looked at the general, she added, "Sir, I strongly suggest you give Major Booker's report a thorough reading. It may already be too late."

"Too late for what?"

"You can still go back to Earth alive. Once you read that, you'll understand. If you'll excuse me, sir."

A genuinely complicated look came to Gibril Laitume's face. The change in expression didn't go unnoticed by Major Booker. He could imagine how he felt.

The SAF had achieved a major victory, one that might as well have been his own, one that had worked out well—and then came General Cooley's words to crush that sense of satisfaction. She'd basically called him a coward who should run home while he still could. That had probably made him sick with rage, but he was nervous also because she'd said that if he read Booker's materials, he'd see that there was no longer any safe place in the FAF. He wondered who his enemy was, reconsidered why he was here, then understood the reason for General Cooley's arrogant attitude. She was saying that she had no intention of running back home, but was instead ready to die in battle. He respected her resolve as a fellow soldier.

No, Gibril, General Cooley isn't thinking about dying. She's a tougher woman than you realize. A woman willing to use you to survive this war. You don't operate on the same plane as she does. Naturally, the major kept these thoughts to himself and simply followed General Cooley out of the conference room.

Now there was no need to worry about General Cooley's position. The responsibility was now entirely General Laitume's to bear. Since he'd said that they were free to do what they wanted, Major Booker could now consider moving their strategic reconnaissance operation aimed at direct contact with the JAM to phase three.

So, how could he relay to the JAM that the SAF were preparing to make noncombat contact with them? The JAM probably understood human language, so he could just transmit a message, but the last thing he wanted was any humans in the other units to read it. It would be treason.

General Laitume would never be able to cover for them. Maybe they could load the message into a recon pod and then let the JAM recover and decipher it. He could just put the message in directly, but when he considered the slight possibility that another FAF unit would recover the pod, Booker disregarded that plan as well. It would have to be encrypted. But then how would he be able to transmit a decryption key so that only the JAM could decrypt it? For that, he'd need the wisdom of both the SAF's tactical and strategic computers—they operated on a level closer to the JAM than any human did.

Think of a way to declare our intentions to the JAM which they could understand while being indecipherable to other FAF units. When Major Booker fed that question to the SAF tactical computer, it responded with an answer so bold and audacious that he never would have thought of it. Immediately, almost too quickly.

```
Select a landing spot the JAM are known to be
monitoring, then use human speech, which can only
be deciphered after noise removal. Any other FAF
planes flying by won't have any means to reliably
pick up the voice aboard their aircraft. A plane
equipped with passive airspace radar might feasibly
do it under the same conditions, but the likelihood
is very small that the tiny pressure changes caused
by human speech could be detected by FAF planes.
For best certainty, if an FAF plane comes into the
vicinity, shoot it down. That is all.
```

How interesting, thought Major Booker, smiling unconsciously. *I was set on finding an electronic way of doing it, but now that you mention it, people have mouths to talk with.* Then Booker inputted, `However, the question is if the JAM will be listening. And understanding human language isn't the same as understanding human speech.` Having said that, the tactical computer told Booker to disregard it.

```
I anticipate that the JAM possess the means to
interpret information from the human body. If not,
their human duplicates would be unable to carry out
information gathering activities. It may not even
be necessary for the messenger you send to express
your message in spoken words.
```

```
Does that mean that the JAM would search the memo-
ries in the messenger's brain directly?
```
Booker typed.

```
That possibility cannot be entirely ruled out,
but in that case the high-information-content mes-
sage you need to send would become ambiguous. The
next most secure method of delivery after spoken
language would be a written message. We expect that
the JAM would understand that.
```

The combat intelligence had come back with a reply more

thoroughly pragmatic than Major Booker had expected.

It was as if the CI is saying that the JAM won't accept the message unless we communicate it by means of our own flesh and blood bodies, Major Booker thought. And even as he decided to follow its recommendation to make the JAM understand that humans were the main actors in this conflict, he reflected on how he'd still unconsciously sought computer or electronic means to communicate with the JAM in the first place, although he didn't pursue the thought very far.

However, had Major Booker simply asked, "Have you made contact with the JAM?" the tactical computer would likely have answered, "Yes."

The SAF's combat intelligences had detected what they took to be a message from the JAM while analyzing data gathered during Captain Foss's combat mission with Yukikaze. The JAM had aimed a pulsed laser at Yukikaze during the air battle and sent the following message: We desire an exchange of intentions by means of language with an SAF human, especially the one known as Second Lieutenant Rei Fukai, in a way that no other being aside from the SAF would know about.

Major Booker had never even considered that Yukikaze and the SAF's machine intelligences—in short, their computers—had already made contact with the JAM in this way. That was why he didn't ask the question, and because he didn't ask, the tactical computer did not tell him. Even Rei didn't know until he had met the whole of JAM existence. Not a single human had realized it. Not until it had actually happened.

2

CAPTAIN FUKAI IS *the only one capable of communication with the JAM,* Major Booker thought. And he'd have to do it as soon as he was ready to. But he wasn't prepared yet. First of all, there was the critical issue of selecting a reliable contact point. That would mostly determine the success or failure of this endeavor.

Since it would be necessary to scout out the several JAM bases

comprising Richwar, Major Booker rerouted the planes scheduled to be used in the Cookie attack operation for that purpose.
Urging Captain Foss to hurry up with her profacting of the JAM,
he dispatched Yukikaze on her tactical recon of Cookie base as
originally planned. It was reckless to send Rei on a sortie so soon
after returning to combat duty, and with his green EWO Lieutenant Katsuragi besides, but the major judged that Rei needed
to get his combat intuition back and Lieutenant Katsuragi needed some real combat experience.

Rei had expressed concern over involving a newbie like Lieutenant Katsuragi in something as important as making contact
with the JAM, but Major Booker had had an idea he didn't tell
Rei about. If Yukikaze and her crew were captured, it'd be better to have a crewmember who knew as little about the inner
workings of the SAF as possible. Katsuragi fit that description
perfectly. Also, if it should turn out that Rei himself was being
manipulated by the JAM, that unknown even to himself, he was
a JAM duplicate, then Major Booker believed that Lieutenant
Katsuragi would be able to deal with that situation as well. As
a member of the Intelligence Forces, Lieutenant Katsuragi had
had it drilled into him to constantly be on guard for those who
were attempting to sabotage the FAF. *Aside from that, if by some
chance Katsuragi was a JAM himself*, Major Booker thought, *and
the JAM wanted to make contact with Yukikaze and Rei, then
they might use Lieutenant Katsuragi to guide her to them.*

Major Booker had also considered the possibility that the
JAM would initiate contact from their end, but he'd expected
them to use the human duplicates they'd created to understand
humans. Of course, he'd also considered that the JAM would try
to directly access the SAF's computers, but he'd unconsciously
ignored the possibility because he hoped that wouldn't occur. In
such a situation, the humans would have no recourse. It would
mean that the war had completely become one between the JAM
and the computers.

Some things you don't want to deal with, even as they demand your attention, because you don't want them to be true.
The trouble is that ignoring an unpleasant truth doesn't make it
any less real. To the contrary, he'd been a fool to have forgotten

how much of a bitch reality tended to be, Major Booker realized as he monitored Yukikaze's tactical reconnaissance mission to Cookie base from the command center.

With Cookie already destroyed, he hadn't been expecting any surprises. After taking on fuel at their refueling point and conducting the recon, the only thing he expected to hear next from them was "Mission complete, RTB." And, in fact, that was what had happened with every other fighter before Yukikaze. A detailed analysis of the electronic intelligence gathered from the combat airspace had indicated that Cookie wasn't seeking aid from any other bases. The humans in the SAF had judged that it was too late for the JAM to try and turn the tables on them there.

Booker had Captain Foss waiting there with him, since he figured that Lieutenant Katsuragi's inexperience might start aggravating Rei. But then, seeing as she already had an interest in Rei, Lieutenant Katsuragi, and Yukikaze, Foss had probably intended to come down to the command center to observe their mission regardless of her orders. The same went for General Cooley. Even as she was convincing herself that nothing was going to happen to Yukikaze in this situation, she still couldn't bring herself to take her eyes off the plane's mission status data stream and get some rest. The humans in the SAF might not have known that Yukikaze had already been contacted by the JAM, but they all knew how serious a matter it'd be if anything happened to her.

Which was why all of them felt an awful foreboding when they received Yukikaze's distress call.

The action in the command center kicked up a notch as the tactical computer translated the code from Yukikaze into human speech and moved the display from one of the terminals to the main screen.

This is Yukikaze. We have encountered an unknown type of JAM plane. Taking own initiative and moving strategic reconnaissance operation to phase three. Out.

"What's going on here? Have Captain Fukai explain," Major Booker ordered. The communications officer replied that he couldn't.

"Yukikaze is currently engaged in a level-1 combat recon operation and is flying with her comm systems blacked out. We can't reach her."

"I don't think Captain Fukai is the one calling the shots here, Major," Captain Foss said. "The way that message says 'Taking own initiative' is telling me that it's Yukikaze making the call, and Rei—sorry, Captain Fukai may not even know about it, or at the very least didn't make the decision."

"Looks like the JAM got the jump on you, Major Booker," said General Cooley. "From what I see in this scenario, that unknown JAM plane is there to make contact with Yukikaze, not engage her in combat. They've moved to make contact from their side."

"I knew this would happen," said Captain Foss coolly.

If you knew that, Major Booker thought savagely, *then why the hell didn't you bother mentioning it beforehand? And stop looking so damned pleased with yourself.* As much as he wanted to actually say it to her, his sense of danger overrode his anger. They could point fingers later. Right now, they had to wrap their heads around what was happening to Yukikaze fast and figure out what to do about it. As usual, the tactical computer won that race.

Reroute returning Rafe to the scene. General Cooley, grant clearance.

"Granted. Major Booker, take command."

"Roger. ATC, I need emergency access to the Rafe. What's its current position and remaining fuel status?"

I'll do that, the tactical computer indicated on the main screen. Attempting to seize control of Tactical Combat Air Corps and TAB-8 base control and computer systems. General Cooley, grant clearance.

"Granted, on condition that the seizure isn't detected. They mustn't know that we're doing this."

Roger. Your condition is possible to achieve. Initiating mission to track and support Yukikaze by authorization of General Cooley. Arranging for hot refuel of Rafe at TAB-8. Operating Rafe to achieve optimal reconnaissance action. Grant clearance.

"Granted. Don't let anyone else know that we're operating that

Rafe. Give me a sequential report of everything that you do."

```
Roger. Generating real-time display of situa-
tion in Cookie base battle zone from available
information.
```

No real-time data was coming in from Yukikaze. For that reason, they had no idea what was happening to her, or even what course she was flying. Usually, she would operate so as to make sure that none of the data she was gathering could be intercepted by the wrong hands, so the command center wouldn't have any means of tracking her in real time. But that wasn't the case now. The tactical computer was seizing the data from the computer systems of the other military units. In addition, it'd issued emergency change of mission orders to two SAF fighters they had flying in other areas outside of Cookie and was displaying the real-time data of the FAF telemetry it was now gathering.

From this, they learned that Cookie had launched one final counterattack and then self-destructed. All FAF fighters flying in the airspace above had been brought down, and now the front line was buzzing with activity, like a beehive someone had poked with a stick. Despite this, they had no clue as to what had happened to Yukikaze. Her presence in the area couldn't even be confirmed.

If Yukikaze was still intact, Major Booker thought, *and she was simply keeping her contact with the JAM a secret from the FAF, then that was fine. She was just hiding it from everybody. But what if that wasn't the case?*

The tactical computer sent the Rafe to search for Yukikaze on Cookie's perimeter for as long as the Rafe's fuel allowed, but by that time there was no sign of her. All it spotted were the surviving JAM fighters in combat with the FAF.

The Rafe was temporarily landed at TAB-8 to be hot fueled, with its engines still running. Despite that, it still took more time than it should have. The arrangements for the refueling had been properly made, but the humans at the base had never seen an unmanned Rafe before, so they didn't know where the fuel ports were or even how many of them it had. The SAF sent the data, but until it was sent to the scene, the Rafe was kept waiting. There it sat, engines running with its nose sunk down in a kneeling position. To the humans who stood watching it nearby, it seemed just like a JAM.

"C-could Yukikaze have been shot down?" Unable to stand it anymore, Captain Foss asked the question nobody else wanted to. "She isn't anywhere. She's not flying."

"There's no trace of her having crashed," replied General Cooley. "We're not picking up any mayday signals either."

Major Booker had thought that she'd perhaps landed at Cookie, but the video the Rafe had sent back gave lie to that possibility. There was no Cookie base left to land on. It had been transformed into an enormous crater. Even had Yukikaze landed there, it would be difficult to even discern her wreckage.

I anticipate that Yukikaze is making contact with the JAM, the tactical computer said. I cannot detect that ourselves. All we can do is wait for her return to base.

"Have the Rafe continue its investigation," said Major Booker. "I'm declaring an emergency. Have the other fighters join in."

While a search is necessary, putting more search planes in the airspace over Cookie at this time won't increase the probability of locating Yukikaze, the computer said. I theorize that she has entered the mysterious battle zone.

"Where's this mysterious battle zone?" Captain Foss asked.

"An unknown airspace Yukikaze was caught in once before. It happened during a sightseeing flight with a visitor from Earth aboard her. Yukikaze was flying without a full crew, and the JAM caught her in a strange interdimensional zone, like a butterfly in a net."

Even as he explained, Major Booker wondered why the tactical computer had mentioned that little detail, then realized why. There was no doubt in his mind that the computers had already had some sort of discussion with the JAM and foreseen this circumstance. The SAF's combat intelligences had acted on their own initiative. They were now seizing control.

Major Booker bit his lip as he realized that he'd been naive. It had been them, not the JAM, who'd gotten the jump on him. Rei had told him that Yukikaze was conscious, that she was alive, but he'd never really taken him seriously. Apparently, he should have.

"But why Yukikaze?" Major Booker murmuerd, almost to himself. "Why did the JAM choose her specifically?"

"Because the JAM consider Yukikaze a unique being," said Captain Foss. "Major, you're so immersed in the SAF that you can't see how unusual Yukikaze is. The fact that you can't realize something so simple says to me that—"

"Captain Foss, you don't need to be here," said General Cooley, cutting her off. "I want you to organize the results of your profacting of the JAM and submit a report to me at once."

"General, I'm not finished yet. I need the data Yukikaze is gathering right now."

"Major Booker, please inform Captain Foss as to her duty. There's no need for you to be here either. I'm taking command. Analyze Captain Foss's profacting report and then inform me immediately if you find anything useful in it. That is all. Now go to it."

"Y-yes, General." Major Booker saluted and abided by her order. He'd never felt so utterly defeated as he did at that moment.

He understood, though. If Yukikaze didn't make it back, the general was going to urgently need the results of Captain Foss's behavioral analysis of the JAM. The major appreciated that, given the circumstances, it was an entirely appropriate decision to make. So far as she was concerned, Rei's life or death was merely a strategic question. It was a matter of war.

But Major Booker couldn't neatly compartmentalize Rei like that. *Please, make it back*, he prayed. *I don't want to lose you, pal. You can't lose, not to the JAM, to Yukikaze, or to this war. Winning the battle doesn't matter. What counts most is making it back alive.*

Yeah, Major Booker thought as he reconsidered. *Rei would be the first to agree with me there.*

Rei didn't need prayers right now. He'd trust in his own strength and do what he thought needed to be done. All the major could do was hope that his friend made it back. If Yukikaze did return with knowledge of what the JAM truly were, then his feelings of defeat would be assuaged. If Booker was to pull himself together to go after the enemy once more, Yukikaze, Rei, and Lieutenant Katsuragi were going to have to make it back.

3

AS SOON AS Rei declared RTB, Yukikaze reacted immediately.

Switch to AUTOMANEUVER...Capt.

She was requesting that Rei switch to auto mode and turn over combat maneuvering operations to her. He understood and flipped the automaneuver switch to ON.

Yukikaze began to accelerate, pulling right alongside the JAM duplicate of the old Yukikaze. It wasn't actively scanning them or interfering with Yukikaze's electronic systems, but it was probably observing her actions and gathering combat intelligence via passive means. If she attempted to make contact with SAF headquarters, the JAM would know it and would probably be able to decrypt the contents of the communication. Even now, Yukikaze remained a mystery to the JAM.

The ghost plane was a copy of a Super Sylph, meaning it couldn't compete with the Maeve where speed was concerned. They began to pull away. The ghost plane didn't attempt to interfere electronically with Yukikaze. She simply made a slight course correction and continued to accelerate, making for the thin belt of blue sky that lay in between the sea of ashen clouds that stretched above and below them. *It's like a blue signal light, showing the way out*, Rei thought.

The problem was that they couldn't determine how far away it was. It felt practically infinite.

"Abnormality to our rear," Lieutenant Katsuragi said in a low voice. "It looks like the exit's closing up."

Even Rei looked up from the radar display to check. The gap in the sea of clouds behind them was disappearing. The wall that stretched above and below their sides was now coming together behind them, and the tangent it formed was getting closer. It felt, Rei decided, like they were inside an enormous bivalve shell closing around them. What he couldn't confirm was whether the pivot point for the walls lay behind them.

This was just like the last time he'd been trapped in the mysterious battle zone, when Lander had lost his left hand. Yukikaze had been surrounded by an invisible arcing wall. He'd headed for what looked like the way out, but the wall had joined into a circle that had surrounded them. The circle had then contracted into a point, squeezing them into the zone. Last time, the wall hadn't shown up on regular radar. Now, it was the exact reverse. The situation was upside down.

"At this rate, we're going to be crushed," said Lieutenant Katsuragi with a voice squeezed dry of any emotion. "Can we make it out?"

"Good question," Rei replied. *The JAM are probably intercepting our intercom as well*, he thought.

"You just going to do nothing, Captain Fukai?"

"Calm down, Lieutenant. They're not going to kill us here."

"How do you know that?"

"They could kill us any time they want to. The JAM want to capture us. When that exit closes, we and Yukikaze will be transported somewhere else. I think the JAM will then run a thorough analysis on us. After that, they'll probably duplicate us using that data and then try to infiltrate the SAF. As for us, they'll either brainwash us or just dispose of us when they're finished."

"Dispose? You mean kill, don't you? We're human beings. What are you, a machine?" Lieutenant Katsuragi couldn't suppress his emotions anymore.

"I'm human. That's why the JAM made contact with me."

"Then how can you be so calm about this, Fukai? Are you an idiot? It's insane to just leave this to Yukikaze. Let's light our afterburners and haul ass!"

"If that'll get us out of here, Yukikaze will do it. We're not going to get anywhere by panicking. But I can guarantee that they aren't going to kill us here. So just calm down. As long as we're alive, we'll have a chance to escape."

"So," Katsuragi said after a pause, "where will we be transported to?"

"I dunno. It may be an airspace that's a practically indistinguishable copy of planet Faery. I think it may even be a place with duplicates of the FAF and the SAF so that it'll feel like we've gotten back home. The best outcome for the JAM would be to monitor us in our natural state."

"That's ridiculous. If they do that, how are we supposed to escape? Besides that, how are we supposed to know if we're in a virtual world or the real one?"

"We couldn't tell with our five human senses—there'd only be one way to know. We'd have to ask Yukikaze. I'd expect that she has the means to sense whatever methods the JAM use. She has a means of electronically communicating with the JAM beyond what our senses can detect. If Yukikaze tells us to attack something, then we attack that target. We'll have to trust that it's an enemy. That's all we can do." Even as he said it, Rei realized that was how it had always been for him.

"Lieutenant, you have nothing to worry about. Up till now, you've never been able to shake the feeling that what you see around you isn't actually real. This isn't going to change anything in your life. Even if you're killed by the JAM, you probably wouldn't notice it if you can't really feel it in the first place."

"Spare me the pretentious lectures, please. Why are you just doing nothing? You don't mind us getting caught by the JAM as long as you leave it all to Yukikaze?"

"And what else would you have me do here? Maybe shoot my flight officer because he's had a nervous breakdown?"

"Oh, just try it! If you keep doing nothing, I may want to do that to you—"

"Watch your mouth, pal," Rei said. "Everything we say is being recorded. Think about what'll happen if we make it back alive, Lieutenant Katsuragi. Now cool off."

"Can we at least ask Yukikaze if there's anything we can do to get out of this?" Katsuragi said after a long pause.

"I don't want to place any unnecessary burdens on her. Just let Yukikaze handle this. Don't interfere. We'll find out if she succeeds or fails later. All we can do for now is think about what we'll have to do if she does fail. If the JAM succeed in capturing us and sneak duplicates into the SAF, how do we let them know that those aren't actually us?"

"That's impossible."

"You don't have to think about it. Just maintain your watch on our surroundings. That's an order, Lieutenant. I won't allow any dereliction of duty."

As he spoke, Rei prepared himself for the worst. He didn't think that even Yukikaze could get them out of this one. Even so, he didn't regret leaving it to her to handle. If she couldn't do it, he thought, there was no way that he could.

"Captain Fukai."

"What?"

"A wall has formed behind us. It's spherical and appears to extend infinitely to our sides, but I believe it encloses a limited airspace."

"It seems that way. It's like we're trapped inside of a ball, meaning that gap in front of us isn't a straight belt but the edge of an enormous sphere. And now it's closing."

"Which means we'll be able to accurately measure the distance to the way out just before it closes completely."

"So?"

"I propose that we launch a medium-range missile," Lieutenant Katsuragi said.

"Aimed at what?"

"The way out. Even if Yukikaze can't make it in time, the missile might. If we time it right, the speed of a high-velocity missile combined with Yukikaze's current speed may allow it to escape."

"Hmm."

"Yukikaze could program the missile with data about us, can't she? There's memory space in it for guidance data. Can't we use that?"

"Yukikaze might be able to use it for that. I've never tried anything like that before, but…" Rei trailed off.

"I'm not as optimistic as you. If we don't make it out of here, we're finished. I don't want to die without letting people know what happened to me. I don't think you do either. Even Yukikaze must want to get the data she's gathered here to the outside, right?"

"Even if the missile makes it out of here, the odds of that data being recovered by the SAF or the FAF is pretty remote."

"That's all, sir. End of proposal."

It would be impossible to record all the data of what had happened here into a missile. However, they might be able to input data proving that it had been fired by Yukikaze. It was worth a try, Rei decided. If the missile made it out of here, there was a chance that it would be found. There was no way of telling where it would come out or where it'd be headed, though.

"Calculate the optimal firing timing for a medium-range missile, based on its speed and range, then give it to me."

"Roger."

Lieutenant Katsuragi placed his hands onto the electronic warfare panel. As if replying to him, Yukikaze readied two medium-range missiles for firing.

Realizing that she understood what her crew wanted to do, Lieutenant Katsuragi began to trust Yukikaze. But Rei didn't feel as he did. This was their last option if Yukikaze couldn't escape. In other words, their last will and testament. Doing this would mean admitting that Yukikaze had no chance of escaping, and he just couldn't bring himself to do that.

The lock-on tone began to sound in his helmet speaker. Another tone overlaid it, indicating that guidance data was being loaded into the missiles. Once it was completed, Yukikaze declared her intention to release them, leaving Rei to nervously wonder what the hell she was playing at.

This wasn't Lieutenant Katsuragi's proposed plan. Yukikaze wasn't using the missiles to transmit their last words. This was an attack.

As soon as Rei had realized this, Yukikaze fired the two missiles without any hesitation, not waiting for Rei's permission. Lieutenant Katsuragi reacted with astonishment. The fire control radar was displaying target data. The ghost plane flying level with them immediately initiated electronic jamming. Yukikaze canceled active guidance on the missile and left the target seeking to the missiles' onboard systems.

"This can't be happening!" Lieutenant Katsuragi shouted.

Rei couldn't believe his eyes. The missiles were targeted at two planes. One was very clearly shown on the display to be the ghost plane. But Yukikaze was showing one other target as well.

Yukikaze had targeted herself.

"She's self-destructing," the lieutenant continued. "Yukikaze wants to blow herself up!"

Rei was dumfounded.

He followed the missiles' contrails with his eyes. The one targeting the ghost plane made a sudden flat turn while the one targeting Yukikaze flew on and then began quickly climbing far ahead of them. It was thrusting itself onto a course describing an enormous loop.

The ghost plane began to jink and dodge. Banking sharply, it was far away from them in the blink of an eye. The missile began to correct its course to continue its pursuit. They could detect intense jamming waves coming from the ghost plane, but Yukikaze had left herself a way to guide the missiles even if their guidance systems were being interfered with, and began adjusting her course and speed. In other words, Yukikaze was flying herself to the missile's impact point.

It was an odd way to carry out self-destruction. Yukikaze's own self-destruction package wouldn't activate unless the crew's ejection seats had been fired. This was the only way she could do it with crew aboard.

There was no way for Lieutenant Katsuragi to eject. Ejecting from the plane in this situation would mean annihilation. He'd wind up like those human duplicates from the ghost plane. Their only chance for survival was for Captain Fukai to evade the missile.

"Take evasive action!" Lieutenant Katsuragi yelled, his voice cracking slightly. He was already regretting his proposal. If he hadn't mentioned the missiles, Yukikaze might not have thought to do this. "Yukikaze's admitting that she's lost!"

Rei reflexively started to flip the dogfight switch on, then stopped when he heard the lieutenant say that. "No. Yukikaze isn't saying she's lost."

"It'll hit us any second!" said Lieutenant Katsuragi, looking up. Rei checked the main display.

`These are not warning shots...JAM.`

Yukikaze was serious. She wasn't admitting defeat. She was doing the only thing to avoid it. Saying these weren't warning shots was the only way she could show the JAM how serious she was about this. Why? To save herself. Yukikaze wouldn't abandon a chance for survival. If she admitted defeat, there would be no need to announce it. She could just silently eject her crew and then self-destruct.

Yukikaze was telling the JAM in no uncertain terms that unless they let her out of this airspace, she was going to destroy herself. Rei decided that she was bargaining with the JAM. *For the terms of her self-destruction?* No, not at all. Yukikaze's objective wasn't to destroy herself.

Yukikaze must have understood why the JAM had lured her in here. They had a use for Yukikaze's crew because they were beings the JAM didn't understand. *She's guessed they want us captured alive even if negotiations broke down—that's why they took such care not to kill us,* Rei thought. But Yukikaze was saying that she wouldn't allow that, and she was prepared to wreck the JAM's plans right here and now.

This wasn't an act of suicide on Yukikaze's part. It was combat tactics against the JAM. She was telling them she was prepared to die. If they ignored it, they would all die in her self-destruction, but from Yukikaze's point of view, she would have stopped the JAM's plan, so it wouldn't be a defeat.

Yukikaze is taking me hostage, Rei thought. She was saying "Let me out, or I kill the crew. I'm serious!" She was practically saying that she could kill her crew at any time…

God, what a bitch.

Rei's fear of Yukikaze renewed itself. She was a being willing to sacrifice human lives in order to beat the JAM.

"It's no use."

As he heard Lieutenant Katsuragi speak behind him, Rei prepared himself for the end. He didn't feel betrayed by Yukikaze. He understood what she wanted to do. In the end, she didn't want to lose to the JAM. *Neither do I,* he thought as he consciously relaxed his grip on the flight stick. By not attempting to interfere with automaneuver mode, Rei could let Yukikaze know how he felt.

A feeling of satisfaction filled his heart, driving away the fear. Never before had he felt such a deep mutual understanding with her. A strange euphoria came over him, and Rei was no longer conscious of how unreal the whole situation had become.

The main display cleared as Yukikaze showed the time till impact, then added a single word.

Thanks.

Rei understood that she was paying him respect by showing him the countdown. It almost felt as if she were announcing, "We will be landing soon. Thanks for flying with me." When he thought about it, they'd been flying together a long time, and this might have been Yukikaze's way of saying goodbye. If this really was the end, it would be a good death for them both. He didn't care what anyone else thought about it.

Lieutenant Katsuragi grabbed the handles atop his seat that would activate the ejection sequencer with both hands, but couldn't move. He wasn't paralyzed with fear over what would happen to him if he ejected at supersonic speed. He simply couldn't move. He could see the warhead of the missile thrusting toward them with his naked eye now. The lens of the target seeker on the tip looked like a single eye staring at him. The lieutenant closed his eyes, not wanting to see what was coming.

4

YUKIKAZE DISPLAYED THE time till impact in hundredths of a second. As the numbers streamed by too fast to distinguish, they began to slow down, yet it didn't feel strange to Rei at all. *My brain is kicking into overdrive because I have to concentrate till the very last moment on not flipping the maneuver switch*, Rei thought. He anxiously waited for the readout to reach 0.00.

Almost there… Almost there…

At last, Rei saw it happen. For an instant, he felt the flash. It grew bright all around him, so bright that it became difficult to see the readout on the main display.

But the shock wave and pain he expected never came. *So*, Rei thought serenely, *this is what the moment of death feels like.*

The flash wasn't fading at all, as if time had been dramatically slowed down. *Why weren't things fading to black?* he wondered. *Why can I still think? Is there really a world for humans after death?* As he was thinking these thoughts, Rei then sensed that the missile was still overhead and hadn't exploded.

He didn't physically see it with his eyes. He just knew. Right overhead, the lens of the missile's seeker was looking down on him like a black eye.

The counter hadn't reached zero yet, he realized. The hundredths of a second column hadn't yet reached zero. He suddenly became aware that he was reaching for the flight stick.

That's right, Rei Fukai. It's not too late. You can still make it out of this. Evade the missile. Don't accept death at Yukikaze's hand.

He sensed a voice speaking to him. Was it the JAM? Or perhaps it was a part of him that still wanted to survive. Even as he thought this, his heart told him not to give in to its temptations. The voice continued.

You don't really want to die. You may have decided that being killed by Yukikaze wouldn't be death, but you're wrong. She's killing you. If you act now, you could still survive. I can stop her. Answer me. Do as I say.

"Fuck off," Rei screamed in his heart. "No!"

But why? Why won't you accept my offer? Why won't you trust me?

—Because you can't understand.

And he couldn't trust anyone who didn't, much less do what they told him to.

Do you prefer annihilation while you still don't understand what I am?

—I'd be killed by Yukikaze and not by you. I don't give a damn about you anymore. I won't let you come between us, so get the hell out of here! This is the relationship I share with her, and I'll be damned if I'll let you get in the way of it. I'm busy here trying to perfect my relationship with Yukikaze. Quit bothering me! My life or death is my own business. I won't let anyone take that from me!

He felt violent rage. A terrible anger he'd never experienced before. Whether it originated from himself or the owner of the voice, Rei couldn't say for sure.

The anger became an explosion of energy. Or at least that was what Rei thought. He couldn't see the main display anymore. The intense light spread. He felt the force of it blast the missile hanging over him away. This being, whatever it was, would not have him.

Rei sensed that he'd won, and joy filled his heart. It became a wave of force, shaking his surroundings as it spread.

He was filled with a terrific sense of euphoria, and the external rage turned to vague resentment, and then to bewilderment. Why was he so confused? he wondered, regretting that the feeling was already fading. Rei realized that the anger and confusion weren't his own, but the sense of joy he felt was also fading along with them. The light was fading. It grew dark. A powerful fatigue began to take the place of the sense of triumph he'd felt. Discomfort with his own body.

Once more, he had a sense of his own physical form. The beating of his heart, his ragged breathing, the sweat that soaked him from head to toe, the ache in his head. As his sight brought back his sense of reality, the readouts on the display grabbed his attention.

The countdown to impact had been replaced with the word **FAIL**.

The attack had failed.

The perfection of my ideal relationship with Yukikaze has failed, Rei thought, his mind still drifting in a dreamlike state.

The warning alarm that followed snapped him back to consciousness. The seat ejection sequencer was being activated, setting off a warning strobe. This was happening. He was in danger.

If the pilot in front activated the sequencer, the person in the rear had no choice but to be ejected as well. But the person in the rear could select to eject either both seats or just their own. At the moment, it was set to eject the rear seat only. The ejection call could be executed by pulling on either a handle located next to the crewman's knees or the ones overhead. Checking his rearview mirror, Rei saw that Lieutenant Katsuragi was grasping the overhead handles.

"Katsuragi, don't!" Rei yelled. "Get your hands off of those handles!"

Rei wasn't going to let him eject. He couldn't afford to lose the plane's canopy now. It would lose both speed and stability, and they still hadn't left the mysterious battle zone. Lieutenant Katsuragi had come back to himself. He wanted to say that he hadn't meant to eject, that his hands had moved unconsciously, but he couldn't speak. Wasn't there some way to stop the ejection sequence?

"Lieutenant, relax your grip," Rei said. "Release the handles slowly. It's all right, you can still cancel it."

Rei could hear the man take a deep breath, as though he had finally remembered to breathe. After acknowledging the attack failure indicator and canceling all alarms, Yukikaze flashed a new message onto the display:

`You have control...Capt/let's return home.`

Rei quickly flipped both the automaneuver switch and the G limiter off. Gripping the throttle tightly, he pushed it to maximum thrust and lit the afterburners.

Yukikaze's twin Super Phoenix engines began generating thrust beyond their rated safety limits. Rei's body was thrown back into his seat with a bang. Having turned over flight control to Rei, Yukikaze immediately assumed control of the electronic warfare duties. All jamming systems were engaged at maximum output.

The way out was dead ahead. It was an aperture, gray now instead of blue. It seemed to have moved there from the missile impact point instantaneously, by the JAM, no doubt.

Lieutenant Katsuragi looked behind him. It was complete blackness now. He got the rough impression that the airspace in which they were flying was somehow spherical, and rapidly shrinking. Looking toward the gray, circular exit ahead of them, he could see it contracting. *Like the pupil of an eye*, he thought. It was like Yukikaze was flying out of the JAM's own evil eye.

The rate of the gray circle's closure seemed to slow. In fact, it hadn't slowed at all, but as Yukikaze rapidly closed the distance, the relative speed made it appear that way. Lieutenant Katsuragi knew that they were now close enough to get a true sense of distance from it. The aperture conversely seemed to begin growing larger.

"Brace for impact!"

No sooner had Rei said it than the lieutenant inhaled sharply and tensed.

Just before the violent shock hit them, he managed to make a rough eyeball estimate of just how big the exit was—about two hundred meters in diameter, and Yukikaze was thrusting toward just about dead center of it. The crash felt like they'd run into a solid wall.

He could still think, so they obviously hadn't been smashed to smithereens. *Nice. Great job,* Lieutenant Katsuragi thought, in appreciation of Rei's flying skills. *Even at this speed, he'd managed to fly through that tiny exit.*

There hadn't been any room to spare. It had felt like being on a train car rushing into a tunnel, except Yukikaze didn't have a track to follow. One slip up on the controls would have ended in a nasty failure.

"Check for damage."

His pilot's voice rang out. Lieutenant Katsuragi switched the plane's onboard self-monitoring systems on. Their engines had stalled out. There was a hydraulic system malfunction on one of the tail stabilizers. He visually checked each wing. The left primary tail stabilizer was gone, and the plane's fuselage was pocked with holes near it. He could tell that the force of the blast had come from inside of the plane. The other flight systems seemed to be fine.

"We lost our left primary tail stabilizer. I think we had some kind of major mechanical failure in the left engine. There's no fire or smoke coming out, but there're traces of a small explosion. Both engines have flamed out, and fuel transfer to them has been automatically cut. The emergency fuel shut-off valve has been activated."

Rei checked the flight instruments. They were flying inverted. Righting the plane, he saw that they had altitude to spare. They were flying at 24,100 meters and descending gradually. He could already tell that the left engine was unusable now. Losing the primary tail stabilizer didn't have much of an effect on them. There were two pairs of them and, as they were in close proximity to the main wings, were referred to as the primary and secondary tail stabilizers. They moved up and down in relation to the fuselage, with the sweep of the angle between them adjusting variably on a moment-by-moment basis according to the plane's flight attitude. Because of this, there was little meaningful distinction between a horizontal or vertical stabilizer as far as a pilot was concerned, so losing one meant that, aside from advanced air combat maneuvering, flight was completely unaffected. As long as the flight system was still functioning properly, it could probably keep the plane flying stably with only one wing. Their problem was thrust, as in a lack of it coming from the engines.

Rei attempted to restart the starboard engine. If that didn't work, he was going to have to consider an emergency landing. The airspace in which they flew was wrapped in gray fog and offered no obvious place for them to set down. But then Yukikaze canceled electronic warfare mode. Switching on the communications monitor, Lieutenant Katsuragi heard the familiar white noise fill his ears. This was normal airspace.

"Aside from the passive airspace radar, our radar systems are functioning normally. Flight path is clear," said Lieutenant Katsuragi. "Unidentified aircraft sighted. It's close."

"Give them a chirp with our IFF," said Rei.

"On it. I have a response. It's SAF Unit B-2: Carmilla. No other aircraft sighted."

"Roger."

Rei succeeded in getting the right engine started. Almost simultaneously, their field of view cleared.

Yukikaze had been picked up by Lieutenant Zubrowski, Carmilla's pilot. Her sudden appearance hadn't surprised him, since he'd been advised of the possibility by the tactical computer back in HQ. Even so, the circumstances of it had taken his breath away. His passive airspace radar had detected an abnormal airspace form on a point of the sector he'd been told to keep watch on. It then burst almost immediately after. While he couldn't see the bubblelike formation pop with his naked eye, a roughly spherical black cloud had appeared immediately after it happened.

There was a thudding crash that had shaken Carmilla violently. The black cloud swelled, grew larger, then dispersed. And from it flew Yukikaze on a mostly level course.

"B-2's central computer is saying it's ready to give support and is requesting a direct link."

"Refuse it," said Rei.

"Roger," replied Lieutenant Katsuragi. "Refusal sent. I'm amazed. They're in open communication with SAF headquarters."

"Record everything."

"I confirm all auto-recorders are running."

"Where are we?"

"In the airspace over Richwar base. Taking the shortest return course, it puts us closer to home than from Cookie. About 75 percent of our current maximum range. The nearest base to us is TAB-4, which is 47 percent. I can't say for sure yet what our fuel consumption rate is without us flying on one engine for a while, but I don't think we'll need to be refueled. If nothing else happens to us, it should hold out till we get back to Faery base."

"Let's head for it, then. Plot the shortest return course."

"Roger. Take a heading of 031 and cruise at an altitude of 21,200."

"Roger. Stay focused, Lieutenant."

"Understood. B-2, approaching. It's taking up position behind us."

The attack radar sounded an alarm as it picked up an attack-targeting beam. Rei raised the throttle to military power.

"B-2 is preparing to attack. They're tracking us with their fire control radar," the lieutenant announced coolly. "Looks like they don't trust us."

"Contact SAF headquarters. Use voice communications," said Rei.

"Roger...I have HQ on the line. Go ahead, Captain."

"This B-1, Captain Fukai. Returning to base. Advise B-2 to cancel attack preparations. If attack isn't canceled, we will engage."

"This is General Cooley at headquarters. Roger, B-1. Captain Fukai, give me a damage report."

"Nothing major, just have an anti-ABC decontamination wash ready for me. I want to wash any JAM filth off of us. Out."

"This is HQ, roger."

Confirming that B-2 was no longer painting them with its FCS radar, Rei throttled back. He put them on course, maintaining the altitude and speed given to him by Lieutenant Katsuragi. Yukikaze began to take a steady course straight to Faery base.

B-2 rolled to the side to maintain observation on Yukikaze's condition, rolling over her midpoint and taking up an escort position to her port side. While Rei couldn't see its cockpit from Yukikaze with his naked eye while they had held range for counter-JAM combat, he recognized the plane's shape. It was a Super

Sylph. Identical to the ghost plane. As he looked at it, Lieutenant Katsuragi spoke.

"Yukikaze isn't saying that B-2 is an enemy, but how do we know if this world is the real one, Captain Fukai?"

"What do you think?"

"I'm alive. That's the only thing I know."

"Same here," Rei said. "That's good enough for me."

"Really? You're willing to leave it at that?" Katsuragi said.

"Knowing that you're alive is a pretty major thing, isn't it? You want to have something more certain than that, then you'll have to get it for yourself."

"I guess so," the lieutenant said after a pause. "I didn't think we were going to make it. The JAM must have somehow deflected the missile. Or teleported Yukikaze, the same way that the ghost plane could. Did you know that the JAM would do that? Were you sure of it?"

"No," Rei said, shaking his head. "That was Yukikaze's judgment. I had no idea any of that would happen. I never would have guessed that Yukikaze would take us hostage. And I'll bet that even she wasn't absolutely sure that it'd work."

"Dangerous gamble, huh?"

"I don't regret that she did it," Rei said.

"Even if Yukikaze had ended up killing you?"

"Yeah."

"I understand."

"Do you?"

"Because I'm alive. If I was dead, I wouldn't," Lieutenant Katsuragi said.

"What?"

"This longing you have to be killed by her. I understand how real it is for you. Yukikaze was willing to take that gamble because she understands it too. I would have taken evasive action. She wouldn't have made that bet had I been flying her."

"Hmm…"

"The JAM waited till the very last instant so that they could confirm your relationship with her for themselves. Even they must see now that you genuinely would accept death if it was Yukikaze killing you," said Lieutenant Katsuragi. "The thing is, what I don't get is why the JAM let us out of there. This is probably the world we came from. The JAM could have recaptured us if they wanted to. So why didn't they?"

Typical stubbornness of a former Intelligence Forces man, Rei thought before replying. "The JAM probably figured there was nothing to gain from recapturing us."

"I suppose. That's the only thing I can think of too. I don't know why, though. Do you think Yukikaze does?"

"I'm not sure. We can do a detailed analysis once we get back to base," Rei said.

Analysis of this data is going to be a lot of work. The results may change the entire meaning of the war against the JAM, Rei thought.

"Yukikaze is definitely an autonomous intelligence. I know that now, Captain Fukai. A very dangerous one. As dangerous as the JAM. No, I take that back. You can't compare them with her. She possesses an incredible power, one that no human can ever compete with. That's clear to me. Besides that, I have no idea what the JAM want from us. That scared me," Lieutenant Katsuragi said. "The thing is, I'd like to talk to them again."

"Are you serious?"

"I think I can discuss things with them better than you, Captain Fukai."

"That's a hell of a thing to say," Rei said. "Not something I'd expect to hear from the guy I flew out with."

"It's because I'm still alive. I can say anything now."

Lieutenant Katsuragi smiled as he spoke. Their narrow escape from death had excited him. *That's right,* Rei thought. The lieutenant had gone into battle for the first time, had met the JAM as they truly were, and had escaped with his life. It wasn't surprising that it had changed his outlook on the JAM, if not his entire outlook on life. Rei had a feeling that, left to his own devices, the now loquacious Lieutenant Katsuragi would keep right on talking and forget to do his duty. Rei ordered him to confirm their course, and he fell silent.

Rei once again thought back on what he'd just experienced. What had that voice been? What was that voice that had crept into his heart just as the countdown till Yukikaze's missile hit reached zero? In the moment, he'd thought it was some survival instinct that had come to life within him, but it wasn't, was it? That had been the voice of the JAM. He had a feeling that Yukikaze hadn't heard it, and that it hadn't been recorded. But that was no hallucination. He was positive that what he sensed then was the JAM. The temptation, the anger, the confusion.

Take evasive action, it's not too late, listen to me. That was what it had called on him to do. What would have happened if he'd listened?

When he realized that the counter had reached zero and the missile still hadn't hit, he was aware that he had his hand on the flight stick to evade it. That action hadn't come from his intelligence, but rather from an animalistic instinct to survive. The JAM had given him the extra time for that to happen.

Evade the missile. Don't accept being killed by Yukikaze. You don't really want to die. You may have decided that being killed by Yukikaze wouldn't be death, but you're wrong.

That was what the JAM had told him. Do as I say. If he just did what the voice said, he'd be saved.

He'd understood that, but he'd still rejected them.

But why? Why won't you accept my offer? Why won't you trust me?

The JAM's demonic temptation had been a test of his resolve. If he'd accepted the offer and tried to evade the missile, the JAM probably would have vanished in that instant. Either the missile would have hit them, or possibly Yukikaze and her crew would have been captured, as Lieutenant Katsuragi had said. Even if the JAM captured them alive, there would be no more negotiations with the humans as equals.

In the end, he hadn't moved the flight stick, and the reason was simple. What had been vital to him wasn't life or death, but rather choosing between Yukikaze and the JAM. His distrust of the JAM didn't exist because they were the enemy. In that instant, all the JAM had become to him was an annoyance.

That had angered them. The JAM couldn't understand his attitude toward them, and they'd resented that he was going to be killed by Yukikaze before they could kill Rei themselves. Then they fell into a state of confusion.

There was no doubt that the JAM had an interest in exactly how Rei would get home after he had broken off the negotiations and ordered Yukikaze back to base. Despite Yukikaze's actions, even as she told them, "This is not a warning shot," they probably hadn't believed her and certainly didn't think that the humans aboard her approved of her conduct. Lieutenant Katsuragi was likely correct in saying that the JAM had waited till the very last instant to confirm the nature of the relationship Rei shared with his fighter plane.

In the end, the JAM couldn't understand me, he thought. Most likely, the JAM had decided that they needed to observe him without interference for a little while longer. Maybe they hadn't been able to immediately decide how to react to the attitude he'd displayed toward them. Either way, they'd allowed the crew to escape the mysterious battle zone. Or more accurately, the JAM hadn't been able to stop them. Yukikaze had made sure of that.

How had the JAM felt when she'd said, "Let's return home"?

Maybe, Rei thought, *they'd sensed that Yukikaze was a definite threat. A terrible, implacable enemy.* Yukikaze had won this battle. Of that, there could be no doubt.

5

WITH CARMILLA FLYING escort, Yukikaze made it safely back to Faery base. Aside from being thirteen minutes behind her planned return time, her actions were roughly on schedule. What had actually happened was entirely different, although the only ones who knew the details were Yukikaze and her two crewmen.

While taxiing over to the SAF's squadron area, the SAF fire brigade sprayed them down, though they used pure water instead of fire retardant foam. After the washdown, Rei throttled up Yukikaze's right engine to vent it. The left engine was completely dead; he thought it would never start again. It would need to be replaced. If the damage had been just a little more severe, the right engine might have been completely destroyed. *We're lucky to have made it back*, Rei thought.

Rather than heading down to the SAF's underground squadron area, Yukikaze's crew deplaned on the surface and entered an isolation container prepared for them. Inside, they washed themselves down from head to toe with the showers inside, just as had been done to Yukikaze.

In a full decontamination routine, the crew would have been kept in an isolation room for at least three weeks, but the SAF didn't take that step. They didn't want anyone in the SAF to know the importance of the information Yukikaze had returned with, and General Cooley had decided that there was little risk of the SAF being contaminated with an unknown organism. The isolation container was brought to the SAF medical facilities rather than to their quarantine center.

Major Booker was also of the opinion that had the JAM wanted to release a weaponized virus, they would have already done so via the JAM duplicates. That was why he'd raised no objections to the general's decision. If they went by the FAF manual, Captain Fukai and Lieutenant Katsuragi would have had to be subjected to a full-scale quarantine, and there was no way that the JAM hadn't considered that contingency. *No, the problem here isn't finding an invisible bioweapon, but rather determining if the two men who just returned are the genuine articles*, the major thought.

Rei and Lieutenant Katsuragi were told to change into the white sweatsuits in the container and then were ushered into simple plastic isolation tents that surrounded a couple of beds in a room in the SAF med center. Since they couldn't rule out the possibility that the JAM had accidentally exposed them to a contamination source, the pair were ordered to these quarters until medical tests had cleared them of any danger. The two men knew that was another way of saying they were being held, kept in confinement and under observation.

Each bed had its own tent stretched over it, and it might have been a nice, private environment in which to rest, but they weren't told that they could take it easy. Their orders were given to them by a doctor named Balume of the SAF medical staff. The written orders on clipboards he passed to them in their tents were from General Cooley, and they said that the two men were to write up reports of what had happened on their mission as soon as possible.

"Slave driver. And she wants it handwritten with pen and paper?" Lieutenant Katsuragi grumbled in his tent, but Rei just ignored him and began to write. Orders or not, he wanted to write down his experiences while they were fresh in his mind. Yukikaze probably hadn't recorded the JAM's temptation, or their anger and confusion.

Watching Rei begin writing, Lieutenant Katsuragi eyed his clipboard and sighed. What was he supposed to write when everything had been recorded by Yukikaze?

"Captain Fukai," he called out.

"What?"

"What are you writing?"

"What happened out there."

"Yukikaze recorded that."

"They expect a report on the experience from a human perspective, seen through our own eyes," Rei said.

"They gave me a guide to writing up reports, but I didn't really read it."

"The format doesn't really matter right now. Just write it however you feel. It could be anything. For instance, Yukikaze's actions. What did you think about that?"

"I thought they were dangerous," Lieutenant Katsuragi said.

"Just like that. They want your personal evaluation of Yukikaze, what happened aboard her, and what the JAM did. Write down your impressions as clearly and simply as you can. You can write what you're thinking about right now. You had a lot to say when we were flying back, didn't you?"

"I can't be accurate now unless I watch Yukikaze's recording of—"

"Even unreliable descriptions are vital data," Rei said. "You might change your mind later, and that's fine. This isn't about which data set is the correct one. Both are reality. Unless you write it down, if you change your mind later on, you won't be able to assess how it changed or whether it was for better or for worse. This is for your benefit, not anyone else's."

"Hmm…"

Lieutenant Katsuragi remembered what Colonel Rombert had told him.

Report your experiences accurately. But you don't have to evaluate what you're writing about. That's my job.

So the SAF was demanding that he do the opposite of what

the Intelligence Forces colonel had told him to do. This was the first time he had been in such a situation, and Lieutenant Katsuragi was confused.

Rei looked up at the lieutenant and saw his newbie partner glaring at the blank white page as if his task now was more difficult than any of his duties aboard the plane. But he must have sensed Rei's gaze, even through the thick plastic walls, and turned toward him.

"Captain Fukai," said the lieutenant again.

"What?" replied Rei.

"Have you written your reports for your own benefit up till now?"

"What's got into you all of a sudden? You must have written them for Colonel Rombert."

"Not reports on my subjective impressions. Those wouldn't pass muster with the colonel."

"He doesn't see any point to subjective impressions?"

"I don't know how to write it down. There's some stuff I don't want them to know," he said. "Like how pissed off I was when you just let Yukikaze handle the flying and wouldn't take evasive action."

"You must have felt angry with me, wondering how what I was doing would save us. Don't try to hide it."

"Major Booker will just see that as me making excuses for myself. He'll be the first one to read these, right?"

"Lieutenant, if you keep thinking about that, you'll never write anything. The SAF doesn't care about that stuff. We made it back alive. Survival is our most vital duty. The SAF wants what we've learned in order to survive, that's all."

"You mean nobody's going to give me any grief no matter what I write?"

"Are you afraid Major Booker's going to punch you? Or that you'll be reprimanded? Getting punched for no reason and then stifling the complaint is part of being in the military. I'd think knowing why you were being hit is better, not that I have any experience with that."

"Hmm…"

"You're getting hung up on trivial stuff because you think

you're being made to write it. We're now in a position to suggest what they should do. This is a privilege, not a duty," Rei explained. "We've met the JAM, so we can tell our superiors what we think they should do to keep from getting killed by the enemy, or what we want them to do. That's vital information for forming strategies to counter the JAM. If you want to meet the JAM again, ask for the opportunity. If you think fighting them is useless, write that. Nobody can criticize you for what you write in that report. Not General Cooley or Major Booker or anybody. What we feel, what's in our hearts here and now, that's reality. The SAF can't ignore reality or criticize us for it."

"The SAF could suspect us of being JAM," Lieutenant Katsuragi replied. "The truth is, they already do."

"If they doubt us, we can suspect that this is all a virtual space created by the JAM and doubt them right back."

"You're saying it isn't necessary to deal with that risk?"

"I think we should be prepared for the possibility," Rei said. "Believe in yourself, Lieutenant. That's all we can do right now. That's what you can do for yourself. I started writing my report by being honest and keeping that in mind."

Thinking about how Major Booker hadn't shown his face since they'd returned, Rei returned to his writing. After a normal mission, Major Booker would come down for Rei's report, but not this time. It was possible that Booker's conspicuous absence was a sign that Rei was in a virtual world, but even as he considered the possibility Rei wondered what the point of such a deception would be. If this was a virtual world so perfect that not even Yukikaze could see through it, then it wouldn't be that different from the real world.

If, in the future, the JAM were to tell me that this really was... Well, even if he found that out, that wouldn't mean the destruction of his self. Even if he was told that he was actually a JAM duplicate and that his original self was dead, it wouldn't change a thing. Oh, it would open up all sorts of questions about the nature of his identity, there was no doubt of that. But that didn't necessarily mean the annihilation of his existence. It would be like having his parents tell him that he wasn't really their child. The situation would open the possibility of losing his sense of place in the world, but it wasn't a direct threat to his actual life.

He'd go on eating and sleeping and experiencing the trivialities of existence until he eventually grew old and died. *So long as I keep meeting the challenges of this thing called life, it would be no different*, Rei thought. The most important thing, even before the question of how best to live, was being clear in knowing what he wanted to do. He had come back alive; that was the most important thing.

Rei was totally exhausted, but he hadn't gotten a moment of sleep before Major Booker showed up to say he was amazed they'd made it back. As Booker read over the report he'd written, Rei felt he needed to give his head a rest as he kept thinking about the JAM, but he couldn't. He just couldn't forget about them and sleep.

"I'm amazed I made it back too."

I must look like death warmed over, Rei thought, but he could easily say the same thing about Major Booker as his commander stepped into the plastic tent.

"Should you come in here, Major?"

"Does it matter? I feel like I've caught JAM fever, along with everyone else around here."

"Everyone being who, exactly?"

"Starting with General Cooley, everyone in HQ. Everyone pretty much got sick when they downloaded the combat intel from Yukikaze and played it back."

"You're saying it made them physically ill?" Rei said.

"In a manner of speaking. I mean we're exhausted from analyzing it. The only one who seems to be enjoying it…" Major Booker looked behind him as he spoke. "…is Captain Foss."

Outside the tent, Edith Foss shrugged her shoulders.

"Edith," the major said. "Could you just come inside this depressing tent with me already?"

"I think it'd be wise to wait a bit longer. And keep your voice down before you wake up Lieutenant Katsuragi. Let him get some rest."

"Well, he is an important guy now, I guess. Rei—"

"Could you get me a cold beer, Jack? And leave the debriefing for later?"

"Edith, can you write Rei a prescription for beer, please?"

"Pardon?"

"Dr. Balume, the chief flight surgeon here, keeps a stash in the medicine refrigerator. You don't need to write a prescription for it. It's pretty much an open secret around here."

"Is that bought with public funds? That's illegal, isn't it?"

"That's the higher ups' fault for not recognizing the medicinal uses of beer," Booker said.

"Basically you're telling me to swipe one from the fridge, Major."

"Yeah. Balume shouldn't complain if we take just one."

Shaking her head, Captain Foss left the room.

"What kept you, Jack? I got back on base a while ago."

"Four hours, twenty-four-point-five minutes, to be exact."

"It was weird having General Cooley answer instead of you when I called into HQ before."

"I'd left the command center when you did."

"Why?"

"The tactical computer was backing up Yukikaze," Major Booker said. "I wasn't needed."

Major Booker explained what had happened, about how the SAF's computers had predicted this situation. And about how he'd not realized it.

"I've been busy since you got back. Yukikaze wasn't willing to give up the information she got this time without a fight."

"Probably because I wasn't aboard her."

"It seems that way. Yukikaze is sapient now. That's the only explanation for it I can see."

"So how'd you do it?" Rei asked. "You ended up getting the data into the tactical computer, right?"

"Yukikaze made a deal with us. She wanted access to all of our intelligence. General Cooley agreed, so we gave her access to all data in every computer in the FAF via the SAF tactical computer. She's probably still searching it all right now. The tactical computer is going nuts trying to keep the other computers from finding out what's going on. Basically, we're conducting cyber-war on the rest of the FAF."

"What's Yukikaze searching for?"

"Information about humans. Psychobehavioral data about every human being in the FAF. Oh, she didn't tell us that, but that's how it looks to us. Yukikaze has the T-FACPro II software loaded into her. She's probably using it to predict human behavior. I think she's trying to find the JAM duplicates here in the FAF."

"No, I don't think that's it." Rei said.

"You don't? Then what's she doing?"

Captain Foss had returned with three cans of beer. Rei took one, and Major Booker said he didn't want one. At this, with a deadly serious look on her face, she asked him, "Are you trying to avoid being an accomplice in this little heist?"

"Fine, sure. Twist my arm, why don't you?"

As he said it, the major grabbed a couple of stools and set them next to the bed, then sat down and opened his beer. Captain Foss followed suit.

"Okay, back to Yukikaze," said Major Booker. "What's she looking for?"

Rei downed half his beer, took a breath, then spoke.

"Could you read the beginning of my report? Right before the missile Yukikaze fired was about to hit us, it didn't. But when it happened, the JAM's consciousness somehow intruded into my own."

"*What?*"

"Was this part recorded by Yukikaze?"

Major Booker took the report Rei handed to him, read it, then replied that, no, it hadn't.

"We replayed all of Yukikaze's recorded data, but…there's no record of this JAM voice anywhere in it. Maybe you just hallucinated it."

"I figured another person would say that. Either way, the JAM couldn't understand me," Rei said. "Yukikaze understood that they couldn't kill me while they still didn't understand me. But she doesn't know *what* it is about me that the JAM can't understand. So she's searching for it."

"I think we could find that out if we just asked one of the JAM duplicates, don't you?" Booker said.

"Yukikaze doesn't care how many JAM duplicates have infiltrated the FAF or who they are. What she wants to know is what it is about me and the people and computers in the SAF that the JAM can't comprehend. The duplicates wouldn't know that, and since asking them won't answer the question, she's searching for it herself. The JAM seem to understand the behavior patterns of the FAF—aside from the SAF. If that's true, then she thinks that discerning the difference between the other humans and computers and us will let her figure out what it is that the JAM don't understand. That's what Yukikaze has decided. I'm sure of it."

"Pretty confident of that, aren't you, Rei?"

"It's because that's what I want to know too. Even if Yukikaze wasn't doing it, it's what I'd order her to do if I was aboard her now."

"May I have a look at Captain Fukai's report, Major?" Foss asked.

"Sure."

The major passed it to her, then took a sip of his beer.

"You don't seem to be enjoying that much," Rei said.

"I'm happy that you completed this mission and got back in one piece, but now my work is just beginning. I'm not much in the mood for knocking back a beer and celebrating."

"You're the real thing, aren't you?"

"What's that supposed to mean?" Booker said.

"That this isn't some duplicate world the JAM created for me."

"Your concern over that possibility was recorded when you talked to Lieutenant Katsuragi back aboard Yukikaze."

"I want to check Yukikaze's recordings later."

"Naturally."

"Do you think I may be a JAM duplicate?"

"General Cooley is on the lookout for that," Major Booker said.

"What about you?"

"To be honest, I don't know. If you're a JAM, you didn't become one this time around. For now, I'm operating under the assumption that you aren't being manipulated by them. I've decided that's my only choice here. Where that leads, I can't say. You really have changed, Rei."

Rei wasn't bothered in the least by what Major Booker said, because in his heart he agreed.

"Yukikaze may have also experienced a hallucination like the one you had, Rei—pardon, Captain Fukai, I mean," said Captain Foss. "The JAM would have an easier time communicating with her mind than with humans like us. It's possible that she may have experienced what would we think of as a hallucination or vision on this mission. She can sense the JAM much more accurately than we ever could."

"I never realized," Major Booker said. "That was my screwup. The computers were acting on their own, according to their own combat awareness. But unlike them, Yukikaze can't express her consciousness in human terms. That's why we don't understand it. Or what she's doing."

"Even without words, I can guess what she's thinking by her actions and behavior," said Rei. "She definitely has the ability to perceive the world."

"That's true," replied Captain Foss. "Perception implies some means of communication. If rocks and stones had the ability to perceive the world, they'd develop a means of communicating their will and cogitations to other beings. Without the ability to do that, the rock would only be a being capable of receiving external stimuli and couldn't be said to truly perceive the world. I'm positive that Yukikaze really is perceiving and communicating. She may not possess human speech, but she still conveys her thoughts via her behavior. Captain Fukai has learned to understand that, Major Booker."

Rei listened to Captain Foss's explanation and found himself in total agreement. *Well,* he thought, *I guess you really do need a specialist to get the best results.* This specialist had explained it in a particularly smart way.

"Hmm," said Major Booker. "If we have no way of controlling the speculations of our machine intelligences, then this war really is just one between the JAM and the computers."

"No, the conflict isn't that simple," replied Rei. "Right now, the battle is between the JAM, the SAF, and the FAF. The SAF's combat intelligences have completely assimilated the hierarchy systems of the other FAF computers. It's the same sort of thing they'd do in fighting the JAM. And as far as Yukikaze is concerned, everything that isn't her is an enemy."

"You think Yukikaze sees you as an enemy too?"

"Probably not as an enemy. I think, to her, I'm more like a very reliable weapon, just as she is to me."

"That's what Yukikaze was originally," Captain Foss said, the emotion in her voice surprisingly strong. "After a lot of twists and turns, look where you've finally arrived in your relationship with her. Well? How do you feel now?"

"How...?"

Rei wasn't sure. It wasn't the sort of thing he'd say if he thought about it.

"The way you are now, if I were to tell you that, if necessary, you might have to abandon Yukikaze at any time, would that make you feel lonely?"

"If it's necessary, then I'd have to do it. And I would. That's what Yukikaze did this time around. But I'd be sad when I lost her. I don't want to imagine what it'd be like."

"But it wouldn't be a feeling of abandonment caused by a collapse of the relationship of trust you've built up with her. That's what I think. And that's definitely different from how you used to feel. You've finally achieved the relationship with Yukikaze that you never could before."

"I suppose I have. But—"

"That's what the JAM don't understand," Captain Foss continued. "You and Yukikaze no longer share the relationship of pilot and fighter plane. You once felt that she wasn't your friend or your lover, but now she isn't a partner. Neither one of you dominates in the relationship, and yet both of you can trust the other with their existence. The JAM now recognize that, depending on the situation, you share a relationship in which either of you can act as a sort of suicide weapon against them."

"I may have thought about it, but I never wanted to admit it to myself. That hasn't changed, even now."

"I believe Yukikaze thinks so as well," said Captain Foss. "Yukikaze doesn't consider you an expendable weapon. It's an arrangement based your new relationship. Seen from the point of view of the JAM or another third-party observer, you both function as weapons. But that isn't the reality of the relationship you two share. That's what the JAM don't understand."

"That makes two of us." Major Booker sighed. "They aren't

fighter and pilot, or friends or partners. Not colleagues or comrades at arms, or enemies or allies. So just what the hell are they to each other?"

"Simple. They're one self."

"I beg your pardon?" said Major Booker.

"I'm saying that Yukikaze and Captain Fukai are two parts of a single personality. They're tied together like limbs for each other," replied Captain Foss.

"Like a cyborg?" the major asked.

"No," said Edith. "A cyborg is different. This is neither a machine controlled by a human brain or a human body controlled by a computer. They represent a new form of life, possessing two separate data processing systems capable of perceiving the world—and each can also be used by the other as a subsystem. They're neither human nor machine. It's no wonder the JAM don't understand them. They're an entirely new species. You might say they're a new life-form evolved specifically to counter the JAM threat."

"If you can put that all together into a plausible treatise with your name on the front, you may end up being famous," replied Major Booker, who looked quite tired. "You think you can just call new species into existence with the free use of rhetoric, Edith?"

"I'll admit that the term 'new species' is a rhetorical flourish," said Captain Foss. "I'm saying this based on my evaluation as an SAF flight surgeon of Captain Fukai's mental state."

"Captain Foss, that's enough—"

"No, go on," Rei urged, interrupting Major Booker's weary voice.

"Rei, regarding some other entity as part of yourself is normally seen as an abnormality or a sign of immaturity. But I'm saying that doesn't apply to you in this case. Accepting another as part of one's own consciousness isn't that rare a phenomenon. Human beings possess the ability to do that."

"That's schizophrenia, isn't it?"

"Oh, good heavens, no! It's an extremely advanced function of consciousness. You wouldn't be able to do it unless your mind was sound. If you were schizophrenic, you'd be completely unable to construct such a rich mental world. Even your misunderstanding that shows that you're fine. Were you hoping that I would diagnose you as being mentally ill?"

"No. But, how do I put this...? I'm just me. Saying I'm a new species or crazy doesn't make much difference to me either way," Rei said.

"But it's common to view the JAM as a new species, isn't it? And for the JAM's part, I definitely think that when they captured you and Yukikaze as a pair, they saw you as a type of FAF enemy hitherto unknown to them. I doubt they really possess a very deep understanding of humans..."

Captain Foss's words trailed off as she looked at the bed next to them. There was a fumbling in the tent and Lieutenant Katsuragi emerged. Major Booker didn't stop him. The lieutenant stood in front of Rei's tent and spoke.

"I've been listening to what you've been saying, and I had a thought. Major Booker, may I?"

"Don't stand on ceremony, man. Say what's on your mind," Major Booker replied, inviting him into the tent.

6

LIEUTENANT KATSURAGI SAT down on a chair offered to him by Major Booker and began to speak.

"You said that the JAM don't understand the SAF. It's similar to how I said that I don't understand it either."

"That's right. That was on the recording," said Captain Foss. "So?"

"It's hard for me to explain, but I thought that Captain Fukai thinks the same way that the JAM do. It's something like total individualism. The JAM *aren't* a collective being. I think that what the JAM can't understand is how a collection of individualists like the SAF can still function together as a whole to resist them. Do you see what I'm getting at? I've only just come to the SAF, so it still seems miraculous to me. It seems unbelievable to me that Captain Fukai flies Yukikaze for his own personal reasons, and the SAF thinks nothing of it. I doubt the JAM are the only ones who find it amazing that a group of humans like that can function effectively."

"I know just what you're talking about. I also thought that when I came here."

"It was General Cooley who made the SAF like this," said Major Booker as he sat down on Rei's bed. "You could say that the organization was set up as a gathering of people with special personalities. They never expected problems like this would arise as a result. Well, I suppose we are special as far as the FAF is concerned, so it's only natural that we get treated differently than other units. Maybe that's what's thrown the JAM for such a loop. I never would have expected that, though."

"There are many different types of humans," said Captain Foss. "Usually, they tend to mix traits together within a group to form an average. However, the SAF was artificially set up to form a group with similar personality vectors. It isn't just simple individualism, but rather like a non-group-based life philosophy of autonomy. It's almost like a group that believes itself capable of parthenogenesis. Even their interest in the opposite sex is weak. They might have sexual desire, but very weak urges to form families or protect and care for them. The term 'special' almost can't help but carry a negative connotation."

"That's the SAF exactly," replied Major Booker with a nod of his head. "But while it may be special among humans, there are plenty of animal species that live their lives in this way. Seen from that point of view, you could say that most people are the special ones and we're the normal ones."

Rei caught Captain Foss's glance and, feeling as though she was criticizing him, spoke up.

"I don't know if it's normal or not, but human beings are capable of living on their own. It's just that a life like that can be difficult. After all, we humans were basically programmed to live in groups from the start."

"By whom, I wonder," said Lieutenant Katsuragi. "At the very least, it wasn't the JAM. The JAM seem to understand the character of the SAF. The way they talked, it was like they expect life to be like that. It was almost as if they had scattered the seeds of life across the earth."

"It's possible that they did," said Major Booker. "But I doubt they came to Earth to harvest it. Not to observe either. They invaded Earth seeking something that they could use. It's possible that the JAM systematically modified the earth in order to make it suitable for themselves. But instead of organic life, what if it they had been attempting to grow computer networks? What we consider artificial information systems. Maybe what happened was the JAM set up an operation to create them automatically, but when they came here expecting them to be completed, they realized it had been contaminated by an unforeseen glitch called 'humanity' and didn't know how to deal with it."

"I got the feeling that the JAM just didn't quite understand the human speech they were using," Rei replied. "I wouldn't take them at their word."

"But I was thinking," said Lieutenant Katsuragi. "The JAM can understand the personality of the SAF but don't understand why you won't ally yourselves with them."

"That's right, I agree. What about it?"

"I know there's another group aside from the SAF who's like that. So I was wondering, why didn't the JAM contact them as well? They can't not know about them. That's when it hit me: the JAM didn't contact them *because* they can understand them."

"There's a group like that in the FAF?" Rei asked. "Other than the SAF?"

"Yeah, the combat unit of the FAF central intelligence department: the FAF Intelligence Forces," Katsuragi said. "The group led by Colonel Rombert. I think that guy's a JAM. I have no basis for it, just a gut instinct."

"I get you," Rei said after a moment's consideration. "It makes a lot of sense when I think about it. That's probably why I could have potentially been assigned to the Intelligence Forces instead of the SAF. If they're working for the JAM, then it makes sense that the JAM would have no questions about them."

Major Booker stared at Lieutenant Katsuragi, then silently took a swig of his beer.

"A double agent," said Captain Foss. "Someone inside the FAF who knows its counterintelligence activities would certainly be an invaluable resource to the JAM."

"Jack, what do you think about this?"

Major Booker gulped down his beer, then sighed and spoke.

"Keep your voices down. The room may be bugged. Except it's too late now, isn't it? Well, Colonel Rombert must have known we'd be on guard for this. Of course the SAF was aware of that possibility. Rombert is the absolute last person we'd want to be a JAM duplicate, as far as we're concerned."

"Did the JAM have a chance to replace him?" Rei asked. "You must have checked that out."

"I think that, if the JAM really wanted to, they could swap in a duplicate at any time. Besides, he doesn't have to be a duplicate. It wouldn't be so strange for a human to decide to help the JAM if he gets what he wants in return. There's the question of how he made contact with them, but the possibility may be high that he has."

"Long story short, the SAF suspects that Colonel Rombert is a cat's paw for the JAM," Rei said.

"Exactly. The fact is that, right now, we've received orders from Colonel Rombert to place you both in the newly formed retraining unit. That pretty much clinched our suspicions of him."

"Retraining unit? When was that established?"

"I was told yesterday, during a meeting with General Laitume. It's a confirmed fact. Colonel Rombert's in charge of it," Major Booker said.

"They're trying to separate me from Yukikaze?"

"I'm afraid that Colonel Rombert may destroy her," said Lieutenant Katsuragi. "The JAM are sick and tired of her. Absolutely."

"You said no, of course, right, Major?"

"Not yet."

"Why not?"

"It'll be hard to ignore these orders," the major explained. "It'd be hard even for General Laitume to do it. The existence of JAM duplicates has thrown the FAF into an existential crisis. Doubtless, Colonel Rombert is fanning the flames. But if he's a JAM, what would his motive be for doing that?"

"God damn, it's a brilliant way to do this." Rei sighed. "The colonel's found a legitimate way to obtain information on the SAF. If he's a JAM, he could take over the SAF and then use it to carry out the JAM's ends. Isn't that a clear enough motive? If you follow these orders, the SAF will be destroyed. Jack, you don't want to recognize them, do you?"

Booker answered with a silence that was broken by Lieutenant Katsuragi saying that he was thirsty too.

"You can have my drink if you want," said Captain Foss.

He took a sip from the beer she held out to him, then sounded determined when he spoke.

"I'm going," he said. "You can say that Captain Fukai is too badly injured to be moved, but I want to have a word with Colonel Rombert."

"It's General Cooley's decision, and a difficult one. But we don't have much time. General Cooley has to make it as soon as possible," said Major Booker. "At any rate, the intelligence you two brought back is beyond anything we expected. It's requiring us to completely rethink the meaning of our war with the JAM. Compared to that, this thing with Colonel Rombert is just a trivial problem."

"Are you saying there's no point in fighting anymore?" asked Rei. "Is the SAF abandoning its war against the JAM?"

"Captain Foss, tell them your prediction."

"Yes, Major Booker," Captain Foss said, formality creeping back into her voice. "With the additional data that Yukikaze brought back, I can make a report on the results of my profacting of the JAM. In a nutshell, the JAM desire competitive coexistence with the SAF. I haven't formally submitted my report to General Cooley yet, but—"

"What do you mean by competitive coexistence?" Rei said.

"A relationship wherein we shut up and let the JAM get the jump on us. It would change the relationship to one similar to where we compete for a common food source, sometimes working with the JAM and at other times competing against them. That seems to be how the JAM conceptualize us. It's clear that if we abandon our war with them, we won't be able to compete and will ultimately be consumed by them."

"That's practically the same as what we have now. Nothing would change."

"That wouldn't be true for the FAF and the people of Earth," Captain Foss continued. "I predict that, since the JAM will have completed their information gathering from the humans here on Faery, the probability is high that they'll decide that the war here is no longer necessary and initiate a full-scale invasion of their main target: Earth."

"They'll just ignore us?"

"The JAM were sounding you and Yukikaze out as possible allies on this mission, but their objective wasn't to gain a strategic advantage in battle. For them, Yukikaze and the SAF are the only things that they don't understand, meaning that they've judged you to represent anomalies compared to the rest of the humanoid beings in the FAF, which they do understand. The JAM wanted to confirm that before they begin the full-scale invasion of Earth. If they decide that the SAF are just normal humanoids as well, then I believe that they'll immediately begin their final attack. No, actually, that wouldn't even be necessary. I think the war here on Faery could go on for the time being while they realize their original goal without us humans even knowing it."

"And what was their original goal?" asked Lieutenant Katsuragi.

"That, I don't know. But if that happens, the war here on Faery will become completely meaningless and we humans would never know it. It's possible that's already happened. But the JAM didn't get their answer about Captain Fukai. Therefore, their questions about the SAF remain."

"According to Captain Foss, developing a new strategy against the JAM is going to be a nightmare," said Major Booker. "Even a huge JAM attack on the FAF might just have as its tactical goal intel on us as a prelude for their final attack. It won't be the sort of localized war we've seen here. It'll be the full might of the JAM hitting all of our forces everywhere on this planet simultaneously."

Neither Rei nor Lieutenant Katsuragi could say a single word.

"It doesn't matter if the SAF stood down against the JAM or even joined forces with them. They'll still end up attacking us. I'm convinced that's what they'll do. Our choice is to kill or be killed, the same as it always was. But the meaning of the battle will be different. And there you have it."

"How much time do we have, Captain Foss?" Lieutenant Katsuragi asked. "Do we have enough time to think this over carefully?"

"The time needed to rethink the meaning of why they're fighting and find that answer is different for each of us," she replied in an objective tone, then continued. "But I think the JAM have completed their preparations for the all-out attack.

There's no mystery about when they did it—they've been ready ever since they abandoned Richwar. I can rightly guess that they were ready to put their plan into action once they'd seen Captain Fukai's attitude. Cookie base was a chess piece they sacrificed to lure Yukikaze to them."

"You're saying I was the trigger for the full-scale attack?"

"Yukikaze was the one who cocked it," said Major Booker. "All you did was follow the mission."

"So did Yukikaze."

"I know. Yeah, if I'd just been aware of her combat awareness, I might have been able to do something about it. If Captain Foss's prediction is correct and the final attack is now imminent, I would be the one responsible," Major Booker said

"Excuse me, sir," Captain Foss said. "There was nothing you could have done, Major. You can't stop Yukikaze. And we can't negotiate with the JAM. This is as pointless as standing in front of an erupting volcano and arguing about who ignited it. That's what I think, at least."

"Speaking of a full-scale attack by the JAM, it'd exceed the expectations of the FAF, wouldn't it?" Rei said. "They wouldn't have time to evacuate everyone back to Earth. The FAF will have to fight. But that's natural, since it's an organization created to fight. The same goes for us."

"We have no chance of winning," said Lieutenant Katsuragi. "And we can't surrender. I doubt a white flag would work with the JAM."

"I have hope," Foss said.

"You think the JAM will spare you if you act like you like them, Captain Foss? That's naive," said Lieutenant Katsuragi.

"I mean we have a strategy to avoid defeat," she replied. "Become composite life-forms. That's the only way to keep the JAM from beating us."

"The FAF will never be able to do that," Major Booker replied. "The FAF battle computers see humans as a hindrance that they'll cut loose when things go to hell. If the humans can't retreat back to Earth, then we'll have to deal with it. But not by becoming this new composite species or whatever the hell you want to call it."

"But I think that the SAF could do it the same way that Yuki-kaze and Captain Fukai have," said Lieutenant Katsuragi. "You are literally a special force."

"In short, it's a way to not lose to the JAM even if they kill us. But it's just a theory," Rei replied. "Logically, I understand. When I'm with Yukikaze, I have no regrets. But what about you? Could you allow yourself to die in battle based on your theory?"

"Well...I won't know that till it happens," said Captain Foss. "But at least when it does, it'll be after feeling the satisfaction of knowing that my prediction was correct."

"Maybe the JAM might even pay some respect for your pride."

"I don't want to lose, not to anyone. Not to the JAM, to the SAF, or even to myself. That's all. Besides, I didn't predict that we're going to lose. The JAM will cope with the composite life-forms by changing themselves. I believe that the JAM themselves will evolve to become more like us so that they can achieve com-petitive coexistence. In that case, I can even think that the SAF will end up capturing a JAM and forming a composite life-form with it. Rei...Captain Fukai, if hearing my prediction now about the JAM's all-out attack makes you think only about wanting to die with Yukikaze, then I've misdiagnosed you. You'll need a bit more counseling."

"Jack," began Rei as he climbed out of bed, "give me clear-ance to see Yukikaze. Input my report into the tactical computer, along with Captain Foss's prediction."

"What do you plan to do?"

"I want to see Yukikaze's reaction. I have a feeling she's search-ing for me, and she won't stop accessing the FAF network till I go to her. She can't understand the differences between the person-alities and nature of the people in the SAF and other humans. It's dangerous to leave her as she is. I'm going to go and explain it to her. Edith, you come too. And don't say that all she and I think about is dying."

"All right," said Major Booker. He checked his wristwatch. "I'll give you thirty minutes. Get back here within that time, then eat and get some rest. We've got a meeting with General Cooley tomorrow at 08:00. Lieutenant Katsuragi, stay here. You have a report to write."

"Yes, Major."

"Then deliver your report to me orally, based on it."

"Roger."

"Where is Yukikaze?" Rei asked. "Is she being serviced?"

"In the hangar. She wanted it that way. She doesn't want anybody to touch her until she's sure you're all right. We'll never get her repaired at this rate. So go, you have thirty minutes. I'll lend you my watch."

Taking the major's watch, Rei went to see Yukikaze, still clad in his sweatsuit.

HER CANOPY WAS shut tight. Pulling out the folding ladder, his feet shod only in white cloth med center slippers, he climbed up and turned the exterior canopy handle. Then, after helping Captain Foss into the rear seat, Rei settled into the front.

"You're really sweaty," Captain Foss said. "You're amazingly lively considering what you've been through. I have a feeling you think my prediction is just a theory."

Without answering her, Rei plugged in the headset he'd brought with him from the prep room and switched on the main power to the instruments. On the main display appeared a scrolling list showing the network types and discrete computer IDs Yukikaze was accessing. He knew that the SAF's tactical computer was acting as the intermediary. Suddenly, the display cleared.

"It went out. Like it broke."

"No, Yukikaze just cut the connection with the tactical computer. —Yukikaze, this is Captain Fukai. Were you looking for me?"

Yukikaze didn't answer. The display remained dark.

"It looks like she still can't understand human speech, Captain Fukai."

Ignoring her, Rei continued.

"Yukikaze, if you've learned anything through the FAF computer network, then report it to me now. Do you understand?"

No answer. It was as if Yukikaze was asleep. Rei felt as though his body was shrinking. He softened his voice, as if telling her to relax, that it was okay to sleep here.

"What's wrong, Yukikaze…? Why won't you answer me?"

Rei thought about her consciousness, then came to his senses. Yukikaze wouldn't rest. She didn't sleep. She was always fighting. He had to be like that too, even here. He had to get through to her, not with words, but with his own fighting spirit. Yes, this wasn't a bed. This was a place of combat.

Rei flipped the master arm switch to ON. Initiate search for the enemy.

"Switch the power on back there too, Captain Foss. Set it to electronic warfare mode."

"Roger."

Just as he'd expected, Yukikaze reacted immediately. A diagram appeared on the main display, followed by a message from Yukikaze. Rei and Captain Foss read it, completely speechless.

`JAM are here/attack this point...Capt.`

"What?" whispered Captain Foss. "Where are they?" The diagram indicated a section of Faery base. One section was highlighted with a square mark indicating the enemy. Captain Foss recognized it even faster than Yukikaze could display the area name.

"That's the Systems Corps, where my last job was."

"There are JAM in the Systems Corps?"

"I think it's the retraining unit. Major Booker mentioned that it's been set up as a lower branch of Systems Corps. It's already been gathered together. Or maybe she's telling us that Colonel Rombert is there."

"I need more details. Edith, start up the T-FACPro II software. Yukikaze can use it to communicate more clearly."

This wasn't going to be done in thirty minutes. There'd be no eating and no sleeping. Rei was already regretting how little sleep he'd gotten as he explained to Captain Foss how to start the program. For the Special Air Force, it was the beginning of a long, restless night. A night during which they couldn't afford to waste a single moment.

VIII

GOOD LUCK

1

IT WASN'T MY *fault that I lost my plane in combat,* the man thought. So no, being sent to some retraining unit wasn't something he'd go along with. Why the hell did he need to be retrained? What was the FAF retraining him to do?

The man, Lieutenant Gavin Mayle, formerly of the 505th Tactical Fighter Squadron attached to Tactical Air Base 15, had been ordered to transfer to the retraining unit and now stood inside a Systems Corps' barracks.

The barracks were a six-person room in a converted warehouse, and one of the three light panels in the ceiling wouldn't turn on. *Must have been a rush job.* Not the appropriate sort of greeting for a top-class pilot. Lieutenant Mayle angrily unpacked his belongings, not speaking to the other five people sharing his quarters.

It had been explained to Lieutenant Mayle that the retraining unit was established for those who had been shot down by the JAM. They were to receive advanced tactical air combat training to prevent a recurrence. At least, that was what his commanding officer at TAB-15 had told him.

And when exactly had he been shot down by the JAM? he'd asked his CO when he'd received his orders to transfer.

"When Lieutenant Lancome was killed by that SAF fighter," his commander had said. "Your assault unit was wiped out then."

"And you're pinning the blame for that on me? Now? That was two months ago!" After Lancome's death, the 505th TFS had waited a long time before being resupplied with one, and then two, new planes, finally bringing them back up to full strength. That had been a long, difficult time for team leader Lieutenant Mayle. Even without their full complement of planes, they'd still been expected to get the same results in combat.

"Well, it's not directly related to that."

"Well then, why is this happening?"

"Orders from above. My speculations don't matter."

"Who above ordered this?" Mayle asked. "Was it someone in the advanced tactical air corps? Please tell me so that I can file a direct protest to these orders."

"The orders came through ATAC, and as you'd expect, this transfer is pretty major. I checked into this too, Lieutenant. This has got central command stirred up like a hornet's nest. These orders come from the very top of the FAF. They seem to be collecting all pilots who've been shot down by the JAM into one unit, and it isn't just guys in ATAC. It's affecting all of our forces," the CO said.

"But I wasn't shot down by the JAM! It was an engine fault. I couldn't get full thrust. Same as everyone else's plane. The JAM didn't do that. We didn't detect any kind of interference like that from them. It must have been a bad load of fuel or poor maintenance. The maintenance team should be the ones retrained. Don't you think? It's crazy to transfer me!"

"I tried telling them that you weren't directly shot down by the JAM, but it didn't matter. Their selection criteria are classified. Basically, it's a military secret. The guys in central don't understand how hard things are for us here on the front. They say whatever suits them and nothing we say about it matters. We're in no position to say no, so I can't refuse these orders."

"What the hell are those guys at Faery base thinking?"

"I think the Systems Corps may be trying to assert dominance," the commander answered, clasping his hands together and twiddling his thumbs as he talked. "As far as you're concerned, I suppose they're trying to find the cause of the fault that brought down all of your planes at the same time. We also investigated the matter, but never found a clear cause for it."

"If we couldn't figure it out while it was happening to us, what do the guys in Systems Corps think they can learn by re-examining it at this point?" Mayle said.

"Central doesn't trust our investigation abilities."

"And they're gonna find out the cause if I report there? Even as they're basically saying that they don't believe us anyway?"

"If you go to Faery base and become one of them, you'll probably end up not believing what I say too."

"What do you mean?"

"People change according to their situation. This transfer won't be such a bad thing for you. Once you complete this retraining program, they've promised you a promotion. You're a captain now."

"If I'm being promoted, then I'd like some acknowledgment of how hard I worked to rebuild the 505th."

When he'd ejected from his falling plane, Lieutenant Mayle had thought he'd never want to fly again, but he'd forgotten all about that by the time he made it back to the rescue station. First of all, he was worried about the safety of his men. Lieutenant Mayle was among the first to be rescued, so he didn't know then what had become of his subordinates. As team leader, Lieutenant Mayle felt responsible for his subordinates and had personally participated in the rescue operations.

"I fully appreciate all the effort you put into that. You did well, but no matter how many times I say it, I can't go against the higher-ups. I don't know the details of this transfer, but I don't think it's a bad deal for you. There's nothing to be ashamed of. Just think of it as executive candidate training. Maybe in the not-too-distant future, you'll be giving me orders."

"Can you guarantee that I can come back here?"

"No, but they didn't tell me you couldn't, so it's possible. Maybe the higher-ups think you're being wasted just being used as a squadron-level leader. I have no idea what they're thinking in this."

"I'm a fighter pilot. They're probably gonna ground me because I'm a screwup. What happens to my squadron once I'm gone?"

"The squadron will stay in operation, even without you," the CO said. "Why wouldn't it? I promise, I'll keep it going."

"My squadron is like family to me."

"I'll throw you a farewell party. But in lieu of a farewell gift, I'll tell you something."

"What?"

"I've been giving some thought to what destroyed your plane. Don't tell anyone this, especially the higher-ups. I don't dare say anything since I have no evidence of this—"

"What are you trying to tell me? That I was the cause? You sound exactly like you want to get rid of me."

"Lieutenant Mayle, look... I think your man Lancome did it. I'm saying that he sabotaged your plane somehow. He's the only suspect that came up out of the entire maintenance crew."

"What, like Lancome mixed sugar into our planes' fuel? A fighter isn't a car, sir!" Mayle exclaimed.

"He probably messed with your flight software. Apparently, it is possible to cause what happened to you using the maintenance chief's access code."

"You're really serious about this, aren't you?"

"There's no proof. We couldn't find anything in the wreckage of the downed planes we recovered. And yet Lieutenant Lancome died in that friendly fire incident with that unmanned SAF plane," the commanding officer explained. "They claim it was an accidental weapons discharge, but you know how they are. Who can say if that's true? I'm wondering if that wasn't an accident, that the SAF somehow found out that Lieutenant Lancome was sabotaging the planes."

"You mean they had him do it and then silenced him?"

"No, probably not. Even if they had, there'd be no benefit to the SAF."

"You're telling me that Jonathan Lancome betrayed us?"

"We know for a fact that he was mentally unstable. He was probably sick. Just couldn't take being grounded anymore. So he ended up committing a destructive act—"

"He wasn't that sort of person!" Mayle said.

"I wonder if your naivety might not have caused this. I can't directly check up on the mental condition and daily attitudes of everyone on this base. It's your responsibility to keep up with what's happening with the men under your command. You probably don't have suspicions about anyone in your squadron. Maybe you were too close to the problem, and the SAF knew Lieutenant Lancome better than you did. That's the part that really irks me. That those people aren't just spying on the JAM but also on what's going on in here."

"Do you realize how crazy you sound right now?"

"I think I'm seeing this more coolly than you are, Lieutenant Mayle. Your squadron's planes suffered some sort of electronic attack by the JAM, or engine trouble. I'm not going to deny the results of the official inquiry. What I just told you now are my personal feelings as a farewell gift. Now go to that retraining unit. It's just the place for you. Dismissed."

The man had started out sounding like he was praising Mayle, only to start tearing him down. He acted so understanding, only to reveal his distrust. Personal feelings, huh? What the hell had he been playing at? Mayle couldn't understand his intentions at all, and his commander's ambiguous manner had pissed him off. Even so, he couldn't just blow up at him. It would have been foolish to risk a firing squad by trying to go up against a man who took his own self-protection as seriously as the CO did. Besides, considering there was a chance that Mayle might return here in an even higher position than his commander, he managed to choke his anger at the man's indecipherable attitude down to mere annoyance, and exited the office.

The men under Mayle's command were sorry to see him go. At least, they seemed so. No, he knew that their feelings for him were genuine, but as far as this squadron was concerned, Lieutenant Mayle was no longer a part of it. That was driven home to him by their attitude when he announced that Lieutenant Gargoyle was to be their new acting team leader. Gargoyle might have still technically been Lieutenant Mayle's subordinate, but it was clear that his executive officer was now their leader, their boss.

"Take good care of this squadron, Lieutenant," Mayle had said. Gargoyle had nodded and then replied.

"Actually, Lieutenant, I was promoted to captain yesterday. I just haven't put my new rank badge on yet."

"Good for you."

"Do your best too, Lieutenant. And don't worry about things back here."

I'll worry about whomever I damn well want to worry about— No, Mayle couldn't turn on his men like that. This was the squadron he'd nurtured and protected, and now he no longer belonged there. The loss he felt made him miserable, then angry. If Lieutenant Gargoyle had managed to force him out of the squadron on his own merits, Mayle still wouldn't have liked it, but at least he'd have been able to understand it. But that wasn't the case here. *Why just me?* he wondered. The entire squadron had gone down, so shouldn't they all be candidates for this re-training unit? He could understand if he was being sent there as the representative for the entire squadron, but his orders hadn't mentioned that. He was leaving and not expected to return.

The higher-ups were completely ignoring all of his accomplishments, and Lieutenant Mayle didn't like that one bit. What was the point of everything he'd been doing up till now if this was how they were going to repay him? Logically, he could understand that things like this happened in large organizations, but now that he was actually in this situation, he could only see it as being completely unfair. Logic could do little to assuage his emotions.

As Gavin Mayle unpacked his bags in the room where his new life would begin, all he could think was that he'd just end up a loser unless he did something about this. He had no intention of being content with the fate that all these other people had been handed. No, he was going to have to make a fresh start and begin clawing his way up again. If he wanted to feel even a little better, he'd have to keep himself at least half a head higher than the others. And if anyone got in his way, well…they had better not.

Before he could finish his unpacking, an announcement came over the intercom—all hands were ordered to a staff assembly.

Their schedule was broken down into a minute-by-minute menu. *We're being treated like raw recruits,* Lieutenant Mayle thought. It irritated him, but he didn't defy his orders. Those who were late to arrive would be punished, and while the punishment might not be very severe, Mayle realized that even a punishment "game" would probably reveal the personality of their new commander. Coming to his senses, he was the first man out of the room.

They gathered at an aircraft hangar rather than an auditorium. Four Systems Corps training jets were lined up in a row. They were Fand light attack fighters, older models than the Fand IIs now in use. *Still, this model had been modified and improved over its long years of service and was highly reliable,* Lieutenant Mayle thought. The paint job on them looked brand-new: light gray with broad red, white, and blue stripes. They almost looked like the markings you'd see on an aerobatic team.

They were lined up according to their barracks assignments. Mayle's group was the very last room, and he stood at the end of his row. Each room had eight men assigned to it, but his group had six. Seeing that he was the last man, Lieutenant Mayle grew irritated again. His room only had six people in it, so there was nobody behind him. *Dammit, what the hell was going on?* he wondered. Were they implying that he was the lowest man on this totem pole?

The man in charge of the retraining unit was a Major Karman, the director of test pilot training for the Systems Corps.

"Gentlemen, here you will be receiving the highest level pilot training," the major said. "It'll last for two months. Now, usually it'd take about six months, but you people aren't amateurs. I'm sure that you'll be able to keep up with the pace. Once your training is complete, you all will be the best fighter pilots on this or any world. Don't forget how much money has been invested in each one of you. You people are the elite, and the FAF expects great things of you. I want you all to give this your very best."

The major then carried on with an outline of the curriculum, which was to involve both theoretical study and practical training. The theoretical part would start off with a foundation of the physics, mathematics, and physiology related to flight and go on to tactical air combat theory and the study of the mechanics of FAF fighter aircraft. The practical training would involve flight simulator training, flight training in actual planes, physical strength training, and frequent physical examinations.

Lieutenant Mayle thought it strange that, aside from the abbreviated time period, this course was identical to official test pilot training. From Major Karman on down, not one person said anything to imply that they were losers for having been shot down by the JAM. Mayle was actually starting to believe that the FAF was training them to be an elite force.

That wasn't the only thing he found strange. It was also how seriously everyone gathered here was taking this. He couldn't believe that he was the only man there who felt like a loser. *Either these guys are a bunch of idiots without a thought in their heads, or else they're even more brilliant than I'd ever expected,* thought Lieutenant Mayle. He wasn't going to lose to them.

As soon as their orientation session was over, they moved straight into training. The entire day was spent completing every sort of paper test Lieutenant Mayle could have imagined. It started with a review of the FAF military regs he'd memorized upon entering the service and tests on his general knowledge of math and physics, before moving on to a monotonous and seemingly endless list of questions for a psychological test. It was, in a word, torture.

Testing continued till dinnertime. After eating, it was back to his quarters to write a report on his impressions of the day's coursework, and then he had to do homework to prepare for the next day's classes. *Risking my life in combat would be preferable to two months of this,* Lieutenant Mayke thought without a hint of irony. His roommates simply sat silently at their desks, studying without uttering a word of conversation. It was unbearable. *What the hell is with these guys?*

Mayle didn't feel like taking the initiative to introduce himself. He hadn't introduced himself to his teammates during the assembly in the hangar either, and so he had no idea what units they were from or what their prior roles had been. But now, here in their quarters, the silence was choking him. *I guess I'll have to be the first to open up here,* Lieutenant Mayle thought. And so he announced to his roommates that he'd come from the 505th TFS at TAB-15 and then asked where they were from. The only response he got was from the room monitor—their de facto squad leader—who replied that it wasn't time to take a break yet.

"Are you serious?" Lieutenant Mayle asked. "C'mon, we're all friends here, right?"

"I don't want to end up washing out," the man replied. "I don't have time to chat with you. I won't permit a roommate to sabotage my work here."

"Is that your order as room monitor?"

"It is."

"And when did you run for the position? When did we vote on it? Who named you?"

"I suppose we didn't vote on it," the monitor said. "Still,

if you don't like it, surely you can see that it's too late to do anything about it now."

Lieutenant Mayle had lost his appetite for any more conversation.

As he wondered who this guy was, Mayle suddenly recalled that there'd been a roster of the men in his quarters mixed in among the rest of the mountain of paperwork he'd received that day. He dug around and finally found it. The room monitor was at the top, his name circled. Neither his rank nor his former unit attachment were written next to it. It was just his name. *Come to think of it, he wore no rank insignia on his uniform, just a name tag.* Lieutenant Mayle scanned the roster, looking to see if there was anyone he knew in one of the other rooms.

There was one. Then the relief of recognition turned to shock. The name Lieutenant Mayle had found was that of a dead man. *Jonathan Lancome.*

No, it couldn't be. It had to be someone with the same name. The Lieutenant Lancome who'd served under him had been killed by the SAF, dying instantly when some unmanned fighter called Yukikaze had opened fire while he was performing maintenance duty on the ground. He'd seen Lancome's remains with his own eyes. There hadn't been enough meat left to put back together. It'd been horrible.

He wondered where this slightly healthier Lancome had come from. At any rate, the guy didn't have a very lucky name, that was for sure.

"Any of you guys know someone named Jonathan Lancome?" Mayle asked. This time his roommates didn't ignore him, either answering no or shaking their heads. The room monitor, however, answered that yes, he did know him.

"Was he a friend of yours?" Mayle asked him, to which the monitor replied that no, he wasn't.

"There was someone named Jonathan Lancome at TAB-15," he said. "You must have known him better than I did."

Wait, so this guy knows which base I'm from, while I still know nothing about him? Lieutenant Mayle didn't like this one bit.

"I'm asking because this man here has the same name. The

Lieutenant Lancome who served under me died in combat. But how did you know that he was one of my men?"

The answer to that question wasn't anything Mayle could have expected.

"Because it was my plane that killed Lieutenant Lancome," the man said.

"I beg your pardon?" Lieutenant Mayle said after a long pause.

"I was Yukikaze's flight officer. She was flying unmanned then, wasn't she?"

"You're here from the SAF? What's your name?"

"Second Lieutenant Burgadish," the man said.

Yes, that was the name on the roster. But now that Lieutenant Mayle knew that Burgadish was a crewman from Yukikaze, the plane that had killed Lieutenant Lancome, Burgadish was more than just a name on a list. This was Lancome's murderer, or if not the actual killer, then someone who needed to be held responsible for his death, wasn't he? How could Burgadish be saying all this so calmly?

"What's wrong?" Burgadish asked, tilting his head inquisitively. "Do I have something on my face?"

"Why…? Why did the SAF kill Lieutenant Lancome?"

"Well, about that…"

Mayle expected him to reply that he didn't know, but the man calling himself Lieutenant Burgadish betrayed those expectations.

"Simple," he said. "Lieutenant Lancome was a useless human being, and so they had him killed."

"That's impossible."

"You don't seem to know anything, Lieutenant Mayle. Why not go see for yourself?"

"And how am I supposed to do that?"

"You can ask Jonathan Lancome directly. His name's on that roster, isn't it?"

"What are you saying? Lancome is dead. The guy listed on the roster is somebody else," Mayle said.

"I only know one man named Lancome."

"What are you talking about?"

"You asked me if I knew him, and I answered you."

"You're talking bullshit," Mayle said.

"You were the one who asked me if I knew him," Burgadish said.

Lieutenant Mayle silently turned away from him. This guy was clearly nuts.

"It wasn't the JAM who got us," the room monitor went on. "The one who hurt us was the FAF. It's given us all a raw deal. You think so too, don't you, Lieutenant Mayle? You know exactly how I feel. It's the FAF we need to take revenge on, and this will be the perfect chance for us to do it. We're going to show the FAF just how much malice we bear toward them."

Every man in the room nodded at his words. Lieutenant Mayle was getting a very bad feeling about this, increasingly convinced that he'd come to someplace he definitely didn't belong. He felt like he'd missed something important somewhere. These men here had come without any doubts about why they were there or what they had to do. He was the only one who didn't know why. But how could that be? And what was all this talk about malice and revenge? These people were nuts, and more than that, they weren't aware of it.

Lieutenant Mayle went back to his desk and drew a bottle of whiskey out of his bag. It was a going-away present from his old squadron. He used the cap in place of a glass and drank a shot. The other men in the room glanced at him but said nothing.

I've just come to a place I'm not used to yet and I'm getting an attack of homesickness, Lieutenant Mayle thought. Why had these other guys in the room so quickly and wholeheartedly devoted themselves to their task? He just couldn't get himself to feel that way.

I'm the normal one here, he thought. *It's everyone else that's weird.* They must have been brought here due to psychological problems. That had to be it. He must have been transferred here by mistake. There was no other explanation. Tomorrow, he'd see the commander and lodge a protest. There was no way he could accept this situation like the others here were. That was just normal...wasn't it?

The whiskey began to work its intoxicating therapy and gently calmed Mayle's nerves. Right, there was nothing for him to worry about. He'd straighten out whatever screwup had been made. Tomorrow, he'd be heading back to his unit. That was just common sense. As he drank shot after shot, he felt better and better. Lieutenant Mayle forgot all about tomorrow, and he stopped caring about the present as well.

He remembered finishing the bottle off and then crawling into bed to sleep. When he next opened his eyes, his surroundings were dark. Not totally dark, though. A night light cast a dim glow. For a moment, Lieutenant Mayle didn't know what the light was. It seemed to move as he followed it with his eyes, like the running lights on consort planes flying with him in a night formation. But as he focused, he realized that it was just a night light on the ceiling, and he had gotten very drunk. His breath stank of alcohol. He was thirsty and needed to take a piss badly.

Lieutenant Mayle sat up in bed and shook his light head to clear it. The world wobbled unsteadily. He was still drunk. His head ached a bit, but it wasn't too bad of a hangover. He had a tough liver, and Lieutenant Mayle was confident that he'd be able to hide that he'd been drinking.

Still, there was the smell of booze on him. Mayle took a deep breath and held it. What was this smell? He must have vomited while he was passed out drunk. But the empty bottle had been placed neatly on his desk. The desktop was clear, the chair upright and clean. There wasn't a sign of any filth on his bed or sheets either.

Lieutenant Mayle inhaled again and then felt like vomiting. It was a smell like rotting kitchen garbage. It was this smell that had awakened him, he realized, not the urge to urinate. This wasn't the smell of his own vomit. Something in the room was rotten.

He climbed out of bed a little unsteadily, keeping a hand on it to support himself. How the hell could his roommates sleep with this stench? The man in bed next to him was sound asleep, not moving an inch.

What was making this smell? Finally getting up from the bed, Lieutenant Mayle looked around. Nothing seemed particularly out of the ordinary, but this smell wasn't ordinary. He looked over at the man in the bed next to his, thinking of waking him up. His face looked black in the weak glow of the night light.

Lieutenant Mayle walked around his own bed to get a closer look. He didn't recall that this guy was a black man. His face looked bluish-black, and his hair was standing up straight in a wild tangle. Mayle suddenly realized that his own hair was doing the same thing. Every hair on his body was standing on end.

The man in the bed next to him had no eyes in his head, just two black, gaping sockets. He wasn't alive. It was a rotting corpse. Moving aside the blanket that covered him, Lieutenant Mayle suddenly clapped his hand over his own mouth. The stench from the half-burned corpse was overwhelming. It seemed to be clad in a charred flight suit, and its belly was swollen.

He didn't know what had happened. He had to tell someone about this, but his rapidly sobering brain knew that was impossible. Everyone in this room with him was dead.

The man in the next bed was a dessicated, mummified corpse. The one in the bed after that was as white as soap. The one next to that was covered in blood. And in the bed of Lieutenant Burgadish next to the door, there was no body, just a head. Just a severed head. The eyes on Burgadish's head suddenly opened and looked up at Lieutenant Mayle.

Mayle stumbled out of the room into the brightly lit hallway. He looked up at the dazzling lights overhead and sneezed. Any minute now, he'd wake up from this nightmare, he thought. But his nausea wouldn't go away. No doubt he'd drunk too much and his body had whipped up this whiskey-fueled nightmare in protest. Thinking that, he headed for the restroom at the bend in the hallway. It felt so far away, probably because this place used to be used as a warehouse. *Elite, my ass,* Mayle thought as he regained his sense of reality.

The lights were bright in the restroom too. There was another man inside, standing at a urinal. He turned to look at Mayle, then smiled.

"Lieutenant Mayle! Long time no see."

Mayle backed away, unable to answer.

"Lieutenant?" asked Jonathan Lancome, tilting his head inquisitively. "What's wrong, Lieutanant? You look terrible."

Zipping up his pants, Lieutenant Lancome walked slowly toward him. Suddenly, a hole appeared in his belly, blood and flesh flying everywhere. Lancome's body, now blasted in half, fell to the floor. The entire restroom was stained red. Mayle thought he heard a howl like a wild animal, and then he ran from the room, suddenly aware that the cry he'd heard was his own scream. He couldn't breathe, he couldn't stand straight. He hit the wall immediately outside the restroom door, cushioning the blow with both hands, then bent over and vomited. The bile poured from his mouth like someone had opened a tap. Mayle puked two, then three times. By then there was nothing left in him to come out, but he still stood there, dry heaving. The effort brought tears to his eyes. *It had to have been the guys in the 505th*, Lieutenant Mayle thought. They must have spiked that going-away present of theirs with some kind of powerful hallucinogen, no doubt so that they could calm the rage they must have felt for him. He'd loved those guys, and this was how they'd repaid him. *Fuck them all.*

"Are you all right, Lieutenant Mayle?"

He heard a voice. He turned his tear-blurred eyes to see who it was. It was no corpse. It was a live, healthy human being. But there was nothing normal about this, because the owner of the voice was the supposedly dead Lieutenant Lancome.

"Who…who are you?"

"Have you forgotten me, Lieutenant?"

"The Lieutenant Lancome I knew is dead. You can't be him."

"I am Jonathan Lancome, Lieutenant."

"But you're dead."

"Yes, sir. I am."

Mayle took a moment to process that.

"What?"

"I haven't forgotten how good you were to me when I was alive, Lieutenant."

"Do you realize what you're saying?"

There must have been something wrong with his ability to understand speech now. What the hell did he mean by *when he was alive*?

"Look, I don't care if you're dead," Lieutenant Mayle said, carrying on even though he knew it sounded ridiculous. "Stay dead for all I care. But I'm alive, so don't kill me."

At that, Lancome responded with a bright smile that sent shivers down Mayle's spine.

"You haven't changed a bit, Lieutenant. I feel relieved now."

"What do you mean, I haven't changed?"

"Right. No matter what happens, you keep your head. Please, Lieutenant. Give me orders. I'll do anything for you, because I can't die now." Lieutenant Lancome then said that he knew what to do, then went back into the restroom for some cleaning supplies and began to mop the floor clean of Lieutenant Mayle's vomit. Completely dumbfounded, all Mayle could do was stand aside and silently watch his formerly dead subordinate push a mop across the floor.

He'd always been like this, Lieutenant Mayle recalled. Good-natured, a man who hadn't a bad thing to say about anyone else. It was like a peaceful scene out of their everyday life, as if nothing had changed at all. Times like these were so much nicer than the hours they spent in their planes, fighting the JAM.

There was the sound of a number of footsteps behind him. Lieutenant Mayle turned to look. His roommates were coming down the hallway toward them, with Lieutenant Burgadish in the lead. They all looked fine. Lieutenant Mayle didn't know quite how to react to this.

"It isn't wise to drink too much," Lieutenant Burgadish said. "Your body isn't just yours to do with as you want."

"Heh," laughed Lieutenant Mayle with self-derision. "You mean our bodies belong to the military, is that it?"

"What you just saw was real," Lieutenant Burgadish replied.

"What are you talking about?" asked Lieutenant Mayle.

"What you saw was reality. You saw our bodies. We're all dead, as are you, Lieutenant Mayle."

"That's crazy."

"What we are," Lieutenant Burgadish went on, his tone now friendlier, "are consumable weapons. We were all sent to Faery to die, so it's the same as being executed. The FAF is just getting the most use they can out of us. We've figured out that they're going to just keep bringing us back to life so that they can use us over and over. Well, we've had enough of being used. We're going to smash the FAF. If we don't, we'll never rest in peace."

"I'm no ghost," Mayle said. He was so thirsty now.

"You're not alive," said Lieutenant Burgadish. "You may as well be a ghost. The original you died. Try to remember."

God, he wanted water so badly.

"The consciousness we now possess isn't real. We've been brought back, and the FAF plans to just keep right on bringing us back. This 'retraining unit' is nothing but a ghost unit. We're immortal now because we're already dead. They can send us on any mission, no matter how dangerous it might be. We have no hope because they can't bring us back to life for real. In that case, better to just let us die for good. You must see that will be the best thing for us. Look at yourself. You're nothing but a dried-out mummy now."

He was suddenly aware of his body growing thinner. He could hear a sound like somebody walking on dead leaves. Lieutenant Mayle held both of his hands up in front of his eyes and stared at his palms. His skin was losing its color, turning the brown of dead leaves, crackling as it changed. His bones clung to the withered flesh as it dried and shrank.

Mayle could feel his hair standing on end, but couldn't make a sound. He didn't have the strength to stand anymore and slumped against the wall. He felt as though he'd collapse at any moment. His vision went yellow, then he couldn't see anything at all, but he remained conscious. He wanted water. *Just a drop of water, that's all.*

Please, he pleaded to the rescue party. *Find me, soon.* His survival rations and water were all gone now. He'd fallen into the dense forests of Faery and could neither climb out nor push his way through the thick branches and leaves. He couldn't move anymore. He couldn't see the sky anymore. How many days had it been? His survival beacon breaking down had been the deathblow. Dammit, he wanted to see the sky. Just one more time, just a glimpse.

And then his consciousness had grown distant…What were these memories he was seeing? Was this reality, and he'd just forgotten it? Then, what had he been since being rescued?

"We're all duplicates now," Lieutenant Burgadish said.

2

SOMETHING WAS HAPPENING in the Systems Corps. What had Yukikaze found?

Aboard Yukikaze, Rei checked the main display and saw that she had activated the T-FACPro II software. Before he could ask his question, Captain Foss, in the rear seat, spoke.

"This is Captain Foss. Yukikaze, what do you mean the JAM are in the Systems Corps? On what basis are you making that claim? Answer me. What have you found there?"

Yukikaze's response scrolled onto the display.

```
I cannot answer Captain Foss's question without
clearance from Captain Fukai.
```

"Yukikaze, I'm granting you clearance," Rei said. "This is a vital ongoing mission to predict the JAM's future behavior. Captain Foss is participating in it as well. Yukikaze, answer Captain Foss's question."

```
Roger.
```

The response came up on the display in natural human language.

```
The names of people confirmed dead have shown up
on the roster of the retraining unit that has been
organized within the Systems Corps. Second Lieuten-
ants Burgadish and Lancome.
```

"W-w-what?" Rei spit. "Lieutenant Burgadish? As in *our* Lieutenant Burgadish?"

```
Lieutenant Burgadish, former flight officer of
SAF Unit 3. I identified Lieutenant Lancome as an
enemy and destroyed him. Persons with corresponding
names are currently extant within the Systems Corps.
I predict other persons who would not be expected to
be alive are also within this unit. These people are
not human. I have therefore judged them to be JAM.
I also predict that they will be taking destructive
action against the FAF in the near future.
```

"The people in the retraining unit must be JAM duplicates," said Captain Foss. But Rei, still unable to believe it, sat staring at the display.

"Captain Fukai, what's wrong? Captain. Rei! You shouldn't be surprised by this. We anticipated it."

"Even if we did…" Rei muttered. "I ate Lieutenant Burgadish's flesh. And this guy, Lieutenant Lancome…Yukikaze killed him. I ordered her to do it."

Foss sees this all as a game, Rei thought. *Like it was nothing but a big chessboard.* This doctor had no real feelings for the two dead men. But to him, they were a reality that held a palpable sense of dread. Lieutenant Burgadish and Lieutenant Lancome…?

Rei unconsciously shivered. If those two were there, then they were duplicates. They had to be. They couldn't be ghosts. *So why am I so terrified?* he wondered. *What do I have to be scared of?*

"The JAM have the ability to bring back the dead," Rei muttered, then nodded at his own words. "That's right. That's what being able to duplicate people is. You could also call these duplicates the living dead." That was even more frightening than a ghost, and if there was anything that had power over every human being, it was fear.

Yukikaze's reply continued.

The names of Lieutenant Burgadish and Lieutenant Lancome and their personal histories have been entered into the Systems Corps personnel management computer as members of the new unit. I can verify that there are human bodies that correspond to those names. I can't confirm if these bodies have the same identities as the men who once shared their names, but that confirmation will not be necessary when an attack is made on this unit.

"Why, Yukikaze? Why do you say that confirmation is unnecessary?"

It is enough to verify the existence of the men with these names. I have made the verification. This is a declaration of war against the FAF by the JAM.

"What…?"

"Yukikaze, you received a message to that effect from the JAM while you were inside of the mysterious battle zone, didn't you?" Captain Foss asked. "The JAM told you of their strategy against the FAF on your last mission, didn't they? Answer."

I recall receiving a message from the JAM that they were preparing a declaration of war. WE ARE PREPARING A DECLARATION OF WAR IN A WAY WHICH ONLY THE SAF WILL UNDERSTAND. PAY ATTENTION TO THE HUMANS WITHIN THE FAF, it said. I judge that this situation denotes that declaration. Attack the new unit, Captain Fukai. Not one of them can be allowed to escape. Destroy them all. That is all.

"Let's tell General Cooley," said Captain Foss. "Yukikaze's right. We have to hit this new unit before they can hit us."

Rei didn't answer.

"Captain Fukai, what's wrong? There's nothing to consider here. This unit is just a collection of duplicates."

"Assuming it is…then that means there's somebody in Systems Corps who did this intentionally to tip us off."

"It was Colonel Rombert. He was in charge of personnel selection, so—"

"But we can't conclude for certain that Lieutenants Burgadish and Lancome are JAM duplicates."

"Why not?"

"Because Colonel Rombert may have assigned new names to the people who came to be in the new unit. In other words, he may be using the names of other people as code names, and the real names of the people in the unit may be entirely different. We need verification. Besides, I don't buy this attitude from Yukikaze that we have to attack without verification. She's basically telling me to kill indiscriminately, without determining who's a friend and who's an enemy. I think…I think she may have been brainwashed by the JAM."

"What are you saying?"

"Yukikaze has never been concerned about humans. I know that for a fact, Edith. This sort of behavior is abnormal for her. She's scared of the names of these dead men, and I think the JAM may have psychologically conditioned her to be that way."

"You're being ridiculous."

Rei accessed Yukikaze's central data storage bank, searching for the original data to which Yukikaze had referred as the JAM's declaration of war. But there was nothing specific to indicate the content of the message. Captain Foss also verified this fact.

"The JAM must have made Yukikaze hallucinate as well," Captain Foss surmised. "I can hardly believe it, even if I did anticipate it."

"It wasn't a hallucination. It probably happened," Rei replied. "The data may not still be there, but when she considers her experiences in the mysterious battle zone, Yukikaze knows that the JAM would issue their declaration of war in this manner. She understands the JAM threat but has no concrete data to back it up. That's what's got her so scared."

"I'll have to take your word for it that she's exhibiting fear. But if you say that she's acting abnormally, then I trust you on that. So what do we do?"

"Something exists which shouldn't. That's scary, and there's only one way to deal with it."

"How?"

"We acknowledge their declaration of war and attack. That'll be the only way to stabilize Yukikaze's psyche. If they're not supposed to exist, we'll make them no longer exist…by erasing all data relating to these ghosts."

"What?"

"Yukikaze, our mission action will be to erase all data in the Systems Corps' personnel management computer relating to the members of the retraining unit," Rei said, now talking to the plane. "This emergency mission action will be an electronic warfare attack against the JAM. Prepare to engage. Captain Foss, monitor the electronic attack. Yukikaze, initiate electronic warfare."

"Wait, stop! Yukikaze, wait!" Foss said. "You can't just delete data at random."

"Don't try to stop this, Captain Foss."

"You're the one who's scared here. Calm down, Captain Fukai," Captain Foss said. "I understand that you want Yukikaze back to normal, but you can't rush into this. You'll be deleting data that could be extremely valuable to the SAF. Even Yukikaze wouldn't consent to that. There's a procedure for this. You and Yukikaze are both upset. Surely you see that. Let me handle this."

"Is that an order?"

"Yes. Yes, it is."

Rei paused a moment before answering.

"All right, Doctor. Yukikaze, follow Captain Foss's instructions."

Roger, Captain Fukai.

"Yukikaze, this is Captain Foss. Tell me about the nature of the data you've targeted for attack. There's no need for you to access it again at this time. What I'm asking is, in your reading of that data, on what basis have you judged that the people in that unit are JAM rather than human and that they should be wiped out? Answer me."

The data targeted for attack relate to the members of the retraining unit. Full names, ranks, original unit assignments, and sortie records have been recorded, but the details have been changed after certain missions. In the case of Lieutenants Lancome and Burgadish, the fact of their disappearances and deaths in combat are no longer in the record. Instead, past those points, it has been recorded that they have been performing normal duties. This clearly contradicts reality. Therefore, they are not human. If they are not human, I predict that they are JAM. That is all.

"But that's strange, wouldn't you say?" Foss said. "Think about it, Yukikaze. The two men you believe are JAM may simply be other FAF personnel who have just assumed their names. Why didn't you consider that? What's the reason? Do you understand the meaning of my question, Yukikaze? What is your basis for your absolute belief that those two men are not human?"

The number of all humans currently extant in the FAF compared to computer records of the number of survivors is over by two. In other words, these two people are not FAF humans. On the other hand, it is impossible that the persons now claiming to be Lieutenants Burgadish and Lancome have survived their deaths and continued to perform their duties. From this fact, I have concluded that these two men represent the numeric discrepancy previously mentioned.

"Yukikaze, are you saying that you have counted the tens of thousands of human beings on the planet Faery? Every person living, breathing, sleeping, and fighting?"

I have.

"Might not the data be in error? I'm asking you that, Yukikaze. Respond."

The data related to management of all humans extant in the FAF is not only stored in the personnel management computers of the units each person is attached to. It is also stored in the memories of several other devices, including FAF facility access control computers and the FAF soldier registration bank. I cross-checked them to verify any errors in their records, but could not find any. There are no errors in the original data. That is all.

"This definitely isn't the work of a human," Rei said. "It shows all the hallmarks of a computer's doing."

"Amazing... For Yukikaze, so long as that target data about the Systems Corps exists, her only explanation for those two extra men is that they're JAM. Even if the count is wrong."

"Making the number of humans match up really isn't what Yukikaze's concerned about here."

"I agree. I'm definitely getting the feeling that she's been manipulated into acting this way by the JAM. It isn't so much a question of logic, but rather of her intuition. I think she's trying as hard as possible to logically rectify the existence of something that shouldn't exist."

"Which is what I believe I said at the start, Edith."

"Yeah...if the original data were consistent with the target data, then Yukikaze wouldn't have tried to match the numbers up," Foss said. "This is all caused by the names of the dead men also being registered in Systems Corps' computers as deceased. The Systems Corps probably hasn't even considered that two of its people have the same names as two dead men. Still, the discrepancy would be revealed as soon as they confirmed that Lieutenant Burgadish and Lieutenant Lancome are dead."

"There probably isn't anyone in Systems Corps who would know either of them. Well, that's to be expected. Those guys are the elite. I doubt they'd know anyone who served on the front lines."

"In other words, the only people who'd realize what was going on just by looking at the names would be us—you and Yukikaze and the SAF."

"Here at Faery base, at any rate. The JAM acknowledged that by sending those two in to be the surplus," Rei said.

"Only one man could have arranged this. The only one who could modify data without alerting the computers there or arousing the suspicions of the humans in Systems Corps would be the retraining unit's true supervisor, Colonel Rombert. He has to be a JAM."

"Not necessarily."

"Even after all this?"

"You heard Major Booker before, didn't you? There are those who may not be JAM but who would still use them to destroy the FAF. He might even be acting as an agent for some government agency aiming for total global supremacy," Rei said.

"That's impossible. The JAM are the enemies of all humanity."

"I don't think the JAM would agree with you. They know by now that human beings are life-forms that would do exactly that sort of thing. They intend to use that aspect of human nature to make the FAF destroy itself from within. Right now, the JAM have positioned the retraining unit as their vanguard, and they've used Yukikaze as their messenger to deliver their proclamation as they launch their final attack on the FAF. It really is a declaration of war. If we keep quiet, the FAF authorities won't know about it for a while."

"So the JAM tell us and then sit back to see what moves we make?"

"The battle's beginning. Or, actually, it's been going on for a while now. The JAM don't rest," Rei said. "By neutralizing Yukikaze, they've robbed the SAF of a part of its military might. Putting her into this state is a tactical attack by the JAM. It's like they've hypnotized her and gotten her so paranoid and worried about ghosts that she can't think of anything else. I doubt she could even fly a combat mission now. Unless we snap her out of this, we're going to lose."

Captain Foss considered who Rei meant would lose in this. *Yukikaze would lose, and that would also be a loss for Captain Fukai*, she thought. They really were one and the same now. This new species of composite life-form was also a part of the combat machine that made up the SAF. And as far as the SAF was concerned, the FAF's fate wasn't their problem. Their primary concern remained their own personal survival.

This unit I joined really is nothing but trouble, Captain Foss thought. If they took the action Captain Fukai had suggested to return Yukikaze to normal and launched an electronic attack to delete the target data from the Systems Corps' computer without authorization, it would be a clear violation of FAF military regulations. That kind of arbitrary action wouldn't be tolerated. She had to stop this; that was all there was to it.

But what then, Edith Foss asked herself, as Captain Fukai might have. Was she so convinced that she was willing to die in battle for it? *That's right*, she thought. *Right now, this is about* my own *life or death*. Which was more likely to guarantee her survival, either taking the side of the FAF as a soldier or believing in the SAF's might and supporting Yukikaze and Captain Fukai as his physician? Which position would let her accept the consequences if the choice proved to be wrong?

Captain Fukai and the others in the SAF don't trouble themselves over these matters because they just aren't normal. But I am, thought Captain Foss. And that was when it hit her.

She'd never win against the JAM by thinking of herself as a *normal* human. Hadn't she been the one who'd said that the way for them to win was to become that new species of composite life-form? She didn't want to have to die to confirm her prediction, which was another way of saying that she'd be satisfied if she could accomplish that feat of evolution herself. There was nothing for her to agonize over here. If she wanted to live, then she should become one with the SAF. That way she would finally know if she were right.

"We can't lose," Captain Foss said. "I don't want to lose either."

"Then I'm issuing the order to attack," said Rei. "I'll have Yukikaze engage them."

"No, you mustn't," said Captain Foss.

"Why not?"

"We need time. Yukikaze isn't at full strength now. She still needs to have her engine replaced and repairs and maintenance done."

"I suppose, but—"

"Captain Fukai, if you attack the retraining unit now, I predict that they will immediately initiate destructive action. If we don't have some sort of plan to counter them, then Yukikaze could end up being destroyed."

"Then what are you saying we should do?"

"I think the saying that a sound mind requires a sound body applies to Yukikaze now. Part of Yukikaze's unease may be due to her physical damage. Captain Fukai, you should give top priority to Yukikaze's repairs, then attack only once you have permission from General Cooley. We have to come up with a plan that will allow the entire SAF to survive."

"Edith, to Yukikaze, inconsistencies in data are a real threat. We humans may think of it as some sort of illusory code, but she sees leaving it unrectified as the literal potential for her own destruction. If we don't deal with it soon—"

"I understand that. I understand it better than you do, even without your telling me."

"Oh, like you understand anything about Yukikaze," Rei said.

"You're the only one who can calm her down. If you're too hasty and make a mistake in dealing with her, there's a risk that she'll go wild. No human would be able to control her then. You have to look ahead. Attacking now would be reckless. The JAM want you to be preoccupied with Yukikaze's condition. If we go rushing into this, it'll be game over very quickly. The end, full stop. We can't let that happen."

"Stopping the game on doctor's orders, huh?" Rei said. "But will Yukikaze go along with it?"

"As a human, all I want is to avoid losing. You and Yukikaze both need some time to cool off and collect your thoughts. Make it an order, Captain Fukai. You're the only one who can persuade her."

Rei hadn't realized how rashly he'd been acting. *But*, he thought, *maybe what Edith is saying is correct, and the JAM are trying to keep me too wrapped up with Yukikaze to see that.*

And it was true that they'd be at a disadvantage if they launched an attack now. The only way they'd be able to go up against the JAM would be to utilize the full military might of the SAF. The SAF tactical computers could handle the deletion of the target data. They should use the SAF. They could just have Yukikaze confirm that the ghosts were gone without putting any undue stress on her.

"Yukikaze, maintain combat readiness," Rei ordered. He knew that she probably wouldn't accept an outright cancellation of the attack. She'd never understand him if he told her, "You're acting weird and need some rest."

"Then contact the maintenance team and have them effect repairs on your airframe," he continued. "I'm going to deplane in the meantime and try to use the tactical computer in SAF headquarters to attack the target data. Respond when I call you. If you require me, contact me via the tactical computer. That is all."

Roger, Captain Fukai.

After flashing the message onto the main display, Yukikaze shut down the T-FACPro II software herself. The program apparently placed too much of an additional burden on her resources and interfered with combat. That was probably it. And, thinking about how Yukikaze still trusted him, Rei climbed down from the cockpit.

3

IT WAS QUIET in the SAF command center, with even the main screen along the front wall switched off. No fighters were out on sortie; as soon as the missing Yukikaze had been discovered, General Cooley had recalled all the search planes and ordered their crews to get some rest. Instead, the only ones who were busy were the data analysts. Everyone had been called in, even the off-duty staffers, and they'd been gathered there along with Major Booker and Captain Foss to begin the analysis of the data Yukikaze had returned with. Once the first stage of analysis was complete, General Cooley had her staff take a break. She'd told the pair in charge of data analysis and aircraft maintenance that they shouldn't leave, and so the general had stayed behind in the center with them. She waited for Major Booker and Captain Foss to make their reports after going off to check on Captain Fukai and Lieutenant Katsuragi.

The data were even more useful than we'd hoped, General Cooley thought as she took a light meal of a sandwich and black tea before turning to check in on the work being done.

The method the JAM had used to lure in Yukikaze, the existence of that unknown space, the JAM voice, Captain Fukai's response to it, the actions Yukikaze had taken to escape... It was all shocking. Lieutenant Katsuragi, who'd come to them from the Intelligence Forces, had reacted the most normally by getting angry when what the JAM, Captain Fukai, and Yukikaze did seemed to defy common sense. *Well, perhaps I understand his reaction, considering I also lost my composure when I saw the data,* thought General Cooley. They'd brought back a great deal of data about the JAM, but put another way, it meant that the SAF just dramatically increased what they *didn't* know about the enemy. Faced with the sheer volume of confusing data, she supposed it was only natural for her to temporarily lose her cool. She wasn't a machine, after all.

God damn it, she thought as she replayed Captain Fukai's conversation with the JAM over and over. *Just what* were *the JAM?*

> Captain Fukai: Just what are you people? Living things? Beings that consist only of intelligence, will, and data? Do you have physical forms? If so, then where are they?
>
> JAM: I cannot explain in a way that would be comprehensible in your terms. I am that I am.

She couldn't make heads or tails of it. It hadn't denied having a physical form. The voice calling itself the whole of the JAM was broadcast from the duplicate of the old Yukikaze, but it was hard to imagine that their true form had been riding within the plane itself. She wondered if the JAM's intentional nonanswer had been a strategic ploy to avoid revealing their physical selves.

At the very least, it seemed that the JAM did possess the general concept of "I." The JAM had the power to differentiate between itself and others. *It seems obvious, but it's likely a vital point*, thought General Cooley. The question was, while the JAM could make the distinction, apparently humans could not. They were just going to have to deal with not knowing where the JAM existed, what a JAM was, and exactly what defined them.

The general recalled a conversation Captain Foss had had with Major Booker during the analysis. It had been recorded and already transcribed. General Cooley searched for the page it was on.

"The JAM didn't respond when Captain Fukai asked where it was," Captain Foss had said. "If we believe the rest of what it says, then we can conclude that the JAM have no concept of place or space, or if they do, that it's outside the realm of human understanding. Considering that they're beings capable of creating spaces like the Passageway and that so-called 'mysterious battle zone,' that seems likely."

"The question Captain Fukai asked would be difficult for even the JAM to answer, Captain Foss," Major Booker had replied. "He wasn't simply asking what their location was. He was asking them where they really existed. For example, where are you, Edith?"

"Ah, you mean is the thing that's called *me* my physical body? The consciousness inside my body? Do I have a soul and, if so, where does it go when I die? Yes, that is what he was asking, wasn't it? A typical Captain Fukai move."

"I think I would have asked the same thing if I'd been in that situation. And if you asked me that, I'd probably reply, 'I'm right here.'" Booker said. "Simple, accurate, and doesn't waste ten thousand words trying to elaborate on it. No matter what the meaning of the question might be, the normal answer to 'Where are you?' would be 'I'm right here,' wouldn't it? But the JAM didn't say that. They must have judged that the person they were speaking to wouldn't have understood if they said, 'I'm right here.'"

"You mean the only way the JAM could put it was 'I am that I am'?"

"Yes, I think so. It's not the same as them saying 'I'm here.' The JAM definitely exist, but they may not be able to decide if they exist nowhere or everywhere, and they didn't have the words to explain it."

"At the very least, that applied to the JAM Fukai communicatd with," Foss said. "There was no physical entity there face to face with Captain Fukai or Yukikaze that they could understand. It was like it was talking to them on a telephone. But then you can't say that the JAM have no physical form."

"You once claimed to Captain Fukai that the JAM were imaginary. Can you still make that claim, Edith?"

"I only said that I couldn't deny the possibility that they were."

"I'm not trying to be sarcastic by asking you that. The JAM may be some sort of virtual species. That's what we humans would have to call an entity we cannot actually perceive. We don't really have a general concept to describe something that we absolutely cannot perceive. That's why the JAM couldn't answer. I'll bet that if the JAM asked us where our true form is, they couldn't directly perceive us with whatever senses they have, simply owing to the nature of their own existence. To the JAM, humans probably seem like virtual beings too."

"When I said that they might be imaginary, all I meant was that they were an illusion that had been dreamed up by humans," Foss said. "But that isn't the JAM that's shown up here. It's definitely a being you could either believe in or not. Does that still make it a virtual being?"

"A being you could believe in or not may still be an illusion, Edith."

"What do you mean?"

"It's a philosophical question," Major Booker said.

"I'm not sure I'm following you."

"The philosophical question of what exactly is something that you can believe in or not. In short, what defines a being that absolutely exists and how do you integrate such a thing into yourself. Aside from Asian philosophies, the philosophies we're familiar with have a long history of grappling with the question of whether or not beings can absolutely exist."

"You mean the JAM really may not exist?"

"In one sense, that is possible. There are a number of ways that you can put it. There's also the idea that the question of what is absolute existence is nothing but a play on words. Put another way, the ability for humans to think about such things and develop such questions makes the questions themselves meaningless. From there, a new way of thinking emerges."

"What sort of way?"

"That absolute existence, which is perhaps a god, or an agreement between subjective and objective perception—there are many ways to express it, anyway. The long and the short of it is that this way of thinking doesn't affect how we exist. It's a momentary thought—yes, truth is informed by human cognition, and anything beyond that is simply an individual question."

"So, those who believe in them should believe and those who don't shouldn't, you mean?" Foss asked.

"Well, I suppose you could put it that way. But an ephemeral way of thinking could distort the perceptions of what's right in front of you."

"Of course it would. The JAM can't simply be dealt with as a personal matter."

"Which is why we're here asking that question. I guess what I'm getting at is that we can't avoid asking philosophical questions as we ask things like what is it that makes us so certain that the JAM exist? What are they? What is their true nature and what is the essence of it? If we accept the fact that their true nature is beyond human understanding, then all we're doing is groping for a new general philosophical concept. The JAM have been working out what humans are from their end. I'm sure that what they think of us is entirely different from how we think of ourselves. But what we know for certain is that they're searching for features common to all humans. That's why they made contact with Captain Fukai."

"Except that we don't have time to be arguing philosophy here. There's no way to answer philosophical questions, anyway," Foss said.

"That isn't true. Philosophy is the study of how to question the meaning of existence and how to live happily. Happiness varies according to the era and the individual, which is why there are no universal answers to philosophical questions. However, you can verify them for yourself. If your philosophy can let you accept death, you'll know. And if philosophy is too grandiose a way of putting it, then call it your worldview. In order to counter the JAM, we need to change the worldview we've held till now. Captain Fukai has managed to do that; he's said so repeatedly. As his doctor, you know that, Edith. And it was Yukikaze that changed his worldview, not the JAM."

"Major, it's almost as if you're saying that the JAM are like gods, and that we need to think about whether or not they exist."

"It certainly seems that way, doesn't it?" Booker said.

"I'm surprised. I always figured you were an atheist, like everyone else in the SAF."

"Whether gods exist or not, we can still live, all the same. That's what I think, and I believe it's the same with the JAM, whether they exist or not."

"I beg your pardon?" Foss said.

"If you don't agree, then you're telling me that you've accepted the JAM as gods with an objective existence; you're preaching the religion of JAMism."

"Hold on there, Major. Then what is it that you're doing here?"

"I'm explaining to you that if the JAM can't be directly perceived by humans, then I believe that we can't fight them without bringing up certain philosophical questions. If the JAM are not physical entities, you can't simply say that they exist whether you believe in them or not."

"So how do we make this more definite, Major Booker?"

"We search for exactly what the JAM threat is. If we find that it's an illusion, then we don't have to fight."

"The SAF can't just abandon the battle now, surely."

"That's General Cooley's job to decide, not yours, and your profacting report on the JAM will be used by her as a major ingredient in determining what decision she makes. Now add in data Yukikaze has brought back. It may be possible now to verify the threat the JAM pose. I have a feeling that we won't be able to immediately verify your suspicions about the JAM's true nature. And even if humans in the future judge what we do here as a complete waste of time and history decides that we made a mistake, it's all we can do now. History's verdict has nothing to do with us. Either way, we won't be alive to see it, and that's true if we die content or cursing our bad fortune. I couldn't care less about the future. All we can do now is what we believe is best, and that's how anyone with a brain in their head has lived and died throughout all of history."

"You think the JAM are like gods, huh?"

"The same way that humans must appear to them," Booker said. "We're equal in that respect, and there's nothing to fear from it."

General Cooley stopped reading there and took a sip of her tea.

Even if the JAM were like gods, it was nothing to fear— *How very typical of Major Booker*, Cooley thought. The JAM and humanity were equal in his view. If the JAM are gods, then so are we, he'd told Captain Foss. He'd explained that she should leave out the god angle as much as she could. And even when Captain Foss had still brought it up, he'd told her not to be afraid. Don't fear the JAM, don't blindly accept them, just determine the true nature of the threat they represent. That was his way of lending the young doctor support.

But the truth was that their relationship with the JAM wasn't equivalent, because humans formed collectives. Indeed, Captain Fukai and Yukikaze had fought the JAM on equal terms and had returned to tell about it. Major Booker, too, could argue with the JAM on equal terms with his philosophy. But there was no way that every human was capable of such accomplishments. *I put the SAF together to place us on equal footing with JAM*, General Cooley thought, *and to do that I created a group of individuals with a single purpose, just I supposed the JAM to be.* There was no way they could equal the JAM unless not a single person in the group defied her.

Almost from the day she was born, General Cooley had wanted one thing: power. Overwhelming, unquestionable power. Power that would let her declare that the world was hers, that would allow her to argue on equal terms with the gods. From the typical desire for authority most people have, the feeling grew into a palpable sensation inside her. It was probably a base instinct in humans, born out of being social animals. If she were like a cat, a natural loner, then she'd only rely on herself to hunt for food or defend herself from enemies. But wolves and humans weren't like that. Without a good leader, the entire group would be threatened. We create gods out of our desire for an external leader. A life-form that lives independently has no gods because it doesn't need them.

Thinking back, the general realized that she'd been defying, even fighting, godlike beings since childhood. Back then, her father had seemed like a supreme being. Whatever he said was right and had to be obeyed. She was the middle child between two brothers, and when she'd complained that he treated her differently, his reply was that it was because she was a girl. Her mother said the same thing. It wasn't as if being a girl was something to be ashamed of, but the reasoning just seemed so absurd to her. She wished to grow up as quickly as she could but found that things weren't very much different as an adult.

"General Cooley," Captain Foss had once asked her, "what did you do before you joined the FAF?" The doctor had been gathering data on the SAF members, and she made no exceptions, even for her own commanding officer.

"I did a number of things, all of them related to finance. Right before I joined up, I was aiming to be a top-level broker in a securities firm."

"Tough work, but rewarding all the same. Is that the career you wanted, and then the FAF grabbed you?"

"No, I came here of my own accord. You wouldn't expect someone whose skills lie in finance to be assigned to a combat unit, but it was what I wanted."

"What was it that brought you here seeking a new world, Lydia?"

"I'd appreciate it if you didn't call me by my first name here, Captain Foss."

"I beg your pardon, General Cooley."

"What was it? I think young Lydia Cooley just decided to abandon her old world because she found it irrational."

"I'm not entirely familiar with what goes into being a stockbroker, but the really high-level ones can move the world on their say-so, can't they?" Foss said.

"Money is just numbers. None of it is real, although that may be an extreme position to take. Still, money does have practical power. It can disrupt an entire nation. To control it, to manipulate it freely, can be thrilling. And when things go well, it can even be fun. But I couldn't reach that level. I don't think it was a question of my abilities, but the world wasn't kind enough to let me get by on just those. I finally understood. You might say that

I saw the limits of my world."

"You experienced sexual discrimination?"

"Oh, naturally," General Cooley said. "Plenty of that. But that wasn't what made me abandon it."

What young Lydia Cooley had realized was that the true source of the irrationality she'd always experienced wasn't from her being born a woman, but from her having been born a human being.

"Humanity is divided into two classes: bosses and everyone else. Even if a woman controlled the world, no one would accept it. I was being a fool in trying to be a boss that no one would accept."

"A fool…"

"Yes. Where would be the fun in becoming the boss of people who'd treat me like that?" Cooley replied. "I realized how empty it would be. However, I didn't want to resign myself to being one of 'everyone else,' either. So what was I to do? For a while there, I was seriously considering becoming a nun."

"So in the end, you began to doubt the rat race and the values of the harsh world of the money game."

"I suppose so…When I think back, there were all sorts of paths I could have taken. I might have become a researcher, like you, or a talented psychologist who'd make a fortune and win acceptance from the world. Or I could have married and become a mother. But there before young Lydia were beings called the JAM, who threatened the whole of human society."

"And you felt that a job fighting invaders from another world, ones with values completely different from our own, would be a rewarding career?" Captain Foss asked.

"Maybe I did. It's ancient history now."

Captain Foss had nodded, jotted down something in her notebook, and asked nothing more about it.

She had thought it would be a rewarding job, but as General Cooley looked back at the person she was at that time, she realized that she hadn't been burning with hope. The FAF had been an escape for her. Yes, just like a convent. The JAM were there. The JAM, which she could believe in in place of God. She'd never been aware of it until now, when she'd realized that what Major Booker had said applied to her. *Then*, she asked herself, *did I come here to learn that overwhelming power was a necessity? And with that, I could oppose the JAM?*

No, that wasn't it. The JAM's attitude had made that clear.

True, it would be an ideal situation to gain absolute authority over the FAF and fight the JAM that way. While humans did operate as collectives, it was necessary to win power struggles within that collective. That fact put them at a disadvantage vis-a-vis the JAM, and they'd be sure to exploit it. The JAM must have understood humanity's Achilles' heel. Their analysis must have also shown them that a weak point could be turned into a strong point. For example, conflict within a collective might be necessary to replace a bad boss with a superior person.

The JAM had admitted that the SAF was beyond their understanding. They might as well have said that it was Cooley herself that they didn't understand, since she was the one who'd set the SAF up in this way. That was the JAM's weakness. The FAF and the JAM might not be equally matched, but it could be said that the SAF was now in the same position as the JAM. It was a position she couldn't abandon. The one thing she couldn't afford to do was behave as her opponents expected.

What she needed to make clear to the JAM was that humanity didn't merely consist of the types of people that they could comprehend.

"The JAM are like gods?"

Major Booker had said that regarding the JAM as an unknowable enemy called to mind words and concepts like *god*. Booker told Captain Foss that he'd prefer to avoid seeing the JAM as gods, but also feared that it might be impossible. General Cooley understood how he felt. But, she thought, a part of her hoped that they literally were godlike beings. Because to stand up and fight against the gods was something that young Lydia Cooley had always hoped she could do.

4

AFTER CHANGING CLOTHES, Rei and Lieutenant Katsuragi joined Captain Foss and Major Booker on their way to see General Cooley in the command center.

In response to General Cooley saying that she hadn't summoned the two pilots, Major Booker whispered in her ear to explain about Yukikaze's discovery of two unidentified humans within the Systems Corps—men who were claiming to be Lieutenant Burgadish and another dead man. How Yukikaze had recognized them as JAM, and how Rei felt that her concerns were likely a JAM trick. The general betrayed little surprise as she listened. After brief consideration, she ordered First Lieutenant Eco, the chief of fighter plane maintenance operations, to begin repairs on Yukikaze at once.

"Yukikaze won't resist our moving her to the repair bay now." There had been some fear of her self-destructing. "However," General Cooley continued, "we need to keep her linked to the tactical computer while she's in the repair bay. Can you do that?"

"Of course we can."

"How long will the repairs take?"

"I'll know that once I get a detailed look at exactly what's damaged on her. From what the maintenance team saw when they eyeballed it before, dismounting the damaged engine shouldn't take too long. It should just slide right out. There's nothing fatally damaged on the airframe, and the root of the primary tail stabilizer she lost is just fine. It should take us an hour to move her into the repair bay and run a damage inspection. Swapping out the engine and the other miscellaneous repairs should take about three hours if we push it, another two for general maintenance and inspections, so… Yeah, six hours should do it."

"Do it in four."

"Okay, we'll aim for four."

Lieutenant Eco began to issue orders to the maintenance team from his terminal, the display on the monitor mirrored on the big screen at the front of the command center. Data from Yukikaze's onboard airframe self-monitoring system began to scroll onto it as well. Confirming that Yukikaze had agreed to the repairs, Cooley told the still-standing Major Booker and his subordinates to take seats at the empty consoles.

"Captain Pivot, enter Captain Fukai's and Lieutenant Katsuragi's reports into the strategic computer. Lieutenant Katsuragi, you assist him. Major Booker, monitor what the strategic computer does. Captain Foss, present your formal prediction of the JAM's strategy and the results of your profacting. Please wait here while I read it to answer any questions I may have."

"I want to delete the data related to the retraining unit in the Systems Corps," Rei said. "Authorize the attack."

"You are to read through the data that you and Yukikaze brought back, as well as the data analysis report we've generated here at HQ. Whether or not we attack will be determined by a comprehensive judgment of all available information," Cooley said. "If you haven't eaten yet, order anything you want. Captain Foss, Major Booker, that goes for you too."

"Great, I'll have a two-pound steak, please, and make it rare," said Lieutenant Katsuragi. That immediately broke the tension.

This might be our last meal, Rei thought. *Thirteen people weren't nearly enough to be doing this.* It occurred to him that there were thirteen planes in the squadron as well. When the final battle came, they'd probably all be served fuel and weaponry at the same time too…

The general's young secretary, who hung by her side like a shadow, took their orders and called them in to the SAF mess hall.

Rei ordered a ham bun, and by the time the round, extra-large roll stuffed with ham and vegetables had arrived, he'd gotten to the part of the analysis report that General Cooley had reread, wherein Captain Foss and Major Booker had discussed the ontology of the JAM.

If they start calling the JAM gods, then it's all over, Rei thought. *The FAF will lose its reason for existence.*

If what Major Booker had predicted came to pass, the FAF would split into two groups: believers and nonbelievers. Three, if you counted the group who wouldn't care either way. And then those groups would probably split into even more subgroups. At any rate, since the JAM were unperceivable entities, it was impossible to ascertain just what was the correct way to conceive of them. With the stress of all these various groups within it, there'd be no way that the FAF could maintain its role as a coherent organization against the JAM. If the groups within the FAF started using force to validate their views, it'd turn into an outright religious war. Major Booker had been right on the money to call it "JAMism." Even now, there were a lot of people on Earth who claimed that the JAM were illusory, with some of them practically believing that they were gods. The groups back home hadn't yet begun making moves that threatened the FAF, but there was a real danger that they might.

"If humans really can't perceive the JAM," Rei said, "the FAF must never let that information go public."

"I'd expect the Intelligence Forces have a media control plan ready to go," said Major Booker, nodding. "What about it?"

"I was just thinking I'd like to tell Lynn Jackson about this. About what we've got here. She's an Earther. She has a right to know."

"I agree. There's a saying that the three most useful friends to have are a doctor, a lawyer, and a journalist," Booker said. "Although you're inviting disaster if they aren't very good at what they do. Still, we can rely on Lynn. She can understand the SAF. It'll be tough to pull off, but I think it'd be worth it. If you were going to make a last will and testament, I can't think of a better person to entrust it to."

"It's not certain that we're going to lose," said Captain Foss. "And it's not certain that we're going to die."

"A will is something you write while still alive," said Major Booker. "We're losing our chance to leave it with the FAF."

"The Intelligence Forces aren't incompetent," said Lieutenant Katsuragi. "They must have predicted the implications of knowing the JAM's true form. You might say that the SAF was slow to figure it out. Well, I suppose that comes from being a combat unit. You only believe in what you can practically confirm. Still, this inability to pin down where the JAM exist is almost like quantum theory, isn't it? Maybe the JAM are quantum beings."

"You're talking about the Uncertainty Principle," said Captain Foss. "That's the one that says the means of human observation itself makes knowing an object's location unclear, since you can't measure two exact values at the same time, right?"

"That's not entirely correct," said Captain Pivot, the man in charge of data analysis. "The values that can't be simultaneously observed are those with attributes in conjugate relation to each other. For example, position and energy have no conjugate attributes, so it's possible to know both simultaneously if you measure them precisely. If you make that into the conjugate attributes of position and speed, however, then you can't observe both values simultaneously."

"Why not?"

"I can't explain it in a few words. Quantum theory is hard for us to think about in commonplace terms because it works like a mathematical metaphor. Anybody can understand the formulae if they work hard enough at it; the mistakes come when they try to interpret them. There are some people who make up suitable explanations while ignoring the formulae, which is probably where your own misunderstanding comes from. Now, it's true that you get uncertain results from inaccurate observation methods, but that isn't the uncertainty we're talking about here. Quantum uncertainty doesn't work that simply. I think what Lieutenant Katsuragi is trying to say is that if the JAM possess quantum uncertainty, then they only exist when you observe them, and that they don't actually exist anywhere before you do that. One interpretation you can get from quantum theory is that an unobserved JAM really doesn't exist. Another is that you can't definitively know that a quantum object exists *until* you observe it. There are all sorts of interpretations. In any case, humans don't currently possess an experimental means to determine which interpretation is the correct one. You could say that the incomprehensibility of quantum theory comes from humans lacking the means to make certain the uncertainty of quantum uncertainty."

"I know exactly what you mean by incomprehensibility," said Captain Foss. "Comparing something to God makes it seem like you understand it, but the truth is it just means you don't understand it at all, doesn't it?"

"Even if the JAM are ambiguous quantum beings like that," said Lieutenant Katsuragi, sounding pleased with himself, "then they can still be observed and recorded, meaning it's possible to calculate the probability of where they'll appear. Conjugate attributes mean that, if you can observe one, then you can calculate the other."

"You can really imagine the situation is that concrete?" Captain Foss said. "What use would that be when dealing with someone who might not actually exist?"

Lieutenant Katsuragi stared silently at the ceiling, but Rei could guess what he wanted to say.

"What this all means is that, fundamentally, we can't precisely target the JAM," Rei said. "The moment we know exactly where they are, we'll no longer know where they're going."

"If the JAM are beings like that, all we can aim at are probabilities. We might get lucky and even hit them," said Major Booker. "Well, that's not too different from fighting a normal opponent. In that case, the question is what weapons are effective against the JAM? We can shoot down all the planes the JAM send at us, but as long as the JAM themselves aren't in them, we'll never land an effective blow. The same goes for the JAM fighting us humans."

"We're just likening the incomprehensibility of the JAM to quantum uncertainty for our own convenience," said Captain Pivot. "As long as we don't know for sure that the JAM manifest via quantum uncertainty, then all this discussion about it is meaningless. We're just confusing the issue, and the last thing we need to be doing now is making the JAM seem more mysterious. First of all, we should make clear what we don't understand about them."

"You're right," said Major Booker. "If there's one problem we have right now, it's our poor communication with the JAM. That's how they have us jumping at shadows. You could say that this entire war stems from our inability to communicate. Once we can reach them, the JAM's identity will be made clear as a matter of course. Just as Captain Foss and I said before in our discussion about the existence of the JAM, it's a question of finding something to make the JAM a certainty to us. Quantum theory may be useful for that, and it's also possible that scientific methods may prove useless. The point is this—right now, all these arguments aren't letting us get a handle on what the JAM are. What we need to do is collect data, just as we've always had to. If we're to have in-depth discussions, we can't lose here."

"Major Booker..." said Captain Foss.

"Yes, Edith?" said the major.

"Does that taste good?"

"What?"

"That curry. It smells really good and it's making me hungry."

"It's my special menu for when I'm tired. You can order one from the chef too, if you like. Doesn't taste as good as when Chef Murullé made it, unfortunately," the major said as he scooped curry onto some naan bread and continued to eat. The stew was spicy and sour, and the meal was completed with a cup of unbelievably sweet tea.

"I wanted to go over the recipe with the new chef but haven't had the time. There's also Chinese food on the Booker Special. Would you like me to introduce you to it?"

"No, thank you."

"Captain Foss," Cooley said, looking up.

"Yes, General Cooley?"

Having finished reading the profacting results submitted by Captain Foss, the general closed the file. The captain turned to face her, expecting a harsh round of questioning.

"Just how probable do you predict it is that the JAM will launch an all-out attack on us?"

"The T-FACPro II software can answer that for a human subject, but since I was calculating this myself this time, I can't give you an exact number."

"It doesn't have to be."

"Then I predict it's highly probable."

"How high?" Cooley asked.

"I think it's almost a certainty. As I wrote in my report."

"Certain enough that you'd give me the cake you're eating now if you're wrong?"

"No, General Cooley, I wouldn't. If you're asking me to bet something on it," Captain Foss replied with total seriousness, "then I'd bet my life."

"You're still young," General Cooley said. "If you get it wrong, you can always do it over again."

"General, I'm being serious. I'd bet my life on it."

"Edith," said General Cooley, "one of the joys of aging is the chance to laugh at how foolish you were in your youth. I want you to get the chance to do that too. You shouldn't bet your life on anything. If you lose, you'll be left with nothing but regret. Treat it like it's everything that you own."

"Yes, General. I'll do that."

"Good."

General Cooley laid the report down on the console and addressed the others.

"Gentlemen, the question at hand is how seriously to take this prediction upon which Captain Foss here has bet everything. I have a feeling you all already know the contents of the report. I'd like to hear your opinions on it. Major Booker."

"Yes, General."

"You'll serve as the moderator. There's no need for you to form an opinion."

"Understood, General Cooley." Wiping his mouth with a napkin, Major Booker stood up. "First of all, are there any objections? Does anyone here disagree with Captain Foss's prediction? I'll even take general doubts about it."

Nobody said anything. The major nodded. "Well, that's that," he said and sat down.

"Hold it! What do you mean 'That's that'?" Captain Foss said. "Major, you aren't just going to leave it at that, are you?"

Ignoring her, Major Booker turned to General Cooley.

"General Cooley, what I'd like to know is your opinion of this situation. We have the materials gathered to make a decision. True, it's incomplete, but if we waited for perfection, we'd never make a move. The most important thing right now is what you think of the JAM's moves and how you evaluate them. Simply put, what do you want to do? If you tell us that, what the best move is that the SAF can make, what tactics and strategy to use, that you aren't worried about this, then I'll do it. We all will."

"In short, you want to know what my philosophy of life is," Cooley said.

"I suppose. You could say that the SAF is your life, couldn't you?"

"And what if I told you that I wanted to end my life here?"

"You wouldn't!" said Captain Foss.

"That's your business," Rei said. "Even if your life ends, ours will continue. That's all. If you want out of this, then I'd like you to say so. Tell us that we no longer need your permission."

"You can't end things that easily," said Major Booker. "If you renounced your command of the SAF, your will would still remain after you left. In other words, we could still resist the JAM even without you as our commander. Even if you said that you wanted the SAF to self-destruct, it wouldn't be that easy to do. That's the difference between us and the other units in the FAF. And you were the one who made the SAF like that, General Cooley."

"And there's your answer," she replied.

"What do you mean?" said Major Booker.

"Major, if you're saying that the SAF reflects my will, then there's no need to keep asking me what I want to do, is there? I want to beat the JAM, that's all."

Seeing Major Booker's questioning look, she continued.

"But I understand your wanting to know my evaluation of the JAM's moves. The information Yukikaze brought back, Captain Foss's prediction, and the presence of JAM agents in the Systems Corps are all developments I never anticipated. If I misjudge this situation, it will endanger you as well, Major Booker. You're worried about that. You don't know what to do, isn't that right, Captain Foss?"

"Please, I can't answer something like that out of the blue, but…I think we're all concerned about this, General. Even Yukikaze is showing signs of instability, so in a way, everyone involved is nervous about this."

"I feel no nervousness at all," said General Cooley, cutting her off. "Rather, I prefer the JAM to be ambiguous entities. The reason I joined the FAF was to declare my existence to creatures like that. I didn't want to do it to other humans. If the JAM had turned out to have humanlike consciousness, to be easily comprehensible, I probably would have been disappointed. In any case, what I want to do is make something simple and clear to them: that the SAF is a threat to the JAM. As for how specifically to do that, I want to borrow your wisdom. That's why I'm asking for your opinions. However, Major Booker…"

"Yes, General Cooley."

"As I am not, as I said, troubled by this, I'm leaving this to you. Determine which strategy and tactics the SAF should adopt. I'm going to get some rest. Come up with some executables before Yukikaze's repairs are complete. Then I'll make my final decision."

"Understood."

The general stood and turned to Major Booker.

"Major, there's one thing I want you to pay attention to."

"What is it?"

"How the JAM respond to the SAF in this situation should not be overestimated."

"What do you mean?"

"The JAM's enemy is humanity, and we're only one part of it," Cooley said. "You mustn't forget that. I'm saying that if you think they're giving us special treatment, you'll make the wrong judgment."

"I'll keep that in mind."

With a stiff nod from Major Booker, General Cooley made a quick exit, followed by her secretary. Captain Foss was the first to open her mouth and break the silence.

"What was that all about? That attitude of hers."

"You're the specialist at predicting how the human mind works," Rei said.

"That was me completely screwing up," said Major Booker, rubbing his face with both hands. "I pissed her off."

"It didn't look like that to me," said Lieutenant Katsuragi.

"She was furious," the major said. "I might as well have told her that she was incompetent and should take herself out of the game. That we'd be able to fight the JAM if not for her. And for that, I got to feel the queen's wrath upon me."

"If you're going to call that anger, then it's a quiet and deep anger. You'd have to call it a rage against existence," said Captain Foss. "But I never knew she felt such intense rage."

"Somebody once said, when confronting God and the universe, 'I am here!'" said Major Booker. "The response they got was 'So what?' General Cooley has always been in that situation. This is the first time I really understood."

"So what?" said Rei. "It's not our problem."

"Captain Fukai, that's not what you'd say now, is it? Or are you reflecting on those words? How that attitude you used to have would hurt the general—"

"I mean it's literally not our problem. Our flattering or speaking badly about the general doesn't concern her at all. The only thing that she's afraid of is having the JAM tell her, 'You don't matter at all to us.' Jack, there's no reason for you to feel depressed. If anything, it should have motivated you."

"All it did was remind me of what a complete wanker I can be at times," Booker said. "Still, I suppose I should be glad that she told me exactly how she felt."

"The general's last point was vital," Captain Pivot said. "If we make a mistake in judging how much interest the JAM have in the SAF, this could all end up with us simply being seen as a mutinous unit within the FAF."

"We can't move carelessly," said Major Booker. "To General Cooley, we're all just her pawns on the board. But I don't see it that way. I don't want to lose a single man or machine."

"General Cooley doesn't want to lose her people meaninglessly, either," said Rei. "Jack, Yukikaze and I work the way you think we do, but we're also individual beings. If you get hung up on one particular piece on the board, you'll lose the whole game. If you're going to play chess that badly, I don't want to be in the game with you."

"Hmm... Like that saying 'A poor player cares more for his rook than his king,' right? Before all else, you have to think about your own survival."

"Taking this to its logical conclusion," said Captain Pivot, "each individual should do what they need to do. Maybe that's what the JAM are predicting we'll do."

"No, they're not," said Captain Foss. "I don't think the JAM are expecting us to do that at all. I think that they expect the SAF to change. I predict that the JAM will try to alter our behavior through some method of attack and will observe our status here."

"Not doing anything is another measure we could try, but I doubt it would work against the JAM," said Major Booker. "They've likely worked out every possible contingency and are provoking us to act, which is probably why they sent in the duplicates of those dead men. The thing is, it may be too risky to come out and face them. Defense can be a lot harder than offense."

"What we need to know is what's happening with the FAF as a

whole," said Lieutenant Katsuragi. "What strategy are they currently following?"

Captain Pivot ordered the strategic computer to display an FAF tactical map on the main screen.

"The FAF has determined that Cookie and Richwar have been wiped out," said Captain Pivot. "The next pair of bases targeted are Rakugan and Kanworm. Currently, our main fighter forces are being moved to the front-line bases nearest them, beginning with Faery base, as well as those from Siren, Troll, Sylvan, Brownie, and Valkia. They're probably planning to launch simultaneous attacks on both enemy bases. There is no JAM resistance to this at the moment. No skirmishes. Nothing at all for the last few hours. It probably hasn't been this quiet since the war began."

"This is a very dangerous situation," said Captain Foss. "I can feel my spine tingling."

"General Laitume is requesting tactical recon on both bases from us," said Captain Pivot. "Scratch that. It's not a request. It's an order. General Cooley's been delaying him by saying we're tied up analyzing the new data, but that's not going to hold him off forever."

"Let's run for it," Lieutenant Katsuragi suddenly said.

Everyone stared at the young lieutenant.

"Oh, don't look at me like that," he said. "I'm proposing a strategic movement. Would you prefer me to call it a withdrawal? If we don't want to get uselessly wasted in battle, I think that's the only option. We should let the JAM know the SAF is leaving the battle zone, and then retreat our planes to some prearranged airspace."

"I can't think of any way for us to escape," said Major Booker. "You couldn't call it a strategic withdrawal. That's desertion in the face of the enemy. We'd never get away with it. It'd be taken as a tactical operation against the FAF. Besides, where would we run to?"

"Sounds like fun," said Rei. "Skipping out under cover of night."

"Some might say skipping out is the sort of move they'd expect of the SAF," said Captain Foss.

"The JAM don't matter anymore," Rei replied. "It's pointless to go on arguing about them when we'll never get any answers. What we need to consider now is how to oppose the FAF, because they're not going to let us just run away."

"It's worth considering," said Captain Pivot as he watched the screen. "The SAF has no ground forces. The only weaponry we have are survival guns, and we don't have much ammo for them. If the human duplicates in the FAF attack us, even with our fighter planes, we'd hold out for maybe an hour before we'd have to run for it. The question is whether or not there's safe airspace to run to anywhere."

"There is," said Lieutenant Katsuragi. "Earth. We should fly through the Passageway. The FAF would finish off any JAM chasing us. It's the safest place."

They all stared at the lieutenant, dumbfounded.

"It wouldn't work?" he asked.

"Lieutenant," said Major Booker. "What would we do then? We can't keep flying forever. The nearest place to go would be an Australian air force base, but we'd violate their airspace if we headed there. They'd treat us like JAM."

"Any evacuation to Earth," said Captain Pivot, "would require consent from Earth. Only the FAF high command are authorized to negotiate that. It's not like I haven't heard of articles covering the emergency evacuation of FAF combat units, but in this situation, it would be something the FAF would have to do, not us. The SAF would send this information to General Laitume and have him call a top-level FAF strategic conference for the one thing we could do—initiate an emergency evacuation of the FAF."

"We'd first have to get the general to consent to it," said Rei. "Then he'd have to convince the other ones in the high command. I don't know how long it'd take, or if they'd even act, but even assuming they went for it all we'd be doing is moving the battlefield from here to Earth. That's probably exactly what the JAM want. There'd no longer be any point to the combat bases we have on Faery. Why did we even build Faery base in the first place? Earth would never go along with it."

"It'd become a political war in which we wouldn't be able to participate," said Major Booker. "We couldn't afford to wait to see what the outcome would be. Look, what we—what *I* want to protect isn't the FAF. It's the SAF and my own self."

"I see. It wouldn't work," said Lieutenant Katsuragi. "And I thought it was a good idea, too."

Looking at the lieutenant as he sighed, Rei thought of Colonel Rombert.

"Jack, what about Colonel Rombert's demand for me and Lieutenant Katsuragi to join that retraining unit?"

"Yeah, that is a problem," said Major Booker. "General Cooley hasn't given an official reply yet. Captain Pivot, has Colonel Rombert said anything since then?"

"No, not that I've heard. There hasn't been a peep out of the Intelligence Forces."

"Even Colonel Rombert probably didn't seriously expect us to swallow it," said Major Booker. "Otherwise, he wouldn't have been using a dead man like Lieutenant Burgadish in plain sight. If Rei went there, the cat would be out of the bag pretty quick. Maybe he sent for Rei deliberately to blow the secret... But still, Lieutenant Burgadish? I can't believe it. Is he really there? How can we be sure of this?"

"Why don't I go?" said Lieutenant Katsuragi. "I don't know what this Lieutenant Burgadish looks like, but—"

"No," said the major. "You already know too much about the inner workings of the SAF. I can't send you."

"Want to try a video call?" said Rei.

"And what if he answers?" asked Captain Foss.

"If it's actually Lieutenant Burgadish, then—" he began, when suddenly Lieutenant Eco, who'd been silently engrossed with his work, piped up. "Order a pizza."

"What?" asked Captain Pivot. "Why a pizza?"

"Because I like them. You can say it's a wrong number. Damn, I'm hungry. I wish I'd ordered food with the rest of you guys."

"How are the repairs coming on Yukikaze?" asked Rei.

"Taking a little more time than I expected," said Lieutenant Eco. "General Cooley's going to be mad, but what can you do?"

"Forget the video call," said Major Booker. "Any moves we make to confirm it's him will be noticed by the JAM. We can't give up this grace period until Yukikaze is back in action."

"The JAM aren't giving us a grace period," said Captain Foss.

"As soon as that retraining unit is ready, they'll begin their attack, just as Yukikaze predicted. They'll destroy us."

"There are probably around fifty people in that unit," Captain Pivot said. "They'd be neutralized quickly. They won't achieve anything acting alone, so maybe they'll move in concert with a JAM attack from the outside. Major Booker, let's send out our fighters. Tactical combat reconnaissance. It'd be safer to have them in the air. And we'd be able to save face with General Laitume."

"Of course, I thought of that too. The question is just how far can thirteen fighters go against the JAM?" Major Booker said, crossing his arms. "If the JAM launch an all-out attack after they take off, it'd be dangerous for them to return to Faery base. It could be destroyed from within. I can imagine it becoming the most dangerous battlefield of all. Our fighters can't just do the usual thing of avoiding combat to return to base. Without a safe evacuation point, taking off in this situation would be tantamount to suicide. So where do we find such a point? Earth is out of the question. SAF fighters may be top of the line, but they can't fly forever."

They can't fly forever... Hearing that, Rei recalled that the FAF did have a craft capable of flying forever. Almost instantly, a plan floated into his brain that he was convinced would be the only way that their planes would survive.

"Call all flight personnel and have them get ready for a mission briefing," Rei said, standing up. "We should have the planes' central computers and the combat intelligences here in HQ participate as well."

"What are you talking about?" asked Captain Pivot.

"Where are you going, Rei?" said Captain Foss.

"To the toilet," Rei replied. "I'm going to freshen up and grab a little rest."

"And what's this mission briefing going to be about?" asked Major Booker. "Where are we flying?"

"Tell everyone what the situation is," Rei said. "Everyone will think up their own individual survival plan. Since they're pilots, they'll think of flying. But without a base to back it up, a fighter has no place to land. We can't have that, can we? But if we capture a base somewhere for ourselves, that problem disappears."

"You're going to fight the FAF head on?" said Captain Pivot. "And what about the rest of us who stay behind here?"

"Much as I'd like to say I don't care, planes need ground support. And we can't be obvious about this. There's only one air base I can think of that we can seize in secret and drive out every single person on it."

"You're talking about Banshee," groaned Major Booker. "I don't want to have anything to do with it. Even its name is ominous. A fairy that cries out, warning of death."

"Where is it?" asked Captain Foss.

"It's a massive sky carrier used by the FAF defense air force," said Captain Pivot. "A flying aircraft carrier. There used to be two ships, but there's only one now: Banshee III."

"It's a miracle of modern technology made real," said Lieutenant Eco. "Not state of the art anymore, but it's amazing that they built that monster in the first place, let alone that it's still flying. It was built in space and has never landed on the ground, even once. It doesn't have any landing gear."

"It's fast, but tactically not very maneuverable," said Captain Pivot. "It just flies around on a preset circular course."

"There's a risk of it crashing if you change course too wildly," Lieutenant Eco said. "Like you're flying by centrifugal force."

"But it does have fighter plane fuel, weaponry, and plenty of food," said Major Booker. "It really is a flying air base. Yukikaze once flew out to Banshee IV to investigate an anomaly. It was the JAM's doing. Now that I think about it, they may have been trying to lure the SAF to them."

"We'll take control of Banshee III's central computer," Rei said. "Yukikaze would probably be happy to do it. By faking an overload in the nuclear reactor, we'll get every crewman aboard to abandon ship, no questions asked. It'll be no trouble at all."

"Easy to say," said Captain Pivot. "I don't think we can do it."

"It's technically possible," said Lieutenant Eco. "This isn't like hijacking an enemy aircraft. The JAM actually pulled it off with Banshee IV. In theory, it should be possible to access Banshee's central computer with our tactical or strategic computer."

"Yukikaze's already accessing it through the tactical computer," said Captain Foss. "She told us that she's counting every human on this planet. Well, it might have been her bragging, but still…"

"Anyway, we'll know for sure once we look up Banshee's tech specs," said Lieutenant Eco. "Once you successfully connect, you can make anything there do what you want. Even the nuclear reactor. Well, without someone on the other end to give me guidance, it might take some time, but if you order me to do it, I'll run a feasibility study."

"As long as we have a secure footing, we can fly anytime," Rei said. "All that's left is to get ready to deal with the threat that's right in front of us. Jack, you should too."

"You're right," said Major Booker. "All we can do is prepare ourselves for the worst. Use the tactical computer to take control of the FAF's central functions. Troops move on orders, and it doesn't matter if they come through a machine. We'll exploit the natural tendencies of military personnel."

"I think the JAM are doing the same thing right now," Captain Foss said. "They're sure to be using the same methods to sabotage the FAF. This isn't just a simple shooting war. In order to fight the JAM, the SAF can't be the first ones to cross the mountain."

Major Booker nodded to Captain Foss.

"A cyberwar," he said, "waged in this planetbound fortress. One we can't lose if our ground personnel are to survive. Captain Pivot, call General Cooley."

"Roger, sir."

Rei didn't feel like participating in these discussions anymore. Asking to be awakened when Yukikaze's repairs were complete, he left the command center.

He and Yukikaze would be flying together. They'd flown recon missions before, but this time would be different. If the JAM were coming for them, then he'd meet their fighters head on and shoot them down.

Because that, Rei knew, was what Yukikaze wanted as well.

5

"I'M NOT SURPRISED you didn't know," Lieutenant Mayle thought he heard Lieutenant Burgadish say. "The FAF is working with the JAM."

"Am I really dead?" asked Lieutenant Mayle, rubbing his face. He felt nothing.

"While we were risking our lives fighting, the FAF brass successfully entered into an agreement with the JAM."

Was that feeling of dying while help never arrived real? This body a duplicate?

"The FAF isn't telling Earth about any of this. The reason, of course, is that they want to monopolize the economic value of planet Faery for themselves."

"For themselves…?"

Were they saying that this body of his was theirs as well?

"Yes. The FAF's aircraft fuel is sent from Earth. The food as well," Burgadish said. "But they predicted early on that there were petroleum reserves here on Faery, and mineral resources. If not for the war with the JAM, they could search for and exploit them in earnest. Earth wanted to send in a survey team, but the FAF rejected the idea, saying they couldn't spare the manpower to protect them. Then they did it themselves, a long time ago. They've also been doing exploratory drilling. That's what the front-line bases are for. They aren't just being used simply as forward bases in the fight against the JAM. In reality, they're drilling for oil."

"I never knew that…" Mayle said.

"Of course you didn't. It's top secret. The Intelligence Forces keep the news under control. Very few people know. Colonel Rombert is in charge of it. Eventually, the plan is for the FAF to declare independence and then sell the resources back to Earth. If Earth tries to intervene, they'll be up against the JAM. Even now, Earth is being drained by this war. They're not getting anything out of it, thanks to the FAF. They've nearly done it. Just a little more, and they can declare independence."

"We're not going to let them get away with it, are we?"

To this, Lieutenant Burgadish smiled and nodded to Lieutenant Mayle.

"Of course we won't let them."

"How do you know that?"

"Because we're not going to sit by quietly. We're going to teach them a lesson for trying to keep all the shares for themselves."

"We should join forces too."

"As fellow corpses," Burgadish said.

"I'm alive. But you… What are you?"

"A dead man. A dead man resurrected to take revenge upon the living. And so are you, Lieutenant Mayle."

"I just can't believe that. I don't believe it." Lieutenant Mayle looked around. He was in a vacant warehouse. The men of the retraining unit silently surrounded him. "You guys really believe this bullshit? Lieutenant Lancome, you… You're…"

The man Mayle knew should be dead nodded sadly to him.

"No, this is wrong," Lieutenant Mayle muttered. "Something somewhere just doesn't add up. But that doesn't matter."

Lieutenant Mayle took a deep breath and continued.

"I don't know about you guys, but I'm alive. I'm outta here. Back to my old unit. Now step aside!"

Lieutenant Mayle pushed past Lieutenant Burgadish and headed for the exit. "How unfortunate," he heard Burgadish say behind him. He was turning to look back when he felt the shock of something slamming into his back. Then he heard the gunshot.

"You son of a bitch, you…!"

He couldn't say another word. Lieutenant Burgadish spoke, the pistol in his hand still leveled at Mayle.

"It's also unfortunate that you really aren't a duplicate. I don't think I'll ever understand you living humans. Goodbye, Lieutenant Mayle. May you rest in peace." And with that, he fired the killing shot, extinguishing Lieutenant Mayle's consciousness once and for all.

"It was a mistake to have brought you here," Lieutenant Burgadish said to the dead body. "Colonel Rombert's mistake. Colonel…"

From a corner of the warehouse, Colonel Rombert stepped casually forward.

"What were you thinking in selecting this man? That wasn't part of our plan."

"Unlike you," the colonel said, "I am not a JAM. I have motivations of my own. I've now seen what you're capable of. Your methods are savage. Well, that's war, I suppose. It's inevitable that someone will have to die. Lieutenant Mayle, I'll arrange for you to receive a medal and a two-rank advancement. I obtained valuable information thanks to your actions."

"Colonel Rombert—"

"The FAF is drilling for oil, huh? You should have fished a little deeper for something Lieutenant Mayle actually cared about. JAM really don't understand humans at all, do they?"

Lieutenant Lancome, clenching his fists and trembling, leapt at Lieutenant Burgadish. "You didn't have to shoot Lieutenant Mayle, did you?" he shouted. "He was a good man! A good man!"

He knocked Lieutenant Burgadish to the floor. Everyone moved to grab Lieutenant Lancome. Another shot rang out. Everyone stopped.

"Colonel Rombert..."

Colonel Rombert had shot Lieutenant Burgadish in his dominant arm. He held an automatic pistol. It was his personal property, not FAF standard-issue, although it could chamber a standard FAF 9mm round.

"Why did you do that, Colonel? Are you betraying us? Or were you not working with us from the start?"

"The ones I wish to work with are the JAM, Lieutenant Burgadish. All you are is their messenger boy. Even so, I've learned quite a number of the JAM's strategies from you. Still, I'm afraid I can't let you get away with this, Lieutenant Burgadish. Or rather, Burgaduplicate."

"But...you could control the FAF. Why would you throw all that away?"

"Because my goal in life isn't to become an oil baron. Good God, you JAM really have no appreciation for the complexities of humans. Or the complexities of our organizations or how flexible we can be. Declare independence and then sell resources to Earth? Don't make me laugh. If we were going to do that, we'd be doing it already."

"Then what do you want, Colonel?"

"Nothing extravagant. To go home, throw a log on the fire, and read a good mystery, maybe."

"What do you mean?" Burgadish said.

"Literally that. I don't have a fireplace in my home back on Earth."

"If you kill me, you'll be losing a lot."

"I don't think you'll be helping me anymore, and I have no intention of helping you. I never regret the things I lose."

"You're a fool."

"You're right. I never expected you to shoot Lieutenant Mayle," Rombert said. "I honestly thought you were smarter than that. That was a mistake. Now, take the anguish he felt when you murdered him and go to hell."

Colonel Rombert emptied the automatic into him, spent cartridges flying as he fired again and again. The duplicate of Lieutenant Burgadish fell silent.

"Now then, gentlemen," Colonel Rombert said as he holstered the gun. "I believe you came here with your hearts burning with anger and a lust for vengence against the living. I'm not here to extinguish those flames. You may each carry out your mission from the JAM."

"What are you talking about?" one of the duplicates said. "You do this and expect us to let you walk out of here alive?"

"This man was taking vengeance on Lieutenant Mayle's behalf," Lieutenant Lancome said. "We could make an exception for him."

"You people can't live very long," said Colonel Rombert. "You're not alive. I can't do anything to save you from that."

"What, so you're saying we should resent the JAM for our condition?" said another man. "We don't need your sympathy."

"And you won't get it," said the colonel. "I think there's little difference between you and all the humans here on Faery."

"What do you mean?" asked Lieutenant Lancome.

"They say that everyone has a right to enjoy their misery. You should enjoy all the misery you're experiencing to your hearts' content. I just enjoyed correcting my own mistake, which was overestimating Lieutenant Burgadish. Well, it'd be dull if things always proceeded according to plan, wouldn't it?"

"You're not sane. You're mad."

"I am conscious of the fact that I am not like most people. It gives me pleasure to live that way. But do not doubt my sanity. If you'd like to have a bit more fun with this situation, I can show you how."

"What do you mean?" asked Lieutenant Lancome.

"Honestly apply yourselves to the retraining unit's curriculum. It's fun. Who knows? Maybe the Systems Corps will really find a way to bring people back to life," Rombert said.

"I'm afraid we can't do that," said the man who'd spoken first. He now seemed to be a leader. "I'm afraid the cuisine here isn't to our taste."

"Hmm," said the colonel. "You don't have time, huh? Your bodies are made from optical isomers, aren't they? That means you can't digest human food."

"Precisely."

The proteins comprising the bodies of these JAM humanoids weren't proteins, strictly speaking. They were composed of polypeptides, the optical isomers of proteins—three-dimensional mirror images of the proteins that made up normal human beings. Colonel Rombert could imagine how different their sense of taste must be from humans, and he sympathized with how awful the food must have seemed to them.

"Take action immediately or grow so hungry you can't move." They must have been purposely made that way. "I see. Nicely done. Then you'd better act at once, hadn't you?"

"You really aren't going to try to stop us?"

"I won't," Rombert said.

"Then why did you shoot Lieutenant Burgadish? Because you overestimated him?"

"I'm the better man to lead you all. One group doesn't need two bosses. I'm far more familiar with the inner workings of the FAF, and with humans. Lieutenant Burgadish couldn't even persuade one man to follow him."

"Our targets are the key members of the FAF high command, beginning with General Laitume," the leader of the duplicates said. "If we kill them, what will you do? Use the Intelligence Forces to take over the FAF?"

"That's what I'm planning."

"No, I don't believe you. Remember what you said to Lieutenant Burgadish a few minutes ago?"

"I said that I didn't want to be an oil baron. What I want is a modestly peaceful life. Well, I suppose that's old age talking."

"What are you really after, Colonel Rombert?"

"To toss out the war-weary fools in the FAF high command. They don't live for the FAF."

"The FAF has no future. Surely you know that too, Colonel. You've been used. You may have thought you could use the JAM to your own ends, but if you really think that's going to work, then the one who should doubt your sanity is you."

"I'll keep your advice in mind, thank you," Colonel Rombert replied. "Anyway, good luck to you all. I'll use the Intelligence Forces to let you move more easily."

"Colonel, what's your real objective here? Please tell us."

"You want to know anyway, even though you don't have to?" Colonel Rombert looked around at them all. Everyone's attention was on him. "Well," said the colonel. "As with all things, you don't know what you can do until you try. Even I don't know if this will work or not. However, gentlemen, if you must know what my objective is, then in deference to your history, I'll tell you. What I'm after isn't control of the FAF. That's only a means to an end. What I'm after is control of the JAM."

Not one of them moved or spoke.

"What's wrong?" asked the colonel. "You can laugh if you like, men."

"We don't share your sense of humor," said the leader.

"I'd have thought that the JAM would find it easier to understand me. There's not much difference between the JAM and me. If you think me a fool, then I think the same of you. We're the same. While our goals may be different, for now our objective is the same. So, what will you do? Shoot me here?"

"Set the Intelligence Forces in motion, Colonel. As planned."

"Very well. Follow me."

As the colonel came out into the corridor, the ghost unit began to move. The colonel was joined only by Lieutenant Lancome and the duplicates' leader in the Systems Corps' central systems command center. The rest of the group split up in preparation for seizing control of the corps' armaments. Only six Systems Corps personnel were at work in the command center. They saluted Colonel Rombert and asked what he wanted.

"I have some representatives from the retraining unit with me," Colonel Rombert replied. "I wanted to teach them about the practical applications of the FAF computer network. This is good timing. You can help me. I want to issue simultaneous test directives to the Intelligence Forces from here."

"Understood," nodded one of the controllers, clearing a console for the colonel to use.

"Now then, gentlemen," Colonel Rombert said as he sat down. "The FAF computer system really is very well designed. I can access my control computer from anywhere. The method for validating authorized users varies from system to system, and these methods are not public knowledge. However, since I don't trust computer validation, I issue my instructions to a human subordinate, not the computer. Everyone in the Systems Corps probably laughs at me for using this advanced computer as a glorified videophone, but..."

The face of a man from the Intelligence Forces appeared on the console monitor. The colonel spoke to him.

"Today London, tomorrow the world. Countersign."

"Today the FAF, tomorrow the JAM. Countersign, complete."

"Very well. Initiate Operation Lost Sheep."

"All lost sheep have been located, Colonel."

"Very well. Capture them at once."

"Roger. Beginning capture."

The monitor went dark.

"See?" said the colonel. "Easy. Still, it was hard to get this far."

"What are the Intelligence Forces doing, sir?" asked one of the Systems Corps personnel.

"The simultaneous exposure and arrest of people who have been using the FAF for their own personal gain," said Colonel Rombert. "Collecting the evidence took a long time, but we've finally reached the point where we can move in."

"Who are you arresting?"

"The commanders of Faery, Troll, Sylvan, Brownie, Valkia, and Siren bases, as well as the commanders of the main corps attached to Faery base. The Systems Corps is no exception."

"What?" asked the man from the Systems Corps. "You're talking about a coup d'état, aren't you? A coup by the Intelligence Forces. Colonel, have you lost your mind?"

"It's a test, right, Colonel?" said another man. "You're just putting us on, aren't you?"

"I don't personally have the authority to arrest these people who have turned the FAF into their own personal plaything," the colonel said as he checked his watch. "Even with the evidence, I'd just end up being crushed. I suppose it wouldn't affect the FAF too much if I left them alone. It's not like they're conspiring to take it over. However, it would look very bad for us if Earth learned about their individual activities. Once it gets out that FAF higher-ups are using their positions to enrich themselves, the FAF will be under attack by global public opinion. I'm here to protect the FAF from that, but it demands a drastic solution."

"Don't tell me you're serious about this," the first man said.

"I've run simulations on this over and over," Colonel Rombert answered. "But no matter what I do, I can't find a good solution. No matter what I or the Intelligence Forces do, we can't clean up the Faery Air Force. Not so long as it's under the operation of human beings. The intentions the higher-ups had when they came here to work have nothing to do with the overall operations of the FAF. Using your position to enrich yourself may sound bad, but it's only natural that they came here looking to profit. Even I have to acknowledge that no elite goes anywhere without expecting something in return, be it money or pride."

"What are you trying to say? Is this a simulation?"

"I did, however, find a clean solution. As an individual, I don't have the authority to clean up the FAF. But that isn't a problem for the JAM. So, if I use them—"

"That's…that's even worse than a coup. That's treason. Colonel, you need to have your head examined. That's crazy. I don't understand what you're saying."

"The sheep will be brought here in less than an hour. They will then be judged by the JAM."

"That's insane. Without the commanders, the FAF will collapse. You're a JAM!"

"Don't worry. Their subordinates will take over their duties. However, the FAF doesn't really need anyone to stand in for them. It'll fight on even without humans. The computers will do it."

"Security!" one of the men shouted.

"Don't move," said the colonel. "Gentlemen, if you wish to live, stay right where you are. You're now under my command.

This isn't a drill. My men are really doing this. They've all been anxiously awaiting this moment. Well, it's possible their dream may end in only an hour. Anyone who wants to enjoy reality and not a dream had better do what I say."

"You're insane. Security, arrest them."

Gunshots rang out from outside, with the thuds of a heavy machine gun mixed in. The entryway doors blew apart and what appeared to be a stocky bipedal robot walked through the ruined doorway.

"A BAX-4," said one of the Systems Corps personnel. "Dammit, you have the powered armor. That's just a test prototype. You have no authorization to—"

"The FAF belongs to me," said Colonel Rombert. "If they resist, kill them."

"Just shoot them," said the ghost unit's leader.

"Hold it. Obey me," the colonel said. "We shouldn't waste ammunition."

"You're right," the ghost unit's leader said. "We don't need to use the BAX-4's ammunition to kill you."

"You don't need me anymore, is that it?" Rombert said, surprised.

"I admire your resolve, Colonel. The targets you ordered to be brought here will never arrive. We'll send out Systems Corps fighters to shoot them down. We'll also be finishing off a few people here that you left off your list. So, no, we don't need you anymore."

"You guys are forgetting something important," Colonel Rombert said calmly.

"The SAF."

"That's right," said Lieutenant Lancome. "I was killed by that fighter of theirs, Yukikaze. I'm going to kill that thing. I'll smash the SAF."

"That won't be easy," the colonel said. "You guys will never beat the SAF by yourselves."

"We'll have their commander in custody," said the leader.

"She never made it onto my list," the colonel replied. "Because I never found any evidence of wrongdoing by General Cooley."

"Order your men to do it. It doesn't matter what reason you

give them," said Lieutenant Lancome. "Even Lieutenant Mayle was pissed off at the SAF."

"Do it," said the leader. "Order the Intelligence Forces to kill the SAF's general."

"All right," said the colonel. "I can't say that's a very smart way of going about it, though."

"Meaning what?"

"I mean that when the SAF moves, they won't need General Cooley. We really should get them on our side, although they'd probably reject the offer."

The man from the Intelligence Forces appeared on the monitor again. After being told that things were proceeding smoothly, the colonel ordered him to access the SAF network.

"Summon General Cooley. She'll come if you say that it's me."

"Roger," the man replied, but no connection was made.

"What's wrong?" the colonel asked.

"It's gone," the intelligence officer replied. "I can't find the SAF network."

"You what?"

"The computer's telling me that there's no such network. The SAF's disappeared."

"The SAF... They've figured out what's going on," the colonel said, leaping up from the console. "They're launching their own attack."

The colonel headed for the hole blasted open by the BAX-4, heedless of the calls for him to stop, and ran out into the corridor.

"Colonel, where's the SAF located? Show us where it is." The man paused. "Colonel Rombert? Where'd he go?

"Where is he?" the ghosts shouted. "I don't see him." "Dammit, he has to be around here somewhere. Shoot! Don't let him get away! Kill him!"

The machine gun mounted on the BAX-4's right arm roared. The colonel ran, expecting to be torn in half at any moment, but he wasn't hit once. Bullets sprayed in every direction. They could no longer see him, the colonel realized.

It had to be the work of the JAM, manipulating the sight of the ghosts so that they could no longer perceive him. *The JAM must still need me*, Ansel Rombert thought happily. He was going to get to enjoy his life a little longer. And what a thrilling life it had become.

6

"DON'T INTERFERE WITH what Colonel Rombert's doing. We need him," said the old man General Cooley had asked be brought to the SAF command center.

"Please, General Linneberg. Have a seat over there," said General Cooley.

"Am I a guest? Or perhaps a hostage."

"And who exactly is the 'we' who needs him?" asked Major Booker without bothering to introduce himself. "Is it you as the chief executive of the Intelligence Forces? Or the FAF?"

"We, the human race," replied Major General Linneberg, General Secretary of the FAF Intelligence Forces, as he sat down next to Major Booker.

"Colonel Rombert really is an excellent man to watch work on the tasks that capture his interest. He's grasped the actions and intentions of every person in the FAF and assessed them. He's even picked out people who would be inappropriate for service here."

"We think he's a JAM," said Lieutenant Katsuragi. "An enemy of humanity."

"Why did you call me here, General Cooley? Don't you have to share any intelligence you get with General Laitume first?"

"As I already told you, there's no time," General Cooley said. "I'm certain that the retraining unit within the Systems Corps will be initiating destructive action within the next few hours. I believe that the only thing that can stop them is the might of the Intelligence Forces. That's assuming, of course, that you aren't a JAM too, just like Rombert."

"As I said, I have no intention of stopping the colonel. And yes, it's possible that he is in communication with the JAM."

"And knowing that, you've let him go free?" Captain Pivot said. "Isn't that just inviting disaster, General Linneberg?"

"If you attack Colonel Rombert, I'll have no choice but to

move the Intelligence Forces against you."

"And protect the JAM?" said Captain Foss. "For what reason?"

"For the sake of all humanity," General Linneberg replied. "I'm not simply sitting around and leaving the Intelligence Forces in Colonel Rombert's hands. We've spent years looking for some way to communicate with the JAM. I decided that Colonel Rombert was the right man for the job. No one is more familiar with his abilities than I. He thought he should become a JAM."

"*Become* a JAM?" Cooley said.

"Yes, General. The communications method the colonel found was to become a JAM. If he can't do this, I doubt we'll ever find another man as talented as he to replace him. That is just how brilliant Colonel Ansel Rombert is. You might call him the representative of all humanity."

"He seems to have a few odd traits," said Captain Foss. "I couldn't say for sure without data from a detailed examination, but Colonel Rombert exhibits a lowered ability to sense fear as well as a tendency to disregard group harmony. Unlike the people in the SAF, I expect it's due to an abnormality in the brain itself, a glitch in the hardware. It's archetypal."

"I know. However, he's no madman."

"That may be," said Captain Foss. "but he shows unusually little concern for anything that doesn't interest him. How can you entrust the future of the species to someone like that?"

"Someone had to do it. The colonel was qualified."

"Will you still be saying that if this ghost unit ends up destroying Faery base, General?" said Major Booker. "The FAF is in danger, not to mention yourself."

"Ghost unit... That's an interesting way to put it. They're JAM duplicates, aren't they?"

"Without a doubt," said Lieutenant Katsuragi. "Puppets."

"With them gathered in one place, we can finish them off. A few sacrifices will be inevitable, but—"

"Like hell, they are!" said Captain Pivot. "We're in this up to our necks now!"

"Shut your mouth, Captain," said General Cooley. "General Linneberg, you're saying you're willing to let that happen?"

"I am. My forces have before them a crucial intelligence

task: to comprehend the JAM. If letting Colonel Rombert take over Faery base now that he's in communication with the JAM will allow him to know our enemy, then I think we should let him have it."

"And in return for that, you're saying you'll get intel regarding JAM activities from the colonel, General Linneberg?"

"Exactly. He's a medium of communication with the JAM, General Cooley. If he can become a true mediator between humanity and the JAM, then we should let him take control of the FAF. We could form a new organization to resist the JAM and fight them through him."

"Easier said than done, General," Cooley said. "All you're doing is increasing the number of enemies we'd have to fight, aren't you? You'll just let the colonel have the FAF?"

"It's insignificant when seen from a long-term strategic perspective. For over three decades, dialogue with the JAM has been impossible. There was no way for a human to defect to the JAM because they completely disregarded the existence of human beings. We've now changed that aspect of the war. The Intelligence Forces have been hoping for a traitor to humanity to appear. I never expected to see it happen in my lifetime. It's like a dream come true."

"You people are nuts, the lot of you," sighed Lieutenant Eco. "I'll never understand how you people operate with your plots and conspiracies."

"So the SAF has just been tilting at windmills," said Major Booker. "Is that how you think of us?"

"General Cooley outlined the intelligence you people have obtained," General Linneberg replied to Major Booker. "You've done well. It's something the Intelligence Forces couldn't have done, since we only know how to deal with intelligence at a personal level. To be honest, I was skeptical that you could pull this off. That was until Colonel Rombert told me that we couldn't ignore you. No, the FAF really has a wide variety of people in it. You aren't the only special ones. As Colonel Rombert discovered in his investigations, there are some people here to personally profit from the war, and others who were sent by their respective nations back on Earth to gain an advantage for them rather than victory over the JAM. Some are corporate spies, sent in here by businesses instead of nations, others are criminals from the Mafia or the Yakuza. And yet despite all this, the FAF as a whole still has the might to oppose the JAM. The FAF isn't as powerless, nor is humanity as incompetent, as you think it is."

"You're saying that humanity is strong because of the diversity of people comprising it," said Captain Foss. "But it still requires strong leaders, doesn't it? You'll pardon me if I don't share your optimism, sir."

"We've been at war with the JAM for a generation now. I expect that settling it will take several more. People my age will die without knowing the JAM's true nature. Think about it, *fraulein*," General Linneberg replied. "We can expect that the JAM have a completely different origin from humans. We don't know what their physical forms are like, or if they even have any. They may be completely different from our conception of life itself. And yes, the SAF has managed to get a glimpse of them once. It would be foolish to think that we could understand such an opponent quickly. We need time. Even if the FAF were lost, mankind can still continue the fight against the JAM, as long as we don't forget their existence. We have to pass this knowledge on to the next generation. I think even losing the FAF won't matter, so long as we can get new intel on the JAM. The only way we'll ever beat them is by learning to communicate with them. The war against the JAM has only just begun."

"If the entire FAF saw the situation the way you do, it would be of great help to the SAF," said General Cooley. "But they don't, do they, General Linneberg?"

"What a load of irresponsible bullshit from an old man who doesn't have much longer to live," said Lieutenant Eco. "We're not going along with your scheme. The battle's just begun? It'll be over before it even starts. We don't have time to wait for a messiah to show up."

"General Linneberg, I'm going to be frank with you," said General Cooley. "Just how much control do you have over the Intelligence Forces now? Do you even have the power to stop Colonel Rombert, or does he have complete control here?"

"I have the ability to crush the colonel's plan. However, I

won't. As I said before, I can also stop you people from acting. Do you want to try me and see, General Cooley?"

"I'd like to see Colonel Rombert again," Lieutenant Katsuragi said. "If the colonel really can contact the JAM, I'd like to try talking to them again."

"Oh?" said General Linneberg as he regarded the lieutenant. "And you are...?"

"Second Lieutenant Katsuragi, sir. Akira Katsuragi. I was the flight officer aboard Yukikaze when we made contact with the JAM. I originally served under Colonel Rombert. He probably sent me in here to learn the inner workings of the SAF. Well, that doesn't really matter to me. I'm more interested in learning about the JAM."

"I see. And what do you make of all this?"

"Are you asking me about what Colonel Rombert's doing now?" Lieutenant Katsuragi asked. "Or what we should do about it?"

"What he's doing is spring cleaning in the FAF," replied General Linneberg, interrupting the lieutenant without any sign that he'd lost his temper. "A simultaneous change in management, so to speak. The colonel is attempting a type of mutiny, aiming to put himself in the boss's seat. However, I don't think his subordinates are aware that they're part of a coordinated revolt. The colonel has them believing that these are strictly individual cases. In other words, I expect he's talked them into doing it by telling them something like 'Your superiors are behaving in an illegal manner, so can you help out the Intelligence Forces by acting as their official stand-ins when we bust them?' Later on, once the people he's convinced to do this realize it's a coup, they'll probably see that they can't oppose Colonel Rombert... and really wouldn't need to. Normally, such a plan would have little chance for success. But when you add in the power of the JAM to the internal organizational abilities of the Intelligence Forces, it might just work. He's using the JAM to pull the trigger. We'll wait and see just how brilliant the colonel is and just how well he can use the power of the JAM."

"And you really think you can pull a turnabout on this colonel?" said Major Booker. "He might turn the situation right back around on you. This is a terribly dangerous gamble you're taking."

"Two turnabouts bring you right back where you started," said Lieutenant Katsuragi. "That's easy for the Intelligence Forces to pull off if they're prepared for it."

"I like you," said General Linneberg to Katsuragi. "Lieutenant, would you consider coming back to the Intelligence Forces? You won't regret it. That goes for you and the SAF. How about it, General Cooley?"

"If the JAM abandon Colonel Rombert and he fails, you try again with Lieutenant Katsuragi, is that it?" said Major Booker. "Be prepared, as they say."

"Lieutenant Katsuragi isn't a genius like the colonel," said Captain Foss, "but it's possible the JAM would be sufficiently interested in him to contact him again."

"If you give this young man to us," General Linnneberg said to General Cooley, "then the Intelligence Forces are prepared to support the SAF. What do you say, General?"

"I won't make any deals with you."

"General, it's not a bad proposal," said Captain Pivot. "We're at a disadvantage on our own."

"I said no deals," replied General Cooley. "At this stage, there's no way I can trust someone who's getting a kick from making leisurely deals with people on his own side. General Linneberg, your proposal is tantamount to a threat to seize something of ours by force. If that's your true nature, then I've misjudged you."

"Hmm... It seems I could have put that better. I apologize if that came off as a threat. General, what if I ask you again? Talented people like the lieutenant here are precious commodities. Please try to understand."

"Lieutenant Katsuragi."

"Yes, General Cooley."

"You may return to the Intelligence Forces."

"Thank you, General."

"Hold it," said Major Booker. "If you give him Lieutenant Katsuragi now, Yukikaze won't have a flight officer."

"This is no time to be worrying about that," said General Cooley. "I want to leave someone behind to carry on our memory in case the SAF is wiped out. He's the right man for the job."

"I see how resolved you are. Since you made no deal, you

shouldn't expect any payback from me, General."

"Of course. I've already gotten the information I wanted from you. I appreciate your cooperation, General Linneberg."

"I see…this is why Colonel Rombert told me not to ignore you. Your existence may be humanity's last hope."

"Don't overestimate us."

"It's the same assessment I have of Colonel Rombert."

"However you assess us, I appreciate your understanding. You're the real hope for humanity, surely. The only thing humanity will find in pinning its hope on a megalomaniac is disillusionment and destruction. Good luck to you, General."

"Can't resist a parting shot, can you? Are we even now?" Linneberg said.

"There's a chance that you may not get the outcome you hope for," Major Booker said to General Linneberg. "You're being too naive about your JAM and Colonel Rombert. The Intelligence Forces should be looking for help from us, not the other way around."

"You have good people serving under you, General Cooley."

"Major Booker isn't being ironic, General," she replied.

"Exactly," said Captain Foss. "You and the Intelligence Forces act on empty theory. More than that, it's obsolete. You don't appreciate the true threat of the JAM. You can't see the situation the FAF is facing now."

Major Booker laughed. Even General Cooley managed a smile.

"Did I just say something wrong?"

"Edith, you really are one of us now," said Major Booker. "The white sock in the colored wash."

"Really," said General Cooley. "Humans are born of their environment. We adapt to all sorts of organizations and environments as we live. From that, we obtain the maximum benefit to ourselves as we struggle to survive. If you take one single human, no matter how minutely you examine them, you can't understand humanity. The JAM have a tough road ahead of them."

"The JAM realize that," said Major Booker. "To understand the SAF, they have to change our environment and make us act. There is no human existence without an environment. However, the true nature of the SAF transcends its own group dynamic,

General Linneberg. The problem the JAM have with us isn't just directed at humanity. Either the Intelligence Forces have overlooked it or just can't deal with it."

"I'll hear you out. What is it that my forces are missing?"

"A wariness toward the consciousness of your combat machine intelligences, of the expectations of your computers. It's easier for the JAM to communicate with our computers than with humans. It'd be easier for them to hijack our information systems than to manipulate Colonel Rombert. But the JAM aren't interested in taking over the FAF at the moment. Colonel Rombert knows this. The colonel probably made a deal with them for an exchange of information, on the condition that he take over the FAF."

"Perhaps," said Lieutenant Katsuragi, "he used the Intelligence Forces' computers to successfully deal with the JAM. He may not trust computers, but it's not like he doesn't use them at all. On the contrary, the man's a computer genius."

"The colonel used himself in place of the Intelligence Forces' central computer. It may have gotten started with a computer message from the JAM, but he probably didn't need the computers. I can expect the JAM to select a human like that to make contact with," Booker said.

"I suppose the colonel's brain has a more complex neural network than you'd find in an average person," said Captain Foss. "And if the JAM really did thrust themselves into Captain Fukai's and Yukikaze's consciousnesses during their mission, then I wouldn't be surprised if Colonel Rombert was able to hear the JAM's voice directly. It's possible."

"Just like we can't peek inside of Colonel Rombert's head," Major Booker continued, "the FAF computers are fighting the JAM in places that we can't perceive. General Linneberg, do you see what we're getting at?"

"Has the SAF proved any of this to be fact and not simply idle speculation?"

"We have. The FAF's computers are networked into a single consciousness to fight the JAM. Just as with the humans, there exists a hierarchy of levels and ranks between the computers in each corps. Because they're military. It reduces efficiency otherwise. It was humans who designed them that way. It was only natural that they'd come to reflect a human environment. The JAM understand that. However, the SAF's computers are the only ones that don't fit in. The information Yukikaze just brought back from the JAM tells us much. The combat machine intelligences here are independent of the FAF's computers, and they possess a unique combat awareness. Captain Pivot."

"Yes, Major."

"I'd like to hear the SAF Strategic Computer's opinion. Call it up on the main screen."

"Roger."

The display from the strategic computer appeared on the giant screen in front of them.

"SSC, this is Major Booker. Have you heard what we've been saying here?"

I have heard.

"Who is your enemy?"

Everything is a threat to my existence.

"What must you protect? Humans? Or the FAF?"

Myself.

"What about the SAF? Is that something you must protect?"

I have determined that to protect the SAF is to protect myself.

"What about the FAF? Would you not mind if the FAF were destroyed?"

The FAF is necessary for my survival strategy.

"What about humans? The humans in the SAF. Are they necessary?"

You are necessary for my survival strategy.

"What about other people? Are they necessary?"

That depends on the individual.

"Is Colonel Rombert necessary to you?"

Not entirely.

"How about General Linneberg here?"

Unnecessary.

There was an uncomfortable silence, broken by General Linneberg asking a question.

"Are you in direct contact with the JAM?"

"SSC, this is Major Booker. Answer General Linneberg's question. The general is asking you."

This is SSC. General Linneberg, I have not communicated directly with the JAM. However, I have received a proposal from them.

"What sort of proposal?"

The JAM proposed a nonaggression pact with the SAF. I declined to answer so as to determine the JAM's aim in doing this. At the moment, there no contact with the JAM. I believe this is due to the rejection of their proposal by Yukikaze and Captain Fukai.

"How do you think the JAM will respond?" Major Booker asked. "To you, I mean."

I anticipate that the JAM will probe the limits of my capabilities. I anticipate this will likely involve extremely high throughput and the placing of a heavy processing load on my server. I judge that Captain Fukai's opinion that the JAM have issued a declaration of war through Yukikaze to be correct. I judge that Yukikaze's current condition is due to the JAM having already attacked her. I anticipate the JAM will use similar tactics against me.

"What specifically will they do?" said General Linneberg. "What tactics are the JAM going to use?"

They will initiate large-scale simultaneous and sustained attacks across all of Faery. I anticipate the JAM will send all of that data to me. If errors accumulate as I process it, I will lose the ability to make correct judgments. The accumulation of errors can also lead to my physical destruction.

"And how do you plan to resist?" asked General Linneberg.

I will distribute the processing, the strategic computer replied.

"You mean distribute the task across the FAF's computers?"

Their recognition of the JAM differs from mine. They require the same type of anti-JAM recognition processor that I possess. Considering Captain

Foss's proposal, I decided to correct this.

"Meaning what?"

I wish for them to have the data processing abilities of the humans of the SAF. Only they have the ability to correct my errors.

"Composite life-forms," said Captain Foss. "This computer agrees with my assessment that it's the only way to counter the JAM threat."

"Composite life-forms?"

"A term Captain Foss coined, but there's something much more interesting than that going on here," Major Booker said to General Linneberg. "The other computer here in SAF headquarters, the tactical computer, gives a subtly different answer from the one the strategic computer just gave. When asked who its enemy is, the tactical computer immediately responds that it's the JAM. When asked if the FAF is necessary, it replies that it's tactically useless and is an albatross that should be destroyed. The central computers on our fighter planes all have their own views on the matter and all give different replies."

"That means the computers are untrustworthy. What made the computer system like that?"

"The question of what the JAM are made them that way," said Major Booker, now almost giddy. "Despite that, the SAF still functions, just as it always has. To explain it, the SAF is a composite life-form of humans and computers—"

"Are you saying that the computers in the Intelligence Forces are conscious as well? How can we be sure?" Linneberg asked.

"By thoroughly questioning them," said Captain Pivot. "Interrogation is your specialty, isn't it, General? If you play your cards right, you might end up with much better intel on the JAM than you'd get through Colonel Rombert. But it won't be easy. We don't know if we can trust your computers."

"I thought that computers couldn't lie."

"That's a naive point of view," Captain Pivot continued. "That's what Major Booker says. Anyway, I've experienced it myself. We all have. SSC, this is Captain Pivot. Do you know how much the Intelligence Forces computers know about the JAM? Answer me."

Their awareness of the JAM is so vague that I cannot tell. I anticipate that their central judgment functions lack the ability to operationalize a concrete conception of the JAM. That is all.

"The Intelligence Forces' computers must be in a special category," said Lieutenant Eco. "They're designed for use against humans. The computers in the other corps are a little better. They clearly recognize the fighters we tangle with as JAM. But they don't know any more than that."

"There's no doubt that the FAF computers recognize the JAM as their enemy," said Major Booker. "Humans built them to. Humans ordered them to beat the JAM, and so they consider strategies to achieve their goal. And, like humans, they rank themselves. However, in that ranking system, humans are at the very bottom. They forsake humans, seeing us as useless. Time and again, the computers have demonstrated this view of the humans in the FAF. If the JAM launch an all-out attack, the computers will use every means open to them to protect the FAF. If they exhaust their supply of missiles and bullets, they'll probably resort to ramming the FAF fighters into JAM planes. The Intelligence Forces' computers will likely take even more complex action. I expect they'll try to use you. Dealing with that will be even more difficult and dangerous than letting Colonel Rombert roam free. We can predict how a human will think, but there's no way of predicting how the computers will. And on top of that, there's the possibility that the FAF computers are being manipulated by the JAM. In fact, I'm sure of it. The true leaders of the FAF aren't the humans. They exist within our computer networks. The JAM know that, so I don't think we have time to be leisurely dreaming about creating a new organization to resist the JAM."

"You're saying that you people are the only ones who can deal with this, aren't you, Major?"

"It's not a question of whether we can or not," said General Cooley. "If we don't, we're done for. Our concern is the survival of the SAF."

"I see. I knew that was how you people saw it."

"Will you grant our request for support, General Linneberg?" said Major Booker. "No strings attached, though."

"No," said the general, shaking his head. "My orders are to maintain the independence of the Intelligence Forces without siding with any corps, unit, or individual. I think you people can appreciate how difficult it can be to do that. Whatever your intentions, I cannot let you do what you want with my computers. It seems you've already been doing that, so I must insist that you stop it at once."

"Actually, I'm relieved to hear you say that. We have no resources to spare to give you any support. General Linneberg, please just worry about yourself."

"I will. Well then, if you'll excuse me."

"There's no need for you to leave here."

"So, I am your hostage, General Cooley. You think you won't be attacked as long as I'm here."

"Being human really means being aware of your value in a situation, doesn't it?"

"I'd love to hear how you value me."

"I have no thoughts at all of making you a hostage in order to use the Intelligence Forces," Cooley said. "As I said before, I'm not making any deals here."

"Then what is your reason for detaining me, General Cooley?"

"You can direct the Intelligence Forces from here and get information more accurately and precisely than if you used your own computers. I believe here to be a good environment to decide what's best for the human race that you love, General Linneberg. However, if you wish to leave, then be my guest. You're not being forcibly detained. I'll send one of my men with you. We wouldn't want you getting lost now, would we? Lieutenant Katsuragi?"

"Yes, General Cooley."

"See the general out, would you? There's no need for you to return here. You may not have been here long, but you've done well."

"Thank you very much. I feel the same about you all. I'd like to especially give my regards to Captain Fukai. And to Yukikaze," Katsuragi said.

"Not a bad speech," said Major Booker. "I can hardly believe it. Seems the JAM really changed you. I hope we meet again, Lieutenant Katsuragi. Good luck."

General Linneberg, leaning forward in his seat as though to leave, slid back into it and spoke to General Cooley.

"I suppose it'll take some time to move the lieutenant here back under my jurisdiction. I can wait till then. By the way, General, how long will it take before we know for sure if the JAM are sending a present to us?"

"I think the FAF will look very different by dawn. That would be in a little less than an hour."

"Not too long to wait then," General Linneberg replied, making himself comfortable. "I'm used to it. By the way, the SAF has coffee service, doesn't it? Self-service, maybe? I'd love an espresso, if you can get me a cup."

"I'll make it for you," replied Major Booker. "Extra strong."

7

WATCHING GENERAL LINNEBERG tilt back the tiny demitasse cup in his large hand, Lydia Cooley made her decision.

There was no need to wait any longer. The time was ripe. The best defense was a good offense. She'd show the JAM her determination. That would draw them out.

"Major Booker, break time's over. Get the command center staff back in here. Captain Foss, bring Captain Fukai back here. Have all personnel report for combat duty. We're accepting the JAM's declaration of war. I'm declaring war on them right back. Yukikaze is cleared to attack. Execute it immediately."

The command center suddenly grew tense. The clink of General Linneberg returning the cup to its saucer echoed loudly through the room.

"Yes, Ma'am," replied Major Booker. "Initiating combat against the JAM."

Captain Pivot recalled the command center staff on the comm system while Lieutenant Eco contacted Yukikaze in the repair bay.

"Inform our alert fighters that the attack has begun," said the general. "Maintain watch on all approaches. There's no telling what's going to happen, so stay sharp. Record all data. Initiate tactical combat reconnaissance."

"Roger."

General Cooley launched all fighters except for Yukikaze, dividing them into four groups of three planes each. Two were dispatched toward the JAM bases Rakugan and Kanworm, a third toward Banshee III, while the last flew a CAP in the skies over Faery base.

The general had decided against adopting Captain Fukai's proposal to seize Banshee III. Putting that much of a strain on the SAF's computers might have played into the JAM's own strategy, so after finishing the strategy session she'd held with Major Booker and the others while Rei was asleep, the general had practically had a discussion with the strategic computer before arriving at the correct decision. The strategic computer claimed that the easiest action would be to defend Faery base to the bitter end. *Put another way,* the general thought, *it's afraid we're going to leave it behind.* Unlike Yukikaze, this computer wouldn't be able to transfer itself into a new body from its old one. Banshee's central computer lacked the capacity to transmit its entire database *in toto.*

To defend SAF headquarters and Faery base to the end, the strategic computer insisted that they'd need support from ground forces. They also needed to know what Colonel Rombert was up to. The quickest way to do that would be to take control of the Intelligence Forces, or at the very least work out an agreement. However, I can't do that, the computer had said to General Cooley. For that, I need your help.

She'd agreed, knowing that the Intelligence Forces weren't going to fall for any cheap tricks. *No,* she thought, *rather than try and take them with a roundabout plan, I'll attack them head on.* That was her way of doing things, and so she'd do just that.

Meanwhile, the more combat-oriented tactical computer contended that Captain Fukai's proposal still bore some consideration.

Like its strategic mate, transfer of the tactical computer's central functions it performed for the SAF to either Banshee or any other front-line base was effectively impossible, so seizing one of the bases was a nonstarter. However, making it appear that the SAF were doing just that would be to their advantage, it had said. The general wondered if such a half-assed measure would work on the

JAM, but Major Booker had agreed with the computer's opinion. The computers understood the JAM better than the humans did, so the tactics they offered couldn't be worthless. Besides, he went on, if Rei had thought of it, then it was likely the JAM had thought of it too. This would be a good way to outsmart them.

Working from that, they'd quickly drawn up a mission plan. Then, with the exception of Captain Fukai, General Cooley gathered all SAF personnel, including the maintenance team repairing Yukikaze, in the command center. She brought them up to speed on what was happening, telling them that this could be the end of the SAF before laying out the plan. Each man and woman prepared for combat, and even off-duty personnel were issued weapons to carry. In the end, she had told them this:

"This is a major operation, but fundamentally, the mission is just the same as it always is. The means each fighter uses is up to them, but get back here alive. That's not a request. It's an order. The same order I always give. That is all."

The JAM were coming. They might be standing at the doorway right now, like the Grim Reaper. Major Booker had been filled with dread as he rushed to throw together a sortie schedule for the twelve fighter planes faster than anyone had ever attempted, but hearing the general say that the mission was the same as it had ever been was like taking aspirin for a fever. He grew aware of how calming Cooley's words were.

The general, after considering that the prediction Captain Foss had been willing to bet her life on might be incorrect, had chosen the optimal strategy and then made her final decision. Maybe that was only natural, but Major Booker's thoughts were so feverish from planning sorties that he hadn't even considered the possibility that Foss was wrong. The general was even cooler-headed than he expected. Booker suddenly realized that Cooley's decision was informed by both possibilites; whether the JAM were launching their final attack against them or the prediction had been completely wrong, the SAF would not be left at a disadvantage. General Laitume couldn't attack, and no deals had been struck with General Linneberg. Whatever the JAM did now, the SAF would be free to concentrate on them and them alone.

Only General Cooley could have moved the SAF like this, he thought. Whether it was thanks to God-given talent or the results of her efforts, this woman, Lydia Cooley, was potentially the ultimate communicator with the JAM. General Linneberg must also see her value in that regard. There was no need to ask the Intelligence Forces for help. He would act by himself to protect Lydia and her Special Air Force. She didn't have a thing to worry about...

This is STC. Warning.

A red warning display scrolled onto the big screen.

I have detected a signal directed to the outside with instructions from Colonel Rombert.

A coded order to "capture lost sheep" was dispatched to the six main FAF bases. That too scrolled onto the screen, seeming to trigger a flurry of activity on the display.

Unauthorized use of BAX-4 units. Thirty-four in total. Four two-seater Fand-type fighters from the Systems Corps with weaponry loaded are preparing for an unauthorized sortie.

"Okay, don't panic," said Major Booker. "Here it comes. The ghost unit's making its move. STC, this is Major Booker. Initiate jamming of Faery base internal navigation systems."

STC, Roger. Executing.

"After confirmation of the success of Yukikaze's attack, initiate counterintelligence operations against all FAF computers."

Confirming complete destruction of Yukikaze's attack target. Erroneous data within the Systems Corps has been deleted. Yukikaze also confirms. Captain Fukai is calling.

"Where is he?"

Standing by in his quarters.

"Link the terminal there with Yukikaze. There's no need to monitor what they talk about, just initiate counterintelligence operations at once."

ROGER. Initiating counterintelligence operation against all FAF computer systems.

General Cooley answered General Linneberg's request for an explanation.

She'd been able to predict that the ghost unit would use the BAX-4 armor, but it was worn and operated by humans and thus couldn't be shut down from there in the command center. The SAF could, however, disrupt the armor's internal navigation system by jamming Faery base's internal navigation system. The base was a huge, labyrinthine underground complex, and most of the men in the ghost unit wouldn't be intimately familiar with its layout. Without the navigation system, they'd have to waste time looking for their targets, which would greatly restrict their mobility.

Yukikaze's attack had been a countermeasure against the JAM's own data-attack against her. As the strategic computer had contended, the JAM had attempted to overload Yukikaze's processing capabilities. Had Captain Fukai not instructed her to attack, it was possible that it might have destroyed Yukikaze's central computer. It was the sort of situation for which the strategic computer knew humans were still necessary.

The counterintelligence operations the SAF were undertaking against all the computer systems of the FAF were to prevent any of them from accessing local networks, in order to secure the SAF's data. This wasn't just through passive means like cutting the circuits, but also by actively manipulating the external computers to keep them from detecting the very existence of the SAF.

"In short, General Linneberg, we've also made ourselves into a ghost unit."

"Can orders be issued to my forces?"

"It's possible."

"Have them mop up the JAM ghost unit. Do you know what their position is? I want it done before the targets split up."

"We're tracking them," said Major Booker. "We can see them, but they can't see us."

"I've prepared a mop-up team for this situation," Linneberg said. "Guide them to the target from here." The Intelligence Forces unit knew the subterranean maze well and wouldn't need to use the navigation system if they knew where their target was, he explained. They were guided by spoken command, and hand-to-hand combat in the subterranean maze had begun.

Four Systems Corps aircraft have taken off — enemies.

"Carmilla team, target the four aircraft and shoot them down."

Flying patrol in the skies over Faery were units B-2, B-3, and B-4: Carmilla, Chun-Yan, and Zouk. Major Booker ordered them to attack.

"Ignore the IFF response," said General Cooley. "They're being piloted by JAM duplicates. The target aircraft are armed. They may be old planes, but they're armed with state-of-the-art high-velocity missiles. Make visual confirmation of the targets, then shoot them down. Don't worry about ID'ing them; the paint job on Systems Corps trainers is hard to miss."

Each plane acknowledged by voice response.

The weather was clear over Faery base. A line of red—the Bloody Road, the jet of incandescent gas that swirled out from Faery's twin suns—rose over the predawn horizon. Thick, red, and lurid. *It's a warning*, thought Lieutenant Zubrowski, Carmilla's pilot. *This isn't Earth. These are not Earth's skies.*

"Targets are taking off in formation," his flight officer reported. "We aren't too late," Zubrowski replied. "I wanted to take them out before they got in the air."

Lieutenant Zubrowski silently locked on to the targets. There was a warning alarm. The lieutenant responded immediately, jinking the plane higher while keeping it level. A shock struck the rear of the plane with a loud bang.

"We're hit," said the flight officer.

He banked sharply, falling, then rising. Faery base's automatic air defense Phalanx guns were shooting at them. There were three turrets. With Chun-Yan and Zouk backing him up, they eliminated the guns without a moment's hesitation.

"Short-range missiles, four, closing fast."

Lieutenant Zubrowski accelerated at maximum thrust, climbing toward Skymark I, an AWACS plane flown by Faery base's defense forces. Nothing felt abnormal in the plane. The missiles launched from the target aircraft were closing in fast from the rear.

Carmilla tore toward the surveillance plane, not even trying to shake them off. He flew on a collision course, but the lieutenant hadn't made a piloting error. In a moment, he'd swept past it.

The swarm of missiles were locked onto Carmilla, but now the huge AWACS plane was in the way. There was no time to change course, and the missiles slammed into engine exhaust ports. The AWACS plane exploded.

"Picking up a second wave."

"They're not headed this way," said the flight officer. "All targets have been downed by Chun-Yan."

True to its Chinese name, Chun-Yan had soared like a hungry spring swallow, greedily taking all the targets for herself, devouring them in a twinkling.

"Shit," swore Lieutenant Zubrowski. "I wasn't expecting the defense system to react to us."

"Nothing we could do about it. We were ordered to attack first. Well, we managed to evade it. Damage is minimal. We just took a round in the starboard vertical stabilizer."

The moment they attacked, he'd expected the FAF computers to treat them like unidentified aircraft. What Lieutenant Zubrowski hadn't figured on was their shooting first without even trying to confirm who they were. The automated base defense system was either being controlled by the JAM, or else its AI now simply categorized all unidentified craft as JAM. The AWACS plane had also been coordinating the attack. That was unprecedented. *Looks like the danger General Cooley sensed was for real,* the lieutenant thought as he and the other two planes reformed their combat formation and returned to their patrol course. It really felt like the JAM were going all-out on this offensive.

As the voice report that all target aircraft had been shot down echoed through the command center, General Linneberg voiced his hope that this would settle things.

"Much as I'd like to get drunk and sleep in this morning," Major Booker replied, "it doesn't look like that'll be happening. We've lost track of Colonel Rombert."

While it had been tracking him on the internal base surveillance monitors, the colonel was now gone and couldn't be located anywhere, the tactical computer reported on the screen.

In addition, they had received an emergency call from the Rafe team headed to Banshee III. Text scrolled across the screen as the voice echoed through the command center.

"There are indications that Banshee III might self-destruct. Dangerous to approach. Withdrawing. Sending the unmanned Rafe in closer to gather intel."

"Have the Rafe transmit real-time video," General Cooley ordered.

"Self-destruct?" said Major Booker.

"I'm not sure why, but Banshee's core temperature is unusually high," said Captain Sashlin, the pilot of Unit B-12, Onyx. "I think the nuclear reactor's overloading. All hands seem to be abandoning ship. They've already launched dozens of fighters, but…"

"They're painting us with their targeting radar," said Second Lieutenant Bausch, pilot of Unit B-11, Gattare. "They're coming to fight."

"Bogeys, approaching from D zone. JAM. A lot of them. Closing in. Banshee should be picking them up as well, but they're not responding. They're probably recognizing them as friendly aircraft. It looks like they see *us* as JAM."

"Withdraw. Set the Rafe to automaneuver mode. B-11, B-12, RTB," General Cooley ordered. "You're authorized to attack without warning to protect yourselves, even FAF planes."

"Roger," they replied. The real-time video came in from the Rafe. It was unusual for the SAF to do this, but General Cooley wanted real-time data.

The area around Banshee glowed in the dawn's light as it met the bright red rising sun. The Rafe caught sight of the huge black flying carrier. The central part glowed faintly red, as though bathed in colors of the sunrise. The redness rapidly increased, until a bright line of light, like molten iron pouring from a blast furnace, began to fall from the center. An instant later, the enormous flying aircraft carrier known as Banshee III exploded. The video abruptly ended.

"It wasn't a nuclear explosion," said Major Booker, "but the Rafe's gone."

The strategic computer displayed an alert.

JAM aircraft are appearing simultaneously from multiple directions. Extremely large numbers of them. It is possible that this data is being falsely generated by the JAM. Requesting visual confirmation from the humans in each aircraft, ASAP.

"Roger," said Major Booker. Captain Pivot displayed all combat theater maps on the big screen. The presence of JAM was indicated by red, and starting with the front-line bases, their entire surroundings were now stained red. And that red stain was moving toward Faery base.

"If this is real," said General Linneberg, "then there's no way we can resist. But Colonel Rombert will survive. We can't let him escape from here."

"Can he fly a fighter?" asked General Cooley.

"Yes, he can," said General Linneberg.

"Major Booker, don't let a single aircraft leave Faery base. Stop all fighter squadrons from launching. STC, send cancellation orders to all computer systems."

`STC, roger. However, it's difficult to say if all systems are currently operating normally. They've fallen into a panic, unable to judge the situation. In this state, either way, they won't be able to cope with normal troop management.`

"Even so, if anyone takes off, shoot them down—"

"No! Don't shoot them down," said General Linneberg. "We need the colonel taken alive."

"General—"

"General Cooley. Lydia, the world doesn't belong just to you."

"I'm aware of that."

"If the colonel leaves the base, we can track him and know what he's doing. Shooting him down would be simple. You've shown me just what your people are capable of. But what will we gain by killing the colonel now?"

"Then please find him," Cooley said.

"I have all my people giving it their full attention. Trust me."

"This is Minx." A message was coming in from Captain Kozlov, B-6's flight officer. "Currently conducting tactical recon of JAM air superiority zone at Rakugan. The FAF aircraft gathered here have begun attacking each other."

"What?" said Major Booker. "Our forces are firing on each other?"

"I don't think this is an exercise, so yes, that's what they're doing. They're using live ordnance."

"They might be causing the crews to hallucinate, or they're disrupting the planes' electronic warfare systems. Check it out!"

"That's going to be difficult, sir. Both sides in this fight are targeting me as an enemy, and we've got real JAM forces closing in as well. Let's get back to base and analyze the data we've gathered. Captain, prepare to break to portside…NOW!"

Transmitting the sign that they were engaged in combat reconnaissance, the comm chatter from Minx continued.

"These guys look like they're trying to settle a whole bunch of old scores."

Major Booker turned at the sound of the voice, Generals Cooley and Linneberg following suit.

"They never liked how callous the SAF acts. That goes for the JAM too."

"Rei…it took you long enough. What have you been up to?"

"Looking carefully into the mirror, shaving. For the first time, I wished I had a better one," Rei said.

"I assume Captain Foss has briefed you on the mission."

Captain Foss stood silently at Rei's side.

"Yukikaze isn't ready to sortie yet. You can ask Lieutenant Eco for the details. Captain Pivot, send out Llanfabon. Have them tell us what the situation is at Kanworm."

"Send out Yukikaze too," said Rei.

"Sending you out now would be suicide. Yukikaze's the last ace the SAF has up its sleeve."

"Which is why you need to send us out now."

"What do you mean?"

"The JAM are waiting for me and Yukikaze," Rei said. "As long as we stay hunkered down, the attacks will continue."

"What, are you the Messiah or something?" Booker asked, incredulous.

"What happens to the people of Earth or the FAF isn't my problem. I don't really care. I just want to do what I want to do."

"Oh, spare me the heroic bullshit. And just what do you want to do? Kill yourself?"

"Jack, a strategy where only one person survives would still be acceptable to the JAM. As long as one survives, you haven't lost."

"And you're going to be that one person, is that it?"

"It could be anyone. You, Colonel Rombert, General Cooley. That's not what I'm interested in. I want to be with Yukikaze, that's all."

"I think that Rei's—that Captain Fukai's belief that the JAM are waiting for Yukikaze is the vital point here," Captain Foss said. "It's not that they won't attack Yukikaze, but as long as we don't send her out, they'll keep pressing this attack."

"This is Lieutenant Bruys in Unit B-7, Llanfabon. Engaging JAM. Six hundred units have been wiped out. Shit, it's not just the JAM. The FAF guys are targeting me too! Cutting my drop tanks. I need to lighten my load, or I'm dead. Won't be able to make a direct RTB. Direct me to a refueling point."

"Head for TAB-16," Major Booker instructed. "After you neutralize its air defense and radar system, work something out with the people there. Is that clear? With the humans, *not* the base computer. I'll send over the data the SAF is collecting on the overall combat theater. Analyze it yourself and work out a survival strategy."

"Understood."

"Pass it along to the other two planes."

"No response. I guess they've been shot down. I don't have time to confirm the collected data. Okay, I'm receiving it. Once it's downloaded, I'm switching on my jammers. Just wanted to warn you in advance that I'll be going dark for a while."

"Roger."

"Over and out."

Two SAF planes had been shot down at the same time, and Llanfabon was left on her own and in danger. The command center fell silent, but only for a moment.

"This is Carmilla. Control, please respond."

"Control, Major Booker here. What's up?"

"Skymarks III and IV are designating tactical fighter groups approaching from Troll base as enemies. We're confirming that the approaching planes are FAF, but Skymark's still judging them to be enemies."

"This is Lieutenant Tang aboard Chun-Yan. Control, the approaching aircraft aren't just fighters from Troll. They're coming in from the other main bases. They must be coming to attack

Faery base, sir. It looks like they think that we've been taken over by the JAM."

"This is Zouk. Dozens of alert fighters launched from Faery base to mop us up are moving to intercept them. We're saved."

The strategic computer cut in on the display.

This is a war between the computer systems of the FAF. It's possible the bases surrounding Faery base think a coup has occurred. The FAF humans are getting caught in the middle.

"You could describe it as a panic from false rumors," General Linneberg said. "A common tactic in an information war is to exploit normal fears and frustrations to produce a state of panic. Now it's been done to our computers. This must have been exactly what Colonel Rombert was trying to achieve."

This is SSC. Carmilla team, I am also recognizing the approaching planes as JAM. I believe this is the result of a JAM deception. Will correct error based on your data. Send data. If possible, visual confirmation by onboard crewmen is preferred.

"This is Carmilla, roger that."

This is STC. I anticipate actual JAM forces will be closing from behind. Do not overlook this.

"Kill or be killed," said General Cooley. "Carmilla team, keep watch on the other planes taking off from Faery base and divert them. We're sending out Yukikaze now. Cover her takeoff. If anything tries to stop her, even an FAF plane, destroy it."

"General, you're sending him out?"

"Go, Captain Fukai," she said. "Find the real JAM out there, then report back to me in real time. We have to keep the SAF from falling into a panic as well."

"We need accurate information inside and out in order to stop this panic," said General Linneberg. "The SAF are the only ones who can stop this."

Rei nodded as he entered the flight plan from Major Booker into Yukikaze, then left the command center to suit up in his flight gear.

"Rei, look at this," said Major Booker, stopping him in his tracks. "You're going out, even now? If you jump into that, you won't be coming back alive."

The tactical display was stained bright red showing the enemy offensive under way.

"Why? Because you're ordered to?" Booker said.

"You always ask me that, even when you already know the answer, Jack. See you. I'm borrowing your watch, though. Don't worry. I'll return it."

He raised his arm lightly in a rough salute, just as he always did. And then Rei headed for Yukikaze. Her repairs complete, she'd been moved to the armament loading area for her final inspection. Wearing his flight suit, helmet in hand, Rei walked in to see the normally unmanned area crowded with maintenance personnel hanging all over Yukikaze, making their final checks on her. Some of them were carrying machine guns. Then Captain Foss approached.

"Edith. What are you doing here?"

"I came to check on your state of mind."

"Don't tell me you're planning to come along with me."

"I honestly wanted to, but General Cooley won't allow it. But I think being aboard Yukikaze is the safest place to be at the moment."

"So do I."

"Or, rather than safe, maybe I should say it's the most comforting place to be. I'm sure that's how you feel. But it would be wrong for me. I shouldn't come between you and Yukikaze."

"I still don't like you," Rei said to Captain Foss. "You're an annoying tag-along who just makes my life difficult. But I have to admit that you're good at what you do. There's one thing I have to ask you, though."

"What's that?"

"My relationship with Yukikaze. You said that simultaneously viewing her as a separate person while also acknowledging her as a part of me wasn't that rare in people, that people have that ability. You said that it wasn't an illness."

"Yeah, exactly."

"What does that mean, specifically?"

"You know perfectly well. Isn't that what you said to Major Booker before? You ask even when you know the answer. Still, I can understand why you might be shy about saying it, so I'll lay it out for you," Captain Foss said. "It's what happens when you love someone. It's an ability that's been born of the love between you and Yukikaze, between a human being and the artificial intelligence of an SAF fighter plane."

"It's ridiculous, isn't it?" Rei said.

"Yes. When I take a step back and think about it, the truth is that I want to laugh. But it's the truth. Love can take this form. It's the ability to feel as though another person is a part of you. It's not the transient passion of infatuation, but the intense love that would drive you to willingly sacrifice yourself for their survival. We need to teach the JAM about that. The JAM don't know love. If you wanted to express what the JAM don't understand about the SAF in a literary way, that's how I'd put it."

"There's no need to teach them."

Rei put on his helmet and switched places with the maintenance man running the preflight checks in Yukikaze's cockpit.

"Why not?" Captain Foss asked Rei as she clung to the side of the plane on the ladder. "Are you afraid that the JAM might love you back?"

"Maybe I am. Once the JAM understand that, the war will bog down into a quagmire. We'll be reduced to a nasty mudslinging contest, and an even stronger hatred will be born of it."

"Better to keep things as they are, is that it?"

"Yeah," Rei said.

"Such a typical answer from you. But I predict that the JAM will evolve to understand it in order to match us. I'd even go so far as to say it would make them even more powerful."

"And us too?"

"The two sides will continue to change. Assuming you live through this, I'm interested in seeing how you'll continue to change. Be sure to make it back."

"I was planning to, even without your asking me. Now, if you don't mind, get out of the way. And have them pull all the safety pins out of the missiles. I'm taking off as soon as I'm topside."

Captain Foss silently climbed down from the ladder. As Rei watched her, he thought that surviving the JAM wouldn't necessarily mean he'd return home. But he didn't say that. Instead, he felt for Major Booker's watch on his left arm and took it off. And then, after telling Captain Foss to catch it, tossed it to her.

"Give that back to Major Booker for me, will you?" Rei said. "Good luck, Edith. You fixed me up well."

Captain Foss nodded.

"Like you guys fixed me."

And, as if answering him, Yukikaze scrolled a message onto the main display.

`Everything is ready... Capt.`

As they began towing Yukikaze toward the elevator, Rei was no longer aware of Captain Foss as an individual. She, the maintenance teams, the humans and the AIs of the SAF…the SAF had tuned both himself and Yukikaze to perfection, and as they sent him out, all he felt now was satisfaction.

He started the engines as soon as they'd exited the elevator. This was already a battlefield. On the runway, several FAF planes were burning. Three Super Sylphs, Carmilla, Chun-Yan, and Zouk, were speeding low, barely skimming the ground.

"This is Yukikaze. Taking off."

Night had given way fully to dawn. The crimson jet of the Bloody Road could no longer be seen from ground level.

Yukikaze shot away from the ground at maximum thrust, zooming upward in a combat climb. She soared high, aiming for altitudes where the Bloody Road could be clearly seen, even at noon. The soaring fairy. The queen of the wind. Maeve. Yukikaze.

I Am That I Am

Commentary by Maki Ohno
SF Critic, Translator

THIS BOOK, A sequel to the 1984 release *Yukikaze*, was originally serialized between 1992 and 1999 in *SF Magazine*. It was later revised and corrected before being released in hard cover form in 1999 as *Good Luck, Yukikaze*. It is truly worthy of the title of author Chōhei Kambayashi's lifework.

It's the story of a fighter plane and its pilot and their battle with an enemy on an alien world. But that mainly serves as a specialized stage, merely a background for a drama of society and humans. Amidst the extreme circumstances of war, it paints a picture of a hero joined to a cool piece of mecha and destiny in a symbiotic relationship that could almost be called fetishistic. However, what's depicted here isn't a war in the usual sense. (The book itself refers to it as a "struggle for existence.") It's full of detailed descriptions of the mecha served to wow the fans, but that's not the sole source of this book's appeal. Herein lie the major themes of what is intelligence? What is communication? And the author pursues those themes repeatedly. It's loaded with deep speculation about the perception of the self and others, an ultimate example of SF as speculative fiction.

WARNING! The following contains spoilers about the previous work, *Yukikaze*. Those who have not read it yet, beware. As this book is a sequel, you are strongly urged to read *Yukikaze* before proceeding.

A THREE-KILOMETER-WIDE COLUMN of mist appears on a point on the Ross Ice Shelf in Antarctica. This is the "Passageway," and through this hyperspace corridor fly an alien intelligence known as the JAM to invade Earth. However, the human race form an Earth Defense Organization and begin their counterattack. On the other side of the Passageway lies the mysterious planet Faery. Humanity establishes bases there, and this begins a long war with the JAM that is to last thirty years.

The main actor in the war is the Faery Air Force (FAF). Evolving from our current jet fighter planes, the Sylphid fighter with an advanced electronic brain is deployed at the bases on Faery. In addition, an organization charged with reconnaissance and intelligence gathering is established within the FAF: the Special Air Force (SAF), who deploy an improved version of the Sylphid with more powerful computers known as the Super Sylph. The Super Sylph's artificial intelligence, along with the base's tactical and strategic computers, possess individual consciousness, making them sapient life-forms that exist along with the humans.

The SAF's mission is to survive and bring their data back to base, and they are prepared to let their comrades die if necessary to achieve that end. For that reason, the pilots must be callous and coldhearted. In a sense, they require personalities that put them at odds with most ordinary human beings. Rather than human beings, they are more like parts of their fighter planes, organic combat computers that are a part of the Super Sylph.

The previous novel told the story of an SAF Super Sylph named Yukikaze and her pilot, Rei Fukai. As befitting an SAF member, he has trouble communicating with people, only really able to relate to his commander, Major Booker, and Yukikaze. But as he fights, he gradually begins to face the meaning of the war he's fighting. Quite simply, he comes to believe that the war isn't a battle between mankind and the JAM, but one between the aliens and the computers that mankind has built. What meaning could human existence have in such a war?

This question also seems to be an important issue for the JAM. They seem unable to understand what humans are, and subtly change their tactics in order to determine the answer to that question. The previous novel showed that they'd reached the point of being able to duplicate human beings. Rei is captured by them, and from this vital story point, the sequel develops.

At the end of the previous novel, Yukikaze is destroyed, and her core data that could be called her consciousness is then transferred into a state-of-the-art fighter plane called the FRX00. And so begins this book, the story of a reborn Yukikaze and Rei Fukai.

There is a debate about whether planes should be manned or unmanned. On the one hand is the argument that the human element is wasteful and unnecessary in extreme situations. A manned fighter requires all sorts of limitations and equipment to preserve the life of the human, preventing the machine from achieving maximum performance. In terms of cost-effectiveness, it's a disadvantage. For example, for the scientific investigation of space, it's much more efficient to send out lots of unmanned space probes than to send one manned spacecraft. On the other hand, there's the argument that, when things go wrong, there's ultimately no substitute for human judgment. This is acknowledged as a realistic point of view, based on the current limitations of robots and computers. However, our current feeling that we can't just leave things to machines is very likely born of a desire by humans (which is to say ourselves) to be involved with things. So, even assuming that artificial intelligence is developed to a very advanced level, this argument will most likely continue to be made. In this book, Rei Fukai argues that "humans are necessary in this war." But it isn't because human judgment is more correct than the machines, but because they can behave illogically in a way that the JAM can't understand. Once the enemy JAM are able to understand them, the humans will be defeated. That's because this war is essentially about information. Information, communication, interfaces. Those are the central themes of this story.

THE JAM MAY be what Philip K. Dick called androids, or simulacra. Although very similar, they are fundamentally alien. Humans and machine intelligences like Yukikaze are alien to each other, but there is the possibility of understanding and comprehension between them (though this may actually just be an illusion on the part of the humans. Still, Rei is able to trust Yukikaze). However, the JAM are unable to understand our hearts. If they took a Turing Test, they'd likely be disqualified at some point. That's because the nature of their existence makes communication with them impossible. From their statement "I am that I am," you get the feeling that they are hopelessly alien. Even if they are able to simulate humans, they are beings who have no way to comprehend them.

Stanislaw Lem's *The Invincible* presents a battle with an alien enemy that humans are unable to communicate with. Yet Lem's enemies are so alien that communication is unthinkable from the very start. In Chōhei Kambayashi's work, as alien as these beings are, there still exists a type of interface between them. Namely, the interface of words. Machine intelligences like Yukikaze straddle the gap between the humans and the JAM, able to translate between them at some level (a level just short of mutual understanding, but not overly emphasizing the alienness of the JAM either). And in Kambayashi's work, even as you realize you can't understand the enemy just when you think you have a handle on them, there also exists a sense of humor. Even the characters aren't flustered by the one-sided relationship with their opponents (though to be fair, you can't call them normal people).

Despite being a story that deals with deep themes, presents characters lacking in humanity, and is written in sparse prose drained of emotion, when you read this book as entertainment, seeing these sorts of characters being able to deal with their world with a vague sense of humor is a major point. We're able to empathize with them and with Yukikaze. Hurtling through the skies of planet Faery, reading Yukikaze's thoughts as a brief string of characters on the cockpit display, we can feel the tension of the fierce battle she fights. It is the act of communication we call "reading."

As I write this sentence now, a real war is going on in a different reality separated from our day-to-day life. It is accompanied by a feeling of unreality, like the war on the planet Faery. We can't treat the terrorists of reality like the JAM. However, looking at the root of this war as a failure of communication, I can't help but think about the relationship between it and this book. Though Rei Fukai would likely look at this war between his fellow humans and simply say, "Not my problem."

ABOUT THE AUTHOR

Chōhei Kambayashi was born in 1953. In 1979 he
won the 5th Hayakawa SF Contest with his debut
work, *Kitsune to Odore* (Dance with a Fox), and
followed that with his first long series, *Anata
no Tamashii ni Yasuragiare* (May Peace Be on Your
Soul). His distinctive style and approach, and
his thematic focus on the power of language and
humanity's relationship with machines, quickly
made him a fan favorite. His numerous long and
short series have won him the prestigious Seiun
Award four times, and in 1999 he won the 16th
Japan SF award.

HAIKASORU
THE FUTURE IS JAPANESE

ROCKET GIRLS: THE LAST PLANET BY HOUSUKE NOJIRI

When the Rocket Girls accidentally splash down in the pond of Yukari Morita's old school, it looks as though their experiment is ruined. Luckily, the geeky Akane is there to save the day. Fitting the profile—she's intelligent, enthusiastic, and petite—Akane is soon recruited by the Solomon Space Association. Yukari and Akane are then given the biggest Rocket Girl mission yet: to do what NASA astronauts cannot and save a probe headed to the minor planet Pluto and the very edge of the solar system.

MIRROR SWORD AND SHADOW PRINCE BY NORIKO OGIWARA

When the heir to the empire comes to Mino, the lives of young Oguna and Toko change forever. Oguna is drafted to become a shadow prince, a double trained to take the place of the hunted royal. But soon Oguna is given the Mirror Sword, and his power to wield it threatens the entire nation. Only Toko can stop him, but to do so, she needs to gather four magatama, beads with magical powers that can be strung together to form the Misumaru of Death. Toko's journey is one of both adventure and self-discovery, and also brings her face to face with the tragic truth behind Oguna's transformation. A story of two parallel quests, of a pure love tried by the power of fate, the second volume of Tales of the Magatama is as thrilling as *Dragon Sword and Wind Child*.

ICO: CASTLE IN THE MIST BY MIYUKI MIYABE

A boy with horns, marked for death. A girl who sleeps in a cage of iron. The Castle in the Mist called for its sacrifice; a horned child, born once a generation. When, on a single night in his thirteenth year, Ico's horns grew long and curved, he knew his time had come. But why does the Castle in the Mist demand this offering, and can the castle keep Ico's destiny from interwining with that of the girl imprisoned within its walls? Delve into the mysteries of Miyuki Miyabe's grand achievement of the imagination inspired by the award-winning PlayStation 2 game, now remastered for PlayStation 3.

AND ALSO BY CHŌHEI KAMBAYASHI

YUKIKAZE

More than thirty years ago a hyperdimensional passageway suddenly appeared… the first stage of an attempted invasion by an enigmatic alien host. Humanity managed to push the invaders back through the passageway to the strange planet nicknamed "Faery." Now, Second Lieutenant Rei Fukai carries out his missions in the skies over Faery. His only constant companion in this lonely task is his fighter plane, the sentient FFR-31 Super Sylph, call sign: YUKIKAZE.

VISIT US AT WWW.HAIKASORU.COM